Blade's Memory

BOOK FIVE

Lindsay Buroker

The Blade's Memory

by Lindsay Buroker

Copyright Lindsay Buroker 2015

Cover and Formatting: Deranged Doctor Design

No part of this book may be reproduced, scanned, or distributed in any printed or electronic form without permission. Please do not participate in or encourage piracy of copyrighted materials in violation of the author's rights. Thank you for respecting the hard work of this author.

This is a work of fiction. Names, characters, places, and incidents either are the product of the author's imagination or are used fictitiously, and any resemblance to locales, events, business establishments, or actual persons—living or dead—is entirely coincidental.

Acknowledgments

Hello, and welcome to the next installment of the Dragon Blood series! I hope you enjoy this new adventure. Before you jump in, please let me thank my beta readers, Cindy Wilkinson and Sarah Engelke, my editor, Shelley Holloway, and the cover designers at Deranged Doctor Design.

CHAPTER 1

As Colonel Ridgewalker Zirkander crouched behind a bush, watching a steam wagon full of soldiers trundle up the road, he felt more like a felon avoiding the law than a military pilot who could claim a distinguished, twenty-year career. All right, *distinguished* might not be quite the word, considering he had almost as many demerits on his record as he had medals and awards hanging on the wall in his office, but he was a respected officer. He certainly was not someone who skulked in the shrubs of his own homeland, especially when it was raining, and water barely above freezing kept dribbling past the collar of his flight jacket and down his spine.

"I don't recognize anyone, sir," Captain Kaika whispered, a spyglass to her eye as she watched the wagon approach. She was skulking with him, while the rest of his squadron, including Tolemek and Sardelle, hunkered in a cherry orchard farther back from the road. "They're infantry, Lionstrike Brigade."

Ridge nodded. He'd spotted the pins on their collars when he had taken a look through the spyglass. Unfortunately, he hadn't recognized the driver or any of the twenty men sitting in the open wagon, either. It wasn't surprising. The army's flier battalion did not often work with ground troops.

"Nobody you've interacted with on your previous missions, eh?" Ridge had hoped Kaika might know someone in the group. She was a part of the elite forces, a unit attached to the infantry brigade that worked out of the same base near the capital.

"I think I've seen that sergeant at the Sensual Sage," Kaika said, "but he doesn't meet my standards, so I've never approached him."

"I was talking about *combat* missions, not... extracurricular ones."

As was the case for most of his travel-weary team, Kaika's rawboned features were smeared with dirt and decorated with scratches and yellow-blue bruises, but she still managed a sultry smile that hinted of a love for those extracurricular activities. "Oh? I thought you just wanted someone we could trust for information, no questions asked."

"I do."

"I'm sure they would recognize *you* if you stepped out there."

"Yes, but based on the intel that you and Apex gave me, I'm not sure I want to be recognized, not until we figure out more of what's going on. If our enemies don't know we're around, we can move about more easily. Maybe we can find the king before anyone ever spots us. Assuming he's still missing."

It had been nearly a week since Apex and Kaika left Iskandia to come find Ridge and the others, and he had no idea if the situation they had reported had escalated while they had been gone or been resolved. He hoped the king was back in the castle and that General Ort had been discovered, as well. Ridge had been gnashing his teeth while awake and asleep, worrying about that idiot Colonel Therrik being in charge of the flier squadrons. Including *his* flier squadron.

Ridge sank lower as the wagon drew abreast of the bushes, its smokestack spitting black smoke into the dreary late-winter sky. One of the men in the back stood up, using a spyglass to scan the bare, muddy farms lining the road. Ridge looked over his shoulder, worried the bare-branched trees would not hide his people sufficiently.

They won't see us, Sardelle said, speaking into his mind.

Because you're using powerful magics to obscure what they see?

Because we moved behind the cider mill building.

Ah. Even better.

Jaxi says she's willing to use some powerful magics if it gets us out of the rain, Sardelle added. *She's concerned about rust.*

I don't think I need anything melted, lit on fire, or blown up right now, but I'll keep her offer in mind, he responded.

That's disappointing, a second voice said. Jaxi. *The flight back across the ocean was boring. Some excitement would not be unappreciated.*

Ridge was getting used to the idea that his ladylove walked around with a sentient sword, one that sometimes shared thoughts directly with him, but he still found Jaxi's presence in his head disconcerting. A few months ago, he hadn't believed magic existed, and now a sorceress—and her sword—telepathically communicated with him on a daily basis. He could accept it; he just wished the rest of the country could. He hadn't forgotten that when they left, some secret organization had been trying to blow up Sardelle.

"He *better* be looking for the king," Kaika growled, staring through the leaves at the man with the spyglass. The wagon had chugged past them without slowing down. "Nobody seemed to be looking very hard for him when we left. I should have been sent out. I even volunteered." She drummed agitated fingers on the pistol that hung from her utility belt, along with a dagger, ammo pouches, and a bag of fuses for however many explosives she had in her pack. "Listen, Colonel. I owe him a favor from way back."

"The king?"

"Yes. You know the elite forces don't take women. That's a rule. I was determined to get in anyway, because my brother... well, I had something to prove, that's all. After being rejected several times, I went to the king for an audience. The line was long, and he wasn't spending much time with anyone. I was afraid he wouldn't even see me. I used the cleaning supplies in the closet outside of his audience hall to blow up an ancient urn—this is what passes as a logical move to a nineteen-year-old woman, yes. That made an impression on him. Fortunately, he was more intrigued than horrified, and he's the one who arranged for me to get orders into the program. I've gotten to see the world, make a difference for our country, and sleep with all manner of exotic foreigners under the guise of obtaining mission-critical information."

"Exotic foreigners, you say? No wonder you feel indebted to him."

Kaika's hand twitched, like she might whack him in the chest, but she seemed to remember that he outranked her. She lowered her hand instead. "Not everybody gets to be a national hero who can crook a finger and get a fantasy bed companion any night of the week. Some of us have to work harder for that. Anyway, that's not my point. I mean I've had the career of my dreams so far and more adventure than any girl could ever crave, and I owe him for that."

Ridge gripped her shoulder. "We'll find him."

"I'm thinking about infiltrating the castle."

Ridge dropped his hand. "What?"

"We need intel. The queen's in there somewhere. If she's not a complete shrub, she might know something. If someone's controlling her with drugs or blackmail, it would take someone observing from the inside to find out. I can do that."

"That's... a more direct approach than I was planning to take." At least to start with, Ridge had simply planned to question some people at HQ and find General Ort so he could get some accurate information on what had been going on higher up in his chain of command—as in, what in all the cursed realms had someone been thinking in handing the flier squadrons over to that hairy-knuckled ape, Therrik? If anyone knew anything about the king, it ought to be Ort or one of the other generals that was regularly in and out of the castle.

"I'm already AWOL, sir," Kaika said. "Let me do this. I'll report back to you, I promise. I heard a rumor that the king was taken somewhere in a flier, so..."

"Ah, so that's why you came with Apex to get us."

Kaika shrugged. "Normally, I handle my own problems, but if I can't *get* to my problems..."

"Everybody thinks of me as a flying rickshaw service." Ridge peered through the leaves of the bush. The wagon had gone over a hill and disappeared from sight, only the black cloud in the air marking its passage. It should be safe to rejoin the others. "I want to gather some intel locally before sending people off in different directions. Give me a couple of hours to mull over your request."

"My request?"

"Yes, isn't that what you were making? As an officer to a more senior officer? A request to infiltrate the castle? Because I'm sure you wouldn't be thinking of going anyway, against said senior officer's wishes, right?"

"Do you really want me to answer that?" Kaika asked.

"Perhaps not." Ridge felt like a hypocrite just bringing it up. Hadn't their mission to Cofahre started with him throwing his mission commander over the side of his flier?

"What local intel?" Kaika asked. "We're still fifteen miles out from the city."

Ridge smiled. "My mom."

* * *

Sardelle kept her hood up and her cloak pulled tightly about her, in part to keep the rain off, but also because she worried about being recognized. She had no idea as to the size of the organization that had been hunting her before they left a few weeks earlier, but she did not feel safe back on Iskandian land, even out in this rural area.

But you felt safe in Cofahre? Jaxi asked. *Those people would happily kill an Iskandian sorceress too.*

Yes, but we can happily kill them right back. It's different when it's your own people hunting you.

These aren't our people. The Referatu are long gone.

I know that, but we were born here. Actually, Sardelle had been born in the mountains, several hundred miles inland, but she had often passed through the capital when she had worked with the army as a mage adviser three centuries earlier, and she knew these lands well. The city had changed a great deal, with its steam-powered machinery and vehicles, but these farms appeared no different than they had in her time, and a twinge of nostalgia came over her. She almost felt that if she went to her parents' house right now, she would find them there, and her brother and cousins and friends, as well. But logically, she knew that she had spent three hundred years in a stasis chamber and that the only relatives she might find would be generations and generations removed.

Ridge jogged up to her side and wrapped an arm around her shoulders. "Are you doing all right? We're almost there. See that windmill up on the hill? The little village where my mom lives is right behind that. We can wash and—" he plucked at his rain-sodden shirt, "—*dry* there. She'll feed us. Might even have pie."

Ridge was scruffier than she had ever seen him, with the rain plastering his short brown hair to his forehead, mud smearing one cheek, and several days' worth of beard growth darkening his face, but when he smiled at her, it still made her weak in the knees. With his clean-cut features and strong jaw, he managed to look handsome even when he *was* scruffy. And that smile—some might call it a boyish grin, even if he was well out of his boyhood years—always had an appealing and kissable quality to it. She made herself smile back, even if the rain and the rest of the situation had her heart heavy. She missed her family and friends, but she had never had anyone like Ridge in her century, and she was starting to think of his pilots, at least the ones they had been working with closely, as new friends.

Even though there wasn't much comfort to be had from two sodden bodies pressing together, Sardelle slipped her arm around his waist. "Pie, you say? Your mother already sounds more hospitable than your father."

She hoped that hospitality would extend to her. She was tempted to ask how Ridge would introduce her, since he had fumbled over the introduction when they had met his father, who had not been overly friendly toward her after learning about her aptitude for the arcane.

"She is. She should be happy to see us. Been a while since I had a chance to stop by."

Sardelle wouldn't get her hopes up as far as his mother being happy to see *her*. If she hated magic as much as the rest of the continent these days, she may not be tickled by the idea of a "witch" for her only son. Apparently, wanted posters with Sardelle's face on them now adorned every other streetlamp in the city, so she couldn't hope to keep her abilities from anyone for long. Though maybe Ridge's mother wouldn't have seen the posters way out here.

"You look glum," Ridge said, watching her face. "Do I need to promise you more than pie? Perhaps a foot rub? Or another type of rubbing?" He waggled his eyebrows suggestively.

Sardelle tried to arrange her features into a less worried visage. She ought to be appreciative that he was going to take her to see his mother, even if it was part of their mission and the rest of the squadron was going too. At least he hadn't spoken of hiding her and her witchy ways when they met. This talk of rubbing sounded promising, too, though perhaps not if his mother would be in the next room.

"It *has* been a while since we had any privacy." Sardelle extended a hand toward the troops ahead of and behind them, Duck, Apex, Cas, Kaika, and Tolemek, though Tolemek might object to being called a troop. "I don't suppose your mother has a guest house?"

"Guest house? Uhm, there's a pottery shed."

"Spare bedroom?"

"There's *a* bedroom. I sleep on the couch when I visit."

"Hm, then we may have to wait for intimate moments. I don't think I want you rubbing anything of mine with all of your pilots spread out on the floor around us."

Ridge scratched his jaw. "Nothing at all?"

"You know I'm not an exhibitionist."

Spoilsport.

Hush, Jaxi.

You've disappointed your soul snozzle terribly.

Didn't we agree that you would stay out of his head, except for emergencies? Sardelle had to keep reminding herself to do the same. On occasion, she spoke to him telepathically, but since he had been born into this same culture that feared all things magical, she tried not to intrude often. To her relief, he accepted that the mind-to-mind communication was useful at times, but he wasn't comfortable with the idea of not being able to have private thoughts.

After the restraint you two showed during the course of the mission through that jungle island, he views a continued absence of rubbing as an emergency, Jaxi informed her. *He's now trying to remember if the pottery shed has a door.*

Jaxi!

"We'll see if we can find a few private moments," Ridge said, squeezing her shoulder.

Sardelle resisted the urge to ask after the pottery shed. Then she would have to admit that her nosy sword had been sauntering through his thoughts.

"Tonight may be the only quiet night we have," he added, his expression turning more somber.

Sardelle knew he was worried about the rest of his squadron—she also couldn't imagine that unstable Colonel Therrik being in charge of a battalion of pilots—and about the king, and about his own fate too. He had broken more than a few rules when he left, and even though they had succeeded in denying the Cofah the source of their dragon blood, they didn't have much proof of the deed, other than the vials they had returned with. The dragon itself, along with Tolemek's sister, had not been seen since flying away from the island. There was also no way to know how much dragon blood the Cofah had stockpiled that Sardelle, Ridge, and the others had never seen. They could still be making more of those troublesome fliers and magic-guided rockets.

"We're getting close," Ridge said.

Sardelle decided to try to enjoy this one quiet night that they might have before heading into the city and trying to locate General Ort and the king—or whatever the plan was. Ridge hadn't shared his plans yet, and she knew Kaika, in particular, was waiting for that. She had gone AWOL to join them and also had to be worried about the fate of her career.

"You didn't grow up around here, right?" Sardelle asked, watching a couple of youths chopping wood behind a house in the distance. "You once said you were born in the city."

Ridge nodded. "A poor part of the city. I always worried about my mom after I wasn't around to protect her. Or at least stand in front of her and attempt to look tall and fierce enough to deter bullies."

"Did that work?"

Ridge touched an old scar on his chin. "Sometimes. More often, she bribed the toughs with her pies in exchange for leaving her alone. Anyway, as soon as I had enough money, I helped her get a place out here. She draws and paints and makes pots and tiles and other artsy things. Seemed like a good area for her. She sells things at the market on the weekends." He raised his voice to call to the front of their group. "Ahn? Take the next right."

Lieutenant Caslin Ahn was leading the soggy group, with her sniper rifle resting in her arms and her eyes alert as she scanned the countryside. That behemoth of a sword that she had retrieved from the ziggurat on Owanu Owanus hung across her back, making her appear even smaller than her five feet in height. She lifted a hand in acknowledgment but did not say anything. Tolemek walked behind her, rain dripping from his long ropes of dark hair. Sardelle sometimes wondered if Cas spoke more to him than she did to others. Either way, their relationship seemed to suit them.

"Did you say pie, sir?" came a plaintive question from behind them. Lieutenant Duck was as soggy and unkempt as Ridge, but he didn't have the facial structure to manage to appear handsome through the damp and grime. His big ears stuck out, flushed red from the bite of the wind. "If that's the case, I'm happier than bees on a flower that you didn't find anyone to talk to on the road and that we've got to get intel at your mom's house."

Lieutenant Apex, a quieter and more introspective man, walked at Duck's side. He didn't say anything about pie, but his expression had grown a touch wistful. Captain Kaika, the last member of their group, walked behind the two of them, the alert set of her face more akin to Cas's than the men's. She looked like someone focused more on her mission than on acquiring baked goods. Sardelle wondered what it said about their group that the toughest soldiers seemed to be the women.

"I can't make any promises," Ridge said, as they turned again, heading up a dirt road lined with cozy cottages. "I didn't write to let her know we were coming, but I wager she'll put something together."

"We spending the night here, sir?" Kaika asked.

Ridge glanced at the sky—the sun hadn't been out since they returned to the mainland, but noon had passed, and the gray clouds were darker than they had been when the squadron first landed. "Most likely."

"You think it's safe to leave your fliers back in Crazy Canyon?"

"I wouldn't ordinarily, but we camouflaged them well, and the weather is dreary. Shouldn't be pirates about. They're too lazy to go out and thieve in the rain."

Tolemek, former pirate and current expatriate scientist, must have heard the comment, because he glanced back. He gave Ridge the squinty eye but did not otherwise comment, perhaps because Ridge was waving them up one of the walkways to a quaint one-story cottage. Thanks to the waterlogged countryside, most of the houses seemed on the drab side, but this stucco structure had perky blue window shutters and trim, a front door painted with a mural of a farmer feeding chickens, and numerous bright, floral tiles embedded in the walls. All around the grounds, barrels and tubs had been turned into pots, some with hardy green plants sticking out and others waiting on spring flowers. A couple of benches sat on a puddle-filled flagstone patio, and Sardelle glimpsed a small pottery shed squatting against the side of the house, numerous ceramic wares stacked around it. From the walkway, she couldn't tell if it had a door or not, but it didn't look large enough for extensive... rubbing.

As she and the others strode toward the front door, several cats ran out of the pottery shed. They darted to the walkway, meowing as they came. Ridge stopped and stared down at them, so Sardelle did too. A white fluffy feline immediately leaned against her leg, leaving hairs on her travel leathers. Oh, well. They had been in need of washing, anyway.

"Problem, sir?" Cas asked, stepping aside so Ridge could approach the door first. She hadn't attracted any cats, but two were zeroing in on Tolemek's legs.

"Nothing unexpected," Ridge said, though he wore a bemused expression. He leaned toward Sardelle to whisper, "There are more every time I come."

Though they appeared well fed, the cats meowed plaintively, and Sardelle wished she had some scraps for them. She crouched down to stroke one of them—the cat had planted itself in the walkway, so it would have been hard to pass without doing so.

"I'm going to be terribly jealous if I don't get rubbed tonight, when the cat did," Ridge murmured.

She swatted his leg. "I thought you were offering to do the rubbing."

"I imagined you being so enthused that you would return the favor."

"Zirkander, you're too old to be so horny," Tolemek grumbled, stepping off the walkway and pointing to the door, clearly hoping someone would knock so they could get an invitation out of the rain. "Can't you save that until nighttime?"

"I'm as fit and virile as you are." Ridge strode past him with a glare.

"But old. Cas agrees." Tolemek nodded to Cas, who merely raised an eyebrow slightly.

"Lieutenant Ahn knows better than to make aspersions about her C.O.'s age." Ridge walked onto the stoop and raised a hand to knock, but the door opened before he touched it.

Sardelle glimpsed a tall, lean woman with a woven band of dried grass and flowers holding back her long gray hair before she flung herself at Ridge. Several more cats flowed out of the house past her legs.

"Ridgewalker Meadowlark, you've been gone for—" The rest was inaudible, because her face was buried in his shoulder.

"Meadowlark," Duck said, then sniggered. "Hearing your C.O. called that is…"

"Inexplicably delightful?" Apex suggested. "Risible? Satisfying?"

"Fun," Duck said.

"Ah, yes. Fun."

"Good to see you, Mom," Ridge said to the top of her head, giving her a return hug. "I saw Dad recently. He's pining for you terribly."

His mother didn't let him go, but she leaned back enough to

snort and meet his eyes. "I'll bet. What's going on here? With all the trouble in the city, I didn't expect to see you. The rumors said you were missing." She searched his face as if the answers might be inked on his cheeks.

"I wasn't missing so much as on a mission with select members of my squadron. We got the news that there was some chaos in the capital, so we decided to check in here before heading to town."

While he had been speaking, Mrs. Zirkander had leaned to the side and started taking in his entourage. "Your... squadron, dear?" Her eyebrows rose as she considered Tolemek.

Kaika, Cas, Duck, and Apex looked like soldiers, albeit scruffy ones at the moment, but Tolemek still had the air of a pirate about him, especially when he wasn't wearing his white lab coat. Sardelle had no idea what she looked like currently. There had been few opportunities for bathing or washing clothes, so all she knew was that her travel leathers were dirty and fragrant after their adventures. She wished she could have met Ridge's mother wearing an attractive dress and with her hair done up instead of simply tugged back in a ponytail in need of shampoo and a brush.

"And a few civilian experts," Ridge said. "Everyone, this is my mom, Fern. Mom, that's Tolemek, Lieutenants Ahn, Duck, and Apex, and Captain Kaika."

Fern's eyes shifted from person to person, following the introduction. Sardelle's stomach fluttered with nerves when the woman looked at her. Fern wore a clay-stained apron over a floral dress and boots practical for the wet weather. Numerous beaded bracelets dangled from her wrists, all made in a cheerful style reminiscent of the decorative tiles embedded in the walls.

Sardelle clasped her hands in front of her, waiting to see how Ridge would introduce her. Civilian expert? Or something less distant? Also, would his mother have seen those posters and recognize her?

You're a powerful sorceress. There's no need to be so nervous.

How would you know, Jaxi? You've never been introduced to a lover's mother.

If I had been, I would have been fabulous.

"Mom?" Ridge extended his arm toward Sardelle and smiled. "This is Sardelle Terushan from a small town over in the Ice Blade Mountains. She's smart, beautiful, adventurous, and she'll have your back in a fight, whether it's on the ground or five thousand feet in the air. She's absolutely wonderful, and I love her."

The blatant, heartfelt words stunned Sardelle, especially after the way Ridge had stumbled over introducing her to his father. His mother seemed stunned too. She stared back and forth from Ridge to Sardelle as her mouth dangled open.

Ridge, his eyes twinkling, lifted a hand to cover his mouth and whisper to Sardelle. "Did I do better this time? I've been rehearsing."

Sardelle tried to swallow, but more emotion than she would have expected swelled in her throat. She nodded.

"How come we don't get introductions like that?" Duck muttered. "We've got his back too."

"You want him to profess his love for you?" Apex murmured back.

"No, that would be weird."

"Then be quiet."

"Ridge," Fern breathed, taking a step toward Sardelle and lifting her arms, "that's so—" She halted mid-step and squinted at him. "This isn't a joke, is it? You know I'm too old for your pranks."

Sardelle wasn't sure what to make of the question, but Ridge only grinned.

"No joke, Mom. I love her. And I think she loves me too. We'll know for sure later when I try to talk her into the pottery shed."

Sardelle flushed and thought about slapping him in the chest, but he had stepped aside so his mother could walk closer.

"Hello, ma'am." Sardelle wasn't sure what else to call her. Fern seemed so informal. Would she prefer to be Ms. Zirkander?

"It's so wonderful to meet you, Sardelle." Fern clasped Sardelle's hands in her own clay-stained ones, her palms lightly callused, the hands of someone who worked for a living, or at least worked hard at her art. "Ridge doesn't usually bring women home, so I can't tell you how happy I am to see you."

"I'm pleased to be here." Sardelle meant it, and her smile was genuine, but she couldn't help but worry what would happen when the truth came out. Ridge hadn't mentioned sorcery in that introduction. Maybe he planned on keeping it a secret, or waiting to share the information.

So, should I not start glowing and throbbing obnoxiously? Jaxi asked.

Please don't.

I won't if he doesn't.

He?

Kasandral. The dragon-slaying sword. He's been glowing vigorously at night when nobody is looking. I think he likes Lieutenant Ahn.

Should I find that alarming? Sardelle asked, aware of Fern looking her up and down. Once again, she wished she were more presentable.

Probably.

"Come inside, dear," Fern said. "Let's get you out of the rain." She let go of one but not both of Sardelle's hands, using the one she held to guide Sardelle to the door.

Ridge smirked as they went by, as if he had expected nothing less than this welcome.

"Uh," Kaika said. "Are we invited in too?"

Fern didn't seem to hear her. "How long have you and Ridge been seeing each other?" she asked Sardelle as they stepped into the house, where the chatter of birds greeted them. Several large bamboo cages hung from the rafters, with colorful canaries, budgies, and cockatiels singing from perches within them.

"Since the beginning of winter," Sardelle said, glancing back to make sure everyone else was following. Ridge was waving them to the doorway.

"And you don't mind that he flies?" Fern raised her eyebrows, leading her around an easel with a half-finished landscape on it, and toward a seating area.

Not so long as he doesn't mind that I manipulate matter with my mind... "Not at all," Sardelle said.

Or have a talking sword?

That too. Though you're more of a telepathic sword than a talking one.

I could vocalize if I wanted to, Jaxi said. *Not that anyone could hear me over the noise of all those birds. And cats. This woman is odd.*

I'd guess she's lonely. Not everybody has a sword to keep them company.

This is true. I'm certain you would be terribly forlorn if I wasn't here for you.

Terribly.

"I know in the past, he's struggled to find someone who can accept that he's always putting himself in danger," Fern said, sitting on a couch and patting the cushion next to her.

"I trust that he's capable up there." Sardelle sat next to her. "I've seen it for myself, in fact. And I put myself in danger, too, so I'm used to that."

"You do? What kind of work do you do?"

Er, yes, what kind of work did she do that she could share? She almost delivered the line Ridge had been giving to the men on base, that she was an archaeologist, but his mother might be knowledgeable on that, given that her husband was a professional treasure hunter. If she started asking about universities and professors, Sardelle would have no idea what to say. "I'm a doctor."

"And you find that dangerous?"

"Well. I have to heal soldiers sometimes."

"Ah, I understand. They can be ungrateful."

"Does she know we're all in here?" Duck whispered to Apex. The rest of the group had moseyed into the living room, and Ridge was shutting the door.

"Unless you give them sweets," Fern added with a wink.

"Or any kind of food," Ridge said. "Mom, can we sleep here tonight? Cadge some of your food? We have to make some plans before heading into the city. Did you know that the king is missing? Or he was? Is that still true?"

"I believe so, Ridge. There's a newspaper on that table over there if you need to update yourself." Fern patted Sardelle's knee and leaned forward. "I apologize for being forward, dear, but is it too soon to ask if you're thinking of marrying my son?"

"Mom," Ridge groaned, drawing out the single syllable into at least three. There might have been more syllables, but he broke it off when he almost tripped over a cat on his way to the table.

"I'm embarrassing him." Fern smiled, not looking the least chagrined about it.

"I wouldn't object to the possibility," Sardelle said, all the while wondering if Fern's birdsong would change when she learned about her talents. "And he's teased me with the idea."

"*Teased* you? Ridge? You're not doing it right."

Ridge had reached the newspaper and was frowning down at the front page. He did not respond. The rest of the squadron was standing or shuffling their feet, and Sardelle felt guilty for getting all the attention while they dripped onto the floor and didn't know where to go.

"What about children?" Fern asked, patting Sardelle's thigh again. "Has he told you how much I would love to have grandchildren? Have you considered having babies? Will it be soon?"

The bluntness of the questions took Sardelle aback, and she had no idea how to answer. It wasn't as if she had never thought of having children, but she had never had anyone she had contemplated having them *with*. And she and Ridge had been so busy—and she had so many people who wanted her dead—that she hadn't sat down to contemplate it lately.

"If it's all right with you, Mom, we thought we'd rescue the king and save the nation first." Ridge was frowning down at the newspaper as he spoke, but he did glance toward Sardelle and mouth, "Ignore her."

"I didn't realize the entire nation was in danger, sir," Apex said.

"It is if the queen is in charge," Duck said. "What does she know about defending a continent?"

"I don't know much about what she knows. In the portraits, she's usually shown reading a book or doing needlepoint. She seems to keep to herself."

"If this article is right, she's in charge now," Ridge said. "I wonder if she's the one who forced General Ort to step down and appointed that muscles-for-brains Therrik to lead the flier squadrons."

"I doubt she has anything to do with military matters, sir," Apex said.

"Well, I want to find out who *is* making those decisions. And who's feeding these stories to the newspaper, as well—stories about me being AWOL and being controlled by a witch who *blew up my house* to warn me of the consequences of disobeying. A decapitated luck dragon was found among the ashes. *Decapitated.* Did you see this, Mom?" He shook the paper in her direction.

Sardelle fought to keep the panic off her expression. Maybe it had been inevitable if the papers had written about it, but she hadn't expected him to bring up witches to his mother.

Relax, she doesn't believe in magic. You're probably fine. But... about your occupation? You probably should have gone with archaeologist.

Why?

She's got some bunions she's thinking of asking you to look at. Since you're a doctor.

Oh. Sardelle had not imagined medical care being a part of her meeting with Ridge's family. *They wouldn't be the first bunions I've seen.*

Unfortunately, I know that.

"Yes, I was very worried about you," Fern said. "The article neglected to clarify that you weren't *in* the house when it blew up."

"Why would they blow it up?" Ridge gave Sardelle a plaintive look. "Nothing they wanted was in it by then."

"You should have gotten a bigger luck dragon, sir," Apex said, his eyes gleaming with humor.

"Maybe he should have rubbed the *real* dragon's belly," Duck muttered.

Fern blinked. "Real dragon? Dragons don't exist."

She also doesn't believe in dragons, Jaxi mentioned.

Yes, I see.

"Right," Ridge said, walking to the couch. "Mom, would you mind making something for my men to eat? We've had a rough few days, and we're starving. Also, we have some classified information to discuss." He tilted his head toward the kitchen door.

Fern looked at Sardelle as she stood up. "Does he show up on *your* doorstep unannounced and ask you to cook for his people?"

Before Sardelle could decide if she wanted to admit to not having notable cooking skills, Ridge said, "We're sharing the same doorstep, Mom. Or we were before it was blown up." Her face twisted in rueful disbelief as he patted her on the shoulder, gently but firmly steering her toward the kitchen.

"Are you?" Fern smiled at Sardelle. "That's wonderful. Ridge, when you're done rescuing people and using my cottage for a safe house, make sure to discuss babies with her."

Ridge grimaced. "Mom, you should have had more kids if you wanted to guarantee grandchildren."

"I tried, but your father was so seldom here. I would have had to tie him to the bed while wearing lingerie made of ancient maps to convince him to engage in *local* mountain climbing expeditions."

"Mountain climbing..." Ridge's grimace deepened and he glanced at his troops. "Mom, we don't want to hear about that."

He shooed her into the kitchen before plopping down beside Sardelle. A gray cat hopped into his lap. Someone must not have closed the door quickly enough, because a number that had previously been outdoors had made their way indoors. Judging by the tilt to this one's head, it was contemplating using Ridge's shoulder for a launching pad to reach one of the birdcages. Sardelle trusted the bamboo was sturdy enough to thwart invasion attempts.

"Sit down, everyone," Ridge said, waving to the other chairs and couches. "Let's try to keep our planning session brief." He nodded toward the kitchen door. Fern hadn't closed it entirely, so Sardelle nudged it gently with her mind so that it *snicked* shut. "As you heard, my mom doesn't believe in dragons or magic."

"Wish I still didn't," Kaika muttered, choosing a plush chair. She flopped back in it, dangling a long leg over the armrest. She had been the last of the group to learn of Sardelle's abilities, but despite her comment, she hadn't seemed fazed by it. Sardelle wished she could hope for such acceptance—or indifference—from all of Iskandia. Duck and especially Apex had been less comfortable with the notion, but after the deadly situations the group had escaped from, they seemed less disturbed by her. Apex still gave Tolemek a lot of guarded glances—one of his concoctions had been responsible for the death of everyone in the village where he had grown up—but he hadn't said a rude word to Sardelle.

While the others settled in, Cas remained by the wall between the front door and a window and peeked outside. Duck and Apex took another small couch, which left a spot for Tolemek on the other side of Ridge. He looked distastefully at his only option for a moment before perching on the edge of the cushion.

"What's the plan, sir?" Kaika asked. She may have appeared relaxed, but her eyes were sharp as they regarded Ridge. "I have some explosives in my pack, and I can get more."

"How will blowing things up help us find the king?" Ridge asked.

"I don't know, but it would make me feel better."

Ridge leaned forward. "Here are our problems, in no particular order." He lifted his fingers to count them off. "First, missing king. Second, that monkey's ass Colonel Therrik in charge of the flier battalion." He clenched his jaw. "Third, General Ort forced to step down by an unknown person. Lastly and worst, the country being vulnerable to attack if the Cofah or anyone else hears about the turmoil here, and I can only assume they'll know soon if they don't already. I want to find General Ort and get his report on what's been happening."

Sardelle didn't mention that the wanted posters and people hunting for her were also a problem, since she knew he had to deal with military matters first, but she certainly intended to do something about that organization hunting her.

"Aren't colonels supposed to report to generals and not the other way around, sir?" Duck asked.

"Probably, but I have an unorthodox method of dealing with the command structure."

Every single one of his troops snorted.

"Finding Ort needs to be our first priority, and—" a slight, pleased smirk crept onto Ridge's face, "—there's someone else I've been thinking about visiting, someone who very likely has some intelligence, given his recent and unlikely promotion. An interrogation could be *most* rewarding."

"You want to interrogate Colonel Therrik, sir?" Ahn asked, her voice laced with skepticism. "He almost broke your neck before we took off for Cofahre. And that was how he felt about you *before* you got him airsick in Crazy Canyon, knocked him unconscious, and abandoned him by the side of the road."

"Yes, Ahn, thank you for the recap. Clearly, I wouldn't be looking to apprehend him physically. At least not in a fair fight. I was thinking of an ambush, followed by him being tied to a chair and convinced to speak to us."

"Convinced with fists?"

Ridge's expression grew wishful.

"Perhaps Tolemek could make a truth serum so it's not necessary to resort to fists," Sardelle said. "I've heard that's in his repertoire."

"It is," Cas said, her tone flat rather than encouraging. Tolemek shrugged apologetically at her.

"No fists?" Ridge laid a hand on Sardelle's arm. "You're ruining my daydream for me."

"Sorry. You can still tie him to a chair, if you wish."

"You don't want to physically confront the colonel, anyway," Kaika said. "I wouldn't even try an ambush. He's deadly in unarmed combat. Nowon was the only one I ever knew who could..." She scowled at the floor for a moment, then took a deep breath for her lost comrade before adding, "He could come out on top at least half of the time, but he was deadly too. Quick, agile, and crafty."

"I'm going to try not to take that as a slight against my own combat skills," Ridge said. "But I do concede your point. Tee, put a truth serum and a knockout potion on my shopping list, will you?"

"I'm not a pharmacy, Zirkander," Tolemek growled. "There's

nothing in the contract I signed about rescuing rulers or picking fights with surly colonels."

If Tolemek's scowl bothered Ridge, he didn't show it. He smiled and said, "Can you have something ready by morning?"

Tolemek's eyes narrowed.

"Tomorrow night? And just to be clear, *I'm* not the surly colonel, right?"

"Fine," Tolemek said, "but I'll need access to my lab. I depleted my reserves in that jungle."

Ridge looked down, seemed to realize he had been petting the cat, which had settled into his lap, and set his hands by his sides. "It might be dangerous for you to be seen in town." He glanced at Sardelle, doubtlessly thinking it would be dangerous for her too. "Colonel Surly was picking the fight with you, not the other way around, as I recall. Maybe I can go with you before checking in on Ort."

"I don't need any help getting into my own lab."

"Or maybe Ahn can go with you."

Tolemek settled against the backrest. "Hm."

Ridge turned toward Sardelle and murmured, "I didn't want any competition for the pottery shed."

Sardelle glanced toward the door to see what Cas thought of the assignment, but she had slipped outside. Sardelle hoped that didn't mean trouble was coming to find them.

"Duck," Ridge said, "I hate to give you the boring and uneventful duty, but someone needs to guard the fliers until we know if it's safe to bring them to the hangar."

It was probably safe *now*, Sardelle guessed, for someone who wouldn't mind reporting in and being added back to the roster under Therrik's command. She could see why skulking around without anybody knowing he was in town would appeal more to Ridge, but hoped he wasn't sinking himself deeper into a tar pit.

"Oh?" Duck asked. "There's decent hunting in Crazy Canyon. I won't mind."

"Good. Apex, I want you to find someone from Wolf Squadron. Don't go into the fort, since we don't want to reveal ourselves yet, but maybe you can catch someone at Wings and

Swords. Find out if Therrik is treating them decently and if they know anything about the king or anything else that's going on around here."

"Yes, sir," Apex said.

"Am I coming along to help with your nemesis?" Sardelle worried that he would get himself pummeled—or worse—if he tried to accost Therrik.

"Actually," Ridge said, "with your unique skills, I thought you would be the perfect person to—"

The kitchen door swung open, and Fern walked out with a pitcher and a stack of cups. She set them down on a low table, said, "Please enjoy some mulled wine, my friends," then returned to the kitchen. She managed to leave the door ajar again.

Sardelle waited until she had returned to the cutting block by the sink before easing it shut.

Ridge leaned close to Sardelle, his shoulder touching hers. "I know you have your own concerns and want to research that organization that was after you, but it might be a good idea to sneak someone into the castle to check on the queen."

Kaika dropped her foot to the floor with a clomp and straightened up. "That's *my* mission."

"I thought it could be both of your missions." Ridge smiled at Kaika and Sardelle, then walked to the table to pour drinks.

Kaika's eyes closed partway as she scrutinized Sardelle. Since Kaika and Apex had returned to Iskandia instead of going to the jungle with the rest of the group, Sardelle hadn't yet had a chance to work with her. Apex may have explained some of her talents, but Kaika hadn't seen many of them for herself. She probably wasn't sure what to think of Sardelle. For that matter, Sardelle did not know what to think of *her*. She had heard that Kaika, after Nowon had been killed, had single-handedly taken out numerous Cofah soldiers in that volcano outpost and then planted the explosives that had blown it up. She was clearly an asset to a military team, but if she didn't like Sardelle—or magic—then working with her would be difficult.

Kaika was still staring in Sardelle's direction when Ridge returned to hand each of them cups. As he headed back to pour more wine, Sardelle thought about brushing across Kaika's mind and trying to read a few surface thoughts, but she always questioned herself when she did that, especially with people who weren't enemies. In her time, there had been laws against such intrusions. Just because there was nobody around to enforce those laws now did not make it right to poke around.

Sardelle sipped from the ceramic mug.

She doesn't hate you, Jaxi said, *but she's under the impression that you're a healer and wouldn't be useful in a fight. She also wouldn't mind if a rogue dragon ate you and she had to console your lover with vigorous sex.*

Sardelle choked on her wine.

Perhaps I should have kept that information to myself. Jaxi's contrite tone was not convincing.

Perhaps you should stay out of other people's heads, especially the heads of allies. At least Sardelle *thought* she could consider Kaika an ally. Ridge could consider her one. That was a certainty.

I'd say so.

I thought she was attracted to Apex.

Oh, she wants to have vigorous sex with him too. She's irritated that he's either not attracted to her or is obtuse about reading her not-so-subtle signals.

Sardelle rubbed the back of her neck. *Is there anyone she doesn't* want to have vigorous sex with?

She thinks Duck is homely and would only consider Tolemek if he got a haircut.

That didn't entirely answer my question.

Jaxi grinned into her mind. *No, I suppose it didn't.*

A warm hand touched the back of hers. Ridge had finished handing out drinks and stood behind her. He took over rubbing the back of her neck and bent low to whisper, "Are the spices in the wine too strong, or is Jaxi making inappropriate comments?"

Sardelle leaned back into his hand. "You've come to know me—us—well in such a short time."

"It's been an eventful couple of months."

Kaika sank back into her chair, looked away from Sardelle—or perhaps the fact that Ridge was massaging her—and stared thoughtfully into her wine.

Even though she knew she should ignore the results of Jaxi's spying, Sardelle couldn't help but ask, *She's not thinking of blowing me up to get to him, is she?*

I don't believe so. She was somewhat mortified by the mother and the idea of making babies with him. I think she's just curious as to how effectively he could make her bed bounce. Now she's thinking about the king.

And making his bed bounce?

Rescuing him.

"You didn't mention what you think of the idea of infiltrating the castle." Ridge glanced at Kaika, then gazed down at Sardelle, a question in his eyes.

"If you think that's a wise course of action, I can probably be of assistance there." Hoping she wasn't being presumptuous, Sardelle touched his mind lightly. *Is there more?*

He pulled a few loose strands of hair behind her ear. *I'm not sure* any *of these actions are wise. Kaika is the one who wants to infiltrate the castle. She believes the queen will know something, or that she'll be able to figure out who's controlling her. She's set on going, and no matter what I say, I can guarantee that she will be gone in the morning. She's extremely capable*—along with the words, Ridge thought of the Cofah volcano base that had blown up as they were drifting away from it in that hot air balloon—*and I could let her go alone, but I'm worried explosives won't be the answer to bringing the king back. With your talents—and Jaxi's talents, of course—you might be able to see more in the castle than she could.*

I don't mind going. There are things to be said for the direct approach.

Good things or impulsive and dangerous things? Ridge asked.

I'll have to let you know after we've stormed the castle.

"That's creepy," Duck announced.

Sardelle dropped her gaze and folded her hands in her lap, certain he had noticed that she and Ridge had been gazing oddly at each other and not speaking.

"When did Raptor add swordsmanship to her list of skills?" Duck added. He had drifted over to the front window with his mug in hand.

"She's passable with a knife, but usually favors her rifle," Apex said. "Or her flier's guns."

Ridge drew back from Sardelle. "I thought she was watching for trouble." He walked toward the window. "She's not cutting up any visitors, is she?"

"No, she's doing practice forms," Duck said. "With that glowy sword. I hope the neighbors aren't looking."

"It's not the first time," Tolemek said. "She said she doesn't trust that dragon not to go back to my peo—the Cofah in some capacity, and that she intends to be ready if it ever shows up here."

An irritated yowl sounded, and Ridge jerked his foot up.

The kitchen door opened, and Fern hustled out with a tray of food. "Did someone step on a cat? What happened?"

"Sorry, I didn't see that one there," Ridge said, frowning out the window.

Sardelle wondered if she should join him, but she only had power over one glowing sword, and the dragon slayer wasn't it.

"That's Mimi." Fern pointed at the spotted cat skulking away.

"Of course it is. Mom, when I moved you out to the country, it wasn't so you could collect *more* stray cats."

"Oh? Was it so my humble cottage could be turned into your secret safe house in the event of an emergency?"

"Well, no."

She shrugged. "Cats happen, dear. That's just how it is."

Cas opened the front door and stepped inside, sweat gleaming on her forehead. "Soldiers are coming."

So much for a secret safe house, Jaxi said.

Chapter 2

Ridge stood in the dark with his back pressed against the cottage wall, his ear toward the window his mom had opened before shooing them outside. Sardelle stood in front of him, her back to his chest, and he resisted the urge to rest his hands on her shoulders. He was too tense. He would end up gripping her like a falcon with talons. He hated hiding from a bunch of soldiers he outranked, or hiding from Iskandian soldiers at all. He should be in there with them, seeing if the locals knew of a place to share a beer, but if he wanted a chance at surprising Colonel Therrik, it would be best if nobody knew Ridge was back on the continent. These troops might be out looking for information on the king, but he found it telling that they had driven straight up to his mother's house.

"Shouldn't we be hiding farther away, sir?" Duck asked. The entire team was lined up against the back of the house. Voices came from out front, where a steam wagon hissed and groaned as it idled. Someone had already knocked on the door. "What if they look back here?"

"I'm not going far while they're talking to my mother." Never before would Ridge have worried that his mom could be in trouble from soldiers, but someone had declared him AWOL, blown up his house, and had General Ort removed from duty. That same someone could have put out orders for soldiers to question people associated with Ridge, and who knew what methods would have been approved for that questioning?

His hand balled into a fist. If he heard so much as a raised voice inside, he would deal with these men, surprising Therrik be damned.

Sardelle found his hand and rested hers lightly on it. "Don't say anything if they look out here," she said softly. "I'll make sure they don't see us."

"I'm not sure if that's comforting or not," Apex murmured.

"It'll be all right," Duck said.

Ridge touched Sardelle's waist. He was still too tense for handholding, but he wanted her to know he appreciated that she was there, looking out for them.

A thunk came from inside. Ridge shifted closer to the window.

"...haven't seen him, ma'am?" someone was asking.

"I told you that he hasn't been by since last fall. If not for his letters, I wouldn't know if he was dead or alive."

Ridge winced, in part because he hated asking his mother to lie on his behalf, and in part because she sounded more sad than indignant. He should have found time to visit this past winter. He hated to think that he had become his father's son and was too self-absorbed in his work to make time for family. Maybe he shouldn't have moved her so far away. But she had always said she hated the city, and she loved painting those rural landscapes.

I never saw my parents often enough, either, Sardelle spoke softly into his mind. *I was always traveling to teach or work with the military.* Her words were a little tentative. She probably wasn't sure if he would want her in his head now, but he liked being able to have private conversations with her. And he didn't have a lot to hide. For good or ill, he tended to say exactly what he thought most of the time.

This time, he did rest a hand on her shoulder. *We always think there will be plenty of time later, but it never seems like there is.*

"Here's how it is, ma'am," the soldier went on—it sounded like there were three or four in there, tramping around. Ridge was glad he had thought to hide all of the cups. There was no hiding the two pies his mother had already put in the oven. "We're worried about the colonel, about the witch controlling him. They say he did some crazy things before disappearing with a handful of our fliers and their pilots."

Disappearing? He'd been sent on a mission by the king himself. Granted, he hadn't taken the commanding officer that he should have taken...

"If you know anything about where he went or if you've seen

the witch, we'd need to know about that, ma'am. For your sake and his. There's no telling what he might do in this state."

In this state, really. Ridge didn't know if Sardelle was monitoring his thoughts, but he probably felt indignant enough that they would ooze out of his skull so that even Duck knew how he felt.

Probably, Sardelle agreed. *Ridge? What happens when your mom figures out... I mean, there's not much chance that she won't see that I'm the witch they're talking about.*

An inside door creaked open, followed by a few more thumps.

My guess is that she's in there rolling her eyes at the notion of witches and being exasperated that these men are intruding on—

"I did *not* give you permission to search my home," came his mother's voice through the window. "What do you think? He's hiding inside a kitchen cabinet? My son is *tall.* I fed him well when he was young."

Even though she sounded more irritated than distressed, Ridge shifted his weight, wanting badly to go in there and put an end to their questions. Maybe he could tie everyone up, steal the wagon, and head into town before they could report back.

I would think that would get you into more *trouble,* Sardelle thought dryly. More tentatively, she added, *What happens when I end up using my talent in front of her or she figures out the truth? Do you still think she'll be asking me about our plans for babies?*

Yes.

She twisted to look up at him. *Are you really that certain?*

She wants grandchildren. Didn't you see all of the cats? If I brought home a fertile baboon, Mom would be lobbying for babies. She had all but given up on me. Ridge paused. *That was perhaps not tactful. My mother would find you far superior to a baboon.*

Is it hard to believe that it was your charisma that originally drew me to you?

Nah, I was surrounded by horny soldiers and hornier inmates at the time. They probably made me look good. I just have to hope you never find any men who are truly charming.

The back door opened. Ridge cursed himself for being distracted by the conversation and dropped a hand to his pistol at the same time as a young soldier stuck her head out. She looked toward the field behind the cottage, then straight at Ridge and his men. He held his breath. He knew Sardelle had said she would hide them, but what if she had been as distracted by their conversation as he had been? The soldier was less than five feet away. She couldn't possibly fail to see them, even with magical intervention.

The soldier squinted toward him, her mouth parting slightly, then shook her head and leaned back inside. The door closed.

"Seven gods, that's creepy," Duck whispered. "She looked right at me."

"Aren't you used to women looking at you and ignoring you?" Apex asked.

"You're thinking of Pimples. I get plenty of loving."

"Sh," Ridge murmured. "Window's open."

But the soldiers seemed to be done with their questioning. After a couple more thumps and an irritated, "No, you can't have any pie," from his mother, the cottage fell silent. The sound of the steam wagon drifted back to them as it chugged down the dirt road and turned onto the highway.

"We better split up and gather our intelligence as quickly as possible." Ridge stifled a yawn. He wanted to order everyone to rest—none of the pilots, in particular, had slept since leaving Owanu Owanus. But time was not on their side.

"I'm ready now," Kaika said.

"Do we meet back here?" Tolemek asked.

Ridge hesitated, worried that being here could bring danger to his mother. Would she let him send her off to visit Aunt Lavender? He let his head clunk softly against the wall. Or maybe he should just report in so the soldiers wouldn't bother her again. Was he being crazy? Running around the countryside and possibly ruining the careers of all of these young officers? But something was very wrong within his chain of command if steadfast and loyal General Ort had been relieved of duty. He had to believe that he was making the right choice, going with his instincts. No, this wasn't just instinct; it was logic.

"Meet back here," he said. "I'll send my mom away so she'll be safe. Once we know more, we'll figure out what to do from there."

* * *

The towering cement wall at the back of the army fort rose up three stories with a fence of pointy iron stakes thrusting from the top. Strong lamps burned in the towers, their illumination focused on the walkway behind those stakes. Now and then, the jangle of a dog's collar and the clomp of boots drifted down from above as soldiers patrolled the barrier.

Ridge wished he could have brought Sardelle along instead of sending her off with Kaika, but he believed he could sneak into the fort without magical assistance, whereas infiltrating the castle would take more skill. He had ultimately decided to send Ahn on that mission, as well, since she was a natural at sneaking around and could scout ahead or watch their backs. Ridge just hoped he hadn't made a mistake in acceding to Kaika's wishes. She had a brash and impulsive streak—he knew how to recognize that since he had one himself. Perhaps he should have tried harder to rein her in. If the others were caught, the entire squadron would be in more trouble than it already was. And Sardelle... He hadn't seen any of the notorious posters yet, but they probably ordered people to kill "the witch" on sight.

Sighing, Ridge fiddled with his rope and looked up and down the street from the shadows of an alley. It was a couple of hours until midnight and chilly, but people were still out, staggering home from the pubs. Tolemek, who was supposed to be creating a diversion, should have rejoined him by now, but maybe he had struggled to come up with something. Earlier, they had found his lab locked and chained, with the contents emptied, so he hadn't had access to any of his usual chemicals. With the king gone, things had clearly changed. Ridge felt like he had been gone for months instead of weeks.

As he listened to another soldier walk past on the wall, Ridge debated whether to try getting in without a diversion. It would be hard to climb up and sneak between those spikes unnoticed, but if he was caught, he might come up with an explanation for his clandestine entrance to the fort. Maybe he could even talk himself into being dragged over to explain himself to General Ort.

Ridge flexed his shoulders and shook out his rope, preparing himself for the climb. Before he had gone more than a step, a faint throat clearing reached his ear. He paused, sinking back into the shadows of the alley. A cloaked figure with shaggy hair approached from the other end. They needed to get that man a hood. That hair alone would identify him at fifty paces.

"Not going somewhere without me, are you, Zirkander?" Tolemek grumbled. Even though they had rescued his sister and saved a dragon from certain death, his mood hadn't improved, at least not noticeably. Maybe he saved his giddy moments for Ahn.

"You're late. I thought you might have decided you didn't care about visiting Ort or Therrik. Or spending time with me, though that's hard to believe. I'm fun."

"You're delusional."

"That's what makes me fun. Travels with me are an adventure."

"You sound like the sword." Tolemek stopped at the mouth of the alley and looked toward the high wall.

"Jaxi, right? You're not talking to the glowing green one, I presume." Ridge hadn't caught more than a few seconds of Ahn practicing sword katas out in the front yard, but the glow of that blade had disturbed him, if only because it would be hard to keep his mother in the dark about magic if swords were beaming at her from the flower beds.

"I don't think it talks. I am somewhat concerned that Cas has been sleeping with it."

"Jealous?"

"No, but it's getting crowded under the blankets. I already had to share her with her rifle."

"Perhaps when all of this is over, you two can shop for a flat with room for a big bed."

"When all of this over, I don't even know what I'll do with myself. I was just starting to like that lab, damn it." Tolemek thumped his fist against his thigh.

"We'll find the king. He'll get you your job back." Ridge waved toward the wall. "Are you ready to go in? Do we have a diversion coming?"

"In less than two minutes. Do you think your general will let me use his kitchen and lavatory supplies? I can't make the truth serum without access to a lab stocked with the chemicals I need, but I can make some crude knockout potions with household items."

Ridge frowned at the idea of trying to interrogate Therrik without any drugs to make him cooperative. He wagered the thuggish colonel had endured all kinds of anti-interrogation training. He probably thrived on pain. And as much as Ridge loathed Therrik, he wasn't going to tear the toenails off a fellow officer.

A soft boom sounded from the other side of the fort, followed by flashing blue and yellow lights that brightened the cloudy night sky above the wall.

"I assume that's our cue." Ridge forced himself to wait a few seconds, in the hope that the guards on this side of the fort would be drawn away, then he jogged for the wall with the coil of rope and a grappling hook in hand. "Not a bad diversion considering all you had access to was the lavatory in that pub."

"I am a talented scientist."

"Modest too."

Thanks to Sardelle, Ridge knew some of Tolemek's alchemical talents were enhanced by his dragon blood and the magic it let him tap into, but he didn't bring it up. He was too busy swinging the rope and readying the hook for a throw.

"You know," Ridge whispered, choosing a target at the top, "this would be much easier if we had a dragon to carry us over."

"I imagine there are many things that would be easier with a dragon. What's the matter? Don't they teach pilots how to throw?"

Ridge narrowed his eyes, then lofted the grappling hook toward the top of the wall. It wrapped around two of the iron stakes on the first try, which was good, but the noise from Tolemek's diversion had already died down, and the clank the hook made sounded painfully loud to Ridge's ears. He did not want to be shot trying to sneak into his own fort. Nor did he want to have to hurt anyone up there. That would be unacceptable.

Still, he took the half second to give Tolemek a smug look. "First try."

"Yes, yes, you're a paragon of athleticism. Now, go. Your general's lavatory is calling to me."

"You're a strange man, Tee."

Not waiting for a reply, Ridge started up. They might not have much time. He skimmed up the rope quickly and squeezed through a gap between two of the stakes, sucking everything in to avoid getting stuck. A jangle floated to him as he dropped down onto the parapet, and he stifled a groan when he spotted a soldier and a hound running toward him.

He faced the dark figure and spread his hands. The soldier had a slight figure. A woman?

"I'm unarmed," Ridge said quickly, in case that might keep her from firing. He believed standard operating procedure was to capture intruders, rather than shooting them, but officers didn't pull fort guard duty very often.

"Step into the light," the soldier said, stopping ten feet away. Definitely a woman's voice.

Ridge did not know if that would help him or not. Based on his past experience, he would be more likely to lure a male soldier away from duty with the promise of a beer and a story. The growling dog, restrained only by the leash its handler held, did not look like it would be won over by alcohol.

Ridge walked a few steps toward the pool of illumination surrounding a lantern. He deliberately kept his arms wide, trying to block the view of the wall behind him. Maybe if Tolemek was able to crawl over without being noticed, he could do something. What, Ridge wasn't sure. He had been almost as disappointed as Tolemek by the locked and stripped lab. Even if Tolemek carried the dubious label of "Deathmaker," his potions and drugs had a tendency to allow for more peaceful solutions than shootouts did.

"Colonel Zirkander?" the woman asked, her mouth sagging

open as she stepped closer to the light. She wore a sergeant's rank and looked to be in her thirties. He highly doubted he would convince her to abandon her post for a beer.

"Yes," he said after throwing away a half dozen complicated stories that he had been working out while waiting for Tolemek. He decided for a simple one that was only slightly untrue. "I heard my house had been blown up. Going in through the gate didn't seem wise."

"Er." The sergeant shifted the pistol away from him. That was promising, but she did not lower it entirely. She wore a conflicted expression, no doubt torn by the need to do her duty and the knowledge that shooting an officer might not be wise.

"I don't suppose you could forget you saw me?" Ridge suggested, even though trying to suborn a soldier made him uncomfortable. She might get in trouble later for not reporting him. How many careers had he already put at risk this month? Starting with his own? "I'm on a mission to rescue the king and gather intel, but I'm not supposed to reveal my presence, lest the people behind his kidnapping suspect I'm coming." No need to mention that he had assigned this mission to himself...

"A mission from whom, sir?"

Whom, indeed. At least she had called him sir instead of immediately ordering him to place his hands on the wall for a search. Tolemek must still be dangling from the rope—his shaggy head had not yet popped up.

"The queen," Ridge said. He almost elaborated, giving her some spiel about how the queen was being forced to pretend to command the nation by some nefarious outfit that was blackmailing her, but that newspaper at his mother's house had been four days old. Since he had no current intel yet, he might say something contradictory.

"Oh." Did that oh sound enlightened? Or skeptical?

The dog growled again. Maybe it could smell the hairs his mother's cats had decorated his trousers with. The dog sniffed the air a few times, then put its paws up on the wall between two stakes. Uh oh. Tolemek was about to be noticed.

"I know your duty is to capture me," Ridge said, stepping

forward, risking getting close to the dog, "but I'm not sure if anyone else is looking for the king. I'm here to check with General Ort, try to get any information he has, then find him."

"They say you're being controlled by a witch, sir. That she has you under her charms." The soldier backed away a few steps, the pistol rising slightly again. She leaned toward the wall so she could see over the side while keeping an eye on him.

If not for the dog, Ridge might have lunged and tried to disarm her. But even if he managed that, what would he do then? He couldn't hurt her or kidnap her, and tying her up would only keep her silent for a short time.

"Come up," the soldier said, directing her words over the wall.

"I'm not being controlled by anyone," Ridge said. "That's the city's new scientist. He definitely doesn't have me under his charms."

Tolemek grunted as he crawled over the wall. Ridge did not look back at him. If Tolemek had some potion in hand, he did not want to draw the sergeant's attention to it.

"I never believed that story, sir," she said, surprising him. "I have to report this, especially since I've been out of the tower for longer than I normally would be, but, ah... I'm not really known for my penmanship when I fill out my reports. My superiors sometimes have trouble reading them. Sir, when you've rescued the king, would you mind coming to visit my son's school? He and a lot of his friends are mad to be pilots and they idolize you." She lowered the pistol.

Ridge blew out a slow breath, lowering his hands. He hadn't dared assume that his reputation would help him here, especially with so many people certain Sardelle was controlling him now, and he considered himself lucky. This never would have happened while sneaking into a *Cofah* outpost. "I would be happy to do that."

"Good. Can I come to the hangar later to set something up?"

"Absolutely."

"Come on, Fang," she murmured, pulling the dog to turn him back in the other direction. She walked away without looking back.

"Does being a national hero and getting preferential treatment ever get tedious?" Tolemek asked.

Ridge bit back a caustic retort—he kept hoping Tolemek would get tired of taking shots at him if he didn't respond in kind. All he said was, "Nah, and you should be tickled about it. You can now have your date with Ort's lavatory."

He pulled up his rope and unwound the hook while he talked, then affixed it and lowered it on the other side of the wall. They couldn't count on the *next* soldier having a flier-loving son.

They descended without further trouble, landing behind a row of barracks. Ridge had chosen this spot for a reason. The general's house was only two blocks away. Sticking to the back routes, he led Tolemek down a well-lit, tree-lined street. Not many people were out, especially in the officer housing area, but Ridge kept his cap pulled low and the collar of his jacket turned up, doing his best to hide his face.

They cut across a lawn, the grass damp with water droplets, and walked to the back of the general's two-story white house. Ridge did not spot the light of any lanterns, but Ort ought to be in bed at this hour. He was not known for late nights out at the pub, nor did he have any family living with him. His three daughters were grown, and his wife had passed away. The lack of lighting was not ominous, or so Ridge told himself.

He knocked softly on the back door while hoping that it didn't mean anything that the dragon luck mat on the stoop had slid off into the flowerbed. When nobody responded, he knocked again, more loudly. Tolemek shifted from foot to foot, watching a pair of soldiers walking up the street behind the house. Alas, there weren't any nice alleys to skulk in inside of the fort. Ridge and Tolemek leaned into the shadows and stood quietly, waiting for the men to pass.

"Let's go around to the front," Ridge whispered when they were gone, though he was not sure if there was a point. He was starting to accept that the general wasn't home.

Further clues suggested he hadn't been home for a while. Letters stuffed the iron mailbox hanging next to the front door, and Ridge's shoulders slumped even before he tried knocking again. Had General Ort left town after being relieved of duty? Maybe he had been furious and gone off to visit his daughters or other friends. But no, that wasn't like him. He was so dedicated to his duty, especially since his wife had passed on, that he was usually in his office sixteen hours a day. This was not a man who would take a vacation because he had been asked to step down. He would have formulated an appeal, fought against whoever had been behind the decision. Ridge couldn't believe he would quietly let someone like Therrik be placed in charge of his battalion.

He leaned to the side of the porch, trying to see through a window.

"Whether he's here or not," Tolemek said, "I need to make some defensive measures before confronting your brutish officer friend."

"Therrik is no friend of mine." Ridge waved and led the way around the house again. He had been by enough times to know the layout and judged the root cellar door on the side would be the easiest entrance to force their way through. "I do recall him chasing you around your lab with a knife, so I can see why you wouldn't want to face him without potions. I hope we can get you into Ort's lavatory."

"Potions. Really, Zirkander. When you don't think I'm a pharmacist, you think I'm a witch brewing elixirs over a cauldron."

With great effort, Ridge kept himself from making a comment about how Tolemek's hair did bring such images to mind. Instead, he pulled out a dagger and slid it between the double doors of the root cellar, trying to unhook the latch. He assumed Tolemek did not have any more of his corrosive metal-eating goo left after their eventful earlier missions.

"I do appreciate you helping me out with Therrik," Ridge said, trying to keep his voice casual and sincere. He *was* sincere; he just had a hard time admitting that he respected Tolemek's abilities and needed his help. It was hard to forget what he had been before Ahn had talked him over to their side, and also about all the people who had died as a result of his "potions."

Of course, it might be easier if the surly bastard ever had a kind word for him. Or even a polite word. Ridge would even settle for a non-judgmental word.

Didn't you shoot down some ship of his and ruin his military career? Jaxi asked, her abrupt presence startling him into dropping his dagger.

"Move over, Zirkander. You're horrible at picking locks."

Ridge picked up his dagger and let Tolemek have his spot, more because he worried he would have to concentrate on whatever Jaxi had to tell him than because he was accepting that he was horrible at anything.

What's your point, Jaxi? I'm sure I was defending Iskandia from a Cofah threat, as usual. If his ship was lurking off our coast, it deserved to be shot down.

Just pointing out that you are, or were, his mortal enemy too.

That's very political of you. Is Sardelle all right? What's going on?

She's fine. We're sitting on some rocks, eyeing the back of the castle and waiting for the night to get later before attempting entry. She wanted you to know.

Thank you, Ridge thought.

She also wants to know if you're *all right. I told her you were trading insults with Tolemek, so she knows all is well.*

For now, yes. Ridge eyed the dark windows of the house, wondering how he was going to get any decent intel when his C.O. was missing and Tolemek did not have the means to make his truth serums.

Tolemek lifted one of the cellar doors. Jaxi did not offer further comments—hopefully, she was not busy burning a hole into the side of the castle—so Ridge followed, groping his way down the earthen steps. He had only been down there a couple of times, but he found his way to the wooden staircase leading up into the house. When he walked into the dark kitchen, his boot collided with something on the floor. It clattered across the tiles. Wincing at the noise, he scrambled after it only to bump into something else on the floor. It rolled to the side and banged into a cabinet.

Tolemek sighed from the top of the stairwell. "So this is the national hero that kids clamor to get into their classrooms."

"I'm better in the sky."

Ridge finally got the pots or kettles or whatever he had run into stilled. He set them on the counter and poked through drawers until he found matches for the gas lamps. He lit one, keeping the flame to its lowest setting. It was enough to illuminate the floor and the pots scattered all over it. That in itself would have been alarming—General Ort didn't let dirt smudge his boots, and his house was always tidy—but Ridge soon spotted something even more upsetting. A throwing knife protruded from an upper cabinet with a cap dangling from it, a cap with a general's rank pinned on the front.

"Blood over here." Tolemek pointed to a stain that had dried on the floor.

Ridge grasped his chin and stared at the mess, fighting off the dread that threatened to smother him. He and Ort sparred with each other more often than they raised their mugs to share drinks, but Ridge had known the man for more than ten years, answering directly to him for almost five.

"Not a lot," Tolemek said, watching Ridge. "They might have kidnapped him, the same as your king."

"They *who?*" Ridge grumbled, but he nodded, appreciating Tolemek's words. Being kidnapped and missing was better than being dead.

Ridge rubbed the back of his neck, wishing he had been around when all of this had been happening. Maybe he would have a clue as to who was behind it all. A story in the newspaper had suggested everyone from the Cofah to pirates to theoretical rebel factions being responsible for the king's kidnapping, but it hadn't mentioned any evidence to support any of the hypotheses. If there were rebel factions around, Ridge didn't know about them. The king was well-liked by soldiers and the common man, and besides, Iskandia had been so busy fighting off the Cofah for decades—for *centuries*—that they hadn't been able to risk internal strife. They were already so outmatched by the empire that their only hope of staying independent had been to create a solidified front.

"I'm going to see what I can make," Tolemek said, heading for a door that led to the rest of the house. He paused with his hand on the jamb. "I assume you still want to visit Therrik?"

"Oh, more than ever." Ridge might have sought out officers he considered friends, and who wouldn't turn him in, but it was doubtful whether those of his rank and below would know what was happening at the highest levels of command—or who was sending down orders from the castle. But Therrik, the wrongfully promoted Therrik, *had* to know something. "And Tee?" he added before Tolemek disappeared into the house. "I *want* a truth serum."

"Anyone ever tell you that you're demanding, Zirkander?"

"All of my young pilots. Most of the older ones too."

"Are you sure the word they used wasn't *trying*?"

"Not entirely."

Tolemek walked out of view, but the words, "All I ever wanted to do was research," floated back to the kitchen.

Ridge hoped he could make something. Even if they were able to surprise Therrik, which Ridge was *not* counting on, he had no idea if they would be able to bring him down or get him to talk. He also wasn't certain they would survive the encounter.

CHAPTER 3

HARBORGARD CASTLE PERCHED ON THE rock-filled promontory on the north side of the harbor, at the opposite end of the city from the bluff that held the dragon-flier base. The rest of the capital had been modernized, with gas lamps lining streets filled with steam wagons, bicycles, and armored military vehicles, but the ancient black rock fortress had not changed much in the three hundred years that Sardelle had been asleep. It was better lit at night, gas lighting having replaced whale oil lamps, and it would be harder to sneak in, so she was searching for weaknesses as she crouched in the rocks with Kaika and Cas. Specifically, she was trying to find secret tunnel entrances that they might exploit. She recalled hearing about them from a fellow mage adviser, one who had worked directly with Queen Ralthori. Supposedly, there were escape passages for emergencies, at least there had been three centuries ago. So far, Sardelle was struggling to sense any such tunnels beneath the rocks. Of course, the conversation going on behind her was a touch distracting.

"You need plenty of saliva in your mouth for lubrication. And don't use your teeth. They don't want teeth down there, trust me. You know about the secret spot?"

Sardelle was glad the question was directed at Cas and not her. She was also glad that night had fallen a couple of hours ago, so the embarrassed flush to her cheeks would not be visible. The technology was the biggest change from the era that she had been born into, but the culture had changed somewhat too. Women hadn't spoken so openly of sex in her time, even the soldiers Sardelle had worked with on occasion.

They didn't speak openly of it with you, *sherastu,* Jaxi thought.

Are you suggesting I was unapproachable?

I'm suggesting that common people don't feel comfortable talking about secret spots with sorcerers. As to your tunnels, they appear to have collapsed long ago. There's a dragon flier in the courtyard at the back of the castle. That's probably how royalty escapes attacks these days.

Are the tunnels completely collapsed? Even if part of one remains, a part next to the castle, perhaps we can cut into the rock above it and slip inside without having to bore a hole into a millennium-old wall.

I'll check.

"Not... really," Cas said after a thoughtful pause—or maybe an uncomfortable one—and a poke from Kaika. She didn't sound like she was certain about the conversation, either, but she *had* been responding to Kaika's questions.

"Girl, you need to know these things. Look, men will give you a spin, because you're a warrior woman, and they find that intriguing, but if you're not as pretty as Freckles over there, you're going to need some bedroom skills to keep them interested. Assuming you're still interested in them, that is. If the sex doesn't have the neighbors complaining because of all the screaming, it might be time to move on."

"I don't think I'm tall enough for anyone to consider me a warrior woman," Cas said dubiously.

"Any man who doesn't want his balls shot off better consider you one."

"Freckles?" Sardelle asked mildly, though perhaps it would have been better to stay silent. By objecting to the name, she was probably setting herself up for teasing, but she felt a little left out. It was natural for the two soldiers to bond, even if they were from different units. They both utterly destroy things—and people—for their jobs.

"You didn't invite me to use your first name, and I don't know your last name," Kaika said.

Since they had originally met when Ridge had left his squadron long enough to boot Therrik from his flier and pick up Sardelle—without warning his people first—that was probably true. There had not been time for formal introductions as they flew across the ocean in separate craft.

"I suppose there are worse nicknames," Sardelle murmured, adjusting her weight against the hard rock at her back.

"That's the truth," Cas said. "Just ask Pimples."

"You're welcome to call me Sardelle, Captain."

"Did you want to comment on the conversation, Sardelle?" Kaika asked. "Care to give us some insights into the colonel's preferences?"

"I don't need to hear that," Cas said.

"Aw, are you pretending you haven't imagined Zirkander naked? I'll do my best to pretend I believe you."

Sardelle wondered if Cas's cheeks were as warm as her own. "I'm more interested in discussing how we're going to get into the castle. It's getting late enough that we could think about trying."

"I have shaped charges, dragon bombs, and a nice stash of thermite that should be able to get us through metal doors and possibly walls of solid stone."

Relieved that Kaika had instantly switched to work talk, Sardelle decided not mention that Jaxi could do those same feats, probably with less noise.

Just because I can burn through a wall doesn't mean I want to, Jaxi thought. *It wears me out and isn't all that fun.*

By all means, we must keep this mission fun.

I sense your sarcasm.

Who, me?

"If I can lead you to an old tunnel that collapsed decades or perhaps centuries ago," Sardelle said, "do you think we could blow our way in without alerting the guards in the tower walls up there?" She waved toward the dark silhouette of the castle. "Our other option is to try sneaking in through the main gate, but it's not open right now, and it's hard for me to build illusions that can hide movement or fool multiple people at once."

"How far is the tunnel from the closest tower?" Kaika asked. "The thermite doesn't make much noise, but the explosives are another matter. I had planned to cut my way in through the sewage grate, but I'm not opposed to blowing things up. Ever."

"No, I've gathered that about you."

"Then we'll get along fine, Freckles." Kaika found Sardelle's shoulder in the dark and gave her a rough shake.

"Sardelle, please."

Is she still fantasizing about a dragon eating me, Jaxi?

Not at the moment. She had some burly young soldier in mind when she was discussing secret spots. It's possible her interest in your soul snozzle was fleeting, references to his nudity notwithstanding.

Would her sewer grate be a better way in?

It depends on how fragrant you believe spies should be. You'll have to swim through effluent after cutting through the bars, and there are two guards in the pumping station.

Sardelle passed on the information about the guards. While it was true this wasn't her mission and she was only along to help, she would prefer to remain undiscovered and not have to subdue anyone.

Kaika digested the information silently before asking, "How do you know this?"

"I can sense the inside of the castle. Actually Jaxi can."

"Jaxi?"

"My sword. She's fond of thermite reactions too. You would probably get along fabulously with her."

Perhaps so, Jaxi thought.

"Uh. That's disturbing."

"Jaxi considers swimming through sewage disturbing. May I show you the tunnel?"

"I would prefer Captain Kaika's route," Cas said.

It was too dark to see Cas's face, but Sardelle sensed a stiffness about her. Was she worried the explosives would make too much noise? Sardelle thought about digging deeper to get a better sense of her thoughts, but she had been doing far too much mental prying of late. She did not want Cas to sense her—as Tolemek had when she had grazed his surface thoughts once—and become offended by the intrusion.

"I can muffle the sound of the explosives," Sardelle said, "so those standing guard in the towers won't hear them."

"Great," Cas said, her tone dark rather than enthused at the idea.

Maybe she was remembering being buried in that rockfall in the pyramid. Sardelle opened her mouth to assure her that nothing that traumatic should happen here, but Kaika spoke first.

"Show me where this collapsed tunnel is, and then I'll decide."

Sardelle almost objected to the notion that Kaika alone would be responsible for the decision, but reminded herself that Kaika *was* the ranking officer on this mission. When Sardelle had worked with the army in the past, she had always held the role of adviser, not commander, so she ought to be used to letting officers take charge. Maybe it was just that she did not know Kaika well yet.

Or maybe it's that I told you she's had fantasies of your lover, Jaxi suggested. *Perhaps I should have stayed quiet about that.*

I wouldn't let that get in the way of the mission. Sardelle headed across the jagged boulders toward the spot Jaxi had shown her earlier. *I'm more mature than that.*

Would someone mature have garnered the nickname Freckles?

Hush.

As Sardelle led Kaika and Cas across the rocky promontory, she kept an eye toward the towers on the back side of the castle, using her senses to monitor the guards there. Two stood watch in each of the three towers closest to the area Sardelle was heading. They were all alert, keeping their rifles close at hand and walking from window to window to peer out at the harbor and the promontory. She hadn't expected sloth and laziness from soldiers selected to protect Harborgard, but it would have been nice. She would have to ensure Kaika set her bombs in a place that the explosion would not be visible from the castle. The sound waves from noise, she could indeed muffle, but when creating an illusion to hide something moving, she had to be able to touch the mind of the person watching, to adjust what he saw as he saw it. That was exceedingly difficult when multiple minds were involved.

You're on the collapsed area over one of the old tunnels now, Jaxi advised. *There were two once, but the other one is completely smashed in. It looks like there might have been an earthquake in the past and that nobody bothered to dig out the passages.*

I see the spot. Sardelle had turned her attention from the towers to the rocks beneath them. About ten feet below the surface, she sensed the opening. In one direction, it was indeed closed off, with rubble filling it from floor to ceiling, the wooden supports long since snapped away. In the other direction, the passage headed straight for the rear of the castle, cutting through the old basalt rock that had been hauled in a millennium if not millennia ago to form the protective harbor.

Sardelle found a dip they could hide in that would protect the three of them from view. She was less certain that it would hide the flash of light that might come with an explosion and thought about volunteering Jaxi to cut through the rock. But that produced so much heat, turning stone into red-hot molten waste, that it, too, might be visible from a distance.

Also, cutting through tons of rock makes my mind throb. It takes a tremendous amount of power, power I might need later if you get yourselves in trouble in there.

I'm hoping that won't happen.

Optimism isn't reality.

Very pithy.

Thank you.

"Straight down ten feet," Sardelle said told Kaika when everyone had climbed into the depression. "Can you cut through that much rock and keep the explosion from flashing so that everyone in the towers can see it?"

"Might as well ask Cas if she can hit a bull's balls at ten paces," Kaika said, already pulling equipment out of her pack.

"I can hit anything's balls at ten paces," Cas said, looking at Sardelle rather than Kaika. For some reason, she had brought the dragon-slaying sword along on the mission, but it was her favorite sniper rifle that she patted lovingly.

"I'm glad I don't have balls," Sardelle murmured.

"That would have been a surprise for old Zirkander." Kaika prodded at the rocks underneath them and lifted some sand to sniff. "Why don't you all find another hole to hide in? It will take me a few minutes to set up. Sardelle, I'll let you know when I'm ready for noise muffling. The thermite won't cut through anything this thick, so I'll probably use the dragon bomb, and those do tend to be loud. I'll try to set it in such a way that it blows downward and doesn't disturb many of the rocks on the surface, but you'll need to be ready for the sound of boulders rolling away, as well as the initial explosion."

"I understand."

Sardelle crawled out of the depression and continued for at least twenty meters before stopping behind a boulder. Even though she'd heard Kaika's training had involved learning how to do controlled demolitions, she could envision more rock than desired shifting and falling away or collapsing into the tunnel below.

Cas stopped behind the same boulder. It might have been Sardelle's imagination, but she thought she glimpsed a slight leaking of pale green light from the end of her sword's scabbard. According to Jaxi, Kasandral, the dragon-slaying sword had been wielded by an Iskandian king fifteen hundred years earlier, but Sardelle did not have any personal knowledge of the blade. It did not have a soul in it the way a soulblade did—Sardelle would have felt that—but it did have a... *presence*. It didn't feel malevolent exactly, but something about it made her not want to touch it. Perhaps that made sense if it had been designed to slay dragons. Her own veins did carry a hint of dragon blood, however diminished over the generations.

"We'll have to look up your new sword in the library when we get a chance," Sardelle said casually, as if to make conversation and nothing more.

"Why?"

"Aren't you curious about it? I've noticed you haven't left it behind anywhere for long."

"Where would I leave it? Back in the fliers? I'm already worried about them being vandalized or stolen while we're gone. At the colonel's mom's house? The soldiers were already there doing a search, so I don't think it would be safe to leave it there, either."

"A valid point," Sardelle said.

Maybe she was dwelling too much on the blade. It made sense that Cas would want to keep it safe, especially since her father had been the one who had brought it to Owanu Owanus with the intent of killing the dragon. He was a dangerous man, and having the sword would only make him more dangerous, especially if the dragon ever showed up in Iskandia with Tolemek's sister. Better to have such a powerful weapon in friendly hands.

"Ready," came Kaika's soft call.

Sardelle closed her eyes, seeing the explosive that had been planted with her mind. It was surprisingly compact. It amazed her what humans had accomplished in the last few centuries, even without the help of sorcerers and dragons. Maybe they had no need for her people any longer; perhaps someone had sensed that three hundred years ago when planning to destroy the Referatu. But no, she had been valuable to Ridge on his mission. Magic could still play a role in this society—if they would let it.

"I'm ready," Sardelle called back.

As Kaika lit the fuse and scrambled away, Sardelle cupped the air around the depression, hardening it into a dense barrier that would contain the sound wave. She made certain it would not keep the bomb from blowing through the rocks they desired.

When it detonated, the raw power railed at her container. She had tangled with a few rockets now and knew what to expect, so she was prepared. An extremely faint boom reached her ears, but she felt certain nobody in the castle could have heard it, especially with the roar of the surf in the distance. The light she had expected never brightened the air, so she assumed Kaika had done something to control that. Sardelle grudgingly admitted that the captain knew what she was doing, and she probably did not need to worry about getting in trouble by following her lead.

Kaika scrambled back toward the site of the explosion, and Sardelle let her barrier dissipate. Cas led the way to join Kaika while Sardelle crawled across the rocks more slowly, checking the guards again. One of them was looking in her direction, and a nervous worm wriggled in her stomach. Was it possible he had seen something? Some rocks shifting? It was a cloudy night, promising of rain, and it was dark enough out on the rocks that Sardelle had trouble even seeing Cas and Kaika. She didn't think the guard could have seen them.

Look closer, Jaxi suggested. *He has a few drops of dragon blood in his veins.*

Sardelle froze. Of course. She had encountered other random Iskandian subjects with dragon ancestors, the blood so diluted that it was unlikely they could ever do much in the way of magic or even knew that they had the power to try, but they might have a few vestigial senses that were superior to those of other humans. That guard might have felt some itch of intuition when she had used her power.

"Sardelle?" Kaika called softly. "Are you coming? It looks like it worked."

The guard was still looking in their direction, but Sardelle risked crawling the rest the way to the hole—she did make sure to stay lower than the rocks, just in case his eyes were sharper than average too. She trusted Jaxi's assessment and did not reach out to examine him more closely, not wanting to risk him sensing her. She would have to hope that whatever he had felt wasn't enough to make him warn a superior that castle security should be increased or that the rocks should be checked. How would he explain what he had sensed to magic-fearing comrades?

When Sardelle reached the edge of the hole, the faint smell of gunpowder or something similar lingered over the tang of the salty air. Kaika had already dropped down, and Cas disappeared soon after, sliding down the slope until it grew vertical, then letting herself fall. She landed without making a sound. Sardelle was not as agile as the two soldiers, but she followed the same route, confident that she could land without breaking anything since she could sense the contours of the rubble filled tunnel below.

Don't be cocky, Jaxi warned and slowed Sardelle's fall. *You have the athleticism of a chubby boulder.*

Though Sardelle wanted to offer an indignant retort, her heel caught on a rock as she landed. Had she come down on it at full speed, she would have fallen on her butt instead of merely fumbling and catching herself on the nearby wall.

"Watch out," Kaika said quietly. "The floor of this tunnel is a mess. There's rubble everywhere, not all of it mine."

"I see that." As Sardelle moved forward to join them, she had to clamber over and around everything from pebbles to waist-high boulders. "Anyone mind if I make a light?"

"Probably not. I assume there's a closed door up ahead?"

"Actually, there's a closed wall," Sardelle said after a quick check.

"Even better."

She was on the verge of conjuring a small globe of light into existence when a pale green glow arose, washing the half-crumbled walls with its illumination. Cas stood in the center of the tunnel, holding the big dragon blade in her hands.

"Is *every*body a witch now?" Kaika grumbled, eyeing the glowing weapon with distaste.

"I'm not a witch," Cas said coolly.

"I prefer the term sorceress," Sardelle said.

"Next time, I'm bringing some of my own people." Kaika headed down the passage, with Cas walking behind her.

Sardelle followed several steps behind, glad that sword would not be at her back.

After about a hundred and fifty meters of scrambling over boulders and ducking broken supports, they reached the brick wall Sardelle had sensed. Judging by the tightness of the mortar and the brightness of the brick, the construction had occurred within the last couple of decades, unlike the tunnel behind them, which seemed as ancient as the harbor itself. Maybe it truly had been the invention of the dragon fliers that had convinced those dwelling in the castle that an underground escape route was no longer necessary.

"We'll be at the basement level, if not lower, right?" Kaika rested her ear against the bricks for a moment, then dropped her pack and dug into it.

"There's a wine cellar on the other side," Sardelle said, "then a food storage area above it and the kitchen above that."

"Good to know. That shouldn't be busy at this time of night."

"The cellars are empty. There are two women in the kitchen washing dishes and mopping."

Kaika looked at her.

"Too much information?" Sardelle had assumed Kaika would appreciate any intelligence she could get before they barged in.

"No. I was thinking Nowon and I should have taken you when we infiltrated the Cofah volcano lab. You're like a really fancy spyglass that can see through walls."

"Thank you," Sardelle said, not quite able to keep the dryness out of her voice. What would her childhood instructors think to have her two decades of training summed up in a comparison to a spyglass?

Kaika donned gloves, pulled out what appeared to be a ceramic pot with a spout, and stuck a metallic ribbon through a hole. Next, she tugged thick goggles over her head. Sardelle had assumed her concoction would work similarly to Tolemek's goos, but perhaps it did not.

"You two might want to stand back again," Kaika said. "There will be some sparks and heat, and a stench that will fry your nose hairs."

"That was going to happen tonight one way or another," Cas said.

Sardelle and Kaika looked at her.

"Either here or via the sewer route." Cas wrinkled her nose.

"Ah."

Kaika lit the ribbon, and Sardelle backed away.

"Lieutenant, if you want to put out your pig sticker, that might be good. Just in case Freckles here isn't as omniscient as she thinks and there's a wine steward selecting a vintage a few feet away."

"It's a dragon sticker," Cas said.

"Yes, whatever. It's glowing like my cheeks after a twenty-mile run. Or an exhilarating night in someone's bunk."

"That turns you a sickly green?" Sardelle asked.

Kaika grinned back at her. "Depends how much exertion was involved."

Cas sheathed the sword, dropping darkness onto the tunnel. Soon, the promised sparks came from the brick wall. Kaika turned her back to them, so Sardelle could not see exactly what she was doing.

Something smellier and less efficient than what I could do, Jaxi said.

I thought you wanted to rest your powers in case we need them later.

That was before Kasandral there started showing off his light-making ability.

Sorry, did you want me to rush to pull you out first in the next room? So you can show off your *glow?*

It would certainly be more attractive than the vomit green light he shines, but I wanted to deliver a warning, not brag about my abilities.

Sardelle shifted her weight, uneasiness creeping into her gut. *A warning about the sword?*

No, about that guard you sensed. He told his buddies that he saw someone moving around out on the rocks, and now security is sending a couple of people out to look.

Any chance you can keep them from seeing that hole? Sardelle doubted she could create an illusion to fool someone from that far away, but Jaxi was more powerful than she.

Probably, but if someone falls through it, he'll probably notice it's there.

Do your best. We'll hurry.

Chapter 4

"Another dark house," Tolemek observed.

He and Ridge stood in the shadow of a tree in the back of another white house, this one identical in layout to Ridge's own one-story, one-bedroom home. His *former* home. They had passed the charred ruins on their way over to this street. He had resisted the urge to snoop in the wreckage or knock on the neighbors' doors to ask if they had seen the diabolical people who had been responsible. He assumed it had to do with the group hunting Sardelle. That group was another reason he didn't want the word out that he was back in the city. Its leaders would probably assume Sardelle was, too, and double their efforts to find her.

"With luck, he'll be sleeping," Ridge whispered. "It's after midnight now."

Tolemek had taken more than two hours smoking up Ort's house with his potion-making projects.

"He may hear us picking his lock," Tolemek said. "Especially if *you* do it."

Yes, that was a risk. Therrik wasn't just infantry; he had served with the elite forces and internal special security. He had probably been trained to wake up at the sound of a squirrel pissing in the woods.

"You don't have your corrosive door—and wall—opening goo, eh?" Ridge asked.

"No household items suitable for making it. That takes some strong chemicals and a special touch."

Special. That described Tolemek suitably enough.

Ridge picked a piece of bark off the tree. "What about your knockout gas?"

"I was able to make knockout grenades and smoke bombs.

Technically, grenades and bombs may be optimistic words, since the fuses were made from boot laces and the chemicals are stored in tea tins filched from the kitchen."

"So long as the contents drop the big hulking muscle-head on his ass," Ridge said. "How do you feel about lighting one of your tea tins and chucking it through that window? We can get him in his bed, knock him out before he has a chance to hear us trying to sneak in."

"How do I feel about it? I feel that you should do it. Also that the tin would bounce off the glass."

Ridge picked up a rock that was part of the edging for the tree. "Tie it to this."

"Someone's going to hear that, Zirkander."

"Does it matter? That someone is supposed to pass out as soon as he breathes in the contents."

"I meant the neighbors. These houses are close together. And how do you know which window fronts the bedroom?"

Ridge pointed at the back window to the right of the door. "It's the same layout as my house. The other one's the kitchen. There's a living room and a small office up front."

Tolemek grumbled something incomprehensible, but he had brought twine along and was able to tie one of his canisters to the rock. Ridge wished he had the prowess to simply jump into Therrik's path, confront him, and then beat meat-for-brains into the ground instead of resorting to trickery, but he wanted to accomplish his self-imposed mission, not get himself killed.

"Here." Tolemek dumped the rock into Ridge's hand, as if to dump all responsibility there too.

Ridge accepted it, looked up and down the row of back yards, and listened for anyone who might be walking or driving down the street out front. The fort had fallen asleep while they were in Ort's house, with the only noise now the sound of the wind whipping a rope against a flagpole down the block.

Ridge crept toward the back window, jerking his head for Tolemek to follow. He had the matches.

As he padded across the lawn, dew dampening the cuffs of his trousers, he stepped as quietly as he could, worried he would make more noise than the pissing squirrel he had thought of earlier. His eyes locked on the closed curtain, hoping he would see if it moved. But he couldn't make out much in the dim lighting. His heart thudded against his ribs as he crept closer, and images of Therrik leaping out the window to strangle him flashed through his mind. Sweat moistened his palms, but he dared not take them from the rock to wipe them off. If he dropped it, the rock might land on the grenade and break it so that its contents flowed out. Even worse than the strangling vision was one of Therrik walking out and finding Tolemek and Ridge unconscious on his back lawn. Who knew what he would do then?

"Stop it," Ridge growled to himself. This was a fellow officer in the king's army, not a pirate or a Cofah soldier. Whatever happened, Therrik shouldn't kill him. Probably.

A few meters from the house, it occurred to him that Therrik might not be home. What if he was working late at the hangar? What if he had a lover he visited off-base? The idea of Therrik with a lover made Ridge curl his lips in disgust, so he changed his thought to, what if Therrik had a *prostitute* he visited off-base?

With the curtains closed, there was no way to be certain. He paused, staring down at the rock. Seven gods, it was just a window. If he wasn't home, the worst that could happen would be they'd break it. So long as no military police soldiers on patrol heard the noise and came running.

Tolemek held up his arm, presumably holding a match and asking if Ridge was ready. Ridge thrust his load toward him. Tolemek felt for the canister, then lit it. Ridge threw the rock, his feet scurrying backward before it struck. In addition to not wanting to be close if Therrik leaped out the window like an attack dog, Ridge did not want to risk breathing in any of those vapors. As the crash sounded, glass shattering and the rock flying through it, he and Tolemek raced back to the tree.

Ridge grasped the bark, watching and listening from behind the trunk. Mostly, he worried about lamps being turned on in other houses, but if one was turned on in Therrik's, that wouldn't be good, either. What if their target escaped his room before he breathed enough of the fumes to be knocked out?

"I feel like a delinquent child throwing rocks at old grannies' windows," Tolemek said.

"Does that mean you're having fun?" Ridge kept his gaze locked on the now-broken bedroom window as he spoke.

"No. My father beat the rebelliousness out of the neighborhood delinquents. Nothing fun about that."

"Bent you over his knee, did he?"

"Numerous times. Did Moe do that to you?"

"*Moe* wasn't around much. My mom withheld pie if I was too bad. That was a heinous punishment."

Tolemek snorted. "Admit it, Zirkander. You were coddled."

"I was an only child. It happens."

Tolemek did not respond to that, other than to glance skyward. Wondering if his sister was out there somewhere? Ridge was not sure whether to hope Tylie would visit Iskandia or not. A dragon could help with a lot of things—the idea of it glaring at Therrik and him wetting himself was quite appealing—but Ridge hadn't gotten the impression that the dragon wanted to be an Iskandian ally. More likely, it would join with Cofah airships in plundering the Iskandian countryside.

"At what point are we going to conclude that we threw a knockout grenade—and a rock—into an empty house?" Tolemek asked.

Ridge sighed, afraid he was right.

"If he was in there, he would have had a few seconds to react before succumbing," Tolemek added. "We would have seen or heard something. Cursing of your name, perhaps."

"I didn't put my name on the rock."

"No? I thought delinquents liked to leave their mark."

Ridge pointed at the house. "How long before it dissipates and it's safe for us to go inside?"

"It probably already has."

"Probably? I only ask because a light went on in that house on the corner—" Ridge pointed, "—and someone might come out to investigate."

"What's the point in going in to question him if he's not

home?"

"Snooping. Maybe there's a nice note about the king's kidnapping in there." Ridge doubted it—as much of an ass as Therrik had been to him at that meeting in the castle, nothing he had said or done had suggested anything but respect for the king, and Therrik didn't seem bright enough to play an actor's role. One wondered how he had made it through officer training.

"Sounds like wishful thinking."

"Stay here, if you want." Feeling the press of time—and the fact that he had accomplished absolutely nothing tonight—Ridge ran for the back door.

He tried the knob, expecting it to be locked and to have to break the rest of the window to get inside, but to his surprise, it turned. "Arrogant bastard," he muttered. "Thinking nobody would be brave enough to rob him."

"Maybe he simply doesn't have anything of value," Tolemek murmured from behind Ridge's shoulder. He must have decided to join in with the snooping after all. Maybe he hoped Therrik had a chemically interesting lavatory. "Or he believes this is a secure base where felons aren't allowed access in exchange for school appearances."

"I'm not a felon. Yet."

"Waiting on the conviction?"

"Sh." Ridge pushed open the door. He found himself reaching for his pistol but forced his hand to open and leave it in his holster. If he shot Therrik, he *would* be a felon.

After the pot incident at the general's house, Ridge stepped carefully into the kitchen, but he did not run into anything. Though he believed Tolemek was right and the house was empty, he paused in the middle of the room to listen. His nose crinkled. The bedroom door stood open, a breeze blowing through the broken window, and the scent of chemicals lingered in the air.

"You're sure they've dissipated enough?" Ridge whispered.

"Yes, but the scent will linger for several minutes."

"Fantastic." Ridge padded through the house in the dark, checking to make sure all of the curtains were closed. He wanted to light a lamp for snooping, but he had to assume Therrik would come home eventually, and getting caught in here—next to the broken window—would not be healthy. "Can you watch the front walkway? Let me know if you see anyone coming?"

"Making me an assistant to your felonious ways?"

"Your bomb was tied to the rock. You're already an assistant in the eyes of Iskandian law."

While Tolemek was stewing over that, Ridge found a match and lit a small lamp. He wasn't sure what he had expected from the decorating eye of Colonel Therrik, but he wasn't surprised by what he got. At least a hundred types of swords, maces, and daggers adorned one wall, while the wall next to the stove held all manner of historical pistols, muskets, and rifles. A third held schematics for military vehicles from horse-drawn wagons to steam-powered armored assaulters. The final wall, the one with the window and the front door, held a single item, a framed cloth embroidered with a pink rose.

"Odd man," Ridge muttered, making his way to the desk.

A disassembled pistol lay on top along with an unpacked weapons cleaning kit. Neither the desk nor the corkboard behind it held any promising messages about the king, ransom notes, or secret deals with the Cofah. He delved into the drawers, but had only made it to the second one when Tolemek stirred at the window.

"Wagon coming. We need to go."

Ridge growled and cut out the lamp. "We haven't found anything yet."

"Perhaps we should have spent less time tying chemicals to rocks and more time—"

"Yes, yes, you can lecture me later." In the darkness, Ridge stepped toward the kitchen and the back door but paused. "Are you sure that's his vehicle and that it's coming here? Therrik seems like the type to walk everywhere. Or double-time it."

"It pulled over to this side of the street and stopped in front of this house."

"Do you have another knockout grenade?" A surge of exhilaration—or was that terror?—raced through Ridge's veins at the idea of springing a trap. Could they yet surprise him?

Throw it as he came through the door?

"Yes, but more than one person is getting out of the vehicle. It's too dark to make out faces, but they're all wearing army uniforms."

Ridge cursed. Knocking Therrik unconscious was one thing, but he couldn't attack an entire squad of soldiers. What were they all doing coming to visit so late at night, anyway? As much as he would like to accuse Therrik of hosting drunken orgies, Ridge hadn't seen any alcohol in the kitchen, and the wall decor hinted more of hobbies that involved war games and firing squads.

"I'm getting out of here before they see me," Tolemek said, his voice on the move. He was already halfway to the kitchen.

As much as Ridge hated the idea of fleeing before he found what he needed, he couldn't think of anything else to do. Maybe they would get another chance at Therrik if they hid outside for a couple more hours.

He remembered the broken window—and the shattered glass and tea canister that would be lying on the bedroom floor—at the same time as he spotted lanterns moving out in the yard beyond the kitchen. Those lanterns were attached to soldiers, military police, the black caps said.

Ridge stifled a groan. The broken window. Someone must have heard it and reported it.

Tolemek cursed under his breath, his hand on the back doorknob. Two of the soldiers were heading straight for the house. "We can't go out there now."

"Well, we can't—"

The front doorknob turned.

Ridge veered toward the bedroom, grabbing Tolemek and pulling him along. "Watch out for glass," he breathed. The front door opened, and he dared not speak again.

Inside the bedroom, he stretched toward the ceiling. There was an access panel to a small attic in his house. He used it for storage. Maybe they could swing up and... no, he didn't feel it. Apparently, the houses weren't *exactly* the same.

Light from the lanterns came through the broken window. A knock sounded at the back door.

"What is it?" came Therrik's irritated voice from the front room.

Ridge looked around for a hiding place. Tolemek was kneeling, patting at the ground. Looking for his tin? Most of the chemical smell had dissipated, so maybe Therrik wouldn't notice it.

Footsteps sounded in the living room—Therrik heading for the back door. The bedroom door had been open when Ridge came in, so he dared not close it. He started for the closet on the far side of the room, but a shadow moved outside of the window—one of the MPs peering in. Ridge pushed his back to a wall and sank to the floor. The bed. It was large and high. Maybe he could squeeze under it.

The idea of being found under there by the military police or Therrik himself made him cringe—what in all the realms would he say? Everyone was sure to come in to investigate, and Ridge and Tolemek would be found. Maybe it was better to turn himself in now.

Even as he had the thought, Ridge flattened himself to his belly and pulled himself under the bed. Glass cut into his palms. He doubtlessly deserved that. This whole infiltration was an idiotic farce. Why had he ever thought he could manage it? He should have sent Kaika. She knew how to infiltrate secret laboratories and outposts. A bedroom would have been no problem.

He wasn't able to push himself as far under the bed as he wished, because a long wooden box lay in the way. He did not want to risk it audibly scraping against the floorboards, so he didn't move it.

Warm air brushed against Ridge's face as he settled in under the bed, his legs and arms pulled as far from the sides as he could manage. It took him a moment to realize that he wasn't alone, that he was face-to-face with his infiltration partner. Ridge was tempted to ask why Tolemek hadn't gone to the closet, since he had been closer to it, but he dared not speak now. When he turned his head, he could see boots through the doorway, gleaming dully as the polished tips reflected lantern light in the kitchen. Therrik's boots.

Therrik had opened the back door. "What is it?"

Another set of boots, smaller ones, joined his, the owner close enough to look out past Therrik. Ridge could hear at least two more people in the living room. Someone groaned, perhaps sitting down in a chair. It was a man's groan, an old man, Ridge judged.

"Someone reported vandalism, sir," an earnest young MP said. "We came to investigate."

The soldier must have pointed toward the bedroom, because both sets of boots strode toward it.

Ridge winced as lantern light stole some of the shadows. Glass crunched under boots. A hand appeared, the MP bending to pick up a shard. Ridge held stiller than a corpse. All it would take was for that man to drop to his knees and look under the bed. His only hope was that the soldier wouldn't think to do that or, if he did think of it, would decide against it, since he would end up with glass in his knees. Still, Ridge sucked in his belly and avoided looking toward anyone on the off chance that they could feel eyes upon them. Given the number of people who had tried to kill Therrik during his career, he probably had very honed instincts.

"Probably those kids again, sir," the MP said.

Again? Had Therrik's windows been broken more than once?

"Kids." Therrik grunted. "Right."

Ridge grimaced. He didn't sound like he believed that.

Soft thumps sounded, like someone patting someone else on the back. "Vann," a woman said, "maybe you should be kinder to those young privates so they don't feel the need to retaliate every time you leave your house."

That voice was familiar. Ridge tried to place it at the same time as he smirked at the idea of Therrik's house being the target of frequent vandalism.

"Maybe the MPs should do their job and not let vandals wander through officer housing," Therrik growled, stepping away from the woman.

"Sorry, sir," the MP said. "We came as quickly as we could, and my men are looking around outside of the house to see if they find signs of the culprit."

Or culprits? Ridge hoped the grass hadn't been muddy enough that his and Tolemek's prints were all over the yard.

"At least they didn't paint lewd pictures on your siding this time," the woman said.

Her voice clicked for Ridge. General Arelia Chason, commander of the Third Signal Brigade. They had their headquarters here in the capital. What was she doing spending time with Therrik? And calling him Vann? Disgusting.

You haven't had any relationships with senior officers? Jaxi asked, her unexpected arrival in his mind almost making him crack his head on the bed.

The MPs were walking around the room again, so Ridge dared not so much as take a deep breath.

A few times, but I'm not Therrik. I'm... He thought about pointing out that he was much better looking and more charismatic, but Jaxi would have a snide comment for that.

Arrogant? she suggested. Maybe she had heard his unvoiced thought.

Nice to spend time with, Ridge responded firmly. *Is there something you want? This isn't the best time.*

Sardelle asked me to check in on you. I'll let her know that you're cozied up under a bed with Tolemek. She may find that disturbing.

She'd only find it disturbing if we were getting cozy in *the bed.*

If you say so, hero.

A thump sounded, Therrik dropping something on a dresser. Belatedly, it occurred to Ridge that he might have asked Jaxi for help. He wasn't sure how far away she could extend her powers, but if she could talk to him, maybe she could brush the minds of others around him, make them think they heard a noise outside and needed to go investigate.

"Do you have any idea who might have wished to vandalize your house, sir?" the MP asked.

"No," Therrik said.

Everyone, Ridge thought.

"Very well, sir. If I can use your kitchen for a moment, I'll write up my report."

"Use my kitchen? We're having a meeting, corporal. Take

your ill-trained troops outside and look for people carrying rocks around."

"Er, yes, sir." The MP clomped out and exited through the back door.

Ridge couldn't relax, not with Therrik still in the room, but he hoped this meant nobody would investigate further. Dust lurked under the bed, and his nostrils kept twitching. He wanted to raise his fingers to his nose, but Therrik might hear even the faintest rustle of clothing.

"I'm going to need to board this up," Therrik said, "and get a broom to clean up this mess."

Ridge clenched his jaw. If Therrik started cleaning, he would doubtlessly end up sweeping under the bed. He was sure to notice the unusual lumps on the floor. Even if he didn't, he would go to sleep eventually, and then how would Ridge and Tolemek escape?

"Not now," General Chason said. "Roalin and Arstonhamer are waiting. They'll think we're back here having a tryst."

"With the MPs watching? I didn't know I had that kind of reputation."

Both pairs of boots left the bedroom and turned toward the living room, then disappeared from Ridge's sight. Unfortunately, in the small house, they couldn't go far. A few more chairs creaked as people sat down.

Ridge had no idea how he and Tolemek were going to sneak out of the house, but if he could hear the words of this late-night meeting, he might gather some of that intel he had hoped to find. Unless Therrik had brought these people over to play dice and drink. That would be disappointing. And surprising. General Arstonhamer ran the infantry brigade, the one Therrik came from, and Roalin had to be Colonel Roalin Porthlok, head of the local intelligence battalion. Ridge knew all of these people from various social gatherings, but he wouldn't presume to invite any of them over for a chat. Even if it had to be the least important thing to worry about now, it rankled him that Therrik apparently *was* someone who could invite them over for a chat.

"All right, Therrik," Chason said, her voice stern now, back to business. "What's the latest update with the queen?"

"And why are there only three fliers sitting up in that hangar?" one of the men asked. "The city is practically defenseless if the Cofah show up."

Only three fliers? Ridge's fingers curled into a fist. Where was all of his equipment? And his people?

Therrik sighed. "She wanted them sent to circle the continent and deal with pirate uprisings."

"*All* of them? Why? And why *our* squadrons? There are flier outposts in all of the major provinces. They can deal with their own pirates. That's why they're there. Leaving the capital—the most populous and most economically viable city in the country—vulnerable to attack is ludicrous."

"We have ground troops, sir." Therrik sounded like he was grinding his teeth while speaking. Good. He deserved it, since he always made Ridge feel that way when speaking to him.

But if Ridge wasn't careful, his own teeth would start grinding. He agreed with whoever that was who was talking—Arstonhamer probably. With the king missing, this was *not* the time to leave the city poorly guarded. What in the hells would ground troops do if the Cofah came in with airships?

"Ground troops." Arstonhamer made a spitting sound. "The Cofah haven't tried a ground invasion for more than twenty years. We need the fliers here. And Breyatah's Breath, where *is* Colonel Zirkander?"

Ridge rolled his eyes. Right here, sir...

"Cavorting with a witch," Therrik growled. "Listen, sir. The fliers aren't gone indefinitely. The queen wanted them sent on a very specific mission."

"Against pirates." Arstonhamer sounded skeptical.

Therrik hesitated. "Yes, sir. She has spies and—"

"Spies? Is that woman truly in charge in there, Therrik? She's never shown a political leaning in her life. Nobody believes someone isn't pulling her strings. You're scratching her itch. You tell us."

"I'm not scratching anything for her, sir," Therrik bit out, even more stiffly than before. "I'm loyal to the king."

"Of course you are, and that's why she's made you her most trusted military liaison. An infantry colonel known for losing his temper and beating privates."

Ridge imagined he could hear the sound of Therrik's grinding teeth from here. He supposed he shouldn't feel pleased at hearing Therrik being chewed out, but he did, damn it. If he hadn't been hiding under the bed, wondering how long he could go without using the latrine, he would have felt extremely smug about the entire situation. He *was* rescinding his earlier envy over the fact that Therrik got to spend time with important senior officers; this was an interrogation, not a gaming night.

"Arelia, you're a woman," Colonel Porthlok said.

"Clearly, with all of your intelligence training, nothing gets by you," General Chason murmured.

"Is it conceivable the queen would choose Therrik for itch scratching? We were debating about this earlier."

"*You* were debating it," Arstonhamer said. "With yourself."

"If he's not sleeping with her, could he be blackmailing her? Or otherwise coercing her somehow? Why is she talking to him instead of going through the chain of command?"

Furniture scraped, then something fell over. "I'm right here in the room with you, sir," Therrik growled. "And I'm not blackmailing anyone. I told you, I'm loyal to the king."

"Now, now," Chason said, her voice more soothing. "Therrik isn't without his merits. He's very firm."

Ridge curled a lip. This conversation had taken an alarming turn. He hoped they would go back to discussing politics and not... firmness.

"But the queen... if she was going to have a mistress. Er, a mister? She could have anyone, you'd think. Would *you* pick Therrik over anyone else?"

"If I were the queen? I suppose strictly on looks, I'd go with that Major Meriak in intel, or Zirkander, if he was around."

Ridge was not sure whether to be pleased or alarmed that General Chason knew who he was and thought he was pretty. Alarmed probably. A faint sigh came from beside him. Tolemek was probably rolling his eyes. Or scowling at him. Or both.

"But she's surely not making her decisions based on looks," Chason went on.

"Surely," Colonel Porthlok agreed dryly.

"It sounds like she wanted control of the flier squadrons. This was a rather unsubtle way to gain that control, but I can see why she would find Therrik more malleable than General Ort."

Therrik growled something. It might not have been a word.

"Unless she tried to pick Ort first," Chason said, "found he wasn't amenable, and that's why he disappeared."

General Arstonhamer sighed. "We all need to be wary of that. He's not the only officer who's gone missing."

Ridge's ears perked. Oh? Who else had disappeared? And had any clues been left as to where? Maybe Ort and all of the other kidnap victims were with the king.

"You think the queen knows anything about that, Therrik?" Arstonhamer asked.

"About where the king is? No, she talks a lot about missing him and being worried she won't see him again."

"We need to find out who's really in command in that castle," Porthlok said. "I'll try to talk to Colonel Forsythe in internal security again. All he said last time was that he had teams investigating, but he was tenser than a ramrod, so I don't know if someone had threatened or blackmailed him too."

"Ahnsung isn't around, is he?"

"The assassin? No idea."

"Someone should check. He'd work for the Cofah if the price was right."

Ridge believed that, but he didn't think there was any way Ahnsung could have beaten them back home. Most likely, he would have had to find passage on a merchant ship leaving the island. Even if that airship had returned to pick him up, that would have been a slower ride than the fliers. Still, Ridge wondered what questioning him would reveal. *Someone* had given him that giant sword and told him where to find the dragon.

A chair creaked, and one of the men yawned.

"Enough for tonight. Therrik, if the city gets attacked while you're in charge of the hangars, you better be ready to pull magic out of your ass."

Therrik did not respond, or maybe he responded with a glower. Footsteps sounded, then the front door opened.

Tolemek prodded Ridge in the shoulder. Telling him it was time to try and escape? From under the bed, Ridge could not tell if those MPs were still out in the yard. Nor was he certain Therrik had gone to the front door. He might have a perfect line of sight of his back door. There was not enough glass missing from the window that they could climb out that way.

More footsteps sounded, making Ridge glad he had not moved. They were near the kitchen.

"Don't let them upset you, Vann," General Chason said softly. "We're all frustrated and irritable right now. Members of the District Council are on their way to the capital to determine if an interim ruler needs to be put in place, since the queen isn't qualified to lead a nation, and Angulus never produced any heirs, but we would all rather find the king. They're right in that we can't risk appearing weak to the Cofah, not now, not when they supposedly have all of these new intelligent weapons."

"I know," Therrik said, his voice sounding more tired and defeated than angry—it was the first time Ridge had heard that tone from him. "Porthlok should have teams out looking for him."

"He has some out there, but he has to worry about external threats too." Clothing rustled, like a coat being put on.

"I tried to tell her not to send out so many fliers."

"What are they looking for? Not pirates, surely. And Porthlok would have said something if the Cofah were on the horizon."

Therrik did not answer.

Ridge wrinkled his nose, trying to ignore the dust tickling his nostrils.

"You can't tell me?" Chason asked. "Even when I defended your firmness?"

Therrik snorted. For a moment, neither of them talked, and Ridge started to wonder what they were doing until a few kissing sounds reached his ears. A fresh wave of dread curled through his limbs. They weren't going to have sex, were they? On the very bed Ridge was hiding under? He could not *lie* here for that, even if it meant risking death.

But the sounds stopped.

Therrik sighed. "Witches."

"What?" Chason asked.

Ridge mouthed the same question.

"They've got some tester for dragon blood, and I guess intel has had an extensive list for a while as to suspected witches and heirs to witches. The squadrons were sent to clean out all of the infected communities existing around the continent, kill anyone found guilty."

The dread Ridge had been feeling turned to a chill of horror. *His* people were being sent on a witch-hunt? As some kind of flying death squad? To kill people who might very well be distant relatives to Sardelle? People who, like Sardelle, might learn to use their powers to defend the country if they were trained? People who were *subjects of Iskandia*?

"*Now?*" Chason sounded almost as incredulous as Ridge, if for different reasons. "When the Cofah are working on super weapons over there? Super weapons they're doubtlessly planning to test on us?"

"Something must have happened. I'm not privy to what's going on in the castle, despite what those two think. Maybe something to do with that dragon that was supposedly found. Or Zirkander's witch showing up and strolling around the city."

"Please. Who actually believes that drivel?"

"Many people," Therrik said coolly.

"Most likely teenage girls who are envious that our eligible pilot hero is now taken."

"There's a report from the crystal mines on file. Go look it up. Witnesses saw that woman flinging fire around and deflecting bullets with her mind."

Ridge had been afraid a report like that would have been filed. He had done his best to squelch all of the rumors before he left, but Captain Heriton had suspected—and feared—Sardelle from the beginning. It hadn't mattered one iota that she had saved the entire outpost from death and destruction.

"I'll look," Chason said. "But this is *not* a national emergency, whatever it is. If there is such a thing as magic, it's been around for thousands of years." She made a disgusted noise and headed for the front door. It opened, but she spoke again before walking out. Ridge had to strain to hear the words—it had started raining, and the patter on the rooftop competed with the voices. "What are you going to do when he shows up again?"

"Who? Zirkander?"

"Yes. Whatever you think of him and his lover, we need him in the sky if the Cofah come. Don't do anything drastic. Or illegal."

"I won't have to," Therrik said, his voice almost a purr. "According to my most recent orders, I'm his commanding officer now. If he wants to fly, he'll do it at my discretion. Maybe I'll send him to hunt down some witches."

Maybe Ridge would borrow Sardelle's sword to turn Therrik into a eunuch.

The door finally shut. Any thought Ridge had of Therrik being a gentleman and walking the general home was squashed when his footsteps started up again—heading for the bedroom. Ridge told himself Therrik could not know that they were there, that he would not have spoken so openly if he had, but he couldn't help but tense.

The boots entered the bedroom, grinding broken glass with each step. A lantern was set on a piece of furniture, and the straw of a broom dangled into view. Ridge bit his lip and hoped Therrik would prove a lazy sweeper, or think he had more stuff cluttering the floor under the bed than the box digging into Ridge's hip.

"Damned rain," Therrik muttered and leaned the broom against the wall and walked out.

The back door opened, then closed. Ridge was so surprised that he had gone outside that he did not react at first.

Tolemek poked him again and whispered, "He must be getting boards for the window. Go."

Ridge needed no further urging. He slid out from under the bed. A thump sounded, and he winced. The wooden box had skidded out from under the bed. Tolemek cursed and scrambled out after it, clutching his knee. Even though Ridge knew they had to get out of there, he caught himself staring at the box. It looked as old as dirt with intricate carvings running along the top of it. The lantern did not provide enough light to tell what the pictures portrayed, but his curiosity got ahold of him. He slid the box the rest of the way out and opened it. There was an old iron latch, but no lock.

"What're you doing?" Tolemek glanced toward the window. "Push that back. Let's go."

Ridge already had it open. Faded blue velvet adorned the interior of the box, covering a layer of thin metal. Otherwise, it was empty. "What's usually in here?" he wondered.

"Probably one of *those*." Tolemek thrust his hand toward a wall filled with ancient axes, swords, and maces, much like the walls in the living room. Then he closed the box, shoved it back under the bed, and raced for the front door.

Ridge chased after him, deciding he was right. As they slipped out of the house and ran to the street, he wished he had found something significant. Even if he had gained information by spying on the meeting, all that information had done was enrage him. A witch-hunt. With *his* people leading it. Dear gods.

At the end of the block, Tolemek jerked to a halt.

Ridge almost crashed into his back. "What?"

"The canister." Tolemek patted himself down. "I pulled it under the bed so the soldiers wouldn't see it, but when I hit my knee on that box I forgot about it." He spun around, looking toward Therrik's house.

"We're not going back."

Banging drifted down the street from the direction of the house. The sound of a board being nailed to a window. Tolemek's shoulders slumped.

"It's a tea canister, right?" Ridge said. "Even if he finds it, he'll just think the vandals threw it with the rock. He won't be able to tell it held chemicals." Ridge had no idea whether that was true, but he tried to sound confident for Tolemek's sake.

"That will be my hope. You may be a national hero that your people want to keep in the sky, but I have no such distinction to protect me from that idiot's wrath."

Chapter 5

Thanks to Sardelle's tricks for diverting people and Kaika having been to the castle before, their group made it to the upper levels that held bedchambers, a library, and private meeting rooms without being seen. So far, the infiltration had not been difficult, but it had not been swift, either. They'd had to duck into linen closets and lavatories to keep from being spotted, and Sardelle felt the press of time. Jaxi was keeping her informed about the guards searching the rocks. Only two men had gone out, but they had lanterns, and seemed to have a good idea of where to look. It would get much harder to sneak around in here if that tunnel was discovered. Having their only escape route discovered would prove problematic, as well.

Maybe you can rappel down the walls, Jaxi suggested.

You didn't even have faith that I could jump down a ten-foot hole. You want me to fling myself down a fifty-foot wall and onto a bunch of sharp rocks?

Captain Kaika brought a rope and grappling hook. Perhaps she could carry you.

Funny.

"King and queen's suite should be at the end of this hallway," Kaika whispered, a set of lock picks in hand. It seemed she had a few ways to infiltrate enemy strongholds aside from explosions.

"Then I'll hope we reach it before we have to spend another ten minutes snuggling together in a linen closet," Sardelle whispered.

"Snuggling? Is that what you call it when someone's giant sword is poking you in the hip?"

"I call it foreplay," Cas said.

Kaika had been leading the way as they crept down the hallway, but she paused to thump Cas on the shoulder. "Good one."

Sardelle wouldn't have guessed that Cas had a ribald streak, but perhaps Kaika inspired it in those around her. Sardelle thought about mentioning that when last Jaxi had checked in on Ridge and Tolemek, they had been hiding under a bed together, but sensed the moment had passed. Comedic timing—and ribald joke telling—was alas not part of her repertoire.

"Watch my back," Kaika whispered and pressed her ear to the door at the end of the hall.

Cas did so, reaching for her rifle, but she paused before touching it and lowered her hand. Yes, even if someone charged up the stairs, they could not shoot the person. These were their own people. Sardelle would have to do her best to create an illusion to hide them, which she could do if only one or two staff members appeared. She kept her mind open, watching the stairs that led up to this level and also checking the rooms behind the doors. Some of them were occupied, and it wasn't so late that everyone was sleeping.

"I don't hear anyone," Kaika whispered. "Sardelle, can you tell if she's inside?"

Sardelle had already done a check of the room behind the door, but the suite had a number of interconnected rooms, and she examined them more closely. "There's a fire in the hearth and lanterns burning, but nobody's in there at the—" A presence stirred on the level below, a wood boy heading for the stairs with a basket of firewood. They had passed the diligent worker a couple of times already. "Someone's coming up," she whispered.

"How long? I need a couple minutes."

As Kaika slipped two slender tools into the door lock, Sardelle searched for a way to delay the boy. He was only steps from the base of the stairs. She could employ an illusion, but if he was delivering wood to the queen's suite, then he would walk right into them.

You haven't given anyone a rash for a while, Jaxi thought.

I prefer to save that for enemies, not innocent servants.

When the youth was halfway up the stairs, Sardelle knocked one of the logs out of the basket he was carrying, bouncing it artfully back down to the bottom.

He's not that innocent. He and a young female groundskeeper were doing frisky things in the woodshed in the courtyard recently. He's feeling guilty because he was supposed to be on shift, and he's hoping nobody will notice that he's late bringing in the firewood.

Telepathically intruding, are you?

I scarcely have to. The guilty thoughts are oozing out of his head.

When the youth bent to pick up the log, balancing the basket on the steps, Sardelle knocked it over. The rest of his wood tumbled out. She felt bad about harassing him so, but perhaps he would believe the gods were teaching him a lesson for his indiscretion in the woodshed.

Comparing yourself to a god? Careful, that's what got the mundanes up in arms about sorcerers three hundred years ago.

Yes, I'm certain they were upset that our people were flinging firewood out of baskets all over the continent.

"Got it." Kaika pushed the door open and slipped inside.

Sardelle followed Cas into the room, leaving the youth to gather his wood in peace, but she kept him in her senses, still concerned that he might be heading for this suite.

"Look around," Kaika said. "It's been weeks since the king's kidnapping, but I heard he was stolen right out of his room, so there might still be clues. And maybe the queen knows something. I'll check her desk for correspondence. Sardelle, will you watch the door? Warn us if someone's coming?"

"Of course."

"Are we sure the queen is even in the castle?" Cas asked. "Didn't you say nobody had seen her? That she hadn't made any public appearances since the king's disappearance, and that it's only hearsay that she's in charge?"

"If she wasn't here at all, I think that's a rumor that would have gotten out," Kaika said, "but it's been several days since Apex and I left to get you. I'm not current on the gossip."

"I don't think they would lay a fire in a room that was going to be empty that night." Sardelle kept the hall—and the wood boy—in her mind, but walked around the sitting room while she did so, also looking for clues.

"Good point." Kaika trotted into the bedroom.

With lush rugs, elegant upholstered chairs and sofas, and a tea service perched on a side table, the sitting room looked more like a staged area only for entertaining guests than a living space where clues might be found. Sardelle entered an office, conjuring a light to illuminate the walls of shelves and the two desks within. She went to the one with the large doily on it and the knitting basket on the corner, glancing at the bookcases as she passed. Most of the tomes were on military history, geography, politics, and economics, with a few lighter texts behind the queen's desk, romances and mysteries and craft books.

I'm guessing she isn't the mastermind behind the king's disappearance, Jaxi said.

You read romances. You don't think you could plan a kidnapping?

Not with a doily sitting on my desk. That would smother my ambition, aggression, and desire for revenge.

Oh? Would that work if I simply draped the doily over your scabbard?

Ha ha. No.

"I wish we could chat with the queen," Kaika said through the open doorway connecting the bedroom to the office.

"So she could ask what we're doing snooping in her room?"

"I wouldn't let her ask the questions."

"I think it's called an interrogation then," Sardelle said, "not a chat."

Kaika drummed her fingers on the doorjamb, then walked in. "I was hoping to find something useful here."

Sardelle slid open the top desk drawer. Kaika went to the king's desk. Perhaps a better idea. If threats had been delivered before he had been kidnapped, maybe he would have a record of them. But wouldn't people have already checked in here? Those leading the search for him?

After finding nothing besides yarn and other craft materials in the queen's drawers, Sardelle turned toward the walls again. If there had been secret tunnels out of the castle once, perhaps there were also secret passages and rooms within it. She reached out, trying to get a sense of the rooms next to the suite. On the outside wall, the one made of stone, windows overlooked the courtyard, but she detected a gap of about four feet between the bedroom and the next room over, one not accessible via this suite. She assumed a door somewhere led to it, but as she probed about more carefully, she did not sense an exit from that room, at least not a visible one.

Sardelle walked into the bedroom to examine the connecting wall with her eyes, searching for a lever or a switch or a painting hanging suspiciously askew.

You might want to figure that out sooner, rather than later. These security fellows are determined, and they're getting close to the hole.

You've hidden it?

Disguised it as well as I could, but our friend with the dragon blood is on the search party. He's having itchy feelings about my illusion.

Even if they left right then, Sardelle feared they would not be able to escape the way they had come. The guards were sure to notice three women popping up among the rocks. Being caught in the castle would not be good, either, not when Kaika had been reported AWOL and Sardelle was wanted dead for witchcraft. Cas would have a hard time explaining that sword too. They would all be charged as traitors who had come to wreak mischief. Or they would be shot outright. Sardelle knew absolutely nothing about the queen, other than her knitting preferences.

She moved a painting and checked behind it for buttons or switches. This wall was made from vertical wooden boards, so if there was a secret door, the cracks would not be easily visible. Though she sensed that gap between the two rooms, she could not start burning holes in the walls of the king's bedroom. There had to be a law against that.

Cas walked in. "What are you looking for?"

"I think there's a secret passage to a room behind this one." Sardelle prodded the andirons in the fireplace, even though that was on the opposite side of the room.

Cas walked along the wall Sardelle had indicated, studying the floor. She stopped halfway along it, bent down, then pulled her sword part of the way out of its scabbard. Sardelle almost pointed out that it wasn't purported to be a divining rod but realized Cas probably just wanted a light. A second later, Cas sheathed it fully and stood up.

"This is the doorway." She nudged the floorboards.

By the time Sardelle joined her, Cas had found a switch. A click sounded, and a panel swung open.

"What gave it away?" Sardelle asked, peering into the darkness.

"There are some faint scrapes on the floorboards where the door opens."

"Ah. Good thinking." Sardelle should have thought of that too. Ah, well. She was a healer, not a tracker or carpenter.

Is that the excuse that will make you feel better about an obvious oversight?

You didn't see the scrapes, either.

No, I was watching our friends outside. They've stopped hunting momentarily and are watching a flier head toward the castle.

Cas entered the dark shaft while Sardelle was communicating with Jaxi. A draft brushed Sardelle's cheeks as a second door was opened. The draft did not smell of must, dust, or disuse. A green glow arose, Cas pulling out the sword for a light again. If her father ever showed up to reclaim that blade from her, he might have to fight her for it.

"You're right," Cas said. "It's another room. Chilly. Nobody laying fires in the hearth in here."

Sardelle joined her inside what looked to be an old nursery with a handsomely crafted but dusty crib along an inner wall. A couple of child-sized dressers also occupied the space along with a desk built for an adult. It rested against the outside wall, one with a shuttered window in it. This room couldn't be *that* secret, but there were not any other doors in it, not visible ones.

Cas went straight to the desk. It and its chair were the only pieces of furniture in the room without dust on them. A soft click came from behind them, Kaika scooting into the room with a lantern.

"Wood boy is in the suite," she whispered.

Sardelle grimaced. She had let the search for the secret room distract her.

"He didn't see me," Kaika added, nodding to Sardelle. "What's this?"

"The pamphlet creation station, apparently," Cas said, stepping back from a drawer. It was filled with small hand-stapled booklets, all with the same cover of forest-green with a silver triangular symbol on the front and leaves at each of the points. "Another craft project?"

Sardelle had never seen the symbol before, but when she leaned in closer and could read the title, her heart lurched. *The Order of the Heartwood Sisterhood, Charter and Mandates.*

Jaxi!

Oh, it's my favorite of the secret, all-women orders listed in that book we were researching. The one dedicated to protecting innocent young men from the advances of lusty female dragons.

It must have evolved into more than that.

Take a pamphlet. Maybe they're recruiting.

Sardelle did remove one and slip it into her bag. When she and Jaxi had been researching possible organizations that might have been responsible for following Sardelle around the city and trying to blow her up, this name had been one of three possibilities. Granted, it had seemed the least likely, but that had been before they found this stash.

"Looking for some bedtime reading?" Kaika asked.

"I believe this may be the organization that's been trying to kill me," Sardelle said.

"To *kill* you?"

"Before we left, some women in dark cloaks were following me around, and then someone blew up the archives building while I was in the basement."

"Oh, I heard about that. One of my colleagues was asked to go investigate. Huh. I knew you were on the wanted posters around the city, but I didn't look that closely at them. Witches, uhm, the idea of magic makes my eye twitch. My trigger finger too."

Sardelle shrugged. She hadn't been looking for sympathy.

"Guess it wasn't that smart for Zirkander to send you here where you might get captured then," Kaika said.

"I believe he sent me so we *wouldn't* get captured. Also, I'm pleased to be asked to help. It's what I was trained to do."

"Help?" Kaika eyebrows rose.

"Yes. I'm a healer and a student of history, as well as a sorceress."

"Hm." Kaika picked up one of the pamphlets. "As a history student, do you know anything about this organization? Is it new or something old?"

"It was founded at least a thousand years ago, but its mission may have evolved. I'm going to have to find a library and do some research."

"What was their original mission?"

Jaxi made a snickering sound in Sardelle's head.

"According to one book, to keep young village men from being lured away by female dragons for mating."

Kaika blinked slowly a few times. "Was that a big problem once?"

"Not from what I've read, but I wasn't there. I'm not quite *that* old."

Kaika frowned down at the pamphlet. "It's a stretch, since we haven't stumbled across any clues yet, but I had the thought that they might have something to do with the king's kidnapping. But I don't know of any female dragons that have been lusting after him."

"As I said, I would like to research the organization more to see what they've been poking their fingers into lately, but that does sound unlikely. I would be more inclined to believe that it was the Cofah who wanted him out of the city. With all that secret weapons research they're doing, they must be preparing for a big attack on someone."

"And we're their recalcitrant former imperial subjects that rebelled." Kaika rolled the pamphlet and rested the end against her chin, scowling at the desk, or perhaps into space. With her voice uncommonly soft, she said, "I'm worried that we're going to learn he wasn't kidnapped at all, but shot and his body stashed somewhere it would never be found."

Even though Kaika did not seem to be the kind of person who required—or ever wanted—comforting, Sardelle risked putting a hand on her shoulder. She did not push it away.

"Is the wood delivery boy still out there?" Cas had rifled through the other drawer and the dressers and apparently not found anything interesting. "How are we going to get out of here?"

Not through your hole.

What?

They found it. One guard is running down the tunnel to see if someone got in, and the other is heading back to the front gate. There's a lot of shouting going on.

Sardelle closed her eyes. "We'll have to..." She trailed off as the buzz of a flier's propeller reached her ears.

Kaika turned off the lantern and opened the shutters above the desk. The room looked out over the grassy lawn in the rear of the castle, as well as a landing pad where a flier was parked to one side. Lanterns burned all along the pathways, and pairs of guards ran down them, the clank of their weapons and armor drifting up to the window. The wall rose too high for Sardelle to see the rocky promontory behind the castle—or the men investigating the hole—but she did not doubt that they were there. More guards occupied the towers and the wall than had before. A few were pointing toward the sky, but most were running, urgency speeding their legs.

"They're starting a search of the castle," Cas said.

"Because their boss is coming home." Kaika pointed to the night sky.

The lights of a two-person flier had come into view. A pilot wearing goggles, a leather cap, and a scarf was guiding it toward the landing pad, and the sight made Sardelle think of Ridge. The person in the back wore a scarf and cap, too, so it was hard to determine features, but locks of long blonde hair had escaped and fluttered behind the woman.

"That's the king's personal flier," Kaika said. "I don't know where the queen needs to fly about to, but it looks like she's taken it over." Her lips thinned with disapproval.

Sardelle was tempted to ask if Kaika had met the queen and what kind of woman she was, but they needed to think about escaping. Some of the guards likely knew about this room and would check it. If not, the *queen* certainly knew about it.

There are soldiers in your hallway. They're searching the rooms, and they're debating whether to search the king's suite next. They're moving quickly. They want to catch the intruders before the queen is on the ground and starts asking how there came to be a hole in the brick wall in the cellar.

"There are guards in the hall," Sardelle told the others. "We can't go out that way."

"I heard them," Cas said grimly.

Kaika risked poking her head out the window. It seemed brazen with the lawn below awash with light and more lanterns moving about on the walls, but they were three stories up, and the wall remained in shadow this close to the roof.

"There's a bunch of ivy on the wall out here," Kaika said. "Maybe the vines are strong enough to support our weight. Hm. I also have some rope. Look, this part of the building extends over to the battlement. We're a little above the walkway. Maybe we can climb across and swing down to land on it. There are a lot of men on the wall, but if we time it right... and get lucky... we might be able to climb over the side and down to the rocks before they catch us."

Those vines aren't as sturdy as they look, Jaxi said. *Just ask your acrobatic lover.*

Noted. Thank you. Sardelle was too busy grimacing at the image Kaika had painted for a lengthier response. The idea of them making it across and down without being spotted sounded incredibly optimistic. As did the idea of making it across and down without falling. The flier was hovering over the yard now, its thrusters activated as it prepared to lower to the landing pad. Sardelle pictured falling from the wall and splatting to the ground right in front of the queen. That hadn't been how she imagined her introduction to the royalty of this century.

"Maybe we could hide in here until things quiet down," Cas said, sounding like she found the odds against them too.

A thump came from the bedroom.

"Don't think we have that option," Kaika said.

Sardelle sensed two armed men searching the bedroom, one

looking in the closets and one... heading for the secret panel.

"They're coming," she whispered. "In here. The window is the only option."

Kaika was already swinging out through it. Not hesitating, she disappeared around the edge. Cas hopped onto the sill and followed. In the bedroom, the secret door swung open. The guard strode straight into the passage between the rooms.

Afraid she would fall if she rushed out the window, Sardelle lifted her hand, trying to think of a way to delay him. If she pushed the dresser in front of the door, he would know someone had been in here. Instead, she focused on the lock. Engineering was not her specialty—as Jaxi would be the first to point out—but she did her best to bend the metal of the latch, hoping it would stick. Then, with her heart beating at triple speed, she climbed onto the sill and peered in the direction the other women had gone. There were numerous vines with ivy leaves tangled all about them, but they did not appear sturdy enough to hang from. Kaika and Cas were creeping along a ledge—more of an architectural decoration—no more than an inch wide, leaning their weight into the wall and using the vines for handholds.

You'll catch me if I fall, right Jaxi?

I don't know. I was amused by that image of you tumbling to a heap at the queen's feet.

The guard grunted and shoved his shoulder against the hidden door, leaving Sardelle no more time to debate the climb. She stepped onto the tiny ledge, only the tips of her toes able to perch on it. Her small pack suddenly felt heavy as it hung from her shoulders, pulling her balance backward. She couldn't imagine how Kaika was doing this. Not only was she taller and heavier, but her pack full of explosives had to weigh three times as much as Sardelle's pack. Kaika had made it to the next window along the wall and was looking inside, probably worried about guards in the bedroom. The curtains had been drawn when they had been in there earlier, but someone might still glimpse a person climbing past on the ledge.

Seeing the window reminded Sardelle to close the shutters behind her so the secret nursery would appear untouched. So long as nobody counted the pamphlets in the drawer.

With her toes already trembling from supporting her weight, Sardelle crept after the others. She used her power as she could, strengthening the ivy so the slender vines would not snap and using air currents to push at her back, to help keep her weight leaning into the wall.

A soft gasp came from farther along the building, past the bedroom window. Kaika's foot slipped off the ledge. She had hold of one of the vines, but the ivy was snapping, pulling away from the wall. Sardelle froze and moved the air currents in Kaika's direction, cupping her from below and pushing against her from behind. With the assistance, Kaika managed to get her foot back onto the ledge. She paused to regroup, taking a deep slow breath, then looked toward Sardelle.

Sardelle, her calves now shaking from the effort of maintaining the awkward position, managed a short nod in her direction, then checked on Cas before returning to her own careful climb. Cas was the smallest and lightest of them all and was not having much trouble. Good. Sardelle had all she could manage to continue along the ledge on her own without worrying overmuch about the others.

As Sardelle reached the bedroom window, the flier touched down. The curtains were still drawn, and she lunged across, hoping nobody was glancing in that direction. She could sense one guard still in there, checking under the bed. As if three women with swords and rifles and packs could hide under a bed.

You never know. Tolemek and Ridge were getting cozy under that bed earlier tonight.

Must have been a big bed.

Kaika had reached the corner of the building and was contemplating the jump to the battlement. There was not a gap, so she merely had to leap down, but two guards were jogging along it. If they looked up at the corner of the building, they were sure to spot Kaika, shadows or not. For now, their focus was toward the rocks outside of the castle. Sardelle wondered how many people were standing around the hole they had made, but she did not break her concentration to check. She was already struggling to focus on the climb and not the words of a conversation floating up from the landing pad. The flier's propeller had been stopped, and she could clearly hear the queen making comments as a guard captain explained the hubbub to her.

"Someone's *inside* the castle?" she asked. "Any idea who?"

"No, my liege. He may be a Cofah spy, but we'll find him. He won't escape."

Cas had caught up with Kaika at the corner of the building. They were waiting for Sardelle before they tried to time a jump. She did her best to coerce her cramping calves and trembling toes to hurry the last ten feet along the ledge. She had to duck under a thousand-year-old leering dragon head to manage it and almost lost her grip. She pushed at herself with an air current again, trying to regain her balance, but a portion of the old ledge crumbled beneath her foot. Struggling to keep the calm necessary to use her power, she grasped at the ivy with both hands and flattened her face to the brick as her right foot now dangled in the air. The sound of the tiny shards of rock trickling down the wall below her seemed horribly loud to her ears.

Cas was only two feet away and might have reached out a hand to steady Sardelle, but she only gazed in her direction, the shadows hiding whatever expression she wore.

"Time to jump," Kaika whispered. "The guards are at the towers. Best chance we'll get."

Sardelle managed a quick nod.

"Any word on the search for the king?" the queen asked from below. She was now walking toward a door while the guard continued his report.

As she passed under a gas lantern, Sardelle got her first good look at her. A woman in her late forties with her long blonde hair clipped back, she had a slump to her shoulders and appeared tired. Whatever her position was right now, she was doing more than knitting and reading mystery novels. She soon walked out of view, but her aura lingered, one stronger and more pronounced than Sardelle would have expected.

Jaxi, does she—

Yes.

Before Sardelle could dwell on her realization, Kaika jumped to the walkway, landing in a crouch, her fingers brushing the ground. The shadows were doubtlessly not as thick down there as she would have liked, and she moved quickly, pulling a coil of rope from her pack. Cas jumped down after her. She had the big sword across her back, but it was so long that the end banged down as she landed. Sardelle winced. With the flier propeller no longer rotating, the courtyard had grown quiet, and that bang seemed to echo along the battlements.

"Someone's up on the wall," came a cry from the yard.

Cursing, Kaika hurried to tie her rope around one of the crenellations. But the nearest two tower doors flew open, and men charged out. She wasn't going to have enough time.

Sardelle jumped down, forming a barrier with her mind even as she dropped. Rifles fired. Bullets would have struck the women, but Sardelle's shield deflected them. That was better than the alternative, but she winced, knowing that even if they escaped, the castle guards would realize that a sorceress had been among the intruders. Maybe it was dark enough that the soldiers might simply believe they had missed. Except that they were running as they were firing, drawing closer with every second. They were sure to notice the barrier when they bounced off it.

"Go," Kaika said, shoving Cas toward the rope.

Without hesitation, Cas slung herself over the wall and disappeared. Kaika waved for Sardelle to follow, even as her hand tapped the hilt of her pistol. Kaika didn't draw it—knew she couldn't. She hopped onto the wall between two crenellations, using them for cover, but from the confused furrow to her brow she had realized the bullets were not making it through to them.

The first soldier reached the edge of Sardelle's barrier. He bounced backward, as if he had struck a wall. His eyes opened wider than full moons as he stared at her. Then Kaika was pushing Sardelle over the side, and she had no choice but to grab the rope and slide down. She ignored the stone wall scraping at her knuckles and the rough rope biting into her palms, and made sure a barrier remained around Kaika.

Watch out, Jaxi barked into her mind.

Rifles rang out from below—*close* below. Sardelle didn't see the bullets speed through the night sky toward her, but Jaxi erected a barrier in time, and they burst into flame, incinerated. Sardelle skimmed the rest of the way down the rope, but as she landed, the air flashed with light, and a boom thundered in her ears. She stumbled on the uneven rocks—or maybe the ground shook and tripped her up—and fell onto her butt.

Cas knelt a few feet away, her rifle in hand, and aimed toward a squad of soldiers running toward them.

"Don't," Sardelle yelled, belatedly realizing Cas wasn't going to. She already would have taken them out if she intended to.

Spotting a soldier pulling back his arm to throw something—a second explosive?—Sardelle hurled a gale of wind at the squad. It struck them like a hurricane, battering them almost as forcefully as a bomb's shockwave would have.

Sardelle scurried away from the dangling rope, looking up toward the wall, hoping to see that Kaika was climbing down and about to land. But the bullets and the explosion had distracted Sardelle. The barrier she had been keeping around Kaika had dissolved.

Kaika was hanging over the edge of the wall, clinging to the stones as men tried to pry her away. Her face contorted with pain, and Sardelle sensed that she had been shot. But what she yelled down was not about her own danger.

"Find the king," Kaika ordered, her gaze raking across Sardelle even as the guards finally managed to pull her away from the wall.

We will, Sardelle promised silently, breaking her rule about telepathic communication to let the words trickle into Kaika's mind.

They're coming again, Jaxi warned.

Sardelle sent another blast of air at the men, then turned and ran for the harbor. Cas was already heading in that direction.

A diversion would be welcome, Jaxi. Sardelle could keep hurling wind at them, but that wouldn't keep the men on the wall from firing or seeing which direction they were going.

Always happy to put on a small show.

Jaxi had no sooner than shared the thought than the sky lit up behind Sardelle. A fiery orange inferno leaped from the ground, incinerating the rope and stretching toward the heavens. The soldiers that had been trying to follow Sardelle and Cas stumbled backward, raising their arms against the intense heat. Even halfway down to the harbor, Sardelle could feel it warming her back. It rose higher than the walls of the castle, and the riflemen standing on the walkway had to flee.

A small *show?* Sardelle asked, running as fast as she could over the jumbled rocks.

You asked for a distraction. They're distracted.

Do any of them have eyebrows left?

They don't need eyebrows to stand guard and shoot people.

Sardelle hoped Kaika had been pulled to safety before the flames had leaped up.

She was. They're taking her to a dungeon for questioning.

How badly wounded is she?

Shot in the shoulder. I suppose how bad that is depends on whether they bring in a healer or just throw her into a cell.

Sardelle shook her head bleakly as she ran. She could not imagine that an intruder with a backpack full of explosives would be treated favorably. A notion of charging back in with Jaxi aflame to rescue Kaika flashed through her mind, and she almost spun around right there.

I wouldn't. Not now. Everyone's alert, and you would have to fight the whole castle. With them shooting to kill and you trying not to hurt anyone, you would only end up dead.

I know. I'm just frustrated. And Sardelle dreaded telling Ridge that she had lost one of his troops. The whole reason he had asked her to go along was to help, and what had happened? Kaika had been slowed down, making sure Cas and Sardelle got out ahead of her. If Kaika had been alone, she would have made it.

Apparently, Jaxi had no words of comfort, because she did not respond to these grim thoughts.

Ahead of her, Cas angled toward the road that led from the

city up to the castle gates. Sardelle had been thinking of jumping in the harbor and swimming away, some notion of hounds following tracks in her mind, but the rough footing made her crave the smoothness of a cobblestone road. She followed Cas, and eventually, they made it off the promontory, though they had to hide twice in a drainage ditch as military vehicles rolled past. Sardelle used her power to keep the drivers from noticing the panting women hunkering beside the road. She and Cas did not speak until they reached the city, ran through a maze of alleys, and ensured they had eluded pursuit.

When they stopped to catch their breath, Cas spun on Sardelle and thrust a finger toward her face.

"What was that? If you were going to break our cover with fire and thunder, then why'd you let them get the captain?"

Startled by the vitriol in Cas's voice, Sardelle said, "I assure you that wasn't my intent."

"Well, now she's going to get shot for being suspected a traitor, and everyone in that castle knows a damned witch was there. They know *you* were there. There's nobody else around who can do all that. And they know you're with the colonel, so they're going to know *he's* here. How are we supposed to sneak around and gather intel when the whole city knows we're here? And what do you think they're going to do to Captain Kaika when they see all her weapons and explosives?"

"They took her to a dungeon," Sardelle said quietly. She did not want to argue and mostly gave the information to reassure Cas, so she would know that whatever happened, Kaika wasn't in danger of being shot, at least not right away.

"Oh, well that makes it fine. I'm sure she'll enjoy her time there before they *shoot* her." Cas whirled around and stalked off down the alley. Sardelle would have followed her—whatever had happened, they had to meet back up with Ridge—but Cas added, "The colonel never should have brought you back from those mountains. All you've done is make everything worse."

Sardelle stood still, letting Cas stalk away. She tried to tell herself that Cas was simply angry and that she would apologize later. Sardelle hadn't realized Cas and Kaika had become that close, but they must have, and she must be scared and angry about losing her fellow officer.

Even though her thoughts seemed rational and were most likely true, Sardelle couldn't manage to brush off the words, to rise above the insult. It stung, and Cas's accusations repeated in her head as she trudged slowly toward the north side of the city and the highway that would lead her into the countryside.

She glanced at a building papered with advertisements and stumbled when she spotted her own face looking back at her. The wanted poster. She recognized the picture from a roster that had been pulled out of Galmok Mountain by the crystal miners. It was her first time seeing the poster, but she couldn't bring herself to stop and read the indictment. She continued onward, trying not to feel like all of Iskandia wanted her dead—including her own comrades. It was hard when she had a long walk ahead of her and nobody to talk to. If Cas hadn't stormed off, she could have informed her of something that may or may not change the course of their mission.

The queen had dragon blood flowing through her veins.

Chapter 6

BY THE TIME HIS BORROWED horse neared his mother's property, Ridge was yawning so fiercely that his jaw kept cracking. He had dozed off several times in the saddle, but that was hardly restful sleep, not when he kept waking with a jerk to keep himself from falling off.

The sky was lightening in the east, promising dawn. He wished it would promise sun too. He was tired of the late-winter clouds and the dampness that seeped through his cloak and made him long for a warm bed, preferably one with Sardelle in it. If she would deign to join him after she learned that his people were hunting witches. No, not even "witches," just people with a very distant ancestor who had been intrigued by a dragon's attentions. Most of them probably had no idea that they had any talent for magic. Tolemek had been using his talent every day and even he had never known it.

Ridge looked over at his silent comrade, trying to decide if Tolemek was being deeply introspective or sleeping in his saddle. "You still worried about that tea canister?"

"I can handle Therrik if he comes for me," Tolemek said, "though I would feel better about handling him if I had access to my lab and could prepare myself for a fair fight."

"By fair, you mean that you would have explosives, tear gas, and knockout grenades to throw at him while he had only his fists?"

"I could give him knockout grenades, too, but I doubt he's bright enough to use them."

"Might be right." Ridge had found his eavesdropping interesting, because it had been a chance to see if Therrik was as much of a badger's teat when he was with other people as he was around Ridge. The answer had been no. Of course, any soldier would behave in the presence of higher-ranking officers, but if Ridge was honest with himself, he would admit that he had goaded Therrik a little when they had met. Still, that didn't explain why he had been such an unbalanced ass with Tolemek. Unless he had known what Tolemek was, that part about him having dragon blood. Could he have? That seemed unlikely, but Therrik had definitely had unkind words for Sardelle, based on her blood rather than on ever having met her.

"Zirkander," Tolemek said, then paused to yawn before adding, "how would you feel if you found out you had dragon blood and it was the reason for your flying skills, rather than any brilliance on your part?"

"I'm sorry, did you just admit I have flying skills? That was almost a compliment. I want to make sure I heard you right over the clomps of the hoofbeats."

"Never mind."

Speaking of goading people... Why couldn't he ever rein in that lippy streak, as General Ort called it? "The dragon blood is a part of you, right? It's still *you* inventing things, knowing the science to make things work when magic alone wouldn't do anything."

"So you would embrace your heritage?"

"I'd be excited about it. It would mean I had an incredibly adventurous ancestor who had been brave enough to get randy with a dragon. You know my dad's dad and my three uncles were all drunks? Every one of them got himself killed doing something stupid. *That's* the kind of blood I have in my veins."

"The blood of stupidity?" Tolemek squinted over at him. "That seems apt."

Ridge touched his knuckles to his cap in a lazy salute. He had set himself up for that one. And after the night they'd had, Tolemek probably didn't have much reason to think him bright. He couldn't believe he had been too cowardly to knock on Therrik's door before throwing the grenade. No, he had thought chucking it through the window with a *rock* was an intelligent infiltration tactic. Although...

He grinned over at Tolemek. "You know what the best part

of tonight was? Finding out that I wasn't the first hoodlum to vandalize Therrik's house. The MP made it sound like it happened all the time."

"That wasn't the best part."

"No? What was?"

"Hearing that Therrik is officially your commanding officer."

Ridge grunted. "And also about how he wanted to send me off to hunt those with dragon blood?"

"No," Tolemek said more soberly.

Ridge clenched his fist around the reins. "I have to round up my people, get them back to the hangar. They need to be here in the capital, right now. The idea of the city having absolutely no air support..." He shuddered. "I think I'm going to have to give up my skulking ways and reveal myself, but damned if I'm going to report to Therrik. I'm tempted to take a flier up the coast and order everyone back in person, but it would take a week to fly all around the country, especially if some of my pilots are inland. I have no idea where those witch communities are. And if I'm gone that long, who knows what would happen back here? No, we need to focus on the king. If we get him back, surely he'll put an end to this stupidity. I hope Sardelle and the others found something tonight."

"I hope Cas didn't shoot anyone she shouldn't have," Tolemek said. "She's been grumpy since we got home. Actually, she was grumpy on the flight back here, too. You would think she would have been pleased we made it off that island alive."

"It's hard coming home to chaos and disruption." Ridge tried to decide if he had witnessed Ahn's grumpiness. She *had* been quiet, and he knew from experience that while others railed and griped at life's frustrations, she was more likely to wall herself off and deal with her problems internally. She hadn't said anything cross to him, though, so he wondered if Tolemek was projecting some of his own disgruntlement onto her. He had done so much work for so long to help his sister, and even though they had succeeded in freeing her, she had left on that dragon's back without an offer to take him along or even a promise to return for a nice family chat.

"Listen, Tee," Ridge said, leaning over to thump Tolemek in the arm. "I appreciate you coming to help me last night. I know you're not on anyone's payroll right now and that you have no reason to follow some crazy Iskandian's orders. But you're handy to have around."

Tolemek gazed over at him, his dark ropes of hair shadowing his face. As always, he looked about as friendly as the deadly pirate he had once been.

Ridge returned his hands to his reins. He'd tried.

"As much as it pains me to say it," Tolemek said after Ridge had given up on receiving an answer, "you helped me get Tylie. I owe you."

That wasn't the response Ridge had anticipated. While he wouldn't mind having Tolemek in his debt, he wouldn't be comfortable with it when that sense of *owing* was misplaced.

"You don't owe me anything," he said. "You know I was only there because it was my duty to rid the Cofah of their big advantage. Your sister just happened to be in the same room as the dragon."

"Nonetheless, you made it possible for me to visit the sanitarium to look for her, and I couldn't have gotten her off Owanu Owanus without your and Sardelle's help."

Mostly Sardelle's help. Ridge had felt largely ineffective on that jungle expedition. Without his flier, he was just another soldier with a gun. But he kept the thoughts to himself. Tolemek didn't show gratitude often, at least not to him, so he had better not fight too hard to dismiss it.

"And I *am* pleased," Tolemek added, "at the thought of Therrik's house being vandalized frequently."

Ridge grinned. "I told you that was the best part of the night."

The hoofbeats of a trotting horse drifted to them, and Ridge turned in his saddle, worried their deeds of the night had been discovered. They were almost to the turnoff for his mother's house, and he thought about nudging his horse to greater speed to make it before they were overtaken.

The lone figure coming up behind them wore a hood and a tightly wrapped cloak. It had a woman's slighter form, and his first thought was that this might be one of those people who had been after Sardelle. But then a familiar warmth brushed his mind, and he knew it was Sardelle. She may not have meant it to, but weariness and worry—and a sense of dread—came to him along with that warmth.

He lifted an arm in greeting, now more worried for her than for himself. And where were Cas and Kaika? His gut clenched. Captured? Worse?

Sardelle pulled her horse to a stop next to his. "I'm sorry, Ridge." She sounded miserable. "We were discovered, and Kaika had Cas and me go down the wall first. I was protecting her, but I'd forgotten about the soldiers outside of the grounds, and I had no idea they had explosives. I was distracted and—I'm sorry. They got her. Jaxi said they put her in the dungeon, but she was shot, and I'm worried she'll be in trouble if we can't find a way to get her out soon. I almost went back in, but the castle was on high alert by then, and I'd already... they know I was there. We—Jaxi and I—made a big display so we could get away. I'm afraid they'll know you're here too now." She was looking past him, avoiding his eyes as she spoke far too quickly, like a soldier reporting to a superior when he knew he was in trouble. Ridge reached over and clasped her forearm. He was worried for Kaika, but he wanted to let Sardelle know that he wasn't upset with her. Hells, he would never want her to feel like a junior officer reporting in to him. He did not even feel worthy of his rank after spending his night hiding under another officer's bed.

"What happened to Cas?" Tolemek asked, his shoulders tense.

"She made it out."

Tolemek peered down the road behind Sardelle.

"I thought she was ahead of me. I didn't pass her on the road."

Tolemek shifted in his saddle. "Did you *see* her get out?"

"Yes, it wasn't until afterward that we split up." Sardelle was gazing past Ridge's shoulder again instead of looking either of them in the face.

"Why did you split up?" Tolemek asked. "Were you being followed?"

"I'm sure Lieutenant Ahn can take care of herself if that was the case." Ridge wasn't sure why Sardelle seemed uncomfortable, but he didn't think she needed an interrogation from Tolemek.

"We weren't being followed, as far as I know," Sardelle said. "She should be fine. She was simply... displeased with me for allowing Kaika to be captured." Sardelle sounded displeased with *herself*.

Ridge groped for a way to reassure her. He was certain that she had done all she could. Maybe Ahn had expected too much. As powerful as Sardelle and Jaxi were, they weren't gods.

No, we're much more useful than gods. We actually care what happens to you mortals and try to help.

We appreciate it, Ridge responded, trying not to let on that he would have rather had Sardelle talking into his head than Jaxi.

She's busy moping. Perhaps you can exchange telepathic endearments later.

"All right," Ridge said. "Let's get back to the house. We can share what we've learned and figure out how to move forward."

He wondered how long they would have until Kaika was indicted. Her record bespoke loyalty and a willingness to sacrifice everything, including her life if necessary, to carry out her missions for Iskandia. He hoped that would buy her time, that they wouldn't go straight to assuming she should be shot as a traitor, but with the kind of ordnance she carried around, being caught skulking around the castle would not be good. He nibbled on his lip and gazed back down the road, tempted to turn around and head straight back to Harborgard to turn himself in. Even if the castle incursion had been Kaika's idea, he could tell them he had wanted the information and that he had commanded her to go. Since Sardelle had been there, they would probably believe that. They might throw him in the dungeon and let Kaika go. Then he could hope they found him too valuable to shoot. He had never interacted with the queen and wasn't sure how she felt about him. Judging by the conversation the senior officers had had in Therrik's house, they at least wanted to see him back flying. But, as was obvious from them needing to get their information from Therrik, they were not in command of the city defenses right now.

"Before you consider anything drastic, I have more information for you," Sardelle said.

He wasn't sure if she was monitoring his thoughts or if the set of his jaw made those thoughts blatantly obvious, but he wasn't surprised she knew his turmoil. He patted her on the arm. "Right, let's get to the house. More rain coming, I think."

Tolemek kept glancing toward the rear as they continued on. Ridge would not worry about Ahn unless she did not turn up at all that day. None of his team could take care of themselves better than she.

As they reached the turnoff for his mother's house, another horse and rider came into view, the thunder of rapid hoofbeats preceding it. This one was coming from the north instead of the city, so Ridge did not worry that it might be someone after them. However, from the uneven hunch of the rider, he thought the person might be injured. He was pushing the horse hard too.

"Busy road this morning," Tolemek muttered.

With uneasiness swimming into his belly again, Ridge stopped his horse to wait. He had sent Duck in that direction to watch the fliers.

"It's Duck," Sardelle said before the rider's face was visible—dawn was creeping across the sky, but darkness still hugged the farmlands. "He's injured. Shot. At least twice."

Ridge cursed. "I was afraid of that." He rode forward to meet his lieutenant.

"Sir," Duck blurted, his voice pained.

When Ridge drew up next to him, Duck almost fell out of the saddle and into his lap. Blood caked his face, and he was clutching his side.

"What happened, Wasley?" Ridge maneuvered his horse around, trying to find a way to support Duck at the same time as they headed for the house. He needed a bed and a healer.

Sardelle was already bringing her horse around to Duck's other side. She reached out, laying a hand on his thigh, probably intending to help right away, but she also nodded in the direction of the house.

"Sir, I tried to stop them, but there were too many." Duck

sounded miserable from more than the pain. "I thought since they all seemed to be women... I didn't really think they would go through with it. They told me to get away from the fliers, but I didn't listen. I tried to grab one, would have had her, but then they threw a bomb and started shooting. Should've treated them seriously right off, especially when they showed up out of nowhere. So dumb. Wasn't smart." He was panting, struggling to relay the story.

"There's a lot of that going around right now," Ridge said.

Sardelle winced, which made Ridge want to wince. He had been referring to his own night's dumbness, not anything she had done.

"So sorry, sir," Duck mumbled.

Ridge patted his shoulder, hoping he would settle down. He could tell the rest of the tale when he was feeling better.

They made it to the house without any more riders streaking out of the darkness, though Ridge wouldn't have minded seeing Ahn arrive. He had hoped Apex might be back, as well, but knew it would take him time to find any of the squadron, especially if he couldn't go on base. Belatedly, Ridge realized he might have sent Apex on a fool's quest. If everyone had flown off on Therrik's witch-hunting mission, there wouldn't be anybody in the city to find.

"The world does *not* want me to get any good intelligence," Ridge muttered as he helped Duck from his horse.

With Sardelle on Duck's other side, they maneuvered him into the house. A few cats slunk out from under the foundation, meowing. Several more waited inside. Apparently, Mom hadn't thought it would be a good idea to take her posse with her to Aunt Lavender's place.

Ridge tried to steer Duck toward the bedroom, but he reached out a hand and stumbled toward the couch. He slumped down on it with a groan, tipping over onto his side.

"Couch it is," Ridge said.

"Saw the quilt on your mom's bed," Duck mumbled as Sardelle lifted his legs onto the couch and grabbed a pillow for his head. "Didn't want to get it all bloody."

"You're a thoughtful patient." Ridge spotted a note on a table by the couch, a request that he feed the cats twice a day. "That'll be hard if I'm in the dungeon," he mumbled.

"Sir?" Duck asked.

"Nothing. Relax, Duck. Let Sardelle fix you up."

"Good advice," Sardelle said, sitting on the edge of the couch and resting her hand on Duck's chest. "Could you get him some water, please, Ridge?"

She did not ask for bandages or towels, but he brought those too. When he returned to the couch, Sardelle's head had drooped to her chin, her eyes closed. Duck's eyes were closed too. He assumed magic things were happening and left without comment.

Tolemek stood by the front window, his fist to his chin. Ridge scrubbed his hands through his hair—it needed a washing. All of him did. He was lucky Therrik hadn't smelled him hiding under his bed. He needed sleep, too, but how could he rest now? He could either go back to the castle and try to get an audience with the queen or, perhaps more effectively, the chief of security. Or he could go check on the fliers and see if anything remained of them. Such as the power crystals. Even though Sardelle had left a map at the Magroth Mines to help the men there find more crystals, it took a long time to excavate tunnels and acquire them. He hadn't had time yet to take her up on her offer of trying to learn how to make them herself.

He shook his head and paced a circle around the living room. Who in all of Iskandia would want to blow up fliers? They were necessary for the defense of the city, of the whole *country*. Women, Duck had said. Could it be the same women who had been after Sardelle before they left? Why would *they* want to destroy the fliers? Even if some organization out there hated sorcerers—not a stretch—they shouldn't hate their own country enough to take away the most effective way of defending it.

Ridge halted in the middle of his pacing. Unless they had figured out what the power crystals were and where they had come from. According to Sardelle, they had been light fixtures in the inner mountain headquarters where her people, the

Referatu, had once lived. A witch-hating organization might object to *that*. Still, to destroy something that was helping all of Iskandia... what idiots. Ridge looked over at Sardelle. She would happily help all of Iskandia, too, if Iskandia would let her.

"Idiots," he breathed, clenching his fist.

Tolemek looked over at him.

Ridge grabbed his rifle and some biscuits and ham from a food pile his mom had left in the kitchen. "I'm going to see what's left of the fliers." Maybe some of those women would be lingering at the scene of their destruction, and he could catch one to question.

Take me, Jaxi spoke into his head at the same time as Tolemek asked, "By yourself?"

"What?" Ridge asked, not quite sure who he was answering.

"I'll go with you," Tolemek said. "There aren't any beds in that canyon for you to hide under. You'll be lost by yourself."

He was probably just looking for something to do so he wouldn't stand there and worry about Ahn all morning, but Ridge nodded, accepting the offer. "There's some grub in the kitchen. Grab whatever you want. I'll meet you outside."

With me, Jaxi said.

Why? Don't you need to stay with Sardelle? Ridge thought of the soldiers who had come by the day before. What if they came back while Sardelle was deep in her healing trance? And why would Jaxi want to come with him?

Watching Sardelle heal people is boring, and I can help if you find some people to question. I can get in their thoughts without you having to brutalize a woman. Not that you'd probably do that, anyway. I imagine you'd be a wholly ineffective interrogator.

Ridge would have liked to object, but it was the truth, wasn't it? When he had first met Sardelle, he had been fairly certain she was a spy, and how had he interrogated her? By folding her towels for her.

Yes, you're very tough. As far as Sardelle is concerned, she can rouse herself if someone comes to the door. She'll be fine against a few soldiers.

You're sure it's all right? Ridge eyed the soulblade. Sardelle hadn't bothered to unbuckle her sword belt before sitting down next to Duck.

It's fine. She knows. Take me.

For a moment, Ridge imagined a dog running to the door, wagging its tail and wanting to go along on the adventure, whatever it was.

You think of me like a dog again, and I'll piddle down your leg.

Er, can you do that?

I'm a mighty sorceress. I can do anything.

Can you do it while being humble?

That wouldn't be as fun.

"Please take her," Sardelle said without lifting her head or opening her eyes.

"Is she threatening to pee down your leg too?"

She didn't answer, and Ridge felt silly for discussing urination while one of his pilots was injured. Being careful not to disturb her, he unbuckled the belt from Sardelle's waist. He kissed her on the top of the head and walked to the door, trying to decide whether he felt relieved or guilty that he hadn't had an opportunity to tell her about the witch-hunt. Or both.

She won't be surprised, Jaxi thought, her tone one of glumness rather than the usual irreverence. *The world has changed much.*

Yeah. Ridge didn't know what else to say. He wished it could be a better place for Sardelle, but he did not know how to make that happen.

The horses were standing in the flowerbeds outside, still saddled, probably waiting for a rub down and food rather than another ride.

"Sorry, fellows. Short trip, then I'll take care of you." He did not know where Sardelle had collected her mount, but his had come from the army fort. It was much easier to head out than it was to get in. When he and Tolemek had ridden through the back gate with hoods pulled over their faces, the guard had not questioned them.

Tolemek walked outside with a small canvas sack that implied he had done a more thorough job of selecting food than Ridge had. Probably wisely so.

"Was all that food for us? The ham? The biscuits? The bread? The cheese?" Tolemek asked, swinging up onto the horse.

A meowing cat reminded Ridge of his mother's note. "I think we're supposed to share it with the cats. Twice a day."

Before climbing onto his horse, he took out a couple of the ham slices he had grabbed and tore them up, dropping them in a pile by the porch.

Tolemek gazed down the road toward the city again before they turned north, but there was no sign of Ahn.

"She's probably walking back," Ridge said.

Tolemek nodded.

They passed farmers out doing chores on the way north, and Ridge waved whenever someone looked in their direction. He kept his cloak around him and the hood up, so he didn't think anyone recognized him. Maybe it did not matter anymore. If Sardelle had been recognized in the castle, people would indeed know he was in the area. Whoever had attacked Duck had clearly known they were back already.

"How do people keep finding us, Tee?" Ridge asked. "There's nothing trackable about the fliers themselves, unless someone could detect the crystals somehow. But it would take a sorcerer to detect something magical, wouldn't it? And an organization that's trying to get rid of sorcerers shouldn't have a sorcerer among them, should it? That would be rather hypocritical."

"You're expecting your enemies to be morally logical?" Tolemek asked.

"Is that unwise?"

"Probably. As to the rest, I'm not an expert, but I doubt there's ever been a sorcerer alive who could detect magic across an ocean. And people have been finding us since we left Iskandia weeks ago. Remember the Cofah waiting along the coast? And somehow Cas's dad knew to look for us on that island."

He's right. I have a range of thirty or forty miles, as far as seeing the world around me goes. I would have to be even closer than that to detect something like your light fixtures.

We prefer to call them power crystals.

I know. It's amusing. I doubt there are many sorcerers who could have detected the landing of your fliers from the capital. I certainly haven't seen anyone capable of that in Iskandia since I was dug out of the rocks.

Any idea how someone would have found our fliers then? Ridge supposed it was possible this organization had scouts up and down the coast, not just in the city. If so, they could be much larger and better equipped than he would have guessed.

Sardelle didn't tell you about the queen, did she?

The queen? Ridge caught sight of dark gray smoke in the distance, several thick lines combining in the sky and being blown inland.

Yes. First off, she has dragon blood flowing through her veins. Second—

"Dragon blood?" Ridge blurted. The queen couldn't be a sorceress. He shook his head. No, it wasn't possible. Who would have trained her? How could she have kept that hidden from the king for years?

Relax, genius. While I suppose it's possible she could have some training, she can have that heritage without being a sorceress or even knowing she has the aptitude. Like your hairy pirate friend here.

"Jaxi chatting with you?" Tolemek asked. "Or was that a response to my comment?"

"Yes. No." Wait, what had his comment been? Something about the range of sorcerers?

"Let me know if she enlightens you on anything important."

From what I've observed so far, Jaxi continued, *about one in a thousand people here has some diluted dragon blood. I doubt many of them could conjure any magic even if they were trained. They're probably considered perceptive by their comrades, but little more. People like Tolemek and his sister, those who still have sufficient blood to have access to more power, most likely have ancestors who were among those who mated with the last of the dragons, back before they disappeared from this world. For someone whose dragon-loving ancestor existed two thousand years ago instead of a thousand, they could never become someone who would be considered a sorcerer, at least not in our time.*

"Just how long have people been having sex with dragons, anyway?"

Tolemek looked at Ridge. "I see this is an important conversation you're having."

Ridge held up a hand so he could think, *Never mind that. Are you telling me that the queen is definitely not a powerful sorcerer?*

Definitely not. She could conceivably know a few tricks, but she wouldn't be a threat in a battle, and she certainly wouldn't be able to sense the crystals of your fliers. However, as I was about to say when you interrupted me, she seems to be affiliated with the Heartwood Sisterhood.

Is that the organization that's been harassing Sardelle?

We don't have proof of that, other than a stack of pamphlets in the queen's drawer, but the organization has been around for more than a thousand years, and they've objected to human-dragon sex since the beginning.

So, are they active again now because they know there's a dragon in the world? Ridge scratched his jaw. Even if he hadn't known about the dragon until he had been sent to Cofahre, the attacks on Sardelle had started just before that. Someone else could have known about the dragon earlier than he had been informed. After all, someone had known to send Ahnsung to try and get rid of it.

Maybe they're concerned that Phelistoth is going to fly over here and sex up all the young virgins.

Ridge shuddered. He hadn't found anything alluring about the powerful creature. Mostly, he had been trying not to crawl under a table and hide when that big reptilian eye had focused on him. But Tolemek's sister had been fearless around the creature. Maybe women would be more likely to be drawn to him.

Technically, the Sisterhood objected to young men being seduced by female dragons.

I had no idea the world used to be so strange.

Says the man who flies about in a mechanical contraption powered by a light fixture.

"You might want to finish it up, so we can plan something." Tolemek pointed to the smoke. "I assume we're not going to ride straight up to the bridge over the canyon."

"No." Ridge pointed ahead and to the left. A few farms still dotted the terrain, but Crazy Canyon was considered a park, and the quarter mile on either side of the canyon was dominated by beach grass and stunted trees. "See that path? We'll take it and head down to the beach and then go into the canyon through the mouth."

Ridge made himself watch the grass on both sides as they headed down the path, though his gaze kept being pulled toward the smoke. They had landed three fliers in the canyon, which meant three crystals that could have been stolen. If he had needed another reason to dread reporting in, he had it. He wondered what rank he would have at the end of all this, or if he would have a rank at all. He couldn't predict what would happen if he showed up at the castle to take blame for Kaika's presence. A part of him wanted to plan another incursion, to sneak in and rescue her without being seen, but that would be one more bullet shot into the already crashing flier that was his career.

Seven gods, you're even more depressing to travel with than Sardelle. Sorry.

As Ridge and Tolemek followed the cliff along the beach to the mouth of the canyon, the air smelled of burning wreckage, as well as salt water and seaweed. When the group had landed, they had perched the fliers on a ledge halfway up a canyon wall, a ledge covered with brush that they had painstakingly used to camouflage their craft. Whoever had found them must have known *exactly* where they were. He didn't believe that Duck had been doing something foolish such as standing naked in one of the cockpits and singing ballads dedicated to lost loves.

That's a somewhat more interesting thought than your earlier ones. Duck naked?

Duck singing. I enjoy ballads.

When they had gone as far through the scrubby growth along the floor of the canyon as they could, Ridge and Tolemek found a place to leave the horses, then continued on foot. Ridge walked softly, trying to listen for the sounds of voices or other signs of humans, but the drone of the ocean made it hard to detect subtle noises.

There's nobody here. Jaxi sounded disappointed.

You're certain? Ridge was disappointed too. It would have been nice if something could have gone their way, if they could have questioned someone from that organization.

Perhaps the answers you seek will be in the pamphlet Sardelle absconded with.

Let's hope.

They had to climb to reach the ledge from this side, and Ridge scrambled over the lip of it first. The sight of smoldering wood and twisted and blackened metal made him sick. Pieces had been blown away and flung all over the ledge, some falling all the way to the stream below. Little of the original shapes of the fliers remained.

He told himself that they were just machines, that he shouldn't be emotionally attached, but it was hard not to mourn their loss. More, it was hard not to be angry at whoever had deprived the capital of craft that could have been used to defend against enemies.

Feeling numb, he walked across the ledge, staring down at the wreckage and looking for... he wasn't sure what. A clue. A clue as to why this had been done and how those women had found the fliers to do it in the first place.

"Zirkander." Tolemek pointed down at something.

Ridge climbed over a log and found him looking at a charred seat that had been thrown clear of one of the cockpits. Someone had pinned a note to it with a dagger.

"Subtle." Ridge freed the paper and unfolded it. He read the short missive, then grimly shared the contents aloud. "Those who fraternize with witches will see all that they love destroyed. It's not signed."

Tolemek stared into the distance, maybe wondering if he would be as much of a target as Sardelle in all of this. Had the queen been the one to close his lab? Was it possible she knew of his blood, as well as his history and reputation?

Jaxi, can those who have dragon blood recognize it in others?

Not necessarily. Sardelle and I can, she because she was a teacher and learned to recognize those who would have talent, and I because I have a powerful enough nose to sniff such details out.

Since she hadn't cared for his earlier dog analogy, Ridge tamped down an impulse to imagine Jaxi as a bloodhound. *For those with the more diluted blood you talked about, it wouldn't be possible to tell?*

Only through deed, or perhaps if they were in close contact for a while, they might get a hunch.

Ridge walked as they discussed, looking for more clues, ones that hadn't been so intentionally left, ones that might tell more.

Someone might figure it out through investigating one's history too, Jaxi added. *Your Apex realized what Tolemek was by researching what he had done and understanding enough science to know that there couldn't be a mundane explanation for all that Tolemek had created.*

Yes, if Apex had figured it out, it was possible that someone else could have. Maybe the queen did more than knitting and making doilies in her spare time.

She also enjoys mystery and romance novels.

Yes, and that was why Ridge had a hard time imagining her as being behind anything. If she had been making pamphlets for the organization, maybe it was because she had been the secretary or head crafts lady. Maybe they had wanted decorative pages full of glitter and embroidered edging.

I don't know anything about her, but underestimating her based on her interests might not be smart, Jaxi suggested.

Yes, you're right. I need more information. I'm guessing. It's frustrating. Ridge kicked a smoldering seat cushion. It flipped over a few times before landing, and something on the bottom caught his eye. He was intimately familiar with every part of a flier—hells, he had helped that engineer at the mines reconstruct one from parts—and he knew there wasn't anything attached to the bottoms of the seats, aside from two metal strips that allowed them to be bolted to the frame.

"Probably just dirt," he mumbled, but he hurried to the cushion for a closer look.

He stared down at it. It wasn't dirt. Half expecting a jolt, he prodded the decorative piece of metal, a round iron pin about an inch and a half wide. Nothing happened.

Jaxi? Is this... something?

Given the definition of the word, I believe that qualifies.

I mean is it magic?

No. I don't sense anything at all from it.

"I found one of your power crystals," Tolemek called from the other side of the ledge. "Do you want me to pry it out of its casing?"

"Yes, thank you." Ridge waved, glad at least one of the crystals had been left but more intrigued by this new mystery. There was something familiar about the angular design stamped on the front. He couldn't have said when or where, but he felt certain he had seen something like it before. The pin itself had a roughness to it, with uneven soldering on the back. It felt *old*. Today, something like this would be made in a factory. And he doubted iron would be the metal of choice. It was heavy for a pin, at least if it was usually worn on clothing and not tacked to seats.

Ridge remembered Sardelle once saying that she hadn't been able to sense that giant owl familiar that they had fought, that she had seen and heard it but not felt it with her mind. *Jaxi, when you say you don't sense anything, do you mean that this pin is no different from any other inanimate object to you, or do you mean you can't tell it's there?*

I can't see it at all, except through your eyes.

Ridge decided not to find it odd that the soulblade was looking at the world through his eyes. How else, he supposed, would a sword "see" anything?

Exactly. The pattern seems familiar to me, too. Like it might be a letter or symbol from one of the old languages. Show it to Sardelle. She's more likely to remember historical minutia than I am.

Is it significant that it's made from iron? I remember Sardelle saying she couldn't sense you through an iron box. Ridge thought of the box under the bed in Therrik's house and the way that had been lined with metal. Had that been iron? It had been too dark to tell, and he hadn't looked that closely. If so, it made him wonder even more what was usually stored in it.

Possibly, but that's not why I don't sense it. For as long as there have been sorcerers, there have been people with the knack of creating magical items that can be used even when the sorcerer is not around. An example is the communication crystals Sardelle made for you.

And the power supplies for the fliers.

Yes. And some sorcerers made items that could hunt other sorcerers or harm them in some way. Magic was never anything that united people, and there were dragon wars long ago, where humans got swept up in the action. Your texts tell you that people used dragons almost like pets or even tools, riding them into battle and ordering them to attack enemies, but there was some revisionist history there. In my time, it was understood that dragons were our equals and allies. Maybe if you go back farther, you will find that dragons were actually running the campaigns and using humans as pets. I don't know for certain, but there were items that were made for hunting dragons—such as Cas's ugly new sword—and for hunting sorcerers, as well. Naturally, it made sense to craft them so said dragons and sorcerers couldn't sense them.*

"Hunting," Ridge mumbled. "Like *tracking?*"

He stared at the pin, then at the seat cushion.

That's possible.

"Son of a hairy teat-kissing sloth," Ridge growled, clenching his fist around the pin. He drew back his arm and almost hurled it into the canyon, but made himself stop before letting go.

Even if it was a tracking device and had allowed his people to be followed across an ocean, it was probably worth researching. He would take it back and show Sardelle. No, he amended hastily, realizing it might still be active. He would leave it here where he had found it and bring Sardelle back to look at it if his description wasn't enough to go by.

"You over here throwing a tantrum while I do all the salvage work?" Tolemek asked, approaching with all three crystals in his arms.

Ridge held up the pin. "Jaxi thinks this is what's been letting people track us."

Tolemek's eyebrows rose.

"I don't suppose you recognize the symbols."

"They're nothing scientific."

"I'll take that as a no."

Ridge dug around in his jacket and found a scrap of paper, actually the back of a card from Wings and Swords promising free beers to pilots on any nights when they returned from a mission. He sketched a copy of the pin, then returned the item to the bottom of the seat cushion. He was tempted to bury it next to some landmark to ensure no scavengers, human or otherwise, would make off with it, but he didn't want his enemies to know that he had found it. He hoped he hadn't already clued someone in by handling it.

"Any idea who planted it?" Tolemek asked.

Ridge stared at him. He hadn't even been thinking about that, but of course someone would have had to stick it there. There had been several times the fliers had been left alone during their mission to Cofahre and those two islands, but if someone had been tracking them since they left home, this had to have been pinned under one of the seats before they left Iskandia. Which meant someone had sneaked onto base and up to the hangars to do it—possible but not that likely. Or someone on the flier maintenance crew had done it. Or—he swallowed. Or one of his own people had done it.

Chapter 7

SARDELLE WOKE TO A TOUCH on her shoulder. She looked blearily up into Ridge's face, then realized she was lying on the floor next to the couch. Between the events of the night and the effort it had taken to remove Duck's bullets and mend the holes they had left, she had been exhausted when she had finished. Collapsing on the floor had seemed much easier than walking to the bedroom. Besides, she hadn't wanted to presume to sleep in Fern's bed.

Soft snores floated down to her from the couch, promising that her patient was still alive.

"Duck looks much better." Ridge smiled down at her. Dark bags lurked under his eyes, and he was in need of a shave, but he still managed to look appealing. His smile warmed her heart—it felt as if a few eons had passed since someone had smiled at her.

"Good," Sardelle murmured.

"I have something I need you to look at." He rested her sword belt on the table beside the couch. "Then you can go back to sleep."

"Sounds reasonable." Sardelle yawned. "Did Cas make it back yet?" A part of her was worried about Cas, but a part of her dreaded seeing her after the harsh words she had spat out the night before.

"No, Tolemek just rode out to look for her. Apex isn't back, either." Concern tightened his eyes, but he did not voice his worries.

He did not need to. Sardelle felt them bubbling beneath the surface for him. Maybe she shouldn't have let Cas stalk away from her. If something had happened after she left, Sardelle would have another reason to feel guilty.

She sat up, intending to push herself to her feet, but Ridge surprised her by sliding his arms under her legs and shoulders and picking her up.

"Are we going somewhere romantic?" she asked, looping an arm around his shoulders, though romance wasn't what she had in mind, not unless she could bathe first. Perhaps continue her nap for a few more hours.

"My mom's bedroom."

"I suppose that could do..."

Ridge looked faintly appalled. "I wasn't thinking of getting romantic in my mom's room. You can rest there while pondering what I have to show you."

After carrying her into the bedroom, Ridge laid her on a sturdy bed made from logs. Despite the rustic appearance, the mattress was comfortable and inviting. Sardelle closed her eyes and leaned her head back on a pillow. Ridge opened the curtains to let the noon daylight in, then sat on the edge of the bed and handed her a card.

"You're taking me for free beers?"

"Look at the back side, at those cryptic scribbles. I tried to draw a picture of the metal device I found pinned under one of the flier seats—what was *left* of the flier and its seat." He grimaced, the image of the wrecked machines scattered across a ledge still at the forefront of his thoughts.

Sardelle sighed, feeling like she should have done something to prevent the possibility of people finding the fliers. Perhaps she could have used her powers to craft a stronger camouflage than what the men had achieved with brush.

"Jaxi thinks it might have been used to track us," Ridge said.

"Track us?" Sardelle examined the back of the card. "Everywhere we've been?"

"Everywhere since leaving Iskandia, I assume. Do you recognize the symbols? I'm afraid my mother is the artist in the family, but I did my best to draw the pin. I didn't want to risk bringing the real one back here. Mom would be upset with me if someone blew up the cats."

Sardelle snorted softly. No doubt. Two had already hopped onto the end of the bed and curled up. "They're letters, not symbols. A and C. The maker's initials perhaps?"

"Oh? Jaxi and I thought the designs were familiar, but she wasn't sure what they were. I just had a feeling I'd seen them before, or something in a similar style."

"You have. Some of the other letters in the alphabet are on the scabbard of Cas's sword. There are two languages on her blade, Old Iskandian and Middle Dragon Script. This is Middle Dragon."

Oops, I should have recognized that, Jaxi said. *I've seen examples of Dragon Script before. Just not so embellished.*

This is almost a calligraphy version.

Do you think Ridge will take me out again? I wasn't very useful, and there was nobody to telepathically interrogate.

I don't know. Did you do anything to irritate him this time?

Does threatening to pee down his leg count?

Yuck. And yes.

"Dragon Script? The dragons wrote things down?" Ridge groped at the air. "I'm imagining Phelistoth's scaled arms and claws here. Or do they call them talons? Either way, I can't see that giant creature holding a pen. Or a quill."

Sardelle smiled. "As you'll recall, dragons *can* shapeshift. But no, this is more the human interpretation of the dragon language than anything they would have written. Dragons themselves were capable of writing, usually using their minds to do so, but they had genetic memories and rarely bothered to record their history, at least not in a way we could understand."

"You said Ahn's sword has this language on it?" Ridge seemed to be trying to picture the symbols on the scabbard. He probably hadn't had a good look at the weapon. They had been busy traveling since retrieving it, and Cas hadn't exactly been showing it off. She always kept it close, not asking anyone else to carry it.

"Yes." Sardelle sat up and touched the side of his face, hoping he wouldn't mind the sharing of the information. She did her best to picture the scabbard in her mind, making the details of those symbols as precise as her memory allowed. She stroked his cheek as she did so, scarcely able to remember the last time they had been alone together. True, Duck's faint snores reminded her they were not entirely alone, but the house was quiet, peaceful. If they hadn't had so much to worry about—Kaika, gods, how was she going to get Kaika out of that castle?—she might have slid her hand around to the back of his head and kissed him.

"Oh." Ridge's eyes widened. "Oh! I've seen those somewhere else. Just last night."

Assuming he meant the language and that her thoughts of kissing hadn't seeped through the link, she asked, "Where?" Dragon Script wasn't common anywhere anymore.

"Under Therrik's bed."

"Uhm, what?"

"Here." He rested his hand atop hers, keeping hers pressed to his cheek. "Can you tell what I'm thinking?"

Much as she had, he formed an image in his mind. She saw a wooden floor with broken glass scattered across it, and a long, oblong box sticking out from underneath a bed. The same two languages appeared on the top of it. The words weren't the same as those on the sword, and she would have to visit a library to find out what they said, but she doubted it was a coincidence that the same scripts had been used.

"You say Colonel Therrik has that box?" Sardelle asked. "How odd."

"Yup, it was hidden under the bed where a normal man puts a collection of souvenir beer steins. Assuming his collection hasn't been blown up. Along with his bed. And his house." Ridge's mouth twisted with rare bitterness.

Sardelle wrapped her arms around his shoulders and kissed him on the neck. "I'm sorry."

"Don't be. It's not your fault."

"Right, your house would have blown up anyway, even if you had never met me."

"It's always a possibility." Ridge rested his hand on the back of her head and smiled into her hair, his bitterness fading quickly, as negative emotions usually seemed to for him. She wished she could let things go so easily. "Did you know Therrik's house is regularly vandalized? The MPs barely even report it anymore." Now he sounded tickled.

"How did a man like that get an ancient dragon-slaying sword?"

Ridge pulled back enough to look her in the eyes, though he wrapped his arms around her waist, keeping her close. "Is that Kasandral's box then?"

"I'd have to take a closer look to say unequivocally, but from what you shared, it seems likely."

"Now I *really* wish we had questioned him. Maybe this has something to do with why he's the queen's new favorite."

"Is he? Hm."

"Yeah, let me tell you about last night."

"I should tell you about my last night too." As much as Sardelle did not want to relive losing Kaika, he might see something she had missed in glimpsing the events through her eyes. "Here. Lie down with me, will you? If it doesn't make you uncomfortable, we can share our memories. The way we did while sitting on that log in Cofahre."

She thought Ridge might object, but he only smiled again and said, "I seem to remember that devolved into you thinking sexy thoughts about my back."

"I'll try to restrain myself this time." Sardelle scooted to the other side of the bed to make room.

"That's not any fun." Ridge lay down beside her, clasping hands with her.

"You go first." It was easier for her to read his thoughts than it would be to share hers with him, since he didn't have any affinity for telepathy.

He closed his eyes and thought about the previous night's events, everything from how they had found Tolemek's lab emptied out and locked up, to the disturbing scene at General Ort's house, to the conversation he had overheard from Therrik's bedroom. She saw and heard what he had experienced and his emotions, as well. He feared losing Ort, not only because of their years working together, but because he had been feeling overwhelmed ever since he dumped Therrik on the road north of the city. He had wanted to confess everything to a superior officer and let someone else take charge. She had no trouble understanding that, even if it surprised her because she had not realized he felt that way; he always seemed so calm and decisive, even when everything was going wrong around him.

He was chagrined but sheepishly amused that he had thrown the knockout grenade through Therrik's window only to realize nobody was home. It amused her, too, and she curled on her side to face him, resting her free hand on his chest and thinking of snuggling closer. She appreciated his humor and would have liked to bask in it for a time. But it was her turn to share, and there would be little to amuse either of them in that story.

She lost herself in the relaying of the events, and even though she did not want to saddle him with her emotional problems, if he wanted to know he wasn't the only one feeling overwhelmed and lost, he would have that from her, along with all of her other feelings. She couldn't hold back the helplessness and desolation she still experienced over being the lone survivor among her people, the dejection she felt every day, knowing nobody in her homeland wanted her there anymore, and lastly, she shared the pain that Cas's rejection had given her, how it had seemed that even the few friends she had made did not want her here. By the time she finished sharing the night's experiences, tears streaked down her cheeks.

"Sardelle," Ridge murmured, shifting onto his side, facing her, and resting his hand on her hip.

"Sorry," she whispered. "I just meant to relay the facts, not complain."

He eased closer to her and wiped her tears with his thumb as he kissed her gently. "First off," he said, his voice hoarse, "you can complain whenever you want. You have more reason than any of us to do so, and you're not even on anybody's payroll. You've been helping us just because... I don't even know why. You redeemed your word to Tolemek and freed his sister. You went to the castle to help me and to help Kaika. Maybe I should have asked if you wanted to continue helping. You certainly don't owe any of us anything." He rubbed her hip and kissed her again. She closed her eyes, needing his touch, his words, like the first day of sun after a long winter storm. "Kaika wouldn't blame you for her getting caught," Ridge said. "She knew the risks when she picked that mission. Everything you're doing for us, it's a favor. I know that. You're right that Iskandia hasn't given you a reason to want to help yet. I wish I could change that. I don't know if it'll ever be in my power to do that, but I'll try."

Sardelle wanted him to know how much it meant to her that he appreciated her, but was not sure if she could manage words, or even what she would say if she could, so she kissed him back instead. Sometimes that was easier than talking. Her salty tears moistened their lips, and for a time, their embrace was one of finding comfort in each other, but the space between them gradually disappeared, with Ridge's leg covering hers. Sardelle shifted closer and slid her hand around his head, loving the feel of his short soft hair as she massaged his scalp. He rubbed her through her shirt, his fingers slipping beneath the hem to find warm skin. His touch made her shiver, and his thoughts did too. Genuine appreciation for her mingled with his desire. He wasn't sure what kept her here, especially when his plans were so sketchy and the odds seemed against them, but it meant everything to him that she was helping his team.

You keep me here, she told him, forgetting to speak aloud—her lips were too busy for that.

He growled softly—there might have been a *good* in there, but it was hard to tell—and shifted atop her, his hands drifting to the buttons of her shirt. As close as they were, she felt everything he experienced. Knowing how much he wanted her took the fire kindling within her from a spark to a flame. She groaned into his mouth and fumbled with his buttons, wanting to run her hands over his muscular shoulders and down his sleek waist to cup his tight—

Ridge paused, his lips lifting an inch from hers.

"Mm?" Sardelle couldn't manage anything more articulate, but she wanted to protest the parting. She had won the war with the buttons and ran her hands up the contoured lines of his arms to his shoulders, barely resisting the urge to dig her nails in and pull him back down to her. They had more clothing to remove, and she didn't care if he had heard the return of one of his men or not.

"Nothing." His lips lowered, attending to more than her mouth this time. She arched up toward him, eager for that attention. But Ridge pulled up again, his breathing heavy as he gazed down at her, lust mixing with an uncommon uncertainty that had just appeared. "Well."

"What is it?" she breathed, though she wanted to tell him to return his mouth to what it had been doing.

"It's just that I'd forgotten that we're in my mom's bed." His face crinkled, and he whispered, "What if she and my dad... I mean they probably don't because they're old, but..."

Sardelle could have laughed at his expression, but she was too busy running her hands over his warm skin and trying to pull him lower again. "Old? Ridgewalker Zirkander, I promise I'm still going to want you between my legs even when we're their age. Much as I want you right now."

"So you think they *do* still do it?" He looked dubiously at the quilt.

"We can use the floor if it'll make you feel better." So long as they used something. She moved her hands around to his belt buckle, brushing him through his trousers, hoping to push any thoughts of his parents from his head.

He groaned, leaning into her hand. "No, no, not necessary." His lips finally returned to hers, and he kissed her deep and hard. They broke only long enough to remove the rest of their clothing, but before Ridge settled atop her, he did pause one more time. "There is that pottery shed outside."

"I hope you're joking." Sardelle imagined knocking over clay bowls and having tools falling from the walls of that tiny shack out there, bare butts being prodded with broken shards of ceramic...

"Uhm. Yes, of course."

He returned to kissing her, caressing her enthusiastically, as if to apologize for his lapse. Still, she could tell that realizing where he was and what they meant to do here bothered him.

"Ridge," she whispered, "we can go to the shed. I just want you. I don't care where."

He met her eyes, his hands stilling. "I love you."

"Good." She looped her arms around his shoulders. She was going to make him carry her if he was taking her naked body outside to reach this dubious love nest.

He obliged, practically leaping from the bed with her in his arms. That made her realize just how much he wanted her and how much this issue was frustrating him. She wrapped her legs around him, wondering what the neighbors would think if they saw a nude couple streaking across the yard. He reached the door, opening it slightly to peer out. Duck was still snoring on the couch, but Ridge paused.

"Did you hear the jingle of a horse's reins?" he whispered.

Sardelle reached out with her senses... and slumped with disappointment. "Apex is back. I think Tolemek and Cas are coming down the highway too."

Ridge closed the door. "No shed."

"No," she agreed, her body hot and frustrated.

I can delay them for a few minutes if you wish to commence with rutting.

Sardelle started to shake her head, but Ridge's eyes widened, and she realized Jaxi must have shared the comment with both of them.

"Rutting?" he whispered.

"That's what it's called if you're a sword with no moist, achy parts."

"Would it be rude to reject her offer?"

"Terribly rude." She leaned closer and nibbled at his earlobe. "And I'd be disappointed if we did. I've wanted you since you kissed my tears and said you'd try to change the world for me." She let her feelings wash over him, so he would know she meant exactly what she said.

Ridge swallowed. "I never want to disappoint you."

"Good."

***

When Sardelle finished bathing and changing into a dirt-free and relatively unwrinkled dress, she eased out of the bedroom and heard voices drifting out of the kitchen. Ridge, Tolemek, Apex, and Cas were discussing how to get Kaika. Sardelle had come up with a plan while she had been scrubbing herself in the small bathroom tub, but she went to check on Duck before heading into the kitchen. She felt slightly ashamed that she had forgotten all about her patient while she and Ridge had been...

Doing unmentionable things to his mom's door? Jaxi suggested.

Even if those unmentionable things had been slightly awkward, especially after being interrupted a couple of times, Sardelle couldn't help but grin. *Yes.*

You should feel more ashamed that the rest of his troops had to spend a half hour chasing a spooked horse all over the neighborhood. I really didn't think your rutting would be so lengthy when I volunteered to cause a distraction.

Sardelle's grin widened. *Neither did I.*

The poor horse is exhausted.

I'll bring him some carrots later.

I'm also confused as to how it's not acceptable to have sex in one's mother's bed but having sex elsewhere in her bedroom is perfectly fine. If a sword could have eyebrows, Jaxi would have been raising hers. *Archly.*

You would understand if you had lived long enough to think of your parents as sexual beings.

Ew, that's disgusting. Here I do you a favor, and you put disturbing images into my mind.

I apologize.

Given the size of your smirk, I don't believe you're sincere.

No? Sardelle asked. *That's odd.*

She touched Duck's shoulder and started to check his wounds, but his eyes fluttered open. A lurch of guilt filled Sardelle at the thought that he might have been awake during the door abuse.

I muffled all the noise you were making, Jaxi said. *I was afraid it would scare off the rest of the horses, and I didn't want to make pirate boy's day any worse. He was already grumpy.*

Oh. Thank you. Have you noticed if Cas is treating him any differently than usual?

I haven't seen any smooching if that's what you're asking. Not that I watch for these things. I'm not a pervert.

You always seem rather knowledgeable about what Ridge and I are doing.

That's because you're my handler. I don't want *to see these things, trust me.*

Sardelle wasn't positive she believed Jaxi, but she let the matter drop. "How are you doing, Duck?"

He shrugged his shoulders and shifted about experimentally. "Better than I expected, ma'am. Did you, ah, magic me?"

"I removed two bullets and cleaned and sealed the wounds. You'll be sore for several days, and I'd keep my movements ginger if I were you, but you should be fine after that."

"That was a yes, right?"

Sardelle braced herself for another rejection of magic. She and Duck had been getting along reasonably well since they had vomited together in the Cofah base, but she wouldn't be surprised if he still regarded her skills with wariness. "Yes."

"Uhm, thanks then. I was reckoning I would die when I was riding back. Just figured I had to warn the colonel first."

Sardelle let out a relieved breath. "You're welcome." She was tempted to ask if she could poke into his thoughts and try to see exactly what he had witnessed in regard to those women, but she doubted he was ready for that. Besides, Duck wouldn't likely want to relive being shot. Touching another person's mind was intimate, too, and she preferred to save that sharing for Ridge.

She patted Duck on the shoulder. "You should get some more rest. Your body worked hard to heal you, so you'll be tired for a while."

"I'm trying, ma'am. I woke up because I was having a dream that I was suffocating." Duck wiped his mouth. "It turns out a cat was sleeping on my face."

"It's probably time to feed them again."

"Could be."

Sardelle gave Duck another pat, then headed for the kitchen. She should have been tired, too, since she had only slept for a couple hours on the floor, but she felt refreshed after her bath. And her exercise session.

Gag.

She knocked softly before entering, not wanting to intrude on secret military plans. Of course, Tolemek was in there, so they shouldn't object to her presence. The men shouldn't, anyway. Sardelle didn't know what she would say to Cas.

Ridge was leaning against a counter close to the door, and he wriggled his fingers in invitation. His drawing and Cas's sword scabbard lay on the table in the center of the room. Cas and Tolemek stood on opposite sides of the table. Apex sat on a counter in the corner, his shoulders hunched and his face tense as he stared at the items. An unexpected reaction. Had they been talking about the sword and how it might be affecting Cas? Sardelle hadn't shared that hypothesis with anyone yet, but maybe Ridge had sensed her suspicion when she had been relaying her story.

"It does look like it would fit," Ridge said, glancing at Tolemek. "That was a big box. And that's a big sword."

"I couldn't see the symbols that closely in the dark," Tolemek said.

"We're debating whether this sword does indeed belong under Therrik's bed," Ridge told Sardelle.

"If I saw the box, I could tell you for certain."

"You can come along next time we infiltrate his house. That was a big bed. Ought to be room for three under it, don't you think, Tee?"

Tolemek gave him a flat stare.

Sardelle walked forward for a better look at the runes. They were definitely Middle Dragon Script. Maybe *Early* Dragon Script. She could be looking at a sword that was more than three thousand years old.

Kasandral doesn't look his age, Jaxi.

Magic can keep you young. Reduces the wrinkles around your hilt.

Sardelle stretched a finger toward the scabbard, thinking she recognized the symbol for mountain. She—

A blast of heat zapped her. Sardelle jerked her hand back. She had barely touched the scabbard, but it was as if she had stuck her finger in molten lava. She stared down at a welt already rising.

I don't think he likes you.

No kidding. She was glad she hadn't tried to pick up the sword by the hilt back in the pyramid.

Yeah, I wouldn't touch the blade if I were you.

Thanks for the warning.

Sardelle glanced around to see if anyone had noticed her reaction, but everyone was looking at Ridge.

"I was thinking it's time for a more direct approach," he said, his earlier humor gone. "Apex didn't find anyone from the squadron. Supposedly Crash refused to go on Therrik's mission, but nobody's seen him. He was marked down as AWOL." Ridge shook his head. "I need to figure out a way to get everyone back to the hangar. End their idiotic quest and get them prepared to deal with whatever dragon-blood-powered weapons the Cofah are planning to fling at us this year."

"I was thinking about that," Sardelle said.

Ridge tilted his head. "You were?"

"It sounds like you need to report in and find a way to work with—or around—Therrik. But there's suspicion on you now, because of me."

Ridge opened his mouth, but Sardelle held up a hand so he would let her continue. She didn't need sympathy now.

"But you're about to escape my controlling clutches." Sardelle wriggled her fingers. "That's what you tell anyone who asks. Pretend I'm gone and you don't know where I went, or say you sent me away. You can blame what happened with Therrik on me, but claim that you're back to normal now."

"You want me to blame my reckless impulsiveness on you?" Ridge had been frowning through everything she had said, and he didn't stop now. "I would have had to meet you twenty years ago."

"Whatever it takes to regain any trust you might have loss. Then you can figure out what's going on from within instead of hiding under beds and spying."

"I'm surprised you told her about the bed, Zirkander," Tolemek muttered and glanced at Cas. Had he not shared that news with her?

"Don't worry, big fellow. She's not jealous of our new relationship."

Tolemek's glare was even flatter this time.

"I *had* been thinking of turning myself in," Ridge said. "Er, reporting in. I'm not actually sure which of those things it will end up being. Or at what rank I'll find myself in the end, if I have any rank left at all. Either way, I figure I'll report in, then go to the castle and try to get Kaika released. I thought I'd say it was my plan to start with. Since I outrank her, they ought to believe that."

Sardelle grimaced. "I can get Kaika out. It's my fault she was captured." She avoided looking at Cas. "Since they know I'm around now, there's no need for me to hold back. I can find a way to her. I'm certain of it."

Really? This should prove interesting.
You may get to melt some holes through walls this time.
Lucky me.

"It wasn't your fault, Sardelle," Ridge said.

"But I think I can retrieve her without you needing to admit to having anything to do with the infiltration."

"Lieutenant Ahn was there, and Kaika was last seen working with my squadron. I doubt anyone is going to believe I didn't know about this."

"I don't know, Zirkander," Tolemek said. "Half of your squad is AWOL. It's gotten trendy. Maybe your superiors will believe that nobody listens to you anymore and that you don't know about anything."

"How comforting that would be," Ridge said.

That drawing is making Apex nervous, Jaxi observed.
Are you sure it's the drawing and not the sword?
He's seen the sword before.

"Ridge," Sardelle said slowly, thinking through the implications, "whose flier seat was that tracking device pinned to?"

Apex winced, ever so slightly, at the word *tracking*.

"I couldn't tell," Ridge said.

"And you left the original device back in the canyon?"

"Yes." Perhaps he caught on to where she was going with the questions, but he added, "You don't have a way to figure out who put it there, do you?"

Doubtful, Jaxi said. *I couldn't even sense it.*

"I believe I could if I had a look at it."

If you believe that, you're delusional.

So long as Apex believes it.

Ah, I see.

Apex's face had grown masked. Sardelle could have poked into his thoughts, but if she found that he had planted it or, more likely, had knowledge of who had, it would be her word against his. He was smart enough to argue his side persuasively. Better to catch him running out to destroy it, or whatever he might try. Maybe he wouldn't do anything. Maybe she and Jaxi were reading him wrong. Sardelle would hate for one of Ridge's people to have betrayed him. He trusted everyone in his squadron, and it would devastate him to learn that he had a spy on his team.

He's guarding his thoughts well, Jaxi said, *but he's definitely feeling guilty about something, and he's afraid too.*

Ridge looked toward the window. They still had several hours of daylight left. "All right. I'll go get it before heading into town. Tolemek, now that we have this closer bed-sharing relationship, are you willing to come back to the capital with me? When I report in, I'm going to have to talk to Therrik, since he thinks he's my commanding officer now. And unfortunately, the rest of the military seems to think that too."

"*Talk?*" Tolemek asked.

"Ideally with your truth serum. No hiding this time. We need to know about the sword and what his link with the queen is—he wouldn't even tell his superior officers, so I'm sure he won't tell me. I could tell he was holding something back though."

"Sorry, but the pharmacy is closed until I get a new lab. I can't make truth serum out of lavatory cleaning supplies."

"Hm." Ridge stroked his chin.

"Maybe you'll have to take me along one last time before escaping my controlling clutches," Sardelle said.

He started to frown, but then lowered his hand. "Yes, of course, if you can see into people's minds, then that would obviate the need for a serum."

Apex's gaze jerked toward Sardelle. Had he forgotten she had that ability? She raised a single brow in his direction and held his eyes.

"Sir," Apex blurted, then lifted his eyes toward the heavens. "I need to talk to you."

"I can go after Kaika afterward," Sardelle said, then stepped back. She had a feeling Ridge needed to hear what Apex had to say.

Ridge frowned slightly—he did not seem ready to embrace her plan—but waved to the living room and nodded for Apex to follow him. Tolemek murmured something to Cas, then also walked out of the kitchen.

Sardelle did not know whether to stay or to pretend some task called to her. A need to feed the cats perhaps.

"Sardelle?" Cas said. "I... I'm sorry about what I said last night."

Sardelle relaxed slightly. Oh? "It's all right."

"It's not. I've been feeling irritated lately, on edge. Like everything is annoying me, and I've definitely felt angry toward you. Almost violent. I had to keep myself from—" Cas shook her head. "I've been short with Tolemek too." She glanced at the table. "He said the sword might be influencing me. I thought it was stupid, but I did have a long walk back this morning to think about it. I don't know. Maybe he's right? Do you think it's... an evil sword?"

Yes, Jaxi said.

"I think it was created specifically to kill dragons, and that might apply to sorcerers too. It does obviously have some enhanced qualities."

Just because he can glow, I wouldn't call him enhanced.

"I would like to research it whenever there's time." Sardelle spread her hand, acknowledging that time was elusive right now. "For now, it might be a good idea to get it back into its box as soon as possible." Maybe they could get rid of it as soon as tonight.

Cas's forehead wrinkled. "You want Therrik to have it? According to the colonel, he's an unbalanced ass at the best of times. And he tried to kill Tolemek when they hadn't even met before."

Sardelle wondered if some of Therrik's rage could have been a result of sleeping with the sword under his bed. If he hadn't kept the case closed, maybe it had affected him, especially when dealing with those with dragon blood.

"We could put it in the box and toss it into the harbor." Sardelle smiled, meaning it as a joke, but maybe it wasn't a bad idea, since the only dragon around was Phelistoth, and he wasn't on the continent, as far as she knew.

She might have meant it as a joke, but Cas's eyes opened wide, and her hand twitched toward the sword. She caught herself before she touched it and lowered her arm, but the haunted expression did not leave her face.

"Or perhaps it could go into a museum," Sardelle said, thinking that might bother her less. If Cas had bonded with the sword in some way, that could explain the attachment. Such bondings could be magically facilitated.

Please, who would bond with that ugly thing? Jaxi asked.

Cas shrugged. "Whatever's best. The colonel—"

A crash came from the living room. Uh oh. Apex may have shared what he knew.

"You what?" Ridge demanded, his raised voice piercing the door.

Sardelle walked out, afraid she would have to grab him by the shoulders to keep him from pouncing on his lieutenant.

Tolemek must have gone outside and taken Duck with him, because Ridge and Apex were the only ones in the room. They stood on opposite ends of the couch, Ridge with his fists clenched, and Apex with his shoulders drooping, his chin down.

"It was when I first learned you were taking Deathmaker on the mission," Apex said, "a criminal who should have been convicted for his crimes and shot—or sent back to Cofahre so *they* could shoot him. I wouldn't have cared which way it went, but to invite him along on a mission?" He turned pleading eyes toward Ridge, but found no sympathy there and dropped his gaze to the couch again. "The hooded woman who approached me the night before we left... She already knew he was going, knew about it all. As soon as she started talking, I knew I had to report her. She asked me to place the tracking device on the flier Tolemek would be riding in, said she would see to it he was taken care of. I refused, sir. I swear." Apex glanced up again, but only for an instant. "I wanted him punished, yes, but I knew what the woman wanted would be a danger to the entire squadron, especially to whoever was flying him. I would never do anything to hurt Raptor."

"But you didn't report this woman," Ridge said, his voice hard.

"No, sir. I put the device under the seat, like she asked."

"Some kind of magical coercion?"

Apex shook his head. "No, sir. When I wasn't cooperating with her, she lowered her hood."

"And?"

"It was the queen."

For a moment, Ridge stood there motionless, gripped by shock, but he recovered and thumped his fist against the couch. "The queen isn't in your chain of command, Anders. You don't take orders from her."

"Technically, the king is the highest-ranking military officer, sir, and she—"

"She nothing. She has a *minor* role in ruling the nation. Usually." He thumped the couch again. He looked like he wanted to kick it across the room.

"But as a subject of Iskandia, I couldn't *refuse* her, sir. She's my *queen*."

"You should have reported to me. Or General Ort. Someone."

"I know, but you... you *wanted* to take Tolemek along." Apex shot him a betrayed look.

"Yes, I did, and he played a valuable role in our mission. I seem to remember him saving *your* life."

Apex slumped.

"You have a way to contact her? Or that organization?" Ridge asked.

"She didn't give one, but I may have deduced... maybe."

"You want to redeem yourself? You go talk to those people and find out where the king is being held."

Ridge stalked to the front door without looking at Apex and strode out, slamming it behind him.

Chapter 8

"I'M GOING TO NEED YOU to come up to the hangar with me," Ridge said, glancing at Sardelle.

They had left Tolemek, Ahn, and Apex back at the house to get some sleep, and they were riding into town, avoiding the castle and coming in on the eastern road. Sardelle had changed into her travel leathers again and wore a cloak over them, the hood pulled low to hide her face. The gray clouds spat a depressing drizzle, so the head covering was logical, but she had to be worried she appeared suspicious or would be recognized. And shot. Ridge reminded himself that she had volunteered to join him, but he hoped that hadn't simply been because she believed he wasn't competent enough to handle Therrik on his own. Even if his and Tolemek's bedroom exploits did suggest that.

Ridge wanted her at his side, though, for this mission and *all* missions. That plan of hers to pretend she was some controlling witch and suggest that he'd had to escape her hold... he hated it. He wanted to make the world—at least his home city—see her value and accept her. He didn't want to do anything that might make it harder for her to gain that acceptance later.

"How will I get on base with you?" Sardelle was gazing up at the bluff overlooking the harbor, probably remembering that, to get to the hangar, one had to get through the guarded gates and then take a tram ride to the top.

Ridge *wanted* to say that he was a colonel and he would walk on base with whomever he liked, thank you very much, but he doubted that would work now that her face adorned wanted posters. His own AWOL status would cast aspersion on him, as well. He couldn't count on the gate guards to have school-age children who wanted him to visit their classrooms.

"By being creative, I hope," Ridge said. "As I recall, you once escaped a secured mining facility with a pack of gear and snowshoes, and nobody noticed."

"Hm. Are you sure Therrik will be up there?"

"There's an office in the main hangar that the squadron leaders share. I don't think Therrik will be presumptuous enough to take General Ort's office down below. But if I'm wrong and he's *not* there, the master communication crystal is, as well as a telegraph machine for leaving messages in the hangars on the other bases around the country. I don't know what the range is on the crystals—"

"Only about fifty miles."

Ridge nodded. He had expected as much. "All right, that won't work. I know I can get in touch with the other flier squadrons through the telegraph. And with *my* squadron, assuming they've reported in somewhere."

"Is that allowed? Or is it just for sharing official orders?"

"It's for sharing intel. I intend to share intel. Such as telling everybody to get their pimpled young asses home, or I'll haunt them after I'm dead."

"Important intel."

"I think so."

Sardelle looked worried for him. Well, that was normal these days. He wondered if a semblance of his regular life would ever return. All this skulking around with his career on the line was making him miss the simplicity of flying into battle against overwhelming odds.

They turned onto a busy street with the sides lined with vendor stalls, their merchants braving the rain in the hope of making some money from soldiers coming or going on errands. It was another hour until the workday ended, but there were enough riders, drivers, walkers, and bicyclers maneuvering about that the vendors did not converge on Ridge and Sardelle. Good.

"There's the gate," Ridge said, glancing to the side. "Do you want me to..."

He stared. Sardelle and her horse had disappeared, though

the hoofbeats still rang out beside him. A second later, they too faded from his awareness, making him certain he was riding down the street alone.

Not really, but I did fall back. I'll need to come in behind you. Jaxi and I will come up with a distraction for the guards.

Will it involve spooked horses? He had heard about the horse chase that had allowed him and Sardelle to finish their passionate moment and couldn't decide whether he felt guilty or was amused. Both, maybe.

Possibly. Go along with whatever it is, please.

Of course.

Ridge continued down the street on his own. A man with a wagon full of wooden luck dragon carvings waved at him. Since the last luck dragon he had purchased from the vendor had not kept his house from being blown up, Ridge ignored him. He would stick to the charm in his pocket, the well-worn one his father had carved him decades ago.

The front gate was open, but two sturdy guards with rifles stood on either side of it. Unlike Sardelle, Ridge had not bothered to bring a cloak to hide his face. He wore his typical olive flight suit, brown leather jacket and cap, and he had bathed and shaved, so he looked the same as he usually did when he strolled through the gate. The guards' eyes widened when they saw him coming. He hoped that wasn't because there was a warrant out for his arrest and they couldn't believe he was ambling right up to them.

"Colonel Zirkander," one blurted with a salute.

"Corporal Miller, Private Brax," Ridge said, reading their names off their jackets and nodding to them. He had seen them at the gate before and might have guessed the names without looking, but he did not know them well. Alas, neither appeared old enough to have school-age children.

"Sir, aren't you AWOL?" Miller also saluted, but it turned into a head scratch.

"And cavorting with a witch," Brax said, his eyes still round.

Ridge was tempted to ride through without explaining himself, but he wanted to give Sardelle time to do whatever it was she intended to do.

"That's an interesting interpretation of events," he said, "but I've actually been on a mission for the king. I would report in to him, but he seems to be missing. I guess General Ort will have to receive my report instead. He'll appreciate that. He enjoys the challenge of deciphering my handwriting."

The guards exchanged looks with each other. He couldn't tell if the looks meant they didn't believe his story, or if they were uncomfortable because they figured they would have to tell him that Ort was missing.

"Sir, nobody knows where General Ort is," the corporal said.

Somebody knew where he was... "Oh? A lot of people have gone missing in my absence."

"Yes, sir," the corporal said glumly. "And all of our flier squadrons have been sent off on secret missions. There's some concern about... well, they're—*you're*—our main defense against aerial attacks."

"Yes, I hope to do something about that. Leaving the city—"

"Help!" someone called from one of the vendor stalls. "My dragons are on fire!"

"There's something you don't hear every day." Ridge turned his mount to face the wagon showcasing the wooden carvings. "Sounds painful."

The soldiers snickered. They took a few steps forward, so they could see the smoke rising from the wagon. Technically, what happened to the civilian vendors was not any concern of anyone on base, but a big fire would be a problem for everyone. Ridge trusted that neither Sardelle nor Jaxi would let things get out of hand.

None of his wares are truly burning, Sardelle said into his mind.

Too bad. There should be a punishment for selling me a luck dragon that wasn't lucky.

The frame of his wagon might be charring lightly. I'll put it out as soon as we're through.

Perhaps you should lightly char his pocketbook.

I had no idea you felt so bitterly about that statue.

It's more for the house that the dragon was supposed to be protecting. Admittedly, Ridge had let himself fall for the vendor's spiel. Oh, he hadn't truly believed that the wooden carvings could change a man's fate, not much anyway, but he had hoped for a little luck when needed.

"Brax," the corporal said. "Go see if we need to contact the fire department or if a wet towel would work."

Though Ridge continued to gaze toward the smoldering wagon, he thought he glimpsed a hint of movement behind him, someone slipping through the gate perhaps.

"I'm on my way to headquarters," Ridge said. "Do you want me to report the fire?"

"No, sir. It doesn't look that bad. And it's raining. How much could it possibly spread?"

Ridge shrugged, not wanting to say anything that would cause the corporal to realize that a fire starting on a soggy, rainy day wasn't terribly likely. Without asking for permission, he nudged the horse forward, as if he had every right to stroll through the gate without being questioned. He usually did. But this time, he waited tensely, expecting one of the men to shout after him.

Nobody did. He trotted the horse toward the stables in the back corner of the fort. He wished he could head straight to the tram and hand the reins off to some private along the way, but this wasn't an emergency, as far as the rest of the base was concerned, so he could not justify that. Besides, the path that led from the stables to the tram was rarely used by anyone except pilots and the maintenance crew. Once he reached it, he hoped to avoid anyone who would question him more thoroughly than a corporal.

He had no sooner than had the thought when he turned onto the street that led to the stables and almost ran over a rangy gray-haired man with the elaborate golden sword-and-musket pin of a general on his cap and a chest full of marksmanship and valor medals dangling from his jacket. General Arstonhamer. The sight of him turned Ridge's conscience guilty, thanks to his previous night's spying, but he whipped up a hasty salute, hoping to ride by without being questioned.

"Colonel Zirkander," the general snapped, stepping into the horse's path and raising a hand.

"Yes, sir?" Ridge said politely.

"Where in all the levels of all the hells have you been?"

"A mission for the king, sir. In Cofahre. So your hells guess is quite accurate." He smiled easily.

Arstonhamer glowered. "If you were on a mission, why do the official personnel reports have you down as AWOL?"

"I don't know, sir. I just got back. I aim to straighten things out."

"The newspapers said you disappeared with a flier squadron to do some witch's bidding."

Ridge knew he should keep his answers polite and respectful, but these people calling Sardelle a witch made his hackles rise every time. "Are we getting our intel from journalists now?"

Arstonhamer's glower turned into a scowl. "You better watch your delinquent mouth or I'll knock you off that horse."

Ridge clenched his jaw to keep from saying something incendiary. More incendiary.

"I assume you're going to report in to HQ."

"Yes, sir."

"I'll stop by there when the workday ends," Arstonhamer said, "to make sure you didn't stray."

"Why would I stray, sir?" Ridge asked, though he probably shouldn't have, since that was exactly what he intended to do. "I need to figure out what's going on. I've been risking myself and my people on a mission, and I come back to find out I haven't been paid all month. I'm going to report in right away."

"See to it that you do." Arstonhamer stepped away from the horse and continued down the street.

Ridge hurried toward the stables, almost laughing at the idea of any pay accumulating for him. When Accounting figured out how many fliers he had lost, he would be lucky if the army's money ever visited his bank account again. More likely, he would receive a big bill. He hoped Sardelle wasn't staying with him for the money.

No, but the cabin by the lake is quite lovely. I look forward to seeing it in the spring.

I didn't realize you were that fond of it. Ridge resisted the urge to look for Sardelle. He definitely didn't want Arstonhamer to spot her. *Most women are unimpressed by the outhouse.*

Indoor plumbing was more of a rarity in my time. Sardelle did the equivalent of clearing her throat in his mind. *Most women, you say? Have you taken many out there?*

Erg, he knew better than to allude to past women to the current woman, especially when he wanted to keep the current woman. *Many? Not many.* Ridge bit his lip, realizing he couldn't lie to someone who was inside his head. *Can you define many?* He only remembered three that he had taken all the way out there, but would Sardelle consider that *many?*

Relax, Ridge, she teased him. *I didn't imagine you were a chaste forty-year-old national hero, pining away and waiting for Fate to deliver me into your life.*

Deciding not to comment further—and risk sticking his foot in his mouth—Ridge dismounted in front of the stable. A private came out to take his horse.

I do hope I'm the only one you've done unspeakable things with against your mother's door.

The image of said things popped into Ridge's mind along with Sardelle's words, and he stumbled and sputtered a little. The private looked at him curiously.

Ridge thumped himself on the chest and coughed. "Still recovering from my last meal at the mess hall."

"Understandable, sir."

Ridge circled the stable and headed for the path leading to the tram. *Yes, Sardelle, I can promise you that I've never whisked another woman into my mother's bedroom.*

Good. A lady likes to think she's special.

You know, you pretend to be more wholesome than Jaxi, but I think you're actually quite well suited to each other.

Sardelle did not answer promptly. Ridge hoped he hadn't offended her.

No, I couldn't formulate a response over the loud snickering that Jaxi was inserting into my thoughts.

Ah. Ridge paused on the tree-lined path. *Are you with me?*

She'd had a horse, too, and he didn't know if she had intended to sneak it into the stable or had already left the creature tied up in front of a building somewhere.

She's behind the stable, munching on an apple and waiting for the attendant to notice her. I'll meet you at the tram.

There would be a soldier operating it from within the hut at the bottom. Ridge would have to chat with him to distract him so Sardelle could sneak on. He longed for the day when they could walk openly together again.

Me too.

"Colonel Zirkander," the tram operator blurted before Ridge could knock on his door.

Given that everyone was greeting him with shocked expressions, Ridge wondered anew about the possibility of an arrest warrant. He hoped they were simply surprised to see him because of the AWOL charge. He also hoped Arstonhamer found some errands to run and didn't think to report seeing Ridge any time soon.

"Afternoon, Sammon," Ridge said casually, pretending there was nothing unusual about his appearance. "Do you know if Colonel Therrik is up there? Apparently, I'm supposed to report to him for duty." His mouth twisted—he had no problem showing anyone who would listen how distasteful he found that.

"He is, sir." Private Sammon gave him a sympathetic grimace. Clearly Therrik had impressed him with his charisma on one of his trips up. "Good luck."

You on? Ridge thought.

Yes. Crouching below the level of the window. The metal floor is impressively dust-free.

We aim to run a tidy base. Ridge headed for the tram door, his nerves dogfighting in his belly. Even though he had argued that it was likely for Therrik to be up top, and he needed to question the man, he wouldn't have minded delaying their meeting. Considering where Ridge had left him when last they had met, Therrik would probably try to throttle him as soon as he walked through the door. He assumed it was hard to interrogate a man while being choked. He would also have a hard time sending telegraph messages with Therrik in the office.

Sardelle was indeed crouching on the floor in the tram. She smiled up at him when he entered. *We'll figure it out. If he tries to choke you, I'll give him a debilitating rash.*

A rash? Where?

In his office.

That's not what I meant.

Speaking of snickering into one's mind... Sardelle did it as effectively as Jaxi.

The tram clanked into motion, slowly rising on its cable toward the top of the cliff. When the roof of the hut disappeared from sight, Sardelle stood up. It would only take a couple of minutes to reach the top, but Ridge extended his arm, offering a hug. Even though Tolemek had his uses, he was glad to have Sardelle along this time. He would *much* rather hide under a bed with her.

"I'm glad to hear it. We wouldn't want Cas to get jealous and believe you're trying to steal her pirate." She leaned against him, slid her arms around his waist, and rested her head against his shoulder. "You smell good."

"Thanks. I bathed. It's been a rare experience lately."

"Is that lavender?"

"Uh. Maybe. My mom makes all of her own soaps, and they tend to be floral rather than manly. Maybe I'll request she make a nice pine resin one for me."

"Scented soaps? I didn't see those when I bathed."

She sounded disappointed. Ridge supposed women *liked* smelling of flowers.

"They're easy to mistake for something else, since she shapes them into things."

"Ohhh. I wondered why there was an army of cats watching me bathe from the ledge. Soap, hm."

Ridge wouldn't have minded standing there with Sardelle longer, but the tram was approaching the top. He hoped Therrik didn't notice that Ridge smelled like a flower. He hadn't realized how strong those cat soaps were.

"You're probably safe unless he gets close."

"Such as the closeness required for throttling?"

"Yes, you should avoid that." Sardelle's eyes grew distant briefly. "There's not an operator in the hut up here. In fact, there's hardly anyone in the hangar. Therrik's in the office and a few maintenance people are in the shop in the back."

Ridge sighed and released Sardelle. "Yes, I've heard about the emptiness."

"I'll wait outside of the office, close enough to get the gist of his thoughts—actually, that will probably be Jaxi. She's the stronger telepath. In order to keep him from noticing her intrusion, it would help if you got him thinking of the questions we want answers to."

"I'll do my best." He did not point out that it would be hard to ask questions if Therrik's hands were around Ridge's throat. He had probably whined about that possibility too many times already. People who faced down Cofah cannons shouldn't complain about meetings with officers in their own unit.

"Perhaps if you met with him while behind the guns in your flier," Sardelle suggested, stopping at the hangar door and waving for him to enter first.

"I would be most amenable to that." As he walked inside, Ridge grinned at the memory of swooping through Crazy Canyon while Therrik threw up behind him.

It's possible there's a reason he wants to throttle you, Sardelle sent in parting.

Ridge was aware of her disappearing into the shadows behind him, but once again, did not look in her direction. It wasn't that hard, since the sight of the bleak cavernous hangar captivated his attention. One two-man flier and two one-man fliers, including his usual craft, hunkered in the repair area. He had never seen the place so empty, so abandoned. Even when Tiger and Wolf Squadrons were both in the skies, the hangar crew would be back here, preparing for their return. But now, the sound of his boots rang hollowly as he walked across the cement floor.

Only a few lamps burned, leaving the shadows thick about the place. Sardelle wouldn't need her magic to hide. Who was here to notice her?

A throat cleared in the office. All right, there was *one*

person who might notice, the person who had approved of this evacuation.

As Ridge strode toward the office, his earlier apprehension faded, replaced by irritation. He was irritated at Therrik, and he was irritated at the queen, too, even if he hadn't figured out what her role was in all of this. It was hard to believe that the king's wife of over twenty years would be spearheading some plan to make her husband disappear and empty the city of its defenses. Why would she? To hand the capital over to the Cofah? How could anyone who had grown up here and endured the frequent and inexorable attacks from the empire think of working with them?

Ridge knocked on the door. The only thing that kept him from barging in and making demands was the reminder of Therrik's training as an infantry soldier who had spent time with the elite forces units. As twitchy as those boys were, he would probably spring for Ridge's neck before bothering to identify him.

"What?" came the familiar growl. Apparently, Therrik wasn't worried that some general had come up to visit him.

"You're in my chair," Ridge said as he opened the door.

The big desk faced the door, so Ridge looked his nemesis in the face as he walked in. Therrik's eyes narrowed to slits. He planted his hands on the paper-filled surface and rose slowly, his massive shoulders flexing. His sleeves were rolled up, revealing corded muscle and tattoos of daggers dripping blood. He could probably spring over the desk from that position. Ridge propped a fist on his hip, hoping to show that he wasn't intimidated. He actually wasn't since Sardelle was out there, though the idea of relying on his lady for protection did make him feel a tad unmanly.

"It's *my* desk now." Therrik smiled, an alarming gesture, even if it was every bit as cold and unfriendly as the rest of him.

"I wouldn't have taken you for a desk man. Pilots like to sit down, but I would have thought all your big muscles would cramp up being forced into inactivity." Ridge glanced at Therrik's forehead, hoping to imply his brain muscle had cramped up, too, but he doubted the man was perceptive enough to see through such a subtle hint.

At what point will you start directing the interrogation toward the questions we wish to know? Sardelle asked politely.

I figured we needed to exchange pleasantries first.

If you goad him into attacking you and I have to reveal myself, I expect he'll be less amenable to answering anything. If he's affiliated with that organization, he'll hate me on sight.

Yes, Ridge remembered the unflattering things Therrik had said regarding Sardelle and Tolemek in that first meeting with the king. He'd never met either of them then. He might have based his hatred of Tolemek on his reputation, but he couldn't have known a thing about Sardelle, unless he had been chatting with the queen back then and *she* had told him something.

For most, it's enough that I have dragon blood. It seems that people in this century don't need any greater reason to hate me.

Ridge would have liked to say something comforting back to her, even if she had stated it without much emotion, but Therrik was opening his bear trap again.

"Where have you been, Zirkander?"

"Cofahre." Ridge almost made a comment about how he had been risking his life while Therrik had been polishing that chair with his butt, but that would remind Therrik about how he had been abandoned. No need to bring that up.

"After that," Therrik said. "Kaika and your scrawny lieutenant came back more than two weeks ago."

Ridge tried to sense if he knew anything about Kaika's capture at the castle, but Therrik did not give any special emphasis to her name.

"We had to deprive the Cofah of the source of their dragon blood, which we were successful at." *I'm going to try and direct him onto more relevant topics now,* he added silently, assuming Sardelle was monitoring his thoughts. "But as Apex would have reported, I'm sure they still have supplies stashed away. Therrik, how could you approve sending both squadrons out of the city? Those weapons are mission-ready. The unmanned fliers and self-directing rockets could show up in our airspace any day."

Therrik had opened his mouth, a protest on his lips, but he frowned at Ridge's last couple of sentences. "Rockets? What are you talking about?"

Ridge stared at him. "How can you not know? Didn't you get Apex's report? The dragon blood samples?"

Since Therrik continued to look puzzled, Ridge started to doubt himself—to doubt his officer. Apex had placed that tracking device. What if he *hadn't* reported in and *hadn't* brought the vials of blood? But even if he hadn't, surely Kaika would have shared all that information with her superiors. Or...

"Wait, was General Ort still in charge then?" Ridge tried to remember exactly what Kaika and Apex had said when they had found him on Owanu Owanus. They'd said Ort had been missing, but maybe he hadn't been when they first reported in. Maybe Ort had received the information and then been kidnapped before being able to brief anyone.

"No, he disappeared shortly after the king did," Therrik said. "*Several* people have disappeared. Maybe you'll be next, now that you're back. I've noticed it's the mouthy ones that go."

"Have you?" Ridge muttered. Ort wasn't mouthy, not generally, but Ridge could see him protesting something like these foolish orders to send both squadrons away. "So, why are you still here? Is it true you're sleeping with the queen?"

Therrik made a choking noise, and his hands, which had been pressed flat against the desk's surface, now curled around the edges.

He's thinking of strangling you, Sardelle informed him. *You predicted that well.*

I'm surprised he's restrained himself for so long. You getting anything from him?

"Listen, Therrik. I don't care if you are." Not entirely true. Ridge liked the king well enough and would prefer to believe his wife was loyal to him. "But tell me someone knows about the dragon blood and the new Cofah weapons. What did Apex report to you?"

"Yes, we know about the dragon blood. Vile stuff." Therrik jerked a thumb toward the back of the office.

Ridge had to rise to his tiptoes and lean to the side to see around him. What he spotted tucked behind the stand for the telegraph machine made him gape. Even without seeing the contents, he recognized the bags that he and the others had used to tote the vials of dragon blood out of the volcano laboratory. They slumped dejectedly in the corner, not looking like anyone had even investigated them.

"What's been going *on* around here?" Ridge thrust his arm toward the bags. "Our scientists should be studying that, trying to make weapons or defenses to counteract what the Cofah are going to launch at us, what they could be flying over here to launch at us even as we speak. Didn't Apex tell you how viable their weapons are? One of those smart rockets, or whatever you want to call them, followed me all through a canyon and nearly killed me." It *would* have killed him if not for Jaxi's intervention.

"I've seen you in canyons. You could crash yourself without the help of a rocket." Therrik waved a dismissive hand. "Even if they're making weapons, they'll be testing them for a while first, I'm sure. They haven't had the dragon blood for long—we would have known about it. It'll wait until after the fliers get back from their mission, a mission you really should join in with. In fact, I insist you join it."

"Does the queen insist I join it? Is she the one trying to get all of the fliers out of the city? To make us vulnerable to our enemies?"

Getting anything from him?

Yes, some. Bring up the sword, if you can.

"What makes you so sure an attack is coming, Zirkander?" Therrik glowered suspiciously.

He's truly wondering if you know something he doesn't, Sardelle thought.

I know all kinds of things he doesn't. "I'm not *sure*, but if we have spies over there, we have to assume they have spies here, spies who are reporting back that we're having a few problems right now." Ridge strode forward until only the desk separated them. "You don't know where the king was taken do you?"

"No."

"Does the queen know?"

"How should I know?"

He's lying. An image of a lighthouse flashed through his mind when you asked.

"You didn't maybe get hired or coerced to kidnap him, did you?" An expression of pure rage contorted the man's face, but Ridge pressed on, hoping to give Sardelle the opening into his mind that she needed. "Maybe you and your big ugly dragon-slaying sword?"

Therrik's muscles had been bunching, as if he meant to leap over the desk and attack, but he froze when he heard those last words.

"That's right. We found it. Funny thing, though. This assassin was wielding it, trying to use it to kill a dragon. Ahnsung. I assume you've heard of him. I shot him. Guess I've got another reason to watch my back. How did an assassin get ahold of your sword, anyway? Or *is* it yours? I know you've got the box under your bed, but I suppose you could have stolen it. I—"

Duck! Sardelle urged at the same time as Therrik exploded into motion.

Ridge ducked—he almost tumbled all the way to the floor in his effort to do so. Therrik sailed over his head, a powerful gust of wind coming from nowhere to add to his momentum and keep him from grabbing Ridge. He flew all the way to the door and bashed against it with his shoulder so hard that the wall rattled. That did not keep Therrik from whirling back toward Ridge.

"I didn't *steal* anything," he snarled, his hands outstretched. He took a step toward Ridge but seemed to be fighting something. The wind had stopped, but some other barrier restrained him. "That sword has been in my family for a thousand years."

Ridge darted behind the desk so there would be one more barrier between them.

"And I wouldn't kidnap the king. I'm loyal, more loyal than you, you smug bastard." Therrik looked down at his hands, confusion replacing some of the rage on his face. Was he just now realizing that something was holding him back?

"Did she ask you to?" Ridge asked, trying to decide if the way Therrik had phrased that denial hinted of that.

"I'm loyal to the king," Therrik repeated, then his lips reared back in a snarl. "Your witch. She's here!"

"You think I'd come visit your tiny, unstable brain on my own?" Ridge asked. "Who gave the sword to Ahnsung? *He* didn't kidnap the king, did he?" No, Ahnsung couldn't have been in two places at once. He had been hunting the dragon.

Yes, but he got there after us, remember? Therrik believes Ahnsung was the one who kidnapped the king. After he refused to do it for the queen.

For the queen. She's really the one behind everything?

Therrik believes she is.

Therrik seethed, his muscles straining against the fabric of his shirt and his face flushed red as he tried to physically fight the invisible barrier that held him.

Why? Ridge asked. *Is she working for the Cofah?*

He doesn't think so. She wanted to get rid of me and of Tolemek, of any magic users on the continent, actually, but apparently, it was our appearance in the city that spurred her to action. The king gave Tolemek a position here and stocked that lab. And he didn't particularly care that I was walking around with you. It enraged her. The king wouldn't listen, saying he wasn't going to prosecute people for their blood. She decided to deal with us—with all sorcerers—her own way. This is the story as it was relayed to Therrik, by the way. I have no way to know if it's the truth. But Therrik's prejudices are clear. He was happy to go along with her insofar as getting rid of us, and even volunteered to get his family's sword out of the crypt, because it could slay sorcerers as well as dragons. He's quite proud that he's descended from dragon slayers.

"I'll bet." Ridge eyed Therrik, wondering if he was about to have a stroke. His face had gone from red to almost purple. *So all of this is about getting rid of people with dragon blood? It has nothing to do with the Cofah?*

With the king gone, she saw this as her chance to ensure all of the Referatu and their descendants were utterly wiped out. As if Iskandia didn't nearly accomplish that three hundred years ago. Sardelle's bitterness seeped through the link, and he could not blame her for it. The next time she was clinging to a wall while the queen walked past underneath, he wagered she would do more than watch in silence.

She didn't kill her husband, did she? Ridge asked. *Was he truly kidnapped or... something else?* If Ahnsung had been involved, it could definitely have been a more final treatment.

Therrik believes he's being stored somewhere out of the way. He doesn't know, but thinks it has to do with a lighthouse. I don't recognize the one he's thinking of. He may not even recognize it. I get the sense that he's never been there, since he did draw the line at being a part of the kidnapping. The queen asked him to do it first, but he wouldn't betray the king, not even to get rid of witches.

He's so noble.

I hate to interrupt, my interrogation specialists, came Jaxi's voice, *but company is coming.*

What kind of company? Ridge would have looked out the window if the office had one, but there wasn't much access to natural light in the hangar when the big rolling doors were not open.

Several soldiers coming up on the tram. I think they're here for you.

Wonderful. General Arstonhamer must have checked up on Ridge. *Sardelle? Can you convince Therrik to step outside for a few minutes? Uhm, Jaxi? Is there any chance you could delay that tram for a few minutes?*

You and Sardelle aren't planning a rutting session before you're parted, are you?

I'm not planning anything that enjoyable, I assure you.

Ridge turned toward the telegraph machine. As he composed a hasty message to tap out, he ignored the puppet-like way Therrik was jerked and ambulated out the door. Ridge had to send his message to every hangar, in the hope that at least some people would come because he asked. Some of them would doubtlessly question why *he* was trying to send orders, when everybody knew he wasn't high enough to order anyone except his own squadron around. He hoped that his reputation might convince some people to at least pass along his message. This was the only way he had to get in touch with Wolf and Tiger Squadrons and request that they come home.

Would you like the tram to be delayed indefinitely? Jaxi asked. *They're starting to get irritated, and the fellow down below is banging against his machine with a wrench.*

Sardelle walked through the door as Ridge sent the last message. As much as he would have liked to keep the soldiers from coming up—especially if they were, as he suspected, military police—they would not be able to hide up here indefinitely. He could have taken the two-person flier and flown off to parts unknown, but he needed to be here in case any of his people *did* return. And he needed to find a way to get Kaika out of the dungeon. In short, he needed all of the doubt to be erased from his name. He just wasn't sure how to make that happen.

Ridge picked up one of the bags of dragon blood, the vials inside clinking. He handed it to Sardelle. "Will you see to it that Tolemek gets this? Maybe he can create some weapons or defenses that we can use to protect the city. Whatever his morals will allow him to make. Since Iskandia is his home now, too, I'm hoping he'll want to defend it."

"I'll give it to him." Sardelle accepted the bag, then squeezed his arm. "As far as clearing your name, if you go through with my plan, that should be easier. I'll disappear, so I'm not seen here with you. Jaxi is trying to adjust Therrik's thoughts so that he doesn't remember my role in subduing him." She winced. "It's not... morally acceptable, but I hope the gods will understand in this case."

"I don't intend to tell them you're some megalomaniacal crazy woman who had control over me," Ridge said.

The soldiers have reached the top and are getting out of the tram, Jaxi informed them.

"Save your career, Ridge. You'll only have the power to do what needs to be done if you're trusted by your superiors. What these people think of me doesn't matter. We can see each other in secret in the future if necessary." She kissed him, then let go of his arm and backed away.

Secret? Ridge didn't want her to have to spend her life in hiding, nor did he only want to see her in secret, damn it. "My mother would be devastated if she never saw you again," he said, because it was the only thing that came to his mind.

As she smiled sadly back at him and disappeared through the door, he wished he had said something far more important. Like that he loved her.

I know you do. I love you too.

Boot steps rang against the cement floor in the hangar. With his shoulders slumped, Ridge walked toward the doorway. He didn't want anyone to notice the telegraph machine or be there to read any return messages that would hint at what he had sent.

General Arstonhamer strode toward the office with six MPs marching at his side.

"A little more force than is necessary for just me, sir." Ridge spread his arms.

"Is it?"

All of the men were stealing covert glances toward the unconscious figure slumped against the wall beside the office door. Even if Therrik did not bear any bruises, his shirt was untucked and his jacket rumpled. Ropes bound his hands behind his back, and a line of drool trickled from the corner of his mouth.

Ridge thought the men would assume that "his witch" had been responsible, but they kept glancing back and forth from Ridge to Therrik. Did they think he had knocked the brawny officer out? That would either be good for his reputation... or the final nail in his coffin.

"Cuff him," Arstonhamer said.

Yup, the nail was looking more likely.

Ridge did not resist. He let them lead him toward the door, though he couldn't help but cast his longing gaze back toward his flier as he went. He wasn't sure if it was because he worried he would never be allowed to fly again or because he could have taken Sardelle and flown away, leaving this mess for someone else to handle. Wishful thinking there.

Say what you need to say, Ridge, came Sardelle's voice, seemingly softer and farther away than it had been before. *I'm going to find a way to get Kaika before it's too late for her.*

Ridge wished he could find those parting words encouraging,

but all he could think was that Sardelle was going to go risk her life, and he had absolutely no way to help her.

Chapter 9

AS NIGHT FELL, SARDELLE LEANED against the wall of the last building on the block, watching the street that wound its way up the craggy slope toward the castle. The bag of dragon blood vials lay at her feet, humming with power. She wasn't sure where to stash the valuable goods while she attempted to extricate Kaika. They needed a safe house closer to town. Of course, they would then risk having that safe house found and blown up.

She considered the castle and the promontory grounds around it, trying to gauge how many men were on duty up there and whether they were anticipating another infiltration. Though she could not see the spot from her position, she had already checked and knew that men were standing guard on the rocks behind the castle, their lanterns shedding too much light for her to think of sneaking in that way. Workers labored at collapsing the rest of that tunnel. The wall in the wine cellar had already been bricked closed again. Sardelle had a feeling a stealthy incursion would not work tonight. Even from far below the castle, she could tell that double the men walked the walls and stood watch from the towers.

What are *you planning?* Jaxi asked as Sardelle observed an ornate wood-paneled steam carriage chugging up the slope. Would it be allowed entrance? It didn't look like a delivery vehicle, nor was it a military truck. She brushed it with her senses and identified a male driver and two female occupants. *Maybe you can wait for the grocery wagon and hide among the cabbages,* Jaxi suggested.

Who delivers groceries at night?

People with worm-riddled cabbages they want to unload before the sun comes back to illuminate their flawed wares?

I don't think anyone would dare send wormy vegetables to the queen at any time of day.

You're probably right. I bet those go to the soldiers. Wasn't Ridge complaining about army food?

Sardelle winced, immediately thinking of Ridge locked up in some dingy cell. If he'd had any notion in his mind of fleeing, she would have suggested that she could have held off those soldiers while he powered up his flier. But she had sensed his weariness, that he was tired of running and hiding and spying from outside of the organization he was supposed to be a part of. She didn't know if he would follow her suggestion, but he wanted to clear his name and return to his unit, ideally taking Therrik's place instead of serving under him, though he hadn't had any idea how he could make that happen.

The castle, Jaxi prompted. *You can ask him later if he received wormy cabbages.*

Yes, that will be what I want to discuss when we're reunited. Sardelle adjusted her position. The cool dampness of the brick wall threatened to seep through her cloak. *I haven't decided on a course of action yet, but was thinking about walking up to the gate, knocking it down, and stomping down to the dungeon to openly haul out Kaika.*

That sounds like a good way to get shot.

I'd assumed you could keep me shielded while I was stomping and breaking down doors.

I could, but what about that instant where you need to transfer Kaika from outside of our barrier to inside of it? Not to mention that they could run ahead and shoot her if they see you coming. Or they could hold a knife to her throat. And what if they figure out how to delay us and if they throw such a barrage of bullets at my shield that I run out of the energy to sustain it?

You? Run out of energy? You melted a ten-foot stone wall.

If you want me to melt the castle, then I'm your sword. Defenses aren't my specialty. It's harder to keep something—or someone—alive than it is to utterly destroy it.

That almost sounded like praise for my role as a healer.

You're a good healer, Jaxi said. *Perhaps you can bribe your way in by assisting a guard with a problem. I think I noticed someone digging at a splinter during my initial survey.*

Or give the soldiers rashes and then offer to heal them? Sardelle watched as the carriage turned around in front of the castle gates and headed for a parking area outside of the walls. Two women had gotten out and were being let into the courtyard, two women in dark cloaks with their hoods pulled up.

I do think trickery would be better than the frontal assault you have in mind. Of course I will shield you, but I worry about this tactic, especially since you won't want to hurt anyone. If you get Kaika but kill five other people, then is anything gained? They'll hunt you more diligently than ever.

I know, Jaxi. Sardelle had not seriously been contemplating an open assault. She was just frustrated, much as Ridge was, at having to skulk around among people who should be open to her help. If only she could make them understand that. *You think the queen is having a meeting with her Heartwood sisters tonight?*

Even as she asked the question, another carriage trundled past. This one had a female driver and a female occupant.

If so, maybe we can get ourselves invited, Sardelle mused.

Jaxi did not respond. Sardelle gave her a mental poke.

You're not the only one out here watching the castle and contemplating ways in, Jaxi informed her.

Oh?

An image entered her mind, one of Tolemek, Cas, and Duck standing on the last dock in the harbor, pretending to be fishing off the end. From their spot, they had a view up to the front of the castle.

Ridge didn't lead me to believe they would be coming tonight. In fact, Sardelle had been there when he said he would find a way to have Kaika released once he reported in.

And yet, there they are. With that sword.

Sardelle grimaced. After their chat earlier, she had believed Cas would leave the thing behind. She had definitely grasped that it was influencing her. So why was it here now?

I don't know, but you could hand the dragon blood to Tolemek. He's probably the only one in town who has an idea how to turn it into something useful.

Perhaps not a bad idea. Right now, Sardelle was more concerned about the queen and the Heartwood Sisterhood—probably since they were targeting her—but Ridge had been agitated ever since learning that Wolf and Tiger Squadrons were out of the city. He would approve of Tolemek finding a lab somewhere and making some weapons to defend the capital. *Do you want to ask Tolemek to lead his team over here? I doubt that fishing ruse will fool anyone. Who fishes after dark?*

Perhaps they intend to employ the wormy cabbage delivery plan. I'm already talking to Tolemek. He's missed my presence in his head.

Oh, I'm sure.

While she waited for the others to join her, Sardelle watched the new carriage reach the gate. A guard came out, made the woman inside identify herself, then waved for her to get out and for the vehicle to park. Sardelle could not tell what the woman had said, but she had not lowered her hood or been questioned for long.

"Sardelle," Tolemek said, leading the trio around the corner. "There's no time to delay. They're planning to hang Kaika at midnight. Actually, the official word is that they're doing it at dawn, but they secretly plan to do it at midnight, so she'll already be dead in case any of her nefarious allies attempt to rescue her."

"Whose words were those?" Sardelle could not imagine the information had been printed in the newspaper.

"Apex was relaying the queen's words from earlier today."

"He's seen her?"

"I can only assume. He didn't deliver the message personally. He pinned it to the door with a dagger while Cas was practicing with the sword out back, then left before anyone knew he was there." Tolemek spoke the words neutrally, but his thoughts roiled near the surface, and Sardelle was standing close enough to feel them. He was worried about Cas and tense—maybe they'd had an argument over the weapon.

"I knew he was there," Cas said coolly, standing apart from Tolemek and Sardelle and watching the harbor and the street. "I thought he would come in, not run off after delivering his message."

"He probably doesn't feel welcome anymore," Duck said glumly, his hands stuffed in his pockets.

"Under his signature he added that he would do what Zirkander asked," Tolemek said, "find out where the king was, and that he wouldn't come back until he had that intel."

Sardelle wondered if they could trust Apex's information. She wished she had been there, so she could have brushed his thoughts while he had been delivering the note. If he had made his peace with Tolemek—and the story Ridge had told of their sojourn through the volcano base suggested he might have—then he might regret planting that tracking device. But if in his heart, he still wished Tolemek dead... he might even now be spying for both sides. Or he might have deliberately delivered poor information. What if Kaika was already dead and this talk of a midnight hanging was an attempt to trap Sardelle and the others? What if he had written the message instead of delivering it in person because he had worried Sardelle would be there to read his thoughts and see the truth?

She rubbed her forehead, the beginnings of a headache blooming behind one eye.

"You're planning to go in?" Tolemek nodded toward the castle.

"Yes."

"We'll go with you."

"Even if it's a trap, we can't risk letting the captain die," Duck said.

So they'd had the same thoughts she'd had.

Jaxi, can you tell if Kaika is still alive? Between the distance to the castle and the hundreds of soldiers and servants inside it, Sardelle could not pick out individual auras.

She's still in the dungeon, yes. Alive.

"I was planning to go in alone," Sardelle said. "I think that might still be best. If there is a trap, or if they're extra alert after last night's mess, then it will be easier for me to only have one other person to protect."

"I don't need protecting," Duck said. "I'm quicker and scrappier than a tiger."

"Which is why you were shot repeatedly last night," Tolemek said, though he, too, was giving Sardelle the squinty eye, probably disliking the insinuation that *he* needed protecting.

"If I hadn't been so quick and scrappy, I would have been hit even more times."

"Uh huh. Sardelle—"

"I know you could be helpful in there, Tolemek, but Ridge has a mission for you." She hefted the bag of vials, though he probably could not tell what it was in the dark.

"Does he," Tolemek said, his voice flat. "Does it involve me playing the role of pharmacist again? Or attempting to use the meager contents of his general's lavatory to make knockout grenades?"

"It's the dragon blood." Sardelle held out the bag toward him. "Ridge is hoping you got a good look at what the Cofah were doing with it and could make some similar weapons—or at least a means of defending against their weapons. He wants you to improvise a lab—you can use his mother's house if you want." All right, Ridge hadn't said that, but she felt certain he would agree if it resulted in weapons for defending Iskandia. Whether his mother agreed was another matter, but they could figure out how to tell her later.

Tolemek accepted the bag, but asked, "This needs to be done *tonight?*"

"Started as soon as possible. He assumed it would take you a while to come up with something."

"A while. Really."

Another carriage is coming, Jaxi said. *There are three women in it, and there's a driver up front.*

Three, you say? Is there any way to delay it briefly? Can the driver see the women or are they separated?

Separated. And delays are my specialty.

"I'm going in to get Kaika," Cas said firmly, then less firmly added, "Do you have a way in? I already sneaked around back, and there are more guards moving around on the rocks than ants."

It's going to drive right past you, Jaxi added. *Fifteen seconds.*

"Stay out of sight." Sardelle waved for the others to press themselves against the wall. "I have a plan."

"Should we be alarmed?" Tolemek asked.

"I would be," Cas muttered.

Duck flattened himself against the wall and nodded at her. At least one person had some faith.

"Do you have any more of those lavatory-inspired knockout grenades, Tolemek?" Sardelle asked.

He dipped into a pocket and produced a tea tin with a fuse.

"Get it ready, please."

Oops, Jaxi said at the same time as a snap came from the road, followed by the scent of something burning.

Oops?

That road has developed a pothole. Another snap sounded. *And a second one. A shame.*

Before Sardelle could comment, the promised steam carriage rolled into view, the frame and wheels made from wood. It was more ornate than the other vehicle had been, with mountains carved into the body, engravings decorating the smoke stake, and flourishes of gold gilding the passenger door. The driver rode in the front in a cab separated from the carriage by the furnace and boiler, so he would not be able to see his passengers. That helped.

The carriage passed the corner of the building, then lurched as the front wheel dipped into an alarmingly deep hole.

Jaxi, Sardelle thought as she jogged for the passenger door, waving for Tolemek to follow her. *That's a crater, not a pothole.*

Have you ever heard someone praise me for my subtlety?

Not in any sense of the word.

Exactly.

"Now, Tolemek," Sardelle whispered, aware of the driver throwing more fuel into the firebox, trying to generate the power to escape the unexpected pit.

A pit. Now you're just exaggerating.

The carriage was locked, but the mechanism was flimsy, and Sardelle snapped it with her mind. As soon as she opened the door, Tolemek tossed his now-lit grenade inside. Sardelle waved, and the door closed. She jammed the lock on the door on the other side. Inside, smoke spewed from the grenade, and the women jumped to their feet.

Jaxi, I should have asked before, but can you pluck their names from their thoughts? And if there's a password or something they're supposed to say to get in? Any details about what they're planning to do in there would be good also.

That information would have been easier to obtain before they started writhing around and grabbing their necks.

I know. Sorry. Do your best.

"Are these loathed enemies, or are we knocking out random guests visiting for a party?" Tolemek asked.

"I'm only guessing, but I think the queen is meeting with her Heartwood Sisterhood friends tonight."

"They're the ones who shut down my lab?"

Inside the carriage, the first woman slumped onto the floor.

"Quite possibly," Sardelle said.

"Then I shall not regret knocking them out."

A door slammed. The driver hopped down to examine the stuck wheel. Jaxi had wisely positioned her rut so that it had captured a wheel on the side opposite from Sardelle and the others, but Sardelle scooted back into the shadows, in case the man walked around. A second woman slumped to the floor. The third had a handkerchief pressed to her mouth. She banged at the door. Sardelle cupped the air around the carriage, creating a barrier the sound could not escape. As the grumbling driver climbed back into the cab and grabbed the controls again, the third woman flopped down on one of the seats.

"Time to take their places," Sardelle whispered. "Duck, Tolemek, I need help removing them."

She opened the door and grasped one of the unconscious women with her mind, lifting her into the air. The headache that had burgeoned earlier increased in intensity. That was surprising since she hadn't done that much yet. Perhaps she hadn't rested enough after healing Duck and experiencing the events in the castle the night before.

"You don't look like you need help," Tolemek muttered, but

he hopped into the cab and grabbed a second woman.

As he was stepping out with his burden and Duck was climbing in, the vehicle lurched. The driver was trying to escape the pothole again. Sardelle floated her woman into the shadows beside the building and set her down. Now she thanked the rain, because there weren't many pedestrians walking through the streets. This would create an odd picture for an observer.

Duck and Tolemek deposited their women next to Sardelle's. With an angry grinding, the carriage finally escaped the pothole. The driver turned hard to try and keep the other wheel from going in. An ominous clank came from under the vehicle.

"Now what?" the driver shouted.

"Same question for me." Tolemek pointed at the women.

"We need two cloaks," Sardelle said, already kneeling to remove one.

"Just two?" Duck asked.

"You and Tolemek will have to stay down here to move the women and do something with them to keep them from running up to the castle to explain what happened."

Without comment, Cas removed the second cloak. The idea of sneaking in with just her—and that sword—at her back did not make Sardelle comfortable, but there was no way Tolemek or Duck would pass as *sisters* of the organization, even with the biggest and fluffiest cloaks.

"Do something with them?" Duck protested. "What?"

"I don't know. Tie them up somewhere. Or take them to a bar and buy them drinks. Whatever it takes to keep them from reporting the kidnapping. Then Tolemek can start on the lab."

The driver had climbed out again and was peering under the carriage. With a lurch, Sardelle realized he might see between the wheels to her comrades—and all of the women lying on the ground.

Don't worry. He sees nothing. But you better hurry and get in. There's nothing left to keep him from driving off.

Sardelle exchanged her cloak for the new one, a fur-trimmed, dark green garment. She waited until the driver climbed into the cab again, then hopped into the carriage. Cas jumped in after her, nearly banging the hilt of that big sword into Sardelle's shoulder.

As Sardelle closed the door, Tolemek and Duck watched with conflicted expressions. Neither appeared happy to be left behind, but at the last moment, Duck waved and made the thumb-to-fingers circle that signified ready among the pilots.

The carriage rolled into motion, this time without clunks or clanks. Sardelle sat in one of the seats, crinkling her nose at the lingering scent of Tolemek's knockout grenade. Though they were moving along at a brisk pace now, she risked opening the door to toss out the tea tin. The driver might find it suspicious if he looked inside later, and she also did not want to pass out herself before reaching the gate.

No, but that is an amusing image, you delivering yourself to the queen's guards without a fight. And returning her missing sword too.

It's Therrik's sword, not hers. But speaking of Kasandral, how are we supposed to explain it? Or hide it? It's bigger than Cas is. If one of the guard's looks into the interior...

Maybe you should have thought of that before inviting Armed, Short, and Cranky there along.

Sardelle slumped back in the seat and wondered if she had been delusional to think this could work.

* * *

"Here you go, sir." The private passed a stick of charcoal through the bars, then surprised Ridge by pushing a corked stoneware bottle through, as well. It clunked against the iron and barely fit, but Ridge soon found himself holding a beer from Bragging Buck Brewing downtown.

"Thank you, ah, Gormen, was it?"

The private smiled and saluted—it was the fourth time he had saluted Ridge since General Arstonhamer had personally deposited him in this cell an hour earlier. Since nobody else was giving him adoring looks here, especially not anyone with any rank, Ridge accepted the private's adulation with more appreciation than usual. Glory was fleeting—hadn't some old, long-dead general said that? Croxton, he thought. The man had also said a hero's reputation survives only as long as his latest great deed. Ridge probably would have gotten along well with that fellow.

"You won't get in trouble for this, will you?" Ridge tapped the bottle with his fingernail before unfastening the wire securing the cork. The last time he'd had a drink had been with his dad in that wretched pirate slum. It had been a poor brew, and the company hadn't been as pleasant as he'd hoped, either, with his father absorbed in his work. As always. Mom probably found the cats better company even when Dad *was* home.

"I'm not allowed to drink on duty, sir. I don't think the regs mention anything about prisoners drinking on duty."

Ridge reached through the bars and patted the private on the shoulder. The young man grinned, apparently never thinking that his legendary prisoner might grab him or try to steal the keys from his belt. Well, Ridge would not do anything to make the kid regret his generosity. Where would he run, anyway? True, he was worried about Sardelle—especially since she had warned him of her intention to return to the castle—but this was his world. He had to find a way to clear his name. Escaping and fleeing would mean he could never come home again. Besides, he still had a lingering hope that he might take the blame for Kaika's actions and get her out of that dungeon.

"What's the charcoal for, sir?"

Ridge took a swig of the beer—Breyatah love the kid, it was even chilled—then set it on the floor. "I got a clue about the king's whereabouts."

"*Really?*" Gormen gripped the bars, his eyes gleaming with eagerness. Eagerness and trust. If he had heard why Ridge had been arrested, it did not seem to have tarnished his opinion yet.

"Thank Fate for small miracles," he murmured, then raised his voice. "Near a lighthouse. That's all I know, but I've flown up and down the western coast and the northern fjords thousands of times, and I've circumnavigated the entire continent more than a hundred. I ought to know every lighthouse we've got out there." Flipping the charcoal in his hand, Ridge walked to the back wall of the cell. The whitewashed cinder block should work well for his needs—not as well as being out there, checking out spots with his flier, but he might figure out exactly where to go once he did find a way out of here. He refused to believe he *wouldn't* find a way out. "There are well over a hundred though, so I'm hoping that making a map will help me remember all the possibilities and mull over which ones might be turned into suitable prisons."

"Oh, that's very clever, sir."

Ridge kept his derisive snort to himself. He hadn't done anything clever all week.

"Maybe I can find an atlas around here to help," Gormen suggested.

"That would definitely be helpful, but don't get in trouble requisitioning more supplies for me, please."

"I'll say I'm developing an interest in geology." The private winked and left before Ridge could point out that his interest should probably be in *geography*.

Not certain the kid would find that atlas, Ridge did his best to draw a giant outline of the continent with the charcoal stick. It had the right general shape, a blob with the Tasagon Handle and Islands extending from the southeast corner, but more subtle details were difficult. It didn't help that the sun had gone down, and the cellblock was dimly lit. Still, he assiduously marked down dots where he remembered lighthouses, pausing to picture each one in his mind and assess whether it might work as a prison. Many were near cities and towns and probably would not be chosen by kidnappers. Plenty of others were remote, perched along stark, rugged landscapes, and a handful of them were only accessible by ship or flier. Those were the ones Ridge considered extremely likely possibilities. The water would be an extra deterrent for escape if the king managed to subdue a guard.

He found himself tapping on one particular lighthouse location about a hundred miles north of the city, in the middle of Fury's Cauldron. He pictured the tiny, craggy island it perched upon. If his memory was being faithful, it would be a five-mile swim to the shore, through a maze of coral filled with jellyfish and reef sharks. If *he* were in charge of a prisoner, he would consider that a good place to deposit someone he wanted the world to forget about.

Ridge circled a couple more possible spots, then stuffed the charcoal in his pocket and started pacing. If he had access to his flier, he could go check those lighthouses right now. Why had he let himself be captured? If he had thought of this earlier, he might have gauged it worth the consequences to ensure he stayed free a little longer. Besides, if he came back with the king sitting behind him in his flier, he might not have to worry so much about consequences. He couldn't count on anything, but it seemed a better bet than sitting in a jail cell.

A door squeaked open, and clanks and grumbles drifted down the corridor. Ridge pushed the beer bottle on the floor into the back corner and stepped in front of it, so nobody would notice and have harsh words for the private.

Gormen and two people Ridge had no interest in seeing came into view, turning to face him through the bars. Colonel Porthlok from the intelligence battalion and Captain Heriton, the officer who had been Ridge's assistant back in the Magroth Crystal Mines, the officer who had been suspicious of Sardelle from the start and who had dug up proof that she was a sorcerer.

Ridge forced a smile. "Hullo, Heriton. I didn't think they were letting you off that frozen mountain until summer."

"Colonel Zirkander," Heriton said politely. "I was called down to act as a witness in an investigation. I'm enjoying the rain."

An investigation about Sardelle, no doubt.

"Either of you fellows mind telling me why I'm being held?" Ridge asked. He did not want to discuss Sardelle. "The MPs failed to mention it. I would like to return to duty and bring our fliers back home, so we'll be ready when the Cofah come."

"*When* they come, sir?" Heriton frowned.

"They've been working on new weapons, and I'm guessing they'll be ready to share them with us soon."

Colonel Porthlok held up a hand. "You're being held because your witch sneaked into the castle yesterday and tried to attack the queen."

Since Ridge had seen the events in Sardelle's mind, he knew she had tried no such thing.

"Why don't you tell us where she is now? If you have any advice on how to apprehend her, your punishment here might be more lenient."

"I don't know any witches." Ridge leaned his shoulder against the wall and crossed his arms over his chest. "And what crime am I being accused of? I assume there must be a crime, because punishment wouldn't be discussed if there wasn't one, right?"

"For starters, you've been AWOL for three weeks," Porthlok said, and when Ridge opened his mouth to protest, he added, "I'm aware of the details of the mission that King Angulus assigned to Colonel Therrik—and what your small role in it was supposed to be. I'm also aware that you dropped Therrik out of your flier and took command of the mission when you had no orders—no right—to do so."

Ugh, someone who had all of the details. "I judged Therrik unbalanced and incapable of leading that mission," Ridge said.

"It wasn't within your rights as an officer to do so. You've been judged maliciously insubordinate by your superiors, in addition to being AWOL." Porthlok threaded his fingers together and rested his hands on his slightly pudgy abdomen. "Perhaps, if you were to verify that the witch was controlling you through some mind-manipulation technique, your punishment might not be as severe. Supposing you also helped us find her."

"Sardelle Terushan," Captain Heriton offered. "That's her name, sir."

"I read the report," Porthlok snapped. "Her name is insignificant."

Ridge glared at the men. Her name was very significant. And so was she.

"Nothing to say, Colonel?" Porthlok asked.

"I don't know where she is." Not *exactly*, anyway. "But let me offer you something else. I've received some intel and believe I can narrow down the places the king might be to about five spots. Let me take a flier out and look for him. If you don't trust me, send someone along to watch me."

"Is this *intel* from your witch?"

Not exactly, Ridge thought again. "No, it's from Therrik. You'll have to talk to him yourself if you want the answer as to why he knows something about the king's disappearance."

Ridge expected Porthlok to scoff, but he clasped his hands behind his back and gazed thoughtfully into the cell instead. "Did you truly beat him in a fight? I wouldn't have expected that from a pilot, or anyone who isn't as combat crazy as he is."

Beat him in a fight? *Therrik?* Ridge managed to keep the surprise off his face, but barely. "Did you speak to him?"

"Before coming to talk to you, yes."

"And he admitted that?"

"Reluctantly, he did."

Why would Therrik lie about something like that? Surely, he would feel emasculated if Ridge beat him in a confrontation. Ridge would love to emasculate him, but without Sardelle restraining him in the office, he doubted he would have had a chance. Maybe Therrik hadn't wanted to admit that a "witch" had bested him. Or maybe he didn't *remember* that a witch had bested him. Had Sardelle done something to tinker with his memory? Or had Jaxi? Sardelle had said something about adjusting Therrik's thoughts. Ridge supposed he couldn't be upset, but he did find it discomfiting to think that might be a possibility for her. He trusted her, but it was chilling to realize that someone might have the power to tinker with *his* thoughts, to make him remember a different reality from the one that had happened.

Porthlok's gaze shifted to the charcoal map on the wall. "If you believe you know where King Angulus has been taken, tell me, and I'll send a team."

"There aren't any flier pilots around."

"And a flier is required to get there?" Porthlok asked.

Ridge closed his eyes. As an officer sworn to the king, he was obligated to help his liege, no matter what the situation. To withhold the information wasn't acceptable. And yet... if he wasn't the one to pick up the king, how was he going to find time to plead his story, to hope for the king's lenience? Not only that, but how was he ever going to get himself out of this cell?

"Your recalcitrance tonight is noted," Porthlok said stiffly.

"Oh, I'm sure it is."

"We *will* find your witch. If she's a threat to the queen—"

"She's *not*." Ridge couldn't keep himself from growling his words. "Show me who she's killed, Colonel. No, show me who in Iskandia she's even hurt? She's a *healer*, not a ... whatever it is you think she is. Just this morning, she saved the life of one of my men."

"One of your AWOL men?"

"He'll report in as soon as he recovers fully. From being shot by some of the queen's new buddies."

Porthlok's eyes closed to slits. "Do you actually know anything? Or are you trying to divert me with lies? I wonder if HQ would mind terribly if I interrogated you."

Ridge did not let any unease show on his face, even though he was sure the intelligence department's method of interrogation was a lot more violent than Sardelle's. "Here's a thought. Treat me like a human being, put me back on the duty roster, and I'd happily share all the shreds of intel I've managed to gather."

"You'll share it, Zirkander. Trust me, you'll share it." Porthlok strode out.

Heriton had been studying the map, but hurried after Porthlok, perhaps not wanting to be left alone with the deranged witch lover.

"Was it worth it, Heriton?" Ridge asked before the captain disappeared from sight.

"Sir?"

"Betraying the woman who saved the entire mining complex from that shaman so you could get a less frigid posting."

Heriton opened his mouth, but clamped it shut again, shook his head, and marched out.

Ridge turned, leaning his back against the bars, and considered his map again. He was also considering that he had made a mistake in letting the MPs collect him. He wondered what the odds of escaping would be without Sardelle's help.

Chapter 10

Sardelle would have preferred not to talk to Cas, since she was emanating displeasure as she stared out the window, but the drive up to the castle was not that long. Already, the old stone structure loomed above them. They needed to solidify their plans. First, she reached behind them with her senses, to make sure the women hadn't woken up and escaped Tolemek and Duck. It would be hard to get in if three escaped captives were running up the street after them and screaming.

Fortunately, Duck, Tolemek, and the women had already disappeared.

"I hope Duck knows I wasn't truly suggesting he take those women to a pub," Sardelle said. "I suspect there would be much yelling and flailing."

"I've heard most of Duck's dates go like that. It should be a familiar run for him."

Sardelle hoped that was a joke. Cas had a reserved and dry sense of humor under any circumstances, and she hadn't even exhibited that since picking up the sword. Maybe this was a sign that she had found a way to deal with its influence. Now that she was aware that it could affect her, she would doubtlessly be more alert of the fact.

"We better put up our hoods," Sardelle said. "I have the password. If they ask, your name is Martna Spranken, and your family owns vineyards in the southern hills."

Cas's expression grew dubious. It could have been because she doubted the information or because she was uncomfortable thinking about how Sardelle had come by it.

Yes, you're welcome for that intel. You remember the name of your girl?

Sai Forgolen, her cousin.

It's too bad you didn't bring Tolemek. It would have been amusing to see him impersonating the third cousin, the chubby one with all of the jewelry.

"Halt," came a distant call from ahead of the carriage, and Sardelle did not reply.

"Cas, can you tuck the sword under your seat cushion?" Sardelle asked. "If it will fit?"

Cas stared back at her.

"In case the guards look in on us. In fact, I'm certain they will." Sardelle knew Cas had a pistol and dagger under her cloak, too, but those might be missed unless the guards searched them.

"They won't see it," Cas said, an odd, almost distant note to her voice. She tugged her hood over her head. "Just as they won't see yours."

"Uhm." *Jaxi, we're positive Kasandral isn't an intelligent being and doesn't communicate with her, right?*

I'm positive he isn't intelligent. I'm not positive that there isn't some kind of communication going on. He does a fine job of glaring at me across the astral plane.

Not heartened by the answer, Sardelle might have asked more of both of them, but the carriage halted. The door opened, the flickering light of lanterns brightening the cabin. Sardelle wiped her damp hands on her cloak and braced herself to create an illusion if necessary. As Ridge had pointed out more than once, she was not an accomplished liar.

"Names," a guard with a clipboard asked, peering inside.

"Sai Forgolen and Martna Spranken," Cas said, sounding bored. Maybe she had more experience with lies. Or was calmer because she didn't mind shooting people who saw through her lies.

"Our cousin got sick and couldn't make it," Sardelle added, though she probably shouldn't have. The guard hadn't asked.

You are *bad at this*, Jaxi observed.

Hush.

The guard frowned at Sardelle. "Remove your hood, please, ma'am."

Sardelle hadn't had a good look at the girl she was replacing but did her best to create an illusion of her face atop her own. Fortunately, only one guard stood in the doorway, looking in. She only needed to fool him. She just hoped he hadn't seen the girl before, or at least did not remember her well if he had.

She pushed back her hood and held her breath.

A few seconds dribbled past as he gazed at her. Far too many, she worried. She didn't sense any dragon blood about him, not like that guard from the tower, but it was possible her illusion wasn't good enough, that she—

"And you," the guard said, facing Cas.

Sardelle rushed to create a second illusion as Cas reached for her hood. So far, the guard hadn't said anything about the sword lying across the seat behind her. Was it possible he didn't see it? As Cas had suggested? At least Kasandral's sheath was keeping that pale green glow from oozing out tonight.

"You're clear," the guard said, stepping back. He waved them toward the wicket gate. "Fronzo is waiting inside. He'll show you to the meeting room."

Sardelle wanted to go to the dungeon, not the meeting room, especially if the queen was waiting in that meeting room, but they could figure that out once they were in. She pulled her hood over her head and hopped out. Cas followed her, that sword slung across her back again.

Sardelle walked briskly through the gate, not wanting to risk someone noticing and stopping them. She almost crashed into a mouse-faced man with spectacles.

"Fronzo," she blurted, hoping she was correct.

He tilted his head and peered down at her. "Madam Spranken?" he asked uncertainly.

Damn, had he seen her before? That was the name she had given Cas, but if Fronzo thought she sounded more like this Spranken woman, Sardelle would go with that.

"Yes," she said, working the illusion again in case the hood hid less than she wanted it to. "And my cousin," she added.

Fronzo hesitated, and Sardelle surveyed the courtyard, hurrying to formulate a plan of action in case this all went awry right here. Numerous soldiers patrolled the walls, but plenty were posted around the yard and in front of the doors to the towers and main building. This would not be a good place to be discovered.

I convinced him you're her, Jaxi thought at the same time as the man said, "This way," and turned toward the main building.

Thank you, Sardelle replied, though she winced anew at the idea of tinkering with people's thoughts. She wondered how those guards stationed all over weren't noticing Cas's sword.

He's bending the light around him, the same way I do to keep from being noticed. Not as strong as an illusion, but it fools most eyes. Yours are an exception.

Again, I'm concerned that this sword is smarter than I thought.

Probably smart enough to object to your plan to stick him in his box and throw him to the bottom of the harbor.

We'll worry about that later. How do we get to this dungeon, Jaxi? Assuming we can get away from our escort here.

"Fronzo, I need to use the lavatory on the way, please," Sardelle said, hoping she didn't risk raising his suspicions.

He sighed. "Of course you do."

Is that suspicion? Sardelle couldn't decipher his tone.

No, I think all of the women ask to use it, and he's not surprised at all. If he's annoyed, it's because he has this duty tonight.

Oh, good. Their escort wasn't suspicious; he was annoyed.

Fronzo led them past the stony-faced guards standing like posts on either side of the double doors leading to the interior. He turned left immediately and chose one of several corridors leading away from the large foyer, then jerked a thumb toward a short, dead-end hallway. Unfortunately, Sardelle did not see any promising stairways leading to subterranean levels, just an open door to a tiny room brightened by a candle.

"You can go first," Sardelle told Cas.

Cas twitched an eyebrow but walked into the room.

How do we get to the dungeon from here, Jaxi?

I'm looking. I thought I had it earlier, but realized the door I found leads to a different dungeon that's only near *the dungeon where Captain Kaika is being kept. There are pamphlets in a holder on the wall. I think they take school children to this one for tours.*

Lovely. Maybe there's a secret door from that one to the other one? You said they're close?

Yes, and I'm looking for that. You may need to bring the bloodhound down here to sniff it out.

The "bloodhound" exited the little room less than a minute after she had walked in. What kind of woman didn't know how to spend at least ten minutes in the lavatory?

One that doesn't care if her soul snozzle is impressed by how much makeup she wears.

I don't know what you're implying, Sardelle said as she headed inside for her turn, *but I hope you're finding a dungeon door while you imply it.*

Not yet. I can see several guards in there with Kaika—and there are two other prisoners too—but none of them are being polite enough to leave, so I can get a chance to see how they do it.

Can't you give them the urge to void their bladders?

A noise of disgust came through ahead of Jaxi's words. *You want me to tinker with a man's bladder?*

How about the part of the mind that responds to urges from it? It should be easy for the soulblade who plucked the information about the family vineyards from a woman's memory in a mere three seconds.

When Jaxi did not respond, Sardelle did not know if she was searching for some guard's bladder controls or steadfastly ignoring her suggestion and hunting for the door herself.

Kasandral would do it, Sardelle teased.

That's not funny. Now, give me a moment to figure this out.

While she waited, Sardelle took her time using the facilities herself, including a thorough washing of her hands and face. Despite Jaxi's comment, she hadn't had an opportunity to apply any makeup in weeks, so she couldn't pretend to check that. She did polish Jaxi's pommel for her with one of the silky towels by the sink.

Oops, Jaxi thought.

Sardelle returned the towel to its holder. *Oops?*

It turns out that the part of the brain that tells a man he has to pee isn't much different from the part that tells him to *pee. It's having the* same effect though. I'm pretty sure he's heading for the door.

I can't believe that in your hundreds of years of existence, you've never made a man pee before.

Really, Sardelle, what kind of soulblade do you think I am? Besides, for three hundred of those years, I was buried under a mountain of rock. Bladders didn't come in my direction very often.

Someone knocked at the door, and Sardelle jumped.

I'm almost out of time, Jaxi. You'll have to tell me how to get down there soon. And Sardelle would have to figure out how to escape the escort, too.

I will.

Sardelle opened the door, expecting an impatient Fronzo. Instead, another woman wearing a hood faced her. It wasn't Cas.

"Sister," Sardelle murmured and stepped out, ducking her head, hoping the woman's needs would delay a conversation—or a who-in-the-hells-are-you question.

"May the forest breeze always bring pleasant winds, Sister," the other greeted and stepped inside.

To Sardelle's relief, a response did not seem to be required. The woman closed the door without further comment. Cas, Fronzo, and another man in castle livery waited at the front of the short hall.

"I'm ready," Sardelle said, though she was already thinking of other ways she could delay until Jaxi told her where to go.

I've got it. First floor, follow the hallway that parallels the king's audience chamber, then turn into the corridor that runs behind it. There are a bunch of doors, and the one at the end leads to stairs that go up or down. Go down, obviously, then all the way through the faux dungeon. Pull on an iron ring dangling from the wall in the back. There's a secret door that opens. Our buddy who is in need of fresh trousers left, but there's another guard in there. Kaika is at the end of a row of cells. Presumably Puddles will be back before long too. You might want to stage your breakout now.

Aware of Fronzo walking ahead of her, leading the way to stairs that went up instead of down, Sardelle could only respond with, *I'll do my best. Thank you.*

Do you need your escort to be overtaken with the urge to urinate as well? Jaxi asked.

The urge or the actual bodily function?

Well, I thought that with practice I could refine things.

But they were already up the stairs, and Fronzo was stopping in front of a door, one decorated with two more guards. Unless Jaxi could encourage the need for a group pee, Sardelle did not see how she was going to walk anywhere except into that meeting room.

"Password," one of the guards stated as Sardelle and Cas approached.

She caught a sideways look from Cas, who probably wondered if this would be the time to fight. Not ideally. If the guards in front of the meeting room disappeared, their absence would be noticed as soon as that other escort came up with the other woman. Even if she spent several minutes in the lavatory, Sardelle knew it would take longer to find those stairs and figure out how to get Kaika out.

"The moonlight glistens on the calm waters of the harbor," Sardelle said, using the term Jaxi had plucked from the real Sai Forgolen.

"That's the *old* one," the guard said, his voice irritated.

"What?" *Jaxi?*

That's all the vineyard girl had floating around in her wine-sodden brain.

"Can't any of you people remember your codes?" the guard asked. "Some secret organization."

He turned to the door, clearly intending to go in and ask someone to come out and verify that Sardelle and Cas belonged. Except that they didn't.

She threw a gust of wind at the door, slamming it shut as soon as the guard opened it. He frowned and started to tug, but then seemed to think something suspicious was going on. He whirled back toward Sardelle. She was already summoning the gust of air necessary to plaster him and his colleague to the wall.

Fronzo stirred. "What's—"

Cas spun on him, slamming the hilt of her pistol into the side of his head. He stumbled backward, and she followed the attack with a palm strike to the nose and a kick to the inside of his knee. He wasn't unconscious, but he crumpled. Neither Sardelle nor Cas had brought rope, but Cas cut strips off the hem of her cloak. In impressive time, she tied the man's wrists behind his back and improvised a gag.

"Better tie his ankles too," Sardelle said, her voice sounding strained in her own ears. Most of her focus was toward maintaining the battering ram of air that had the guards flattened against the wall. They tried to reach for their weapons, but she slammed their knuckles against the unyielding stone behind them. Holding them this way took a lot of energy, and she worried about the consequences. What happened when that other woman walked up the stairs? Or what if someone already inside the meeting came out?

"We dragging them somewhere?" Cas asked.

"We'll have to. Here, come tie up these two. I'll hold them."

One of the guard's lips curled back, as if he wanted to deny that she could do that. His lips were all he could move. The other one wasn't fighting her power so fiercely. He was staring at her with his eyes round.

The room across the hall from that one is empty, Jaxi said.

Good, thanks.

The guard who peed is back, so you'll have two to deal with down there.

Understood.

So long as they could *get* down there. Sardelle heard voices from the floor below and winced. The other "sister"? Keeping the guards pinned down was taking all of her concentration, so she could not check. She did manage to lower her hand to open the door behind them. A dark sitting room lay inside, a few chairs and tables just visible in the gloom, along with another door open in the rear. Sardelle couldn't tell if it was a meeting room or the living area of a bedroom suite. It hardly mattered. She couldn't imagine it or the door keeping those guards for long once they figured out how to escape their bonds.

"Done," Cas whispered. "Someone's coming."

"I know."

Again using the wind, Sardelle pushed one of the guards across the hall as she stepped out of his way. She wished she could shove them both in at once, but she lacked that kind of precision control. The headache that had blossomed earlier throbbed in sync with her heartbeat now.

I think it might have something to do with proximity to the sword, Jaxi said. *You haven't done that much today.*

I don't know—I haven't rested much since last night, either. Besides, I haven't been very far from that sword since we found it. She maneuvered the second guard into the room, pushing both of them to the far side before knocking their legs out from under them. Perhaps it was a vain hope, but she hoped they would have trouble moving across the room and thumping on the door to get attention.

A woman's laughter floated up the stairs. "It's always a delight visiting, Hasham."

Someone inside the meeting room asked something, but the door muffled the words. That made Sardelle extra aware of how close everyone was and how unlikely it was that this kidnapping would go undiscovered.

"Can you knock them out?" Cas whispered as she dragged Fronzo across the threshold on his back.

"Not when they're this alert."

Cas did not say anything else, but Sardelle imagined her wishing she had Tolemek there. His knockout potions never failed to work. Of course, Sardelle could have done damage that would have caused the men to lose consciousness, but she was loath to beat them up any more than she had already. Whatever these people accused her of, she did not want any of it to be true.

As soon as Cas dumped her load and came out, Sardelle closed the door. She took a step toward the stairs, but the laughter came again, closer this time, and she sensed that woman was half way up already. She grabbed Cas's arm and pointed the other way down the hall. She had no idea if there would be another set of stairs that would take them back down to the main floor, but they would have to chance it. As she and Cas ran in that direction,

Sardelle focused on the locking mechanism of the door of the room that now held the guards. She melted it, hoping that would give them a few more seconds.

The woman and her escort had nearly reached the top. There wasn't time to get to the corner. Sardelle grabbed a door, wincing when she found it locked. Cas grabbed the knob on the opposite side of the hall and shoved the door open, charging inside. Sardelle leaped after her, worried those coming onto the landing had spotted her, and also worried that they would notice the lack of guards.

"What?" someone in the room blurted. "Who are you?"

Cas glanced back, a question in her eyes. Sardelle didn't know the answer—what to do with the bald, frail man in the middle of dressing. Sardelle grimaced at the idea of beating him into submission, especially when *they* had been the ones to barge into his room. She brushed the surface of his mind, hoping to find some tidbit that would give her an idea as to how to assuage his suspicions in a way that would let them walk out again in a minute.

He's the castle bookkeeper, Jaxi said at the same time as Sardelle discerned that their appearance worried him, not because they were intruders but because they were wearing those cloaks which meant they were a part of the queen's special group.

"Sorry," Sardelle said, smoothing her features. She was not going to panic because she was in the middle of an infiltration that was growing less likely to succeed with each passing minute, not her. "I don't think you heard us knock."

"I—ah." The bookkeeper glanced toward the door, but seemed more concerned by the trousers around his ankles.

"The queen sent us to inquire about..." About what? Uhm. "Funding for a special project."

"Another one?" The man wrestled his trousers up to his waist. He struggled with his belt, and they were in danger of slipping down again. The burden of slim hips.

"Yes." Sardelle tried not to make it sound like a question.

"To the Trim and Tight Landscaping Service again?" Sarcasm thickened his voice. He succeeded in fastening the belt and propped his fists on his hips, recovering his equilibrium.

Cas had stirred at the name of the company. Recognition? From the name, Sardelle was imagining some kind of sexual services business, but she supposed the queen wouldn't need to hire prostitutes to service her sisters.

Those types of perks were not mentioned in the organization's encyclopedia entry, Jaxi shared.

Good to know.

However, I haven't yet had an opportunity to look over that pamphlet you took from the queen's desk.

"How much does she need this time?" the bookkeeper asked.

"Five thousand nucros." As Sardelle plucked the number out of the ether, she scanned the hallway outside. It was empty. She did not know whether to assume that meant it was safe to leave. They probably weren't going to find *safe* tonight.

"The job was completed to the queen's satisfaction," Cas added.

"Glad to hear it. That's been very expensive landscaping." The bookkeeper waved them toward the door. "I'll get to work on it."

Sardelle nodded toward Cas, then strode out the door. They jogged down the hallway, Sardelle slowing down only enough to see if anyone was on the stairs and make sure the guards hadn't escaped their prison yet. They were still there, wriggling their way across the floor toward the door.

Worrying they had already been reported as missing, Sardelle took the stairs three at a time. Jaxi guided her toward the audience hall and the hallway behind it. Twice, she and Cas had to duck into rooms or closets to avoid guards patrolling the building. If not for her senses, they would have stumbled right into them. At least none of these rooms contained bookkeepers or anyone else.

Jaxi's directions proved accurate, and they found their way into a very tidy and dust-free basement dungeon. Sardelle headed straight for the back, searching the gloom for the iron ring.

"Are those brochures?" Cas asked as she walked past the entrance. As Jaxi had promised, a holder supported a stack of papers, and there was a chalkboard, as well as illustrations and photographs next to neat handwriting that described how the dungeon had once been used to house enemies of the nation.

Once. Right. "I believe they're educational pamphlets," Sardelle said. "To be handed to schoolchildren."

"Must have missed that field trip when I was a student."

Sardelle tugged on the heavy iron ring, the kind that might have once secured chains to the wall. It did not move. *You're sure this is the spot, Jaxi?*

Yes, apply more muscle. Or get Cas to do it. Her little arms are surprisingly strong.

Sardelle glanced at Cas, but another question popped into her mind first. "You don't know anything about the Trim and Tight Landscaping Service, do you?"

Cas nodded curtly. "One of several fictitious business entities that my father uses to send invoices and collect payments."

"Invoices?" Sardelle couldn't wrap her mind around the notion of receiving an invoice in the mail from an assassin.

"He's an organized man. The fictitious names allow people to hire him without their household knowing about it. Sometimes someone within the family is a target."

Sardelle was starting to wish she hadn't asked. She tried twisting the ring instead of pulling it, and it gave slightly.

"That's it," she whispered, remembering the guards that would be in the real dungeon on the other side of the wall. "Ready for another fight?"

A sickly green glow spilled onto the stones. "Ready." Cas had drawn the sword.

Sardelle hesitated. "We're not eviscerating, beheading, or castrating anyone, remember?"

"If Kasandral can cut through dragon scales, I'm guessing it can handle iron bars."

A logical argument, though Sardelle did not like the way the green glow reflected in Cas's eyes.

I can handle iron bars too.

I have no doubt of that, Jaxi.

"Here we go." Sardelle checked on the placement of the

guards before tugging on the ring. She doubted the dark green cloaks would explain their presence down here.

She expected them to be in the same spot as they had been a moment before, but was surprised that they had moved away from the door entirely and drifted down one of three rows of cells. To check on Kaika? Sardelle tugged on the ring. They might not get a better chance to sneak in.

The stone slab swung open more quickly than she expected. Sardelle charged through, a barrier in place in front of her in case she was wrong, and someone with a gun was waiting. But she was assaulted by smoke, not bullets. The hazy air slipped around her shield, stinging her nose and making her eyes water.

"What's—" Cas started to ask, but a muted *bang* came from down one of the rows of cells.

A figure strode toward them, smoke swirling. Sardelle lifted a hand, prepared to defend herself again. The person who marched out of the smoke *was* armed, with a pistol in each hand, but she lowered them.

"Sardelle?" Captain Kaika asked. Soot smeared her face, and a dark bloodstain marked her wrinkled shirt, the same one she had been in the day before, but she looked ready to chew up some rocks and spit them out rather than tumble onto a fainting couch. "Is that you?"

Sardelle pushed back her hood. "How did you know?"

"There's a ball of clean air hovering around you."

Sardelle wrinkled her nose. "Not that clean."

Behind her, Cas coughed. "We came to rescue you, Captain."

"Good, because until you showed up, I didn't know where the door was." Kaika peered back over her shoulder. "I was going to ask one of them, but, uhm, they're going to be too busy digging themselves out of that rubble to chat."

"How in all the realms did you get ahold of explosives down here?" Sardelle asked.

"Made them. If you're ever running a dungeon, make sure you do a *thorough* search of the prisoners, and don't dismiss any powders or liquids they've tucked away in dark places."

"I shall keep that in mind."

Kaika coughed a few times and wiped tears from her eyes—they were leaving clear tracks down her sooty cheeks. She grasped her shoulder where she had been shot, but all she asked was, "Did you bring a cloak for me?"

"Sorry, that would have been a smart idea, but we didn't think of it. Also, we've been harried and rushed for most of our infiltration." Sardelle stepped back into the show dungeon, waving for Kaika to follow. "Speaking of that, we should go. I'm afraid that noise will have been heard, and there have been other... disturbances as a result of our entrance too."

Cas snorted noisily.

Kaika had walked out of the smoke-filled dungeon, pushing the door shut behind her, but she halted before taking another step. "I'm not leaving until I talk to the queen."

"Talk? Or interrogate her?" Sardelle asked. "I don't think either is a good idea. We're seconds away from being discovered as it is, and she's up there in the middle of one of her sisterhood meetings." In truth, Sardelle hadn't searched the auras in that room, so she could not say for certain that the queen was in there, but it seemed logical. If nothing else, she needed to hand out all of the pamphlets she had made.

"You know where she is? Perfect." Kaika strode toward the stairs, her pistols still gripped in her hands.

Sardelle rushed to catch up with her, grabbing one forearm. "There are soldiers everywhere. You'll be seen before you get to her."

"Define everywhere."

"All of the halls. We barely made it down here without being noticed. We had to hide multiple times. We're fairly certain they let the news leak out that you were being hanged tonight, in order to ensure we—your allies—tried to break you out. They're setting a trap, if they haven't already."

"I was to be hanged tonight?" Kaika lifted her sooty brows.

"Or at dawn. Apex was fuzzy on the details."

"You find out where the king is being held yet?"

"We have a lead. Therrik thought he had been taken to a lighthouse."

"Oh." Kaika used the muzzle of one of the pistols to scratch her chin. "There are a lot of lighthouses in Iskandia."

"Yes, it's not a perfect lead."

Cas jogged to the bottom of the stairs and tilted her head toward the door at the top. What had she heard?

Jaxi?

The guards upstairs haven't been noticed yet, though they have thumped at the door a few times. The meeting is underway in the other room. They're probably sacrificing some chickens or something noisy.

Is anything else going on?

There are a lot of soldiers on the ground floor, both inside and out. They might be setting that trap you were thinking about.

So, Sardelle thought, *it would be hard to get out?*

Remember that notion you had of shielding yourself and charging past legions of soldiers shooting at you?

Yes...

That could still happen.

Wonderful.

"*She'll* know where he is," Kaika said. "Without a doubt."

Sardelle did not know if Kaika was trying to convince herself, or if she had heard something that verified their suspicions. Either way, there wasn't time to ask.

Kaika spun toward her. "If we have to fight our way out of here, can you keep us alive? I heard you can stop bullets."

"I would prefer not to fight, but I can shield us from fire, yes. Not indefinitely, mind you."

Kaika nodded. "Good enough."

"Wouldn't you rather escape, let me heal your wound, and try to contact the queen another time?" Sardelle asked.

"No." She strode up the stairs.

Sardelle followed while wishing she had a better feeling about all of this.

* * *

"We were outnumbered, at least twenty to one," Ridge said, sharing his second or third tale with Private Gormen, who was now off-duty. After finishing his shift, the young soldier had returned with the promised atlas, and Ridge had double-checked his map and his memory. The atlas did not mention lighthouses, but seeing the contours of the coast helped him remember two more spots that could serve as out-of-the-way prisons. Now, he just had to figure out how to get out of this cell and up to the hangar, so he could grab that two-person flier and hope he wasn't shot down by the city's artillery weapons as he took off.

"Their airship was armored, with some shaman protecting the balloon too," Ridge continued. "It was my first encounter with magic. Before that, I'd been like my mom, believing it didn't exist. It's hard to maintain that belief when an airship starts flinging bolts of lightning at your flier."

"What'd you do, sir?"

"Started flying on top of their balloon, so they couldn't target me. Crash and the Milkman—he's retired now—flew under it, tried to find a way through that armoring and to their engines. When the shaman was distracted with them, I swooped down, did a strafing run on their deck. Flew right between the ship and the balloon. Managed to cut through some of the supports, too, so the back of the deck was dangling down, and the shaman was too busy trying not to fall into the ocean thousands of feet below to bother with me. About a hundred other Cofah wanted to shoot at me, but I snugged right up to the balloon, so they realized they were cutting holes into it with each shot. Finally, I took a nice handmade explosive, a gift from the artillery fellows, and tossed it at the tank delivering hydrogen to the balloon. Got out of there about half a second before the biggest explosion you've ever seen."

The on-duty guard, who was stationed up the hall and out

of Ridge's sight, let out a low whistle. Ridge didn't know if his storytelling was doing anything useful—wouldn't it be easier to escape if the guards weren't paying any attention to him?—but had some vague notion of establishing a rapport with the men. The bars on the cell door and the window were quite sturdy, so he could never escape without human intervention. He couldn't bring himself to ask either of them for a key, both because it would be deleterious for their careers and because he was skeptical as to whether they would let him go, but with time, maybe he might find an opportunity to slip a key off one of their belts. Especially if he could get the on-duty fellow to come join him and Private Gormen for a drink—Gormen had brought a second bottle of beer when he had returned with the atlas.

"That was in the early days of Cofah airships," Ridge said. "Back when we were all using hydrogen, before we realized it was too easy to blow up. There were even non-combat-related accidents where the gas simply caught fire through some crew error and took the ship down. We've all switched to helium now. As I saw on my last mission, the Cofah have fliers, too—they stole our design, the bastards. And some other weapons. Any future battles are going to be tough. They always had superior numbers, but we had our fliers, which are of course far more maneuverable than their plodding airships. Things won't be easy going forward."

Ridge resisted the urge to rail about the lack of fliers defending the city at the moment.

"Sir," came a terse greeting from the out-of-sight guard.

The off-duty one's eyes widened as he looked up the hallway, and he shifted the bottle of beer behind his back.

Had Colonel Porthlok come back to start his interrogation? It was late for that—it had to be nearing midnight. Ridge hadn't expected more company until at least dawn. Maybe he had run out of time and should have been trying harder to find a key.

"This how you guard a prisoner, Private?" a gruff male voice asked.

Ridge slumped against the wall. He recognized Colonel Therrik's voice before the man walked into view, glowering at Gormen.

"No-no, sir," Gormen stammered. "I'm off-duty, sir. I was just..." He waved vaguely at Ridge.

"I asked him to keep me company," Ridge said, hoping to keep Therrik from contemplating some punishment for the young soldier, not that he particularly wanted to draw Therrik's ire toward himself. Whatever had brought the man here at this hour, it couldn't be anything good. Maybe he wanted revenge for the beating he believed he had received at Ridge's hands. "You know how needy I am," he added. "I get terribly lonely if I don't have anyone to tell my stories to."

Therrik grunted, then jerked a thumb toward the exit. "Take your beer and get out of here before I report you."

Gormen flashed a quick salute at Ridge—an action that made Therrik scowl—then darted around the big man. He looked relieved that reporting was all that Therrik had mentioned. Given his reputation for pummeling young privates and academy cadets, that wasn't surprising. Ridge wondered if *he* was about to be pummeled. He almost joked that Therrik should be nicer to young people, so that he wouldn't be the subject of vandalism so often, but clamped his mouth shut before the words could escape. As far as Ridge knew, Therrik had no reason to suspect he and Tolemek had been anywhere near his house. It would be better for his health if Therrik continued to believe that.

"I heard you were drawing on the wall in here like a three-year-old." Therrik held a lantern up to the bars and stared at the map at the back of the cell.

"Now, Colonel, I take exception to that comment. I believe I have at least the artistic skills of a five-year-old."

"You're known for being delusional."

Ridge looked at the map. "A four-year-old?"

Therrik's face remained stony, his dark, dull eyes offering no hint that he appreciated the humor.

"You heard about the lighthouse too," Therrik said, his hard gaze shifting toward Ridge.

Too? Ah, right. Therrik wouldn't have sensed the information being plucked from his mind. But if he thought Ridge had some intel that he needed, did that mean he had come for an interrogation? An unsanctioned one? Or maybe Porthlok had secretly sanctioned it.

"I've been all along the coasts," Ridge said carefully. "I don't think I have any more information than you do, but I can only think of a few lighthouses that would make viable prisons, especially if someone wanted to hide someone extremely recognizable for the long term."

"And you want to search them."

"Seems like a logical approach. A lot of the problems we have would go away if King Angulus returned." And his flier squadrons, but Ridge didn't want to risk bringing that up again. He did wonder if Therrik had been back up to the hangar and had seen if any messages had been returned.

"I don't suppose *you* would go away," Therrik grumbled.

A few sarcastic comments floated to mind, but Ridge kept his mouth shut. Grumpy Therrik was an improvement over cruel Therrik, and he was waiting for the man to tell him why he had come. No need to distract him with clever repartee.

Therrik fished in his pocket. Ridge anticipated everything from brass knuckles to a garrote wire to some compact torture device. What he didn't anticipate was a key, though maybe he should have. After all, torture implements would be easier to use without bars in the way.

"I'm out of beer," Ridge said. "No need for you to come in."

"I bet you swilled it without even thinking that it might be poisoned."

"I would have thought that in a Cofah prison, but Private Gormen seemed genuinely interested in my tales."

"I'll bet." Therrik shoved the door open.

Ridge tensed, all too aware that he didn't have Sardelle to help him this time.

But instead of stepping in, Therrik stepped back. "Get out. Go find the king."

Ridge looked from him to the key, noting a piece of tape around the fat end. This wasn't the same key as the guards wore on the rings on their belts.

"Is this authorized?" Ridge asked.

"What do you think?"

"I'm not sure what to think. I figured you came to beat me into a pulp."

Therrik's eyes brightened, and his fingers curled into a fist. "I would be happy to do that. Maybe it would make your escape look more real."

"Uh, that's not necessary." Ridge would have preferred to wait until Therrik left before venturing out—in the tight corridor out there, he would have to get uncomfortably close to the man to squeeze out of his cell. But he might not get another chance, or Therrik might change his mind.

Ridge took a breath and stepped through the gate. He noticed two things: that the guard at the head of the corridor was not there... and that Therrik grabbed him.

Ridge jerked his arm up in an attempt to block, but Therrik threw his weight behind the attack, his hands a blur. He knocked aside Ridge's arm, even as he smashed Ridge into the bars beside the gate. Hard metal bit into his back, and his head clunked against iron. Ridge got his arms up to protect his throat, but all Therrik did was pin him there, his hands curled into Ridge's uniform jacket.

"I don't believe you bested me, you untrained chair jockey," Therrik growled. "I can't see it, but you better be the man those starry-eyed privates think you are." Therrik shoved Ridge and let him go.

Ridge gripped the bars to keep from falling. He would love to slam a fist into that sneering face, but he was too busy trying to figure out what was going on to truly be angry.

Therrik thrust a finger toward his nose. "If you don't find the king, *don't* bother coming back."

Without waiting for acknowledgment, Therrik stalked up the corridor. He slammed the door on his way out and did not look back.

Ridge couldn't begin to figure out that man—and a big part of him wondered if Therrik was setting him up to be shot, letting him go so the MPs would see him as an escaped prisoner and unleash the hounds on him. But he willed his legs into motion, anyway. This might be his only chance to find the king. If he didn't... Therrik wasn't the only one who could make Ridge's life miserable—or make it *over*—when he came back.

CHAPTER 11

SOMEONE HAD NOTICED THE GUARDS were not at their post.

Sardelle grimaced, but was not surprised. At least twenty minutes had passed since she and Cas had stuffed them into that room. If Kaika wanted to barge into the queen's meeting, they should have gone straight there from the dungeon, but Kaika had insisted on stopping in the kitchen to make explosives. Technically, it was a storage pantry in the back of the kitchen. Enough of the staff had been working in the main room, its ovens fired up and a giant mechanical mixing machine clanking and churning, that hiding had been necessary.

"We should go," Cas grumbled, pacing. In the pantry, she could only go three steps before turning around. Every time she spun, Sardelle worried the hilt of her sword would catch on one of the flour bags stacked against one wall, tear it open, and make a mess. "There have been too many delays already. Trying to get into that meeting is going to get us killed."

"I agree," Sardelle said.

Cas stopped and stared at her. "You do?"

They were alone in the pantry, waiting for Kaika to return. Kaika had made up her explosives with impressive speed, but then she had insisted on leaving Sardelle and Cas behind while she sneaked back to the dungeon and planted a bomb. "It'll be a distraction when we need it," she'd said, "and it should finish the job the other one didn't quite manage: collapsing the rubble in my cell so people think I'm dead under the pile, and they don't come looking for me."

Sardelle questioned how viable of a distraction it would make. Would the noise even be heard? It seemed nobody had heard the first explosion. Either the dungeon was not directly under a part of the castle where anyone was working, or when the architects had designed it a thousand years earlier, they had ensured it was insulated enough that the residents did not have to listen to the cries of torture victims.

Sardelle nodded to Cas's question. "We were able to get her. I think we're spitting in Fate's face by lingering."

"Yes. Exactly." Cas went back to pacing. "It would be one thing if we could fight these people, but we can't. I understand the captain's drive to find the king, but..."

Sardelle held up a hand. "Someone's coming." She stood next to the door, listening with her ears and her mind.

"That woman really wants her flour." Cas pressed herself into a corner between two shelving units, the sword scabbard clunking against the wall. Kasandral might be invisible to most people, but the blade was definitely there.

The last time the cook had headed for the pantry, Sardelle had distracted her with the subtle suggestion that a taste of the boar turning on the spit would be far preferable to retrieving flour for cookies that were destined to go upstairs to the meeting instead of being consumed by the kitchen staff. Sardelle reached out, intending to make another suggestion, but a second figure jogged into the range of her senses. Kaika.

Afraid she wouldn't see the cook and would crash right into her, Sardelle almost spoke to her telepathically, but she worried she would startle Kaika when the captain needed her concentration. In the half second she was debating this, Kaika came across the cook. Even though Sardelle had her ear pressed to the door, she did not hear anything. Only her senses informed her when the cook had been subdued and dragged off.

"Kaika's back," Sardelle whispered, and eased the door open.

Few lamps burned in this back half of the kitchen, but she could tell the cook was nowhere to be seen. Kaika strode out from behind some cooling racks with a ball of twine and a grin. "We're all set."

Sardelle checked on the cook, found her tied and gagged in the corner, and shook her head. With or without explosives, their plan, such as it was, had to be close to tumbling down around them.

"Where's the meeting?" Kaika whispered. Other staff were still working at the front of the kitchen.

"This way." Sardelle headed for the door they had come in earlier.

Kaika gripped her shoulder before she could push it open. "Thanks for helping me," she whispered. "Again. When we find the king, I'll make sure he knows what you did and that you were loyal to him too."

Sardelle nodded, though she wasn't sure she *wanted* the king knowing what she had done here, which had included snooping through his wife's possessions and breaking into his castle twice. She also wasn't sure Kaika had any sway with him. Would he even know who some captain in the army was? Sardelle kept the thoughts to herself.

With Jaxi helping to guide her again, she led the others through hallways that eventually took them back to the stairs. Every time soldiers were in their way, Sardelle's group had to divert—or find a way to distract those soldiers. She teased one into leaving his post with the scent of cookies baking in the kitchen, and Jaxi convinced a couple of others to run to the lavatory.

"We would be smacking right into them if it wasn't for you, wouldn't we?" Kaika whispered after they hid in an alcove while a group of four marched past. Sardelle had cut out a gas lamp and deepened the shadows so they hadn't been noticed. "I had balls of a time getting back to the dungeon without being seen."

Two men's voices drifted down from the top of the stairs, and Sardelle did not answer.

Jaxi, did they find those guards yet?

Not yet. I've been muffling their sounds. One has been banging on the door with his knee. The man who escorted you up almost has his hands free. Two officers are arguing in the hallway. They're about to knock and go in to ask the queen if she dismissed the guards.

"We have to go," Sardelle whispered. She wanted to explain herself, but there was no time.

Trusting the others would follow, she charged up the stairs. Before she reached the top, she battered the officers with wind and knocked them away from the door. As with before, she made a prison of compressed air to hold them, but only one was held utterly immobile. The other growled and batted at the air with his hands. Even though it should not have been effective, he created eddies, pushing against the current.

Dragon blood, Jaxi warned.

Is it the same man from the tower? Sardelle would have preferred to *teach* him rather than beat him down, but she doubted a recruiting speech would be well received.

I think so. He—

Kaika surged past Sardelle and hefted a rifle over her shoulder. Sardelle hadn't seen her grab it, but she clubbed the man in the head while he was still struggling to defeat the magic. Afraid she would get in Kaika's way, Sardelle focused on the second one. She forced him to his knees and waved to Cas to tie him.

Kaika had stomped her officer into the ground and was kneeling on his back, employing her twine. It was silly to think about now, but Sardelle lamented that the man would likely always consider her an enemy, and she would never get a chance to talk to him about magic. She would probably never get a chance to talk to anyone here about anything except execution orders for herself.

Sardelle helped Kaika and Cas drag the men into the room next door to where they had already stored other guards.

"You two go first." Kaika waved at their cloaks. "Since I'm not dressed as a whatever, I'll lurk and come in behind you if I can. Holler if you need help." She waved a lumpy package, one of her handmade explosives.

"When does the one in the dungeon go off?" Sardelle asked.

"Soon. Might not want to loiter."

Right. Sardelle adjusted her hood, pulling it low over her eyes, and tried the door. It wasn't locked. Of course not—people had been guarding it, and cookies were on the way.

Sardelle walked into a room full of tables and rolls of... was that wrapping paper? Maybe it was craft paper. Voices drifted out from an open door that led to a second room in the back, with a crackling hearth and several occupied chairs visible through it.

"Looks like we're late to the meeting," Cas murmured. She was right behind Sardelle.

Sardelle eased closer, hoping to catch a few words before revealing herself. She would have preferred not to reveal herself at all, so she walked around one of the tables and hugged the shadows near the wall instead of approaching straight-on.

"He's disappeared from the city," someone was saying. "We don't know where he went."

"What does our spy say?"

Spy? Both of the speakers had been women. Sardelle was about to examine the room with her senses to get a further feel for the occupants, but a woman in a chair close to the door peered out. The queen. Shadows or not, she looked directly at Sardelle and Cas.

Don't forget she has dragon blood too, Jaxi said.

I haven't forgotten. Does she sense my power? Or yours?

Actually, I think she noticed that Kasandral strolled in.

Great. Sardelle lifted a hand in greeting, as if she had just arrived, and walked into the room. *Shouldn't that sword have a problem with her blood, the way it does with mine?*

He should, yes.

None of the sixteen women seated inside had their hoods pulled up. Most of them had taken their cloaks off altogether and draped them over chairs. Sardelle felt conspicuous with her hood up, especially when every single woman turned to look at her. Every woman and one man. Apex was perched in a chair in the corner. Sardelle was so surprised to find him here that she couldn't think of anything to say. *Our spy.* Was he truly? He looked miserable, plucking at the seam of his chair cushion, but he had clearly been invited to the meeting.

Behind her, Cas sucked in a sharp breath.

He's here trying to get what Ridge asked for, Jaxi said, *the king's location.*

You're sure he's not here telling *them about Ridge?*

No, he's pretending to be their spy, but he's not giving them anything important. He regrets the choice he made. He still hates Tolemek, but it stung him to lose Ridge's respect, and he wishes he hadn't been impetuous. He wants to make it up to Ridge.

All right. We'll see if we can all get out of here.

"Good evening, sisters," Sardelle said. Since nobody had stopped staring at her, she doubted she would get by with simply slipping into an empty chair. The queen was seated close to the doorway, so Kaika might be able to rush in and grab her if she had room. Sardelle took a couple of steps farther inside to make way. "Are we late?"

"Who *are* you?" the queen asked.

"Sai Forgolen," Sardelle said.

The queen stood. "No, you're not. Lower your hood."

A boom came from the depths of the castle. The floor shuddered, and several women leaped to their feet. Apex stood, also, reaching for his waist, but he did not have any weapons belted there.

Without looking, Sardelle was aware of Kaika lunging into the room and grabbing the queen. Sardelle waved a hand toward the fire, throwing oxygen into the coals. The flames doubled in size with an audible *fwoop*. She cut off all of the lamps in the room.

Behind her, someone grunted. Flesh smacked flesh. Sardelle winced, imagining the queen receiving the same barrage of blows that the officer had. At least Kaika hadn't blown up anything in the room yet.

"What did you do with King Angulus?" Kaika growled.

If the queen replied, Sardelle did not hear it.

"Witch!" someone cried.

"I prefer sorceress," Sardelle muttered, raising her hands to keep the women back. Several were grabbing for short swords or daggers, and two lunged toward her. Sardelle formed a barrier through the center of the room, one that would keep everyone on the far side behind it. Only a couple of the women could reach her, and she glared at them, trying to dissuade them from doing so. She could feel Jaxi's power pouring into her, making it easier than usual to maintain the barrier while concentrating on other tasks at the same time.

In the corner, Apex took a step toward her. She turned her

glare on him. He lowered his hands, his body slumping.

Kaika cursed, and the queen stumbled back into Sardelle's vision. She had produced a stiletto, the slender blade dripping blood. Sardelle channeled a pinpoint gust of wind at her. It struck the queen's hand and knocked the weapon out of her grip. It flew away, landing in the side of one woman's chair and sinking in to the hilt.

"*Antyonla masahrati!*" the queen cried.

Sardelle had no idea what she had said, but her skin crawled, and she knew right away that the words contained some power. Power over *what,* she could not guess, not until Apex yelled, "Look out!"

She didn't know if the warning was for her or for the queen or someone else, but Jaxi yelled a similar warning inside her head. Sardelle leaped to the side. She was careful not to lower the barrier, lest the other women all be able to attack, but utter shock went through her at what she saw.

Cas had drawn Kasandral and held the giant glowing blade aloft over her shoulder. She wasn't facing the queen. No, she had Sardelle in her sights. Alarm and confusion twisted Cas's face, but there was no confusion in her body. Without hesitating, she swept the blade toward Sardelle's neck.

Sardelle threw herself into a backward roll, no longer worrying about the barrier. How could she? The blade swept through the air she had just left, nearly carving her head from her shoulders. She just avoided slamming against one of the chairs as she jumped to her feet, yanking out Jaxi.

Shouts came from all around her, but Sardelle had to concentrate on defending herself. Cas had already advanced, and she swept that giant blade around as if it were as light as a rapier. Jaxi flared to life, glowing red in contrast with Kasandral's green, their mingled light driving all shadows from the room. Metal screeched as the blades met, motes of energy flying like sparks from a raging fire. Jaxi guided Sardelle's hand, blocking with speed and agility Sardelle never could have claimed on her own. Cas's skill and speed were uncanny, too, enhanced by her blade. Kasandral's glow increased, as if it was hungry, as if it had craved this moment for all eternity.

Don't get melodramatic on me, Jaxi said. *Let me handle this. Make sure none of those women are trying to get to your back.*

They're too busy fleeing this— Sardelle winced as the blades came together in another clash, their energy burning her face like heat from a fire, *—chaos.*

Jaxi did not reply. Most of the women were running out of the room, but Sardelle glimpsed the queen pulling something out of her pocket. Some vial? Something that would knock out Sardelle? Or kill her?

Sardelle thought about trying to fling another surge of wind at her, but with her entire body involved in the fight, in leaping chairs and maneuvering around tables, she struggled to concentrate on anything else. A couple of times, she spotted a tiny opening, a place where she might have darted in and stabbed Kasandral's wielder, but that wielder was one of Ridge's ace pilots and someone who Sardelle had been starting to think of as a friend before this sword appeared in their lives.

The queen lifted her arm to throw something. Sardelle did not know where Kaika had been—fresh blood streaking down her cheek promised someone had been troubling her—but she appeared in time to bowl into the queen. The two women toppled over a chair, upending it as they went down behind it.

The action distracted Sardelle—and maybe Jaxi, too—for Kasandral slipped past her defenses. Sardelle jumped away, but not before the glowing blade bit into the back of her hand. The fiery pain of a sun burned through her flesh, and she almost dropped her own blade.

Sorry, Jaxi said tersely.

She seemed to take the slip as a personal affront. She flared with crimson rage, and Sardelle found herself surging back into the fray. Her blade slashed toward Kasandral—and Cas—with such speed that Jaxi blurred, too fast to see. Sardelle had no idea how Cas blocked the assault, but she managed, each blow met with steel, the squeals of clashing metal so harsh that Sardelle's ears hurt. Though not nearly as badly as her hand, which burned as if venom had been poured into her blood.

Apex had left his corner and had his hands out, as if he wanted to jump into Sardelle's and Cas's battle, to stop it somehow. Sardelle couldn't object to the intent—if someone could disarm Cas, this would probably all be over, at least for the moment—but she worried he would simply get in the way.

A chair toppled behind Cas. Kaika and the queen? No, there was a man over there too. A guard. Someone must have heard all of this noise. More guards poured into the room. Kaika was pulled from the floor by her armpits. Something fell out of her shirt.

"Let me go," Kaika snarled, fighting the men who held her. "You knocked my—that's a bomb, you idiots. Get back, get back!"

They didn't let her go; they didn't even seem to hear her. Their only focus was to pull her away from the queen. Sardelle imagined the ceiling crashing down and crushing all of them. She wanted to flee the room, get the queen and everyone else out, but she couldn't extricate herself from the sword fight. As Cas pressed her back, Kasandral's assault relentless, Sardelle couldn't even spare the thoughts to examine the bomb.

"Cas," Sardelle yelled, hoping she could somehow get through to her. "We need to get out of here. Go out the door."

Jaxi, can you do something about that package?

It's just lying there, the powder inside half spilled out. I think a fuse would have had to be lit.

Kasandral kept slashing toward Sardelle, its fury somehow unleashed by those words the queen had chanted. Cas's face remained contorted, the struggle written plainly on it. Sweat streamed from her temples and dripped from her chin. She didn't *want* to kill Sardelle, but the sword would not relinquish its hold on her. And Sardelle had no idea how to break it, short of killing her.

A clank came from the other side of the room. Kaika had clobbered one of the guards, and he fell back, stumbling against a table that held a lantern. Time seemed to slow as the glass holder wobbled, tipped, and fell. It shattered, oil and flame spilling onto the powder on the floor.

If Sardelle had been given another half a second, she could

have dropped a shield around the bomb and contained the explosion. But time did not wait for her. Flame burst from the powder and ignited the rest of the package.

Since Kasandral was still slashing toward her face, Sardelle could neither stop and stare, nor run and hide. With Jaxi in control, she kept blocking, parrying, and advancing and retreating, even though furniture was being hurled through the air. Men flew back, too, those who had been too close to the explosion. Light and heat seared the room, the flames from the hearth as nothing in comparison. Dust filled the air as stone tumbled down from the ceiling. Then a massive block crashed down behind Sardelle as she was defending a fresh onslaught from Kasandral.

She could not compensate in time, and her heel caught on the jagged stone. A booming snap came from the floor. The wooden boards sagged beneath her, further assaulting her balance. She flailed, and could feel Jaxi's power trying to keep her upright, but more boards snapped before she could recover. The giant stone dropped through the floor to the level below, and Sardelle's legs fell through the hole it left in its wake. She caught the crumbling rim under her armpits, but realized she would have to let go. Cas stood above her like an axe man. With one arm, Sardelle lifted Jaxi to block, even as her legs dangled in air underneath her, and all of her weight hung from her other arm.

Let go, Jaxi ordered as Cas's blade plunged down toward her.

Sardelle couldn't have resisted if she had tried. As she fell, she glimpsed movement behind Cas. Apex lunged in and grabbed her around the waist. Cas whirled toward him, that blade blazing more brightly than ever.

Sardelle fell below the level of the floor and did not see the rest. But she heard the scream of utter agony as she landed on a table ten feet below, pain slamming her back. Before she had gathered her wits, the table broke. She dropped through it, falling another three feet as broken wood scraped at her arms. Finally, she landed hard on a stone floor, the dark room strangely quiet after the chaos she had left. Or maybe it had grown quiet upstairs too. Dust and pebbles dribbled through the hole in the floor, but the sounds of fighting had stopped. So had the scream of pain.

Apex? she asked in her mind, not sure if the question was for Jaxi, not sure if she wanted an answer.

You don't.

Shit.

I know.

Sardelle pushed herself to her feet. With Jaxi's help, she could have jumped up, caught the rim of the floor above, and pulled herself back into that room, but she had visions of having her head cleaved off as she did so.

She dropped the sword, Jaxi said.

Good. Sardelle headed for the door, anyway. That blade had more magic in it than she had guessed. Maybe it had once slain enemy dragons and sorcerers, but she could not imagine how the Iskandians had used it centuries earlier without putting their own people at risk.

He didn't attack the queen. It's possible there is a way to teach him not to strike against allies.

Teach him? You told me the sword isn't sentient.

No, he's not. The magic wrapped up in the blade may allow commands to be imprinted, allies to be identified. Or it may simply be that you have less-diluted blood in your veins than the queen, so Kasandral chose you as his first target when he was roused.

Sardelle found a set of stairs and took them three at a time. Distant shouts came from other parts of the castle, but she did not hear boots thundering in the hallway above her yet. Occasionally, stone shifted and clattered to the floor. Maybe the soldiers were being warned to stay out until the rubble settled.

They're blocked. That room isn't the only one where there was a collapse. You may have a few minutes to escape without being noticed.

When Sardelle reached the top of the stairs, she saw what Jaxi meant. She had to crawl over waist-high rubble to travel down the hallway to the meeting room—what was *left* of the meeting room. The doors on the left side of the hall appeared undamaged, lucky for the guards they had stuffed in those rooms, but the right side was a mess. A broken beam lay across the hall, the jagged tip thrusting through the doorway of the meeting room. Sardelle debated asking Jaxi to incinerate it but decided to squeeze above it instead. With dust still sifting down from the ceiling, the area did not appear stable.

The ceiling in the outer room had dropped, crushing most of those tables. She hoped the guards who had been trying to pull Kaika out had escaped. She couldn't bring herself to check beneath the rubble for bodies. People weren't supposed to die, damn it. Why had she gone along with this? She should have foreseen that nothing good could come from directly confronting the queen.

You couldn't have foreseen that your ally would try to kill you, Jaxi said.

No? Sardelle asked as she crawled across the rubble toward the inner door. Weak coughs came from inside that room. *That sword has been giving me indications that it wanted me dead all along. I ignored them because there hadn't been time to find a library and research it yet.*

You have the heart of a scientist; you like proof before condemning people—and swords. It's not a bad thing.

A compliment. A sure sign that Jaxi felt remorse over all of this—or knew there was worse news to come.

The rubble rose to chest-height in the doorway to the inner room. All of the lanterns had been extinguished, and the fire in the hearth must have been smothered, too, because Sardelle could not see anything. She conjured a globe of light and floated it in through the gap.

She glimpsed Apex's eviscerated body, his face upward, his eyes unseeing. He was already dead with no chance of healing him. Tears welled in her eyes and regret formed a lump in her throat.

Groans drifted out from under a rubble pile in the back, and Sardelle forced herself to look away. She sent her senses outward, bracing herself for the further death she might discover. Intense feelings of pain washed over her from different sources. She realized with a start that she was on top of Kaika, who had been in the doorway when the ceiling had collapsed. The queen was... Sardelle swallowed. The queen was dead.

By the gods, Jaxi. Sardelle almost added that there was no way either of them would be able to show themselves in the city—or on the continent—again, but with dead or dying people all around her, that was too selfish a thought to share. *Help me burn the rubble away, please. Be careful of those underneath it.*

Got it. Cas is over by the hole in the floor, sitting down with her head in her hands.

While Sardelle was debating if she wanted to approach Cas, Jaxi started incinerating stone. Sardelle decided to work on that instead. She could sense that Kaika was alive, but that she was in pain and struggling to breathe. Sardelle backed up and started lifting rocks away with her mind. Oddly, her head did not throb as much as it had earlier.

Maybe because Kasandral is buried, Jaxi said. *That ought to shut up his brutish glowing.*

Focused on extracting Kaika, Sardelle did not respond. She almost jumped when she lifted away a rock, and an unexpected hand stretched up toward her. She hadn't reached Kaika yet. It was one of the guards.

Aware of some of the distant shouts growing closer, and of bangs and thumps as people tried to clear away enough stone and debris to get to this level, Sardelle rushed to pull him out. He groaned, but his eyes did not open. That might be for the best. Surely, he would not be an ally here when he woke up.

Next, she reached Kaika. Her eyes were open, pain mingling with determination on her face. And grime. Sardelle had never seen someone so dirty outside of a boiler room.

As soon as her arms were free, Kaika pulled herself out. Fresh blood seeped from the bullet wound from the night before, and countless scratches and bumps marred the rest of her. Sardelle pulled carefully, not wanting to do more damage.

"What in all of the cursed realms happened?" Kaika whispered.

"Your bomb, I believe."

"That only went off *after* everything fell apart. After Ahn started attacking you." Kaika's brow furrowed with confusion.

"It was the sword," came a soft, emotion-choked voice from the doorway. Cas slumped against the frame. "It—I... Apex." Tears welled in her eyes, as she glanced toward the hallway. She looked like a rabbit poised to flee—or a woman about to face the executioner's axe.

Maybe that wasn't entirely inaccurate. Ridge would not react well to this. Hells, Sardelle's own emotions were such a tangle that *she* didn't know how to react, either.

Get out of here, Jaxi advised. *Figure it out later. People are coming. People who aren't going to be happy about the queen's death. I've moved or incinerated enough rubble that those who survived should be easy for them to retrieve.*

"The queen," Kaika said, pointedly not looking at Cas. "Did she make it out?"

"No," Sardelle murmured.

Kaika smashed a fist against her thigh. "All of that, all of *that*—" she thrust her hand toward the rubble-filled room, thoughts of Apex at the top of her thoughts, "—and I didn't even get the information I came for? We still don't know where the king is?"

I actually did get that information while Kaika was pummeling the queen and asking, a more precise location than Therrik knew about. Jaxi shared the thought with Sardelle.

"He's being held in a lighthouse on an island a hundred miles north of the city," Sardelle said. "We'll need a flier to get there."

Kaika stared at her. "What? How long have you known?"

"Two seconds," Sardelle hurried to say before Kaika could accuse her of not sharing earlier and keeping all of this from happening. "Jaxi took the information from the queen's thoughts as you were questioning her."

Kaika's stare shifted downward, to the soulblade belted at Sardelle's waist.

"All right then." Kaika did not appear relieved or happy, just more determined than ever.

"One more pull, men," came an order from the base of the nearby stairwell.

"Come on." Kaika climbed to her feet and shambled toward the door. "There's nothing left for us here."

Despite her words, she paused in the doorway, casting a long look back toward the room before walking out.

Chapter 12

Cas disappeared soon after they escaped the castle, and Sardelle found herself riding through the dark countryside with Kaika, the world silent around them save for the clip-clop of the horseshoes. Dawn would arrive soon. Even though wisdom had suggested a swift retreat, Sardelle had gone hunting for Ridge after slipping out of the castle. Kaika had stuck to her side, knowing they needed a pilot—and a flier—to get to the king. But Ridge had been nowhere to be found. Three times, Sardelle had made Jaxi scour every aura in the army fort and the hangars atop the cliffs. Jaxi had promised she would have found him—she was familiar with his aura and had chatted to him often, after all—if he was anywhere within fifty miles. Sardelle had refused to believe his people had shot him and that she couldn't sense his presence because he was dead. He was too important to the Iskandians. The army wouldn't have shot him. Unless the queen had ordered it before stepping into that meeting, as some punishment for associating with sorcerers.

Sardelle closed her eyes—she had barely been seeing the road ahead, anyway. She hoped she had not made the wrong choice in leaving the city. Jaxi had said she'd sensed Tolemek and Duck back at Ridge's mother's house when she had been looking for Ridge. It seemed a logical meeting point, and Ridge would know to look for them there.

Kaika twisted in her saddle, frowning at the road behind them.

"Trouble?" Sardelle did not sense anyone riding up on them, but she had not been checking the farmhouses and fields to the sides of the road.

"She *better* not have gone back for that sword."

"Cas?"

"Yes, *Cas*. Lieutenant Ahn. It's bad enough if she's hiding to avoid a court-martial, but if she tries to get that magic-cursed monster blade out of the rubble, I'll blow her higher than she's ever flown."

Cas hadn't looked back toward the sword when they had been leaving the room or sneaking out of the castle. Sardelle could be mistaken, but she believed whatever bond Kasandral had placed on her had been broken with Apex's death. Maybe the sword itself had even felt contrite—if that was possible—over killing the wrong target.

You're attributing a brain to that over-sharpened steel rod. It doesn't have one.

It has... something. You admitted yourself that it's more than we believed. And you've called it by name and given it a sex since the beginning.

Only because something that chooses to glow such a hideous shade of green has to be male.

That's a lovely prejudice you have.

I seem to remember you having a similar thought about whoever designed Ridge's hideous green plaid couch.

No, I said only a man would buy *that couch. And I was right.* Sardelle sighed wistfully. As strange as it seemed, she missed that couch. And she missed Ridge, too, even if less than twelve hours had passed since they had been parted. She had grown used to having him nearby, being able to touch his mind, to take comfort in his solid presence. The emptiness was noticeable.

Maybe you can buy him another one when you find a new place to live. If you can find the designer who came up with that pattern. He's probably been dead for a couple hundred years. Or maybe he was shot for crimes to the eyes.

Sardelle was not in the mood for jokes and could not muster a smile or a retort.

"You don't think so?" Kaika asked.

It took a moment for Sardelle to remember their conversation. "That Cas went back for the sword? No. I doubt she's hiding from the law, either." She might want to hide from Ridge; she looked up to him, as all of his young pilots did, and he would not react well when he heard about this. "She shouldn't be punished for what happened. She wasn't in control."

"Wasn't in *control*? She tried to *kill* you. She *did* kill Apex."

"I saw her trying to fight the sword's influence even as she was attacking me," Sardelle said.

"No officer in a military court is going to believe that, that the *sword* made her do it."

Sardelle feared that might be a truth. Even if the queen and her Heartwood sisters had been leading this witch-hunt, from what Sardelle had seen, the majority of Iskandian subjects had never seen magic used, not real magic, and most did not believe it existed anymore, if it ever had. She had no idea if there had been any actual witnesses to Apex's death, but more likely, she would be blamed for it, even if someone had seen Cas land the killing blow. Sardelle had a feeling she was going to be blamed for everything that had happened in that castle. And even though the queen had died, others in that organization had survived. Her heart grew heavier whenever she tried to imagine the future, because she doubted she could stay here, not if she didn't want to be hunted day and night.

"I can't believe you're so calm and serene about everything," Kaika said, slumping in her saddle.

Serene? Sardelle felt tired, depressed, and resigned. Definitely not serene.

"I didn't really know Apex that well," Kaika went on, facing forward again, "but I wouldn't have minded knowing him better. He was bookish and oblivious but handsome. I figured I could have worked on the rest, if he'd ever given me indication..." She shrugged. "Well, he didn't, and that's his loss, but I still thought he was an all right fellow. Not sure how he got captured and taken to that meeting, but—" She shrugged again.

Captured? Oh, right. Kaika had not been there when Apex's betrayal had been unearthed. Well, Sardelle would not speak of it. Perhaps Ridge would prefer that it not be remembered. That was what *she* would prefer. After all, what choice had Apex had, given that the queen herself had asked a favor of him? It must have been an impossible situation, one that meant betrayal no matter what he did.

"Cas wouldn't have been there if I hadn't insisted we go to that meeting," Kaika said. Earlier, her voice had been loud, rough, and agitated. Now it was so soft that Sardelle could barely hear it. "That *sword* wouldn't have been there."

Sardelle did not know what to say. That she had been blaming herself too? "I don't think any of us made the best decisions tonight."

"I never do. Nowon was the brains in our duo. He would have had some clever way to—" Kaika's voice broke off into a muffled choking sound, an attempt not to cry. She looked away and rubbed her face. "I've always been the impulsive one. Too impulsive. Too stupid."

"I doubt anyone who can make explosives from within her dungeon cell could be deemed stupid."

"Fine, then ridiculously unwise. Is there a word for that?"

"Besides unwise?"

"Yeah."

"Injudicious?"

"Sounds classy. I'll take it." Kaika rubbed her face again.

Sardelle did not have to see her face to know that tears streaked it. She was like Ridge, someone who used humor to cover up that she was hurting. Maybe it was a military trait, something about not being perceived as weak or vulnerable.

Sorceresses get to cry, because if anyone mocks them, they can incinerate buildings.

You speak from experience, Jaxi?

Maybe.

"Is it selfish that I'm wondering what's going to happen to me now?" Kaika asked after a time. Her voice had grown steady again, but the dejected slump to her shoulders remained. "If I can't find the king... and even if I can... I've been caught breaking into the castle, was responsible for the explosion that killed the queen, and oh, I've been AWOL for the last two weeks. If Nowon were here, he'd look at me like I was pathetic. He wouldn't say it, because he never did, but his eyebrow would twitch ever so slightly, and I'd know."

"If it helps, I'll probably get blamed for most of what you

played a part in," Sardelle said. "Come up with a plausible excuse for your AWOL status, and you might retain your career."

"I doubt it."

"Your crimes are minor compared to being a sorceress." Sardelle tried to keep the bitterness out of her voice. After all, she'd just been praised as being serene. One couldn't be serene and bitter, could one? Serenely bitter?

"Witch," Kaika said.

"Pardon?"

"We call you people witches, remember? Sorceress sounds too noble. Or maybe it's just harder to say."

"Like injudicious?"

"Exactly."

To Sardelle's surprise, Kaika leaned over and punched her in the shoulder. It took her a moment to realize it had been a friendly comradely punch, rather than an attempt to unhorse her. Kaika even smiled—at least Sardelle thought it was a smile. The woman truly needed to be allowed into the washroom first when they reached the house.

"You're all right," Kaika said. "For a witch."

Sardelle resisted the urge to correct the word. "Thank you."

Aw, you made a friend.

Too bad I lost another one.

You didn't know Apex that well, Jaxi said.

I was thinking of Cas, because I'm not sure she'll be able to get over what she did and to work around Ridge again or to look me in the eye. Sardelle wondered how Cas's relationship with Tolemek would be affected. He could probably understand the idea of unforeseen consequences due to the tools one chose to wield, but Cas might not realize that. *I'm upset over Apex's loss, too, especially since it will hurt Ridge.*

Cas isn't lost, especially if she left Kasandral behind. I do wonder if we should have taken him and thrown him into the deepest part of the harbor.

I got a welt just from touching the scabbard. Sardelle rubbed her finger at the memory. Earlier in the night, she had done her best to heal the cut she had received in the fight, but she had a feeling there would always be a scar there that no amount of magic could heal.

True. Just so long as that Therrik doesn't end up with it again.

That would be fine if he put it in storage, or the family crypt, wherever it was he got it.

Maybe more of the castle will collapse before people can dig it out, and it will simply be left under a few tons of stone for all of eternity. Jaxi beamed contentedly.

I'm not sure we should pray for the further devastation of a one-thousand-year-old building that's on the historic register.

I wasn't praying, just smiling as I contemplated Kasandral's entombment.

Dawn brought them to the house, where they were welcomed by a rooster crowing in the yard across the street and a foul-smelling bluish smoke wafting from the chimney.

"Tolemek must be at work already," Sardelle said.

"Does he ever sleep?" Kaika stifled a yawn of her own.

"I don't—"

A shriek came from within the house. Sardelle nearly fell off her horse. It had been a woman's voice, not Tolemek's.

"Who is *that*?" she asked, stretching out with her senses.

"Mrs. Zirkander?" Kaika guessed.

"She's supposed to be staying with a relative," Sardelle said, even though she had already identified the people inside the house. Tolemek, Duck, and Ridge's mom, along with at least a dozen cats, the caged birds, and some other small creatures that had not occupied the house previously. What had happened? Tolemek couldn't have been here for more than a few hours.

"Does she know that?" Kaika dismounted, then waved for Sardelle to hand down her reins. "Go check. I'll take care of the horses."

"You're either being generous, or you don't want to deal with Ridge's screaming mother."

"You're perceptive, as well as serene." Kaika gave her a lazy salute and led the horses around to the back of the house.

Another shriek pierced the early morning quiet as Sardelle opened the front door and peeked inside.

"There are snakes everywhere," Fern cried.

She was spinning around the living room, one hand over her mouth and one pointing. Several new cages and terrariums had been added to the collection of living creatures inhabiting the cottage. They housed snakes, giant spiders, and a venomous lizard Sardelle thought she recognized from Tolemek's lab. At the least, one like it had occupied a terrarium the time she had visited.

Poor Duck stood in front of Fern, patting the air in a placating manner, a placating manner that clearly wasn't placating.

"There are snakes in my house, young man. Snakes. And spiders. Poisonous spiders!"

Sardelle thought about pointing out that venomous was the more accurate adjective, but decided that would do little to calm the woman. Where was Tolemek, anyway? Hiding somewhere and leaving Duck to deal with Fern's wrath?

"Yes, ma'am," Duck said. "I know. I helped carry them in."

"You *helped*?" Fern gaped at him.

"It's just temporary, Mrs. Zirkander," he said. "Until Tolemek can find a real lab again. Uhm, the colonel said you wouldn't be back for a while..."

"I came to check on the cats. And to make my son food. But there's that man, that strange man with all the hair, in my kitchen." She flung her hand toward the door. "And the *smells* he's making in there! Those fumes will kill my birds." This time, she flung her hand toward the cages in the rafters.

Sardelle crept in, following the wall toward the kitchen. Maybe it was cowardly, but she thought she might leave the explaining to Duck and check on Tolemek. Fern spotted her.

"Sardelle." She rushed over and intercepted her.

"Yes?" Sardelle asked. After the night she'd had, she did not want to be interrogated about spiders, but she forced a smile.

"You look tired." Fern clasped her hands, then wrinkled her nose. "And you smell of smoke."

"That's what she gets for traveling with Captain Kaika." Duck smiled, but raised his brows in a question when he met Sardelle's eyes.

"I'll explain soon." Sardelle knew someone would have to share the details as to what had happened, and that it was either up to her or Kaika, but she couldn't bring herself to blurt out that Apex had died. She needed to sit down first and brace herself with coffee, since she felt like doing nothing except sleeping after being up all night again.

Duck's expression grew worried, but he did not question her further.

Now you've got him thinking something happened to Ridge and that you don't want to share it in front of his mom.

I'll explain soon, Sardelle promised.

"Please, you can use my bathtub to wash up. So long as there aren't snakes in it." Fern curled a lip toward a terrarium as she wrapped a sinewy arm around Sardelle's waist. "Come, this way. I'll heat some water for you and make tea. Or do you prefer coffee?"

"I—ah." Emotion thickened in Sardelle's throat, surprising her and making it difficult to get more words out. It had been so long since someone had mothered her, and she hadn't realized how much she had missed it until Fern's solicitous arm came around her. With a pang of longing, she realized she wanted this, wanted to be welcomed by someone, to be part of a family again.

"Nobody offered me coffee," Duck said as Fern steered Sardelle toward the kitchen. "I was *shot*, remember?" Duck clutched his shoulder, though neither of his wounds seemed to be bothering him anymore. That reminded Sardelle that she needed to attend to Kaika's injuries before falling asleep. Kaika was so stoic that one could easily forget she *had* injuries.

As Fern pushed open the kitchen door, she pointed back at Duck. "You move those snakes and spiders out to the shed in the yard, and I'll bring you coffee and apple bread."

"Oh?" Duck brightened. "A lot of apple bread?"

"I brought the ingredients over to make several pans. Ridge forgets to eat, so I have to fatten him up when he's here. A woman likes something on a man to grab on to, right, dear?"

Sardelle flushed, the memory of grabbing on to things in Fern's bedroom coming to mind. Ridge wasn't exactly skinny;

he had all of those nice, lean muscles to hold on to. "I'm fond of his current physique."

Duck grimaced. "I'll get to these cages. Anything to keep from hearing about the colonel's physique."

The familiar tingle of dragon blood washed over Sardelle as she stepped into the kitchen. Six vials hung in a rack on a counter next to Tolemek, who was hunched over a microscope, oblivious to the fat gray cat butting its head against his jaw. Another cat sat on a stack of sketches while watching a hairy-legged spider amble across a rock in a small terrarium.

One of the exterior doors thudded shut, and Fern peeked back out into the living room. "Ridge didn't come back with you, dear?"

Sardelle winced. "No. We were separated. The MPs took him."

"Oh. Well, he'll tell a few stories and charm his way out of any trouble."

Sardelle wasn't so sure about that. She was glad she had an excuse not to mention that Ridge wasn't with the MPs anymore and wasn't anywhere that she could sense him. Since Fern did not believe in magic, there was no point in bringing that up.

"I'm in need of a blacksmith to craft a delivery mechanism for my concept," Tolemek said without lifting his head.

"Is he talking to me or to you?" Fern whispered to Sardelle.

"Is there a local blacksmith?" Sardelle asked.

"Datlesh, several blocks away."

"Then I think he's talking to you."

"Is he always so rude?"

Tolemek frowned over at them, dark circles under his eyes and a frown riding his lips. "Your son has given me an impossible task, no time to do it in, and no resources with which to do it."

"So, yes." Grumbling, Fern headed for the stove. She frowned at all of the equipment cluttering the counters on either side and a kettle boiling something miasmic. "How am I supposed to make that young man something to eat with all of this... *this*?" She batted at the blue steam wafting from the kettle, then threw open the windows.

"Is Cas with you?" Tolemek asked Sardelle. "I didn't—" He glanced at Fern and lowered his voice. "I didn't sense that sword return." He waved vaguely toward the yard.

Sardelle hadn't realized he could sense it too. She groped for a way to tell him that Cas hadn't come back again, but knew she would have to explain the whole night once she started. Maybe it was just as well. The story would not grow any more pleasing for having been delayed.

"Come out into the living room for a couple of minutes, please," Sardelle said. "I'll tell you what happened. Uhm, Fern, the coffee would be welcome. Thank you."

A moment ago, Tolemek had been complaining about not having enough time, but he did not hesitate to walk away from the microscope and lead the way to the living room. His face was grim. He knew something had happened.

Sardelle took a deep breath and followed him, bracing herself to share the news.

* * *

Dawn found Ridge sailing among the low-hanging clouds off the Iskandian coast, appreciating the sea breeze tugging at his scarf, the thrum of the propeller in his ears, and the subtle vibration of the flier under his butt. This was where he was meant to be. He wished he could forget the trouble he had left behind, but he kept worrying that he hadn't been able to contact Sardelle and let her know where he was going. He also worried that he was on a duck hunt when the ducks had all flown south for the winter. He was going entirely on what Therrik had believed. Who knew if anything reliable existed in that brain?

Even if Therrik was right about the lighthouse, there were more than a hundred of them to search. He had already visited two and found them empty aside from surprised lighthouse keepers he had roused from bed. He refused to feel dejected until he checked the one on that island he had been thinking of, as that seemed an ideal spot. But he couldn't help but realize it could take weeks for him to investigate all of the lighthouses, even if he ruled out half of them as impractical.

Ridge dipped below the clouds so he could gauge how far up the coast he had gone. He had passed the town of Crasgar's Bay, and the waves churning and breaking against the rocks below told him he was flying over the thirty-mile-long Fury's Cauldron.

"Twenty more miles to the island lighthouse," he said, knowing the spot was right in the center of the Cauldron. Briefly, he wondered why he had spoken aloud. He had his communication crystal activated in case anyone tried to contact him, but he had already flown out of range of the base. There probably wasn't much point in having the device active, except that he hoped he might chance across some of his people on the way back from their fool's mission. When he had left, he hadn't risked lighting lamps in the hangar or checking the telegraph machine, not when he had worried that the MPs would catch up with him at any moment. No, he had pushed open the rolling doors, then run straight to the two-man flier. He was certain Therrik hadn't had any authorization to let him go—his disappearance had probably already been discovered. Had there been fliers and pilots to spare, someone might have sent one after him, but there was no one in the city left to chase him into the skies. He wouldn't likely suffer further punishment until he returned. If he didn't find the king, he wasn't sure if he dared return at all.

Before he could lament his fate further, movement in the distance caught his eyes. A dark shape flew through the gray clouds, its size too great to belong to a bird. The craft was heading in his direction, toward the capital, so hope rose in his breast. Maybe one of his people was returning.

Ridge tapped the crystal. "This is Colonel Zirkander from Wolf Squadron. Identify yourself."

Initially, Sardelle's communication crystals had only gone out to Tiger and Wolf Squadrons as a test, but everyone had seen the practicality of them—so much so that nobody had questioned too much exactly what technology had produced them—and they had been installed in all of the military fliers across Iskandia. Thus, Ridge expected a prompt answer.

Instead, only silence came back to him. He repeated the call. The dark craft rose, the clouds obscuring it from view. An uneasy feeling replaced the hope Ridge had felt. He nudged his flier upward, picking a route that would let him intercept the craft if it did not change its route. It *might* be a non-military flier—there were a few handfuls of decommissioned and private ones out there, such as the two craft that were maintained by Harborgard Castle. But it might be something else too. The clouds and the early morning light had made it hard to tell the color, but it definitely had dark paint, dark paint that reminded Ridge of the unmanned fliers that had tried to shoot him and Sardelle down in Cofahre.

Seeing one here wasn't entirely unexpected, but it was surely unwelcome. He had hoped they would have more time to retrieve the king and get the squadrons back to the city.

As he searched the sky, the clouds whispered past his face, leaving droplets of moisture on his goggles. He wiped them with his scarf. With the visibility poor, he would need all the vision he could claim to spot another flier up here. Since his own propeller buzzed in his ears, he would never hear an enemy approach, not until a machine gun rang out, so his eyes were all he had up here. His eyes and his intuition.

If he were dealing with another human being, he might have weaved around, expecting the other pilot to take evasive moves to avoid being found, but those unmanned fliers had used simple patterns, almost like machines obeying a punch-card program. He didn't doubt that the vial of dragon blood attached to the control board gave the craft uncanny intelligence, but it couldn't replace a human brain. He hoped.

The dark shape, its body almost identical to a one-man Iskandian flier, soared into view again. It was still flying south, in the direction of the capital, but at a higher altitude than Ridge had anticipated. He grimaced. If it fired from up there, it would have the advantage.

He pulled back on the flight stick, climbing at the same time as he carved to the side, knowing he needed to reach it but hoping to make a harder target as he closed. If it was a scouting craft, it might not be programmed to fire, but he couldn't bet on that. It had twin guns mounted above the nose, and he squinted, spotting something else on its belly, something black and blocky.

"Seven gods, is that a camera?" Ridge thumped his hand on the side of the cockpit. His people were supposed to be developing an aerial camera, and he'd seen prototypes on dirigibles, but they hadn't managed anything lightweight enough for the fliers yet. "Damned Cofah don't need to worry about weight when they don't have pilots," he growled.

The bangs of a machine gun rang out like hail on a tin roof. Cursing himself for having been caught staring at that camera for too long, Ridge threw his craft into a barrel roll, then banked into a thick cloud. Belatedly, he decided there was probably no point in trying to hide from something without eyes. That dragon blood would allow the unmanned craft to sense him in the same way as Sardelle would.

Nonetheless, his swoops and rolls kept the bullets from striking him. As he came out of the cloud on the far side, he pulled up, climbing hard, hoping to rise above the enemy craft. Despite the fire, it had not diverted from its route to chase him.

"Must have more pictures to take," Ridge grumbled and turned to chase it. He was *not* going to let it sail in and collect images of the capital, especially not when he had left the hangar door yawning wide open, where the empty interior would be all too visible.

"You are *not* going home," Ridge announced, accelerating after the craft. "Or back to some mobile base." It horrified him to think that a landing dirigible or carrier ship might be waiting fifty miles off the coast for its return.

He jammed one hand into his pocket to rub his wooden dragon figurine, then focused all of his concentration on the craft. The wind railed at his face, burning his cheeks as he struggled to catch it. He hated to think that the Cofah might have made a craft that was faster than his, but his was a two-seater and had a pilot. The other flier had nothing except the camera and the guns to weigh it down.

Ridge tilted his wings slightly to take advantage of wind

gusting from the rear. He wasn't sure if that was what helped, but he finally closed on the Cofah craft, cutting in on a diagonal approach rather than from straight behind its tail.

At first, it did not make any evasive moves, and he rested his thumb on the trigger for his machine gun, thinking he might get an easy shot. Then, as he pulled within range, it dropped down, spinning through the clouds. At the first dip of the nose, Ridge reacted. He cut the angle tighter and gained ground. Though he was still at the edge of machine-gun range, he fired, hoping for a lucky shot. He thought he clipped a wing, but that was not a vital target. He needed to take out that camera—and the vial of dragon blood powering the craft. The latter would be protected by armor, but he fired again, aiming for the body.

The craft veered again, but he clung to it like a leech stuck on a man's ankle. Thanks to the crashed flier he and Sardelle had dissected, he had a good idea of where that vial should be. He swooped left and right as they dove, trying to hit the body from the side. His bullets riddled the fuselage. Smoke wafted from the tail of the craft. As its dive turned into a plummet, both craft dropped below the clouds, and the rocks of the Cauldron came into view. Ridge probably should have felt fear at the speed he was maintaining and at the rapid way those rocks were approaching, but the exhilaration of the hunt thrummed through him. He fired again to make sure that craft smashed into the sea, never to report back to its home. He would pull up well before he risked crashing himself. He glimpsed that camera on its belly and fired at that. It was knocked off, smoke rising as it flew away from the craft. Good. It could not be retrieved.

As he was about to pull up, certain the unmanned flier would crash, a massive boom rang out. A ball of orange flame exploded right above the sea. Startled, Ridge yanked on the flight stick. The shockwave slammed into the belly of his craft. He would have been bucked from his seat if not for his harness. As it was, the force of the blow rattled his teeth—and every nut holding his flier together. For several seconds, he had no control of the craft, and he envisioned his wings being torn off and the body tumbling into the sea.

Finally, the steering responded to him and he flattened out, skimming scant feet above the waves breaking below. Water sprayed the side of his face, and he gulped and glanced back. The flames had disappeared, leaving only bits and pieces the size of confetti floating on the surface. Unless he had struck the dragon blood vial and that had somehow caused that much energy to be unleashed, he couldn't see how such a powerful explosion could have been the result of anything on the plane blowing up.

"Note to self," Ridge said, ignoring the tremor in his voice. "The Cofah unmanned fliers are rigged to explode if it becomes clear their mission will fail."

He wished he had foreseen that. He had very nearly been taken out by that trap. Even worse than death would have been being killed by something without a brain.

"Embarrassing," he muttered and was suddenly glad he was out of Jaxi's range. She would have had even more biting comments.

A creak came from the frame of his flier. Ridge sighed and veered toward the coast. He would need to land and make sure he hadn't taken any serious damage. He looked around to get his bearings, then twitched in surprise. The whitewashed tower of the island lighthouse rose up less than a mile away.

Instead of heading toward the mainland, he veered in that direction. Had he been in his one-man flier, he could not have landed on the compact island—there was little more to it than the lighthouse in the center, a few tufts of grass in a small yard, and the rocks raising it up above the surf. But so long as his thrusters hadn't been blown off in that explosion, he would have room enough to land this craft.

Ridge wiped droplets of water from his goggles and tried to determine if anyone was home. It had grown light enough that he could not see if a lamp burned in the lantern room, but a keeper ought to be on duty around the clock. A bunkhouse and storage area hugged the base of the tower. He thought he spotted a figure in the window—someone looking out toward him. In case he was correct, he offered a cheerful wave.

He swept around the tower once to make sure nobody with

guns was waiting in the grass. If a kidnap victim was being held here, he would doubtlessly have guards. Not that he could go anywhere. The shoreline was barely visible from here, and nothing about the churning waves and sharp rocks said a swim would be advisable.

Not seeing anyone outside, Ridge activated the thrusters and lowered to the ground. The port side one gave a hiccup and only operated at half power. He gritted his teeth, trying to compensate and keep the flier level. A bevy of seagulls squawked and flew away.

"Critics," Ridge grumbled, finally feeling his wheels bump against the ground. He came down hard on one side, but did not think he had done any more damage.

The door in the base of the lighthouse opened. Two big men with short hair, broad shoulders, and nondescript clothing walked out. One was missing an eye. The other had a nose that had been broken at least three times. Right away, Ridge knew two things. One, these were not lighthouse keepers, and two, this was the right place. What he didn't know was how he was going to avoid being shot. Damn them—why couldn't they have come out looking belligerent and thugly while he had been in the air? Now it was too late to turn the flier toward them and put his machine guns to use.

Chapter 13

AWARE OF THE GOONS WATCHING, Ridge climbed slowly out of his cockpit. Normally, he would have a pistol and a dagger as part of his flight uniform, but Therrik had been too busy shoving him against the bars to offer the use of a weapon for this adventure. Ridge might be able to come out on top in a physical fight with one of the big men, but both watched him carefully, the butts of their loaded rifles resting on the ground next to them. Those rifles were Mark 500s, the type of sniper firearm Lieutenant Ahn favored. Ridge hoped that didn't mean these men were acolytes of her father, but he wouldn't be surprised to find that Ahnsung was tied in with the kidnapping somehow.

"Either of you fellows have a wrench? Any mechanical skills? Got a small problem." Ridge waved in the direction of the explosion, hoping they had seen it. If he was lucky, they might believe the aerial skirmish had brought him to this island rather than a search for the king.

The men exchanged glances, then looked back at him without responding. Ah, a friendly group of kidnappers.

He patted the side of his flier. "No wrenches? No beer, either, I suppose?"

"Early in the day for drinking," one finally said. His voice was rough, as if he had been punched in the throat a few times in his life, as well as in his nose.

"It's never too early in the day for a drink, especially if you've been shot at recently." And if you've been up all night, Ridge added silently. He scratched his jaw and pretended to look at the men for the first time, then he squinted up at the lighthouse. "You two the keepers here? You sure you don't have any tools? I took some damage when that other flier blew up. Need to check the thrusters. You probably noticed that wasn't the smoothest landing you've seen."

They looked at each other again. Maybe they shared a brain. Ridge kept his stance easy and offered an amiable smile whenever they glanced in his direction.

"No tools," the broken-nosed speaker finally said. "Fix your flier and get out of here."

Well, at least they weren't shooting him outright. While he watched them out of the corner of his eye, Ridge pulled his tiny toolkit out of the cockpit. Even though he knew the contents by heart, he prodded at them, thinking in terms of finding something that would help him overcome those two. There wasn't much, neither for tackling enemies nor for fixing the flier. The lightweight pliers, screwdriver, and wrench were about useful enough to pull a splinter out of the hull if necessary. He squeezed some patch tar out of its tube and rubbed it between his fingers. In theory, one could use it to plug a leak for the duration of a short flight.

He walked around the flier, checking out the thrusters and inspecting the rest of the fuselage while he stole glances at the men. They hadn't gone back inside. They had walked over to the rocks to talk to each other, but they were definitely keeping an eye on him.

With the waves crashing below them, Ridge couldn't hear many of their words, but he caught his name. It might have been his imagination, but he thought he heard the words "kill him" come out too. He hoped the entire sentence was, "He's the brave and noble Colonel Zirkander, so we *can't* kill him," but he wasn't going to bet on it.

Ridge hammered at the dented thruster housing while formulating a plan not to be killed. The only way he would have the advantage would be from the air. If he could keep those two from running back into the lighthouse, he should be able to shoot them down before they shot him. Maybe. He would definitely have better odds on that than on trying to overpower them from the ground, especially when he did not have a weapon. The problem would be keeping the men from running inside to the safety of the lighthouse. It was built from stone, and his bullets wouldn't do much to damage the sturdy walls. Another problem was that they hadn't actually done anything to him yet. Even though he was ninety-nine percent certain they had been placed here to guard the king, Ridge did not have proof of that. It would be nice if Angulus would pop his head out the door. Ridge wished he had Sardelle along to sense through the walls. He would even settle for her snarky sword.

Ridge pulled a few pieces of shrapnel out of his wings and decided that was all he could manage from here. The thrusters did not play a role once he was in the air, and he could manage another lopsided landing if he had to. He rubbed the patch tar he hadn't used, his body heat keeping it from hardening. A thought popped into his mind. Perhaps he might patch something else on this island.

Without asking permission, Ridge ambled toward the lighthouse door. He forced himself not to run or hurry, though he worried they wouldn't let him get close enough for his plan.

Sure enough, Broken Nose called out, "Where are you going? I told you, there aren't any tools in there."

"Need to use the lav," Ridge said without slowing down, even though sweat was trickling down his spine. Both of those rifles swung in his direction. "You've got one of those in there, don't you?"

"It's not for visitors. Use a rock." The man jerked his rifle toward the jagged black boulders that comprised most of the island.

"I've got to do more than piss." The door was only five steps away now. "It'll just take a minute, then I'll head out." Three steps. Two.

"Stop right there." Both men jerked their rifles to the crooks of their shoulders and sighted along the barrels.

Ridge halted, one step from the door. "Easy boys." He turned slowly toward them, his hands up. He kept his left fingers curled enough to hide the goo on his palm—and to keep it warm with his body heat, so it wouldn't harden, not yet.

"You'll go *now*."

"You're sure I can't..." Ridge tilted his head toward the door.

"No."

Ridge sighed and lowered his hands. "Look, I'll pay not to use the rocks." He dug in his pocket with one hand and, holding his breath, stuck his other hand out and leaned against the door, flattening the patch tar to one of the hinges.

He had barely touched the metal when a shot rang out. He jumped and skittered backward. Belatedly, he realized it had been a warning shot, the bullet burrowing into the ground at his feet. Both muzzles were pointed at his chest now, so he didn't try to approach the door again.

"Let's kill him," the heretofore silent one said. Ridge had liked it more when the man hadn't been speaking.

"It's gods-blighted Zirkander, you idiot. We can't shoot him."

"I can." Silent grinned unwholesomely.

Ridge hadn't managed to cover the hinge with as much of the patch tar as he had hoped to, but at least it was sticking. Hands spread, he stepped away from the building. "All right, I'll go."

The pair of muzzles followed him as he crossed the small lawn back to his flier. This time, he didn't bother pretending he wasn't rushing. When he reached the craft, he couldn't pull himself into the cockpit quickly enough. He fired it up, relieved when the propeller and both thrusters roared to life, the crystal glowing intensely from its casing as it poured magical power into both components of the craft. There wouldn't have been room for a typical wheeled takeoff.

From the higher position, he knew all of his actions wouldn't be visible to the men on the ground, so he slumped down slightly and peered up at the top of the lighthouse, toward the windows in the lantern room. He wasn't truly expecting to see anyone, but his heart lurched up into his throat. The familiar broad features of King Angulus looked down at him through the glass. Angulus didn't wave—it looked like his arms were pulled behind his back—but he was standing up and definitely alive.

A surge of certainty filled Ridge, the belief that his plan was right. He took off, staying low in the cockpit so the goons wouldn't be able to target him easily. Unfortunately, the flier wasn't impenetrable to bullets, so he could be shot through the lightweight hull, but this was a risk he had to take. Being in the air bolstered his confidence somewhat, as did the fact that he had machine guns, versus their pump-action rifles. They shouldn't have more than ten shots each.

"Not that ten shots couldn't kill a man," Ridge muttered as he rose.

He soared toward the clouds, pretending he meant to fly off, that the guards would never see him again. He glanced back and spotted them lowering their rifles and walking toward the door. It wouldn't take them long to figure out how to pry off the patch tar, so he had to discombobulate them before they did. Besides, they would have less cover out in the open.

Ridge banked, the sky tilting, then the ocean and the island filling his vision again. Even though he had shot countless enemies during his career, his heart hammered with dread and fear at the idea of shooting people on the ground, Iskandian people. But they had chosen their fate. He had to harden himself to that.

First, he rubbed his dragon figurine for luck. Then, like death itself, he swooped down, thumb on the trigger. The men realized what was happening immediately. One sprinted for the door, while the other dropped to one knee to shoot. Ridge slumped as low as he could while still being able to see his targets. He aimed for the shooter first, unleashing a round of ammunition.

A bullet slammed through his windshield, passing so close to his head that he nearly lost his cap. Hells, maybe these *were* some of Ahnsung's people. He zigzagged in the sky, trying to make himself a more difficult target while he continued inexorably downward. He kept firing, twin streams of bullets hammering the ground as he sought the plane he needed, the angle that would allow him to hit the men. But they were sprinting around now, doing a good job of avoiding his run, and there was no way to pivot the guns without turning the craft.

Another bullet slammed into the hull under the cockpit. He had no idea if it made it through, but imagined it wedged into his seat cushion.

One of the men shouted. He was pulling at the door latch. Ridge allowed himself a grim smile. Maybe that would teach him the folly of denying a man use of the toilet.

The men stopped firing as his flier neared the ground. Ridge wobbled the wings, hoping they would think he had been shot and was out of control. Indeed, they must have believed the flier would crash right into them. They abandoned their rifles and raced for the rocks overlooking the churning water. He peppered the ground with bullets before pulling up at the last second, the grass stirring from the wind the flier created.

He rose quickly, gaining altitude, then turned so he could make another run. The men were scrambling down the rocks. One leaped into the water. Ridge angled downward again, speeding straight toward them. The second one shook his fist and yelled obscenities that Ridge could not hear over the wind blasting past his ears. Fists and obscenities were far less worrisome than bullets. Ridge fired again, his rounds slamming into the rocks all around the man. He leaped from his perch, splashing into the water. Both men disappeared under the surface.

Ridge swooped past the island again, giving the all-is-right hand signal to the lighthouse windows. This time he didn't see the king. Was there someone else inside guarding him? Someone who had yanked him into some room after seeing his comrades assaulted? Ridge would have to prepare himself for another fight when he landed, but he made another pass before heading back to the lawn. He spotted the guards swimming toward the distant shore. Judging by the uneven strokes, neither was a natural, and one must have been hit, because he was paddling with one arm. Ridge couldn't muster any sympathy for them, not when they had been holding the king hostage.

After making sure they were heading away from the island, he brought his flier down again. He hopped out before the propeller had stopped spinning and raced to the dropped rifles. He would go in armed this time.

With one of the rifles slung across his back and the other in his hands, ready to fire, he ran to the door. He was about to pull out his knife to pry free the patch tar when the door flew open so forcefully that it was like an elephant had kicked it.

Half expecting an army, Ridge aimed the rifle and wished he had some cover to hide behind. The grass swaying at his calves would not do much to stop bullets.

But only a single unarmed figure strode out of the lighthouse. Iron shackles hugged the king's wrists, though the chain that should have bound them together had been broken, the ends dangling. His usually short and tidy hair had grown shaggy, and a few weeks' worth of beard had sprouted on his usually clean-shaven jaw. Though unwashed, he did not appear gaunt or injured, aside from some bruises on the knuckles on his right hand.

"I'd hug you if you weren't aiming a gun at my chest," Angulus said.

Ridge hastily lowered the weapon and snapped up a salute. "It's just as well, Sire. I think there may be a rule about soldiers hugging kings. Impropriety and all."

"I think that's only if the soldier is doing the hugging."

"Oh? If I were a king, I wouldn't mind hugs, especially from female soldiers."

Had General Ort been there, he would have kicked Ridge under the table—or under the grass—and warned him not to be so familiar—or lippy—with their liege. But Angulus didn't seem offended.

"I bet." The king looked toward the waves breaking to the north. "That was a Cofah flier?"

He had seen the battle? Ridge held back a grimace. He would have preferred not to have witnesses for his nosedive into an explosion. "An unmanned one powered by dragon blood, yes, Sire. It had a camera."

Angulus's jaw clenched. He scanned the gray sky, as if more fliers might sail out of the clouds at any moment. "You came here alone?"

"Yes, Sire."

"Is the rest of your squadron defending the city? I assume there are more Cofah out there."

"Ah, it's not my squadron at the moment. Why don't you

climb in, Sire? I'll tell you what's been going on while we head back."

Angulus sighed. "I'm not going to like this story, am I?"

"*I* didn't when I got back from the Cofahre mission. Perhaps you'll be a less discerning audience."

"That the mission where you misplaced your commanding officer?"

Ridge had hoped the king might have forgotten that detail. "Uhm, yes, but there were extenuating circumstances."

"Such as that you didn't like Colonel Therrik?"

"Such as that Colonel Therrik is an ass." Ridge almost felt guilty saying that when Therrik had been the one to let him out of jail. The ease with which he had escaped the base suggested that it hadn't been a trap, as hard as that was to believe.

"But a loyal ass," Angulus said.

"I've... come to realize that, Sire. Do you, ah, know who kidnapped you, by chance?"

The creases at the corners of Angulus's eyes deepened. "My wife," he said tightly. "She didn't approve of the heinous outbreak of witches in the city. Her words."

"Witches? Sardelle and... Tolemek?" Thanks to the conversation he had eavesdropped on before the Cofahre mission, Ridge knew the king was already aware of Sardelle, so he didn't worry about mentioning her. He figured Angulus had put the pieces together on Tolemek too.

Angulus nodded. "Yes."

"Tolemek may be even more offended than Sardelle at being called a witch. Witches are girls, aren't they? I admit I'm still a neophyte when it comes to magic."

Angulus slanted him a look the Ridge could not read. "My wife even suggested that *you* might be a witch."

"I've been told I don't have a drop of dragon blood in my veins. But either way, I'd prefer to be considered a wizard. Or a warlock. Something with manly connotations. Or male ones at least."

Angulus sighed. "My willingness to use Tolemek may be what really riled the queen up, but your woman's presence in the city got her antsy too. She's always hated any hint of magic, any hint that it might come back into the world and be more prominent. As paradoxical as that was."

"Oh? Why is that?" Ridge stopped below the cockpit, wondering if he should offer the king a boost up. Angulus was stocky, strong, and in his forties, so he ought to be able to handle climbing up, but it seemed like there might be some rule about making one's king clamber into a flier on his own.

Angulus jumped, caught the lip of the passenger pit, and pulled himself up easily. The flier creaked as his weight settled into it. He was a big man and never would have made the qualifications to be a pilot. With their combined weight, it would be a slow trip back.

"It's not widely known," Angulus said, giving Ridge a long assessing look. Wondering if he could share some secret with a mouthy pilot?

Ridge could keep secrets, but he didn't want to be seen as nosy or pry into something he shouldn't know, so he pulled himself into the cockpit and belted himself in. He spotted the two guards sitting on a wet rock about a quarter mile from the island. It might have been his imagination, since it was hard to see details at that distance, but he thought one was pointing at a black triangular fin cutting through the water. He hoped so. Those two deserved sharks.

"Her mother was a witch," Angulus said after such a long pause that Ridge had given up the conversation as finished.

"What?" He twisted in his seat.

"She thinks I don't know. Her mother knew potions and had a few magical tricks, nothing like your Sardelle, I don't think, but enough."

"Sardelle is from another time," Ridge said, though discussing her with the king made him uncomfortable. Even if he had originally mentioned her name, he still had a sense that he should do his best to keep people from knowing what she was. Still, if anyone could make it acceptable for her to stay in the city—to stay with *him*—Angulus would be the person.

"Yes, I read Captain Heriton's report. Anyway, Nia's mother

used her skills to convince my first wife to commit suicide. You remember that?"

"I remember the suicide, Sire, that the papers said she walked off one of the castle towers and fell to her death. It was almost twenty-five years ago, wasn't it?" Ridge had been fifteen then, and Angulus wouldn't have been much older. Nineteen? Twenty? He had been prince at the time, his own father still alive and ruling; Ridge remembered that.

"She was *coerced* into walking off. I never believed she would have committed suicide, so I investigated it. I was so obsessed that my father got fed up with it and sent me off to serve in the army. I loved my first wife very much." Angulus looked wistfully toward the sea, not searching for enemy fliers this time, Ridge sensed. "When I returned from five years of duty, my father had arranged a new marriage for me. He'd let me choose the first time—he always hated arranged marriages, since his own had been a shambles—but he was sick by then and wanted to make sure grandchildren were on the way to secure his legacy. Little did he know Nia would never have children." Angulus shook his head.

"So, if the queen's mother arranged your wife's death, does that mean she had something to do with the new marriage?"

Angulus nodded. "Nia has never admitted to it, but I think her mother gave potions to my father and made him amenable to the idea. Nia's mother was nothing if not ambitious, far more so than Nia was. She never actually *wanted* to marry me." The king's lips twisted, his eyes edged with bitterness. "She was seeing a young officer at the time and didn't want to give him up. You've met him."

Ridge could only lift his shoulders, not having the vaguest idea as to who he knew who might have attracted the queen's eye more than twenty years earlier.

"Therrik," Angulus said.

If Ridge hadn't been strapped in, he would have fallen out of his seat. "What? *Why?*"

Angulus spread his palm toward the sky. "Who can understand the fancies of women?"

Ridge could only shake his head.

"I don't think I was an... unreasonable husband, but we never loved each other, not the way my first wife and I did, and probably not the way she and her strapping young soldier did."

"Ugh, Sire, could we not talk about Therrik's... straps?"

"She eventually learned what her mother had done to arrange the marriage, and she's been an advocate of destroying everyone and everything tainted with magic ever since. I didn't realize she felt quite so strongly as to have orchestrated all of this, but when I hired Deathmaker... That may be what pushed her over the edge. I can't say that I don't understand our people loathing him for his crimes, but I have to make my decisions based on logic, not emotion. I have to think about what's best for the kingdom, and I don't have to tell you how outnumbered and outgunned we are by the Cofah. These last couple of decades have been less difficult than the previous ones, thanks to the fliers and the crystals, but now that the Cofah have figured out how to make equal—if not superior—aircraft and weapons..." Once again, his gaze drifted toward the sea where the unmanned flier had crashed. "I couldn't pass up the chance to have a brilliant weapons maker on our side."

Ridge wanted to object to the idea of Tolemek as *brilliant*, but he supposed it was true, at least insofar as making toxic death went. And hadn't he himself sent the dragon blood to Tolemek so he could make something useful? He was making the same choice the king had. Did that make him logical? He hoped so. Sometimes, such as when Apex looked at him with feelings of hurt in his eyes, Ridge wondered if he was the one in the wrong, the one betraying his people.

"We just have to destroy all of the dragon blood they have left, Sire. All of their clever weapons—and the flier designs they *stole* from us—rely on using that for an energy source. We took a lot of it when we left that volcano facility, and we found the source of it so they won't be able to get more in the future. They'll only have what they stockpiled and stored in different facilities." Ridge raised his eyebrows, silently asking if the king knew this much of the story. According to Apex and Kaika, the king had already been kidnapped when they had been reporting in.

"Does that mean that you or the assassin my wife hired succeeded in killing the dragon?" Angulus asked.

Ah, so he did know about the dragon. "We succeeded in freeing it from a Cofah lab, Sire."

"So it could fly back and join forces with their army?"

"I'm hoping it's not in the mood to join forces with their anything." Ridge remembered the way both Tolemek's sister and the dragon had considered his team of Iskandians to be enemies and wondered if that was a vain hope. "Its only loyalty seems to be to Tolemek's sister."

Angulus blinked. "It's not *here*, is it?"

"On the continent? I don't think so. They flew off across the ocean together. Sardelle did extend an invitation to the girl to come to her for instruction. Apparently, Tylie is quite the talent."

"I'm now envisioning a girl riding a dragon landing in the castle courtyard. That will *really* distress the queen."

"Would Tylie be welcome if she did come? By you?" Ridge almost asked about Phelistoth, too, but he wasn't sure how he felt about inviting a dragon to roost here. His mother would probably try to feed it and invite it in the house with the cats.

"Better here than in Cofahre. I don't know how to make our people accept them, but we can't let the Cofah have any more advantages." Angulus thumped on the side of the flier. "Get this beast in the air, Zirkander. I need to see what's going on at home, and you need to tell me where your squadron is."

"Yes, Sire."

As Ridge piloted the flier off the ground, he allowed himself to feel carefully optimistic about finding a solution that would allow Sardelle to stay with him, but it was hard to think that far in the future. Not with the wreckage from that unmanned flier sitting at the bottom of the Cauldron, one of what could be hundreds of fliers poised to attack his homeland.

* * *

Sardelle woke slowly, aware of several voices speaking softly around her and the chirp of birds in the rafters. She had fallen asleep on the couch after healing Kaika, sending her to the bedroom to sleep, and informing Duck and Tolemek what had happened in the castle. She did not know how much time had passed, but had a sense that she had slept hard.

"I wouldn't have expected a powerful sorceress to drool," someone observed. Sardelle did not recognize the voice. "That's not mentioned in the fairy tales."

Confused and worried, she wiped her mouth and opened her eyes. Sunlight slanted in the window, framing two male figures and making it difficult to see their faces.

"She doesn't usually." That was Ridge. He lowered a hand, touching the top of her head gently, and her worry faded. As long as he was here, she didn't care who the other man was. "I hear it was a rough night."

She still couldn't see his face. Had someone told him about Apex?

No, Kaika just woke up too. I just hinted of trouble. I didn't think he would want to hear about dead pilots from me.

No, probably not. Sardelle supposed it was cowardly to wish that Jaxi *had* delivered the news, so she wouldn't have to.

I did tell him that you were worried and that he had better stop here to see you before delivering his cargo to the capital. He came into my range earlier this afternoon, Jaxi added.

His cargo? Sardelle sat up at the same time as Ridge settled onto the couch beside her.

He wrapped an arm around her shoulders and pulled her close, resting his face against her hair. She wasn't sure if the hug was for her sake or for his, but she returned it, sliding both arms around his waist, relieved to have him back close.

You're canoodling in front of the king, in case you didn't realize.

I—*oh*. Sardelle pulled back enough to look at Ridge's face, then toward the stocky figure beside the couch. "You found him?"

An obvious question, she supposed, but she *had* just woken up. She couldn't be expected to be at her sharpest. She shifted toward the edge of the seat, thinking she should get up and curtsy. Or genuflect. Hells, what was the proper protocol in this century?

"Yes," Ridge said. "Kaika was relieved to see him but also distressed that she didn't get to come along on the rescue. I explained that she wouldn't have fit in the flier, but..." He hitched a shoulder.

"All of the women here seem distressed," the king observed, looking around the living room.

Sardelle's first thought was that Cas had returned and that was who he was talking about, but Ridge's mother hustled through, carrying a basket of towels, her face tense. She blurted a quick, "My liege," before passing through into the washroom.

"That's my fault for not warning my mother that a king was coming to visit, Sire," Ridge said. "Apparently the snakes and spiders are further adding to her distress."

I could have given her a couple of hours' warning if she believed in me, Jaxi said.

Sardelle stood up and went with a curtsey, bowing her head. Genuflecting had gone out of style centuries before her time, and she took a guess toward less formality in this age rather than more. "My liege, it is an honor to meet you." It was going to be less of an honor to explain that his wife had been buried under a pile of rubble, and that it had been a result of her snooping around in his castle.

"Is it?" The king sounded amused. King—what was his name?—Angulus. "Who ruled Iskandia in your time?"

Your time. He knew more about her than she did about him. That probably wasn't a good thing.

"King Astarak," Sardelle said.

"I believe he was my great, great, great and a dozen more

greats uncle. Any resemblance?" Angulus turned his head from side to side, offering her a good look at his broad features. He would be handsome when he got a shave and into clothes that were not torn and didn't smell of sweat and mildew. He was younger than she had first realized, perhaps in his late forties. With his stocky build, he looked more like a warrior or someone who did manual labor for a living, rather than a man who sat at a desk—or on a throne—all day.

"Astarak was short, skinny, and had big teeth that made people compare him to a rat," Sardelle said, though she wasn't comfortable with the familiarity. Even if she had been in the castle long ago and spoken to her King Astarak, this wasn't her king or her world anymore. And as she had seen and heard all too clearly, she was not welcome here as an ally—or anything else.

"Oh," Angulus said. "I believe I'll hope for a lack of resemblance then."

"He was friendly and well-liked by the people. After watching his three older brothers die to assassins, he figured he had better have the personality in the family. They were troubled times."

Angulus sighed. "Yes, they all are."

Ridge? I don't know where I stand or what he knows, or... I know nothing.

Nothing at all? Ridge twitched his eyebrows upward as he stood and took her hand. *Just how long were you asleep?*

From his humor—and the king's, as well—he definitely had not been told about Apex yet. Or the queen. Ridge was obviously pleased to have found Angulus and brought him back. And, if the king had been stuck in a lighthouse for weeks, that could account for the ease with which he carried himself now. He must be relieved to be free.

I need to let you know what happened last night, Ridge. It's... not good.

Ridge's expression sobered. *I saw Duck sitting on the fence out back, staring into the mud like he's lost his closest friend. I haven't been out to see him yet.*

Sardelle closed her eyes, not wanting to have to tell Ridge

that his assessment of Duck was accurate, nor did she want to hurt him, or have him disappointed in her. Yet, she feared it was inevitable. *If only we had known you had the king's location...* She frowned at him, wondering how he had found the right lighthouse. *We needn't have stayed in the castle at all. If we hadn't gone to see the queen...*

"What happened?" Ridge murmured, squeezing her hand. Silently, he added, *I'm sorry I couldn't find you to tell you I'd gotten away and that I was leaving. I was afraid there would be pursuit. There still may be.* He grimaced toward the front door. *I tried contacting Jaxi, in case you were monitoring me, but she must have been busy.*

He was locked up in a jail cell, Jaxi said. *I didn't think anything would be worth monitoring there. Besides, we were sneaking into the castle then. I did inform him that you were here as soon as he flew back into range of my senses.*

I know, Jaxi. It's fine. Sardelle shifted her attention back to Ridge, though she glanced at the king to make sure he wasn't looking at them suspiciously for simply staring silently at each other. Some of the cats had found him and were rubbing past his legs. He had bent to pat one.

If we can find a quiet place, I could explain, Sardelle told Ridge. *Or show you what happened, I guess. I don't know if I can explain exactly.*

That bad, huh?

Sardelle could only nod.

I have bad news of my own, but I'll let you go first. We're not going to be able to stay here long. Need to get the king back to the castle and see if I can talk him into giving me command of my squadron again. I'm hoping that some of our fliers are already on their way home. I don't think we're going to have much time.

A door clicked open, and Ridge's mother walked into the room again, this time with two neatly folded towels and a bar of cat-shaped soap on top.

"My liege," she said and dropped to one knee, her head bowed as she held out the towels. So much for Sardelle's guess on genuflecting. "Please accept the use of my modest bathing facilities before you return to the city."

"Is your mother telling me that I smell, Zirkander?" Angulus asked.

"I believe so, Sire. Politely."

"My kidnappers only had enough water for drinking. They weren't open to bathing sessions."

"Perfectly understandable, Sire."

"Mrs. Zirkander, I don't want you to go to any trouble," Angulus said as the cat he had been petting noticed he had stopped and started bumping against his leg again. "I'd thought to have your son fly me straight back after he told his powerful allies they need to hurry back to town to help with the defenses. Assuming they're willing to do so." He lifted his brows toward Sardelle.

Her mouth dangled open. Was he asking for her help? Or simply acknowledging that Ridge wanted her help? She would have been honored either way, but knew his feelings would change as soon as he learned about his wife.

"Powerful allies?" Fern mouthed and frowned toward Sardelle.

"Yes, Tolemek," Ridge said. "I'm hoping that the addition of snakes to the house is a sign that he's been working hard on weapons to fight the Cofah, and that they're not something you decided to add to your collection."

"Absolutely not." Fern sniffed—and seemed to forget that Angulus had looked at Sardelle at the mention of powerful allies.

One more omission that would come out eventually, changing the way these people looked at her. Sardelle kept her face neutral, though inside, she wilted a little more.

"Sire," Ridge said, "I think you should take the bath offer. Your staff will be more amenable to following your orders if you smell good. Or at least less bad."

Angulus hesitated, but then accepted the towels. Fern's arms must have growing tired from holding them out.

He picked up the soap bar. "Is this a cat?"

"It is, Sire," Ridge said, "and it'll leave you smelling like flowers. I haven't yet discussed the notion of creating some manly scents with my mom."

"Manly scents?" Fern's brow wrinkled.

"I was thinking of pine trees. Or gun oil. Or the smell of a cockpit."

"What does a cockpit smell like?" Sardelle asked, drawn in, despite her grim thoughts.

"Wood, leather, sweat, desperation."

"Sexy."

Angulus looked dubiously at the cat soap, but let Fern lead him away to the washroom. Sardelle wondered if he usually bathed himself or had servants to handle the scrubbing. After being imprisoned in the bowels of a lighthouse for weeks, even sitting in a small tub of tepid water and self-scrubbing would probably feel like bliss.

"Sardelle?" Ridge asked softly.

"Yes, uhm." She looked around the living room, but with Tolemek banging and clanking things in the kitchen and Ridge's mother wandering through, it would not provide as much privacy as she would like for this. Outside, the sun had broken through the clouds. It might be warm enough for sitting quietly and sharing thoughts. "Kaika is in the bedroom. Let's go sit on that bench on the side of the house."

Ridge kept hold of her hand as he followed her out the front door. Though he had joked easily enough with the king, now that they were alone, she could sense that his humor was more a reflex than a genuine show of pleasure or amusement. Weariness pulled at his limbs like shackles, and she felt guilty since he had come back to find her sleeping. He must have flown through the night. He probably had not slept at all since she had seen him last. And not much before then, either.

They stepped off the walkway and wandered to the flagstone patio next to the pottery shed. A stone bench, shrubs and flowers growing in ceramic pots, and a small fishpond made it a pleasant spot. Someday, Sardelle hoped to be able to share it with Ridge when there wasn't unpleasant news to deliver.

"Are we talking?" he asked. "Or..." He pointed at her eyes, then his, then back to hers.

"I don't think I have words for last night." She sighed and sat on the edge of the bench.

"All right." Ridge flopped onto the other half of it. "Not quite as comfortable as the bed for sharing thoughts."

"No, but sharing thoughts on the bed led to sharing other things, as well."

"You don't think that can happen here?" Ridge nodded toward the wooden structure leaning against the house. "I've been having naughty thoughts involving that pottery shed since we first got back."

Despite his smile, he appeared too tired for naughty thoughts and certainly for naughty actions. Besides, he would not be in the mood when she finished. She just hoped he would still be talking to her. She didn't think he would blame her for what had happened, but she couldn't help but think what a waste it had all been, since he had deduced the king's location on his own.

"Come here," he murmured, perhaps reading the conflicted thoughts on her face. He lifted his arm, and she leaned against his side, resting her head on his chest.

"Ready?" she asked softly, feeling this time that she needed to warn him first.

"Yeah." He sounded nervous.

As soon as she started sharing her experiences from the night before, she wondered if words might have been better. Before she got to the point where they had walked in and found Apex, tears were pricking at her eyes. She hadn't cried yet, not seriously, so maybe it was fitting, but she wondered what it said about her life that every time she did this with Ridge, she ended up in tears. Still, being in his arms and having him stroke her hair was comforting. She should have been trying to comfort *him*, but she did not know what she could say or think that would accomplish that.

"I should have figured out a way to keep Kaika from going to the castle in the first place," Ridge said when Sardelle finished. "Nothing good came from that mission."

Except that they had learned of the queen's involvement in the Heartwood Sisterhood. Sardelle knew she shouldn't be relieved that the woman was dead now, but she couldn't help but hope it meant those people would try less hard to come after her. At the least, they should have access to fewer resources now. If only Sardelle could have achieved that without Apex's death.

"I shouldn't have yelled at Apex, either," Ridge murmured, his words barely audible. "Should have kept him with Duck. Should have..."

Sardelle lifted her face enough to see his, to see the moisture glistening in his eyes. She wished she had thought to bring out something alcoholic to share with him. That seemed to be his preferred method for dealing with death and devastation. But perhaps there was no time. He had spoken of trouble on the horizon, and the king wanted to be flown back to the capital soon.

She laid her palm against his cheek, rubbing the stubble on his chin with her thumb. "I'm sorry," she whispered and kissed him. It was the only solace she could offer, and it seemed so inadequate.

Ridge pulled her closer and rested his face against the top of her head. "I'm afraid things aren't going to get any better."

She brushed his thoughts, and he shared his experience with the reconnaissance craft—and his belief that many more of those craft were out there, perhaps along with a flotilla of airships out at sea. Airships armed with those awful target-seeking rockets and who knew what other devastating weapons.

"I need to talk to Angulus," Ridge said, "get him back to town and pray he'll give me permission to walk back onto base. And that he'll walk with me to the radio tower and send a message to the other bases, one they can't ignore."

"I doubt everybody ignored *your* message." Sardelle leaned back so he could get up.

"I don't know. I haven't seen any friendly fliers in the sky yet, and we're close enough to the coast that we ought to see them heading to the capital." He shook his head and stood.

"Ridge? Is the king... He seems approachable. Are you and he close enough that—"

"He'll forgive his wife's death? I don't know. We're not close. You may have noticed my family isn't exactly royal. Most of them aren't usually sober, either. And I've never chatted with him before without General Ort or one of my other superiors along, kicking me in the leg under the table to make sure I stay properly respectful."

Even though his expression remained grave, Sardelle smiled at the image.

You should ask him how respectful he was being when he was dangling from that vine and eavesdropping outside of the king's greenhouse.

"If it's any consolation," Sardelle said. "I've known a lot of people with royal blood who consider drinking their predominant hobby. I don't think that predilection has much to do with bloodlines and nobility."

Cas is on her way back. She's several miles out, but I thought you should know.

Trepidation seeped into Sardelle's stomach. If Jaxi had sensed her from this far away... *She doesn't have that sword, does she?*

No, I can sense familiar auras even if they're not carrying ancient swords with bad attitudes.

Good to know.

You also might want to know that Kaika is in there talking to the king.

In... the washroom? Sardelle knew Kaika had a lustful nature, but she couldn't imagine her propositioning the man in the tub.

Jaxi issued a mental snort. *No, in the living room. She's telling him what happened while wringing her hands and avoiding his eyes.*

She's braver than I am.

By the way, Jaxi added. *We would have beaten him, in a fair fight. Kasandral. I wasn't trying that hard because I didn't want to eviscerate Cas.*

I never doubted you. Sardelle did doubt whether fighting fair was one of Kasandral's tenets, but she did not add that thought.

"From what he told me, she's not—she wasn't—the love of his life," Ridge said after a thoughtful moment. "Perhaps eventually he could forgive those who caused that loss." He nudged a loose flagstone with his boot. "He is rather proud of his castle though. So is the city. You don't know how many committee meetings he has to suffer through just to get the approval to paint a wall. I'm afraid the king may not forgive you two for collapsing that back corner."

Ridge's words sounded light and playful, and he brushed a few strands of hair behind her ear, but his smile was forced, and his eyes remained grim. She could tell he wasn't sure how this flight path would end up looking. Even if the queen and the king had not been soul mates, Angulus would surely miss someone he had spent more than twenty years of his life with.

She sensed Ridge's hope that the king could put the need to defend the city above personal grudges, that Angulus would see the wisdom in getting all of the fliers back home so they could be sent out to do some reconnaissance of their own.

Ridge stroked her hair a few times, then sighed and headed toward the front door. Sardelle tried not to feel guilty that so many of her thoughts had been about her own future and about personal repercussions for her actions, when all of his involved protecting the city.

That's what you get for falling in love with a noble man.
I know.
If it helps, he is rather insistent in his thoughts that he *get to lead the way in protecting the city.*
He knows he's the best person to command the fliers.
And he likes that fact.

Sardelle smiled slightly. *I know* you're *not calling Ridge narcissistic.*
What does that mean?
Nothing, Jaxi. Nothing at all.

Chapter 14

RIDGE EYED THE OPEN WINDOW, the sound of Captain Kaika's voice drifting out as she described the previous night's events to the king. Her voice was tense, and she stared down at her clasped hands as she sat on the edge of the couch while he stood and listened with his arms folded across his chest. Ridge was tempted to listen, as well, so he might hear the king's reaction and be prepared for it the next time they spoke. Ultimately, he decided that he should not spy on King Angulus twice in the same month.

Since they looked like they might be discussing events for a while, Ridge continued on around the side of the house. His first thought was to check in on Tolemek—and the noxious blue smoke wafting from the kitchen windows. It was too soon to ask if he had come up with a weapon to use against invaders, but Ridge hoped he was making progress.

Before going inside, Ridge spotted Duck in the back yard, still sitting on the fence. He had no idea what words of comfort he might offer, especially when he felt responsible for Apex's death, but he detoured in that direction. Duck did not look up as he approached.

Ridge leaned against the fence beside him, wishing he had something useful he could say. Comforting people wasn't his strong suit, unless getting them drunk counted. But he dared not do that now, not when he could be called to leave any minute. Too bad, because he wouldn't have minded a stiff drink. Apex's face kept entering his thoughts, that hurt expression he had worn when Ridge had told him to fix the problem he had made. Now all Ridge could do was wish he had handled that better. Sending the man off alone... what had he been thinking? He had been angry. He *hadn't* been thinking.

A cat stalked past, hunting a moth. A couple of yards over, a lady feeding chickens stole glances in their direction. After landing in the closest field he could, Ridge had done his best to hustle Angulus to the house without attracting attention, but he was sure a few neighbors had spotted him. That was another reason to leave soon. The last thing Angulus needed was a bunch of rural folk coming to him about problems with neighbors stealing cows or letting dogs run through their chicken pens.

"You going to be able to fly?" Ridge asked. "I'm going to do my best to make sure there are some fliers in our hangar come dawn."

"Yes, sir."

"I know it's hard to lose people—*friends*—especially when..." He stopped himself from saying the death had been meaningless. Apex had been there, trying to redeem himself, trying to do what Ridge had asked. That wasn't meaningless. What was meaningless was the queen's bloody tirade against anyone who might have the slightest ability to perform magic. He should have been enraged by her actions, but it was hard to feel rage toward a dead person. "It's just always hard," he finished when Duck looked at him.

"Sir, I don't understand... I mean, I probably would have done the same thing if the queen had come up to me and told me to stick a tracker on my flier. Are you even *allowed* to refuse royal orders? What else could he have done?"

"He could have told me about it, and I would have stalked into the castle and shoved that device up the queen's big, padded—" Remembering that the house windows were open, Ridge lowered his voice and amended his last word to, "—nose."

Duck managed a brief half smile. "You probably *would* have done that, sir." His smile faded quickly, and he stared down at the mud. "I owed him a beer. Never got a chance to get back to town and buy it."

"A life lesson. You should never delay the mutual consumption of alcohol."

"I know people die, sir. We've lost friends before, but it seems to make more sense when you're defending your country, fighting back those Cofah bastards, you know? This was just—to get randomly shot by some castle guard... such a waste."

Ridge lifted his brows but managed to keep from asking who had told him that version of the story. Kaika? He didn't think Sardelle would have lied to protect Ahn's reputation or to make things easier, if only because she was a lousy liar, but perhaps Kaika had wanted to spare contention among the officers. It might not be a bad idea, since they were going to have to fly together again.

"Apex was a good man," Duck went on. "His anger with Tolemek... I understood why he hated him. I didn't have that personal connection to Tanglewood, but it was horrible, sir. I... It doesn't make sense to me, why good men die young and evil men who are murderers will probably live to be old, crusty geezers." Duck glanced toward the kitchen window.

Hatred didn't roil off him, not the way it had for Apex when they had first left for the mission to Cofahre with Tolemek in the back of Ahn's flier, but Ridge doubted Duck would ever be friends with the former "Deathmaker." So long as he was willing to use any weapons Tolemek came up with to defend the homeland.

"Fate and fairness don't usually go hand-in-hand," Ridge said, "but you know some of those Cofah who fly against us are probably good men, too, men who are just following orders, the same as us. Over there, we'd be considered the murderers. It would take wiser men than us to decide what's good and what's evil. We're better off following orders and accepting that the world doesn't always make sense. Then coming home and drinking beer." He patted Duck on the back. "We'll have one together when this is all over, all right?"

"Yes, sir." A yawn almost swallowed Duck's last word.

"Go get some sleep. I think the bedroom's open."

"Yes, sir."

Ridge wouldn't have minded a spot to rest for a few hours, either, but as soon as the king finished talking to Kaika, he would want his ride back into the city. Ridge wondered what version of the story she was giving *him*. He also wondered if he might have liked things better if he had also received that version. Knowing it had been Lieutenant Ahn's hand that had slain Apex did not make anything easier. He didn't blame her—as soon as Sardelle had frowned doubtfully at that sword, he should have found a way to lock it away somewhere that nobody could use it. But he did worry that Ahn would blame herself, and he didn't think anything good could come of that. What if she never came back at all?

She's actually turning onto this street now, Sardelle whispered into his thoughts. She was leaning against the wall at the corner of the house. Had she heard him talking to Duck? Or maybe she was eavesdropping on the king's conversation, as he had thought to do.

We had this discussion before. Sardelle smiled at him. *It's not eavesdropping if I happen to be standing nearby while you're discussing things in a normal tone of voice in an open area.*

Yes, I do remember that. Does the same rule apply if you're hanging from a vine while listening?

Whoever would listen while hanging from a vine?

Never mind. I better go meet Ahn. She doesn't have that cursed blade with her, does she?

No. We left it in the rubble at the castle.

Rubble that would eventually be cleared. He grimaced. If the king was still talking to him after he heard the full story, Ridge would have to lobby for someone to have that thing taken out to sea and dropped in the Forbidden Trench.

As Ridge circled toward the front of the house, he watched Sardelle walk through the kitchen door. A great plume of smoke wafted out as she entered. Once everyone cleared out of the house—and there was no risk of the king overhearing any yelling—Ridge expected a lecture from his mother. A loud one.

Ahn stood in front of the house, looking at the front door, as if debating whether she truly wanted to go up and knock. He could understand the sentiment. Her short hair was tousled, her clothes ripped and stained, and her slouch hinted of weariness far greater than anyone as young as she was should feel. He did not see a horse, so she might have walked the entire way. She held an envelope, the creamy, smudge-free paper contrasting with her dirty hand.

When she spotted him, she stood straighter, her hand twitching upward. It didn't make it all the way to a salute. Instead, her shoulders slumped again, and she stared bleakly at his boots.

Ridge walked over, having no more idea of what to say to her than he had for Duck. For lack of a better opening, he started the same way.

"You going to be able to fly? I'm trying to get our machines back. I got the king—" Ridge pointed his thumb toward the house, "—so that might happen more easily now."

Ahn blinked a few times and stared at the front door. That probably was not the opening she had expected.

"Yes, sir," she said. "I mean... I can if you need me to, but I..." She looked down at the envelope, took a slow breath, then held it out to him. "I came to report for punishment and also to resign my commission."

Ridge looked at the envelope without moving his hand to accept it.

"I know I'll still be tried by military law... when that time comes, but I can't go back to—" She swallowed and looked down the street. A couple of chickens were wandering in the dirt lane, pecking for bugs. "I figure if I'm going to be killing people indiscriminately, I might as well be working for my father."

"Ahn," Ridge said, then gripped her shoulder. "Caslin. I can't promise that there won't be repercussions for the choices we've all made here—especially me—but see what they are first. Don't assume—look, I get it. The queen gave some order, and the sword leaped to obey. You were just the one holding it."

"I *chose* to be holding it, sir." Ahn dropped her gaze again. "It had some pull I don't understand, but I should have seen through that. I don't even *like* swords. They're barbaric. Who chooses to kill someone like that?" Her voice cracked on the word kill, and she blinked again, this time not with surprise but to stave off tears.

Ridge released her. He had no idea what to say. He thought about offering her a hug, but he was probably part of the problem, since he represented authority—as ironic as that may be—and she expected punishment. As difficult as he found it to admit, Tolemek was the better person for her to talk to right now. Of everyone here, he could truly understand what it was like to be powerless to stop deaths one was responsible for.

"Let's worry about it after we've dealt with the Cofah threat," Ridge said. "I shot down a reconnaissance flier this morning, so you better believe more will be coming. In the meantime, Tolemek is in the kitchen, sooting up the walls and hopefully not asphyxiating my mom's cats. Maybe you should check on him."

From the mixed expression on her face, she wasn't as certain as he was that Tolemek was the right person for her to see, but she said, "Yes, sir." She took a step toward the door, but paused again and lifted the envelope. "Will you accept my resignation? For after the battle?"

"No, I won't. You know I hate paperwork. You'll have to see if General Ort will take that."

"Isn't he still missing?"

"Yes, he is. Just try giving it to him."

Before she could object further, Ridge pointed her toward the kitchen door, so she wouldn't walk through the king's meeting. Sardelle must have told Tolemek that Ahn had arrived, because that side door opened, and he stepped out.

Ahn was only a few steps from the house, but she hesitated, dropping her gaze to the walkway. Tolemek crossed the distance and wrapped her in a hug, lowering his face to the top of her head. Ahn tipped forward, leaning her forehead into his chest, but she did not return the hug. Her arms drooped at her sides with her shoulders slumped. Ridge couldn't remember seeing anyone look so dejected.

Tolemek murmured something and led Ahn toward the house. She shambled along slowly, but at least she went with him. When Tolemek glanced toward Ridge, Ridge nodded once. He doubted the former pirate cared about receiving his approval, but Ridge would give it, anyway. He truly believed Tolemek would be the best person to comfort Ahn. To his surprise, Tolemek returned the solemn nod before they disappeared inside.

Left alone in the yard, Ridge rubbed his face and looked up at the sky. The clouds had returned, and their somber gray matched his mood. He wondered if the gods would laugh at him if he prayed for the Cofah attack to be delayed for another six months.

A distant buzz drifted to his ears, and he slumped. He had a feeling the gods were about to mock him.

He walked out into the street, hopping a few puddles, then turning for a view of the sky in the direction of the propeller noise. He found the source against the gray backdrop, and his heart lifted. This time, the flier was bronze. It was too far away to see the pilot or the animal snout painted on the nose that would identify the squadron, but Ridge found himself grinning, anyway. It had to be one of his comrades on the way back from one of the other bases. Someone had heard his message and was coming.

He almost waved, but the pilot would never see him at this distance. Besides, who would be looking down at a tiny community plopped down in the middle of a bunch of farmland? Instead, he scanned the sky behind it, longing to see other aircraft coming into view. He would take any help he could get, but a single one-man flier wouldn't add much to the empty hangars.

As the bronze craft flew overhead to the west, Ridge spotted a few dark dots on the horizon. He grinned again. Maybe the gods were finally on his side. That looked like five—no, six more fliers. Maybe they belonged to his squadron. It felt as if an eternity had passed since he had seen Crash, Blazer, and Thasel. He'd even give Pimples a hug if the kid walked up right now.

But his grin faded as those aircraft flew closer, the buzz of their propellers audible now. These fliers were not the same bronze as the first one. Their dark paint filled Ridge with dread. Even worse, there were heads visible above those cockpits, so they weren't automated. Fliers piloted by real people with real and cunning human brains were chasing whoever was in that single Iskandian craft.

"Cofah," he whispered and sprinted for the house. "Sardelle!" he cried, having already decided in that split second that there was nobody else here that he wanted in the seat behind him to help catch those craft before they annihilated the Iskandian one.

* * *

Sardelle gripped the sides of her seat, not complaining when the wind whipped the tail of Ridge's scarf into her face. She was too busy panting from their wild sprint across people's yards, around barns, and through pigpens in order to reach the field with the flier in it. She couldn't hear or see the Cofah craft Ridge had spoken of, and she hoped they could catch them before it was too late for the Iskandian pilot.

I could take care of that for you, Jaxi said.

Sardelle hadn't had time to grab anything else from the house, but she had belted the soulblade on as she ran. *What?*

The scarf. You've seen me cut through steel vault doors and ancient pyramids. A thin, little scarf would be a simple matter.

I don't think Ridge would be amenable to that. He uses the end to wipe his goggles during flight.

I could incinerate those specks of engine grease that trouble him, Jaxi suggested.

Sardelle imagined Ridge's alarm when flames burst from his goggles.

You're awfully chatty right now, Jaxi. The flier lurched into motion and bumped across the uneven field. Sardelle buckled herself into the harness. If this was like their last battle, she might end up upside down at some point. *Feeling perky?*

You know I like to go into battle.

Sardelle did not share the feeling, preferring the healer's tent to a battlefield, but it pleased her that Ridge had asked for her in between ordering Tolemek to finish making something brilliant and ordering Cas, Duck, and Kaika to ensure the king got back to his castle. There hadn't been time to wait for objections—or counter orders—for which Sardelle was also glad. She'd only glimpsed Angulus's face on her way to grab her sword, but it had been much less expressive than it had been when she had first awoken, *before* he had known his wife had been killed. He could have been thinking anything behind his stony facade. She hoped that it wasn't about how he would avenge the queen's death.

"Can you sense them?" Ridge called over his shoulder.

I'll check, Sardelle spoke into his mind, abashed that she hadn't already thought to look. In the minutes that had passed while she and Ridge ran to the field, the fliers might have escaped her range, but Jaxi ought to be able to sense aircraft at a greater distance.

Yes, I can. And I do. They're about halfway back to the city. The ugly black ones are shooting at the bronze one.

Sardelle was about to relay the message, but Jaxi added, *I told him too. He appreciated that I identified the Cofah aircraft as ugly. He also appreciates that I'm along.*

You got all that when he's busy flying and worrying about his man?

It may have been a general sense of appreciation for the information. I extrapolated.

Sardelle snorted.

She leaned to the side, searching the sky ahead with her mind, as well as her eyes, the former being more effective since she didn't have goggles. The wind teared her eyes and tried to whip hair free from her braid, but she located the six Cofah aircraft flying in a triangular formation. The one soaring at the point was doing the most firing at the target ahead of them. Sardelle could see little more than a bronze smudge at this distance, but she could tell that dark gray smoke wafted from the belly of the craft. The Iskandian flier had already taken damage. Enough to bring it down eventually? She couldn't tell.

Stiff wind came from the sea, and cold rain droplets flew sideways, stinging her cheeks. She flexed her fingers, both to keep them warm and because she was ready to use them. She wanted to help, wanted to prove to King Angulus that she was worth keeping around—and alive. And, as always, she wanted to help Ridge keep his people alive. She didn't want to see him lose anyone else.

The craft vibrated enough to make Sardelle's teeth rattle. Ridge was pushing it to its maximum speed and then some.

Sardelle took slow breaths, telling herself to remain calm, that he knew what he was doing. Seeing bullet holes in the hull had made Sardelle pause, but Ridge had climbed in without hesitation. If he believed the craft flight-worthy, it must be. Still, she hadn't been able to keep from thinking that her powers might not be enough to save them if they crashed.

I believe we're close enough that I could bother them, Jaxi said at the same time as the fliers grew closer, their dark shapes hugging the clouds. *Do we want rashes to inconvenience them? Or fireballs to utterly destroy them?*

If six of them are chasing one lone Iskandian flier on our continent, I believe Ridge's vote would be for fireballs.

Yes. I approve of this relationship of yours.

I'm so glad.

The rattling of their flier increased, and Sardelle gripped the edges of her seat again. Ridge was pushing to close the distance, but she doubted they could before the other fliers reached the city. Would the Cofah dare enter the space over the capital? She wasn't sure what the full capabilities of the artillery weapons down there were, but knew some could reach high enough to strike low-flying craft.

Almost close enough for pyrotechnics, Jaxi purred.

Even though Sardelle was alarmed at their speed already, she closed her eyes and concentrated on the air behind them. She assumed the rattling was due to the strain of the engine rather than any problem with their velocity—and she hoped that assumption wouldn't get them killed—so she channeled the wind, trying to give them a tunnel to fly through, one that the other aircraft did not have.

"Wolf Squadron 74 to home," Ridge spoke to the communication crystal, the wind almost stealing his words before Sardelle heard them. "This is Colonel Zirkander. Is anybody manning the desk?"

A silent moment passed, and Sardelle could feel his disappointment. He couldn't even warn the city as to what was coming.

"What do you want, Zirkander?" came a rough voice over

the crystal. It was muted and tinny, but Sardelle recognized it as soon as the speaker added, "And is this thrice-cursed rock magic, too?"

Rock? Was that oaf referring to her master crystal? She had painstakingly crafted that over a week.

"Quit whining, Therrik," Ridge said. "There are six enemy fliers heading for the city. They'll be there any minute. If any of our fliers are back, get them in the air. Get your infantry buddies on the guns too."

Therrik's only response was a curse.

So good to know he's got our backs, Ridge thought. *Do you hear me? Is that you helping back there? This is great. We're making incredible speed.*

I do, and I am.

Good. Thank you. Ridge massaged the trigger of one of his guns. *Almost close enough to—*

Flames burst from the tail of the rearmost flier in the formation. Clouds of black smoke poured into the sky. Jaxi cackled.

The pilot craned his head around. Even across the distance and even though the man wore goggles, Sardelle could see the horrified expression contorting his face. He veered away from the formation, descending rapidly. Whether he would be able to land or if a crash was inevitable, Sardelle did not know. Even if these people had marked themselves as enemies, she found she much preferred fighting against the unmanned fliers.

I do too, Jaxi said.

Your cackle suggested otherwise. Sardelle fed more wind into her tunnel, propelling Ridge's flier to even greater speeds. They cruised through the smoke the flaming craft had just left. Ridge took a few introductory shots at a flier in front of them.

That wasn't a cackle. It was an expression of pleased satisfaction that I was able to toast one of these mechanical monstrosities.

I see. Sardelle focused on the bronze flier, testing the air currents around and behind it. The craft had slowed down, and the others were gaining. Perhaps if she could give it a boost, it would make a difference. The buildings of the city had come into sight on the horizon, and she could just make out the bluff where the hangars overlooked the harbor.

I may have also been slightly amused when he turned around and tried to blow out the flames, Jaxi added.

I'm quite certain he was only pursing his lips in horror. Can you shield that Iskandian pilot up there? He's too far away for me to do it.

I can shield his entire flier while making waffles and buffing my pommel.

Feeling cocky, are we?

Ridge had found his range with the machine guns and was laying into the two remaining fliers in the rear of the formation. They noticed and took evasive measures, as did the two in front of them. The leader of the formation continued after the bronze flier.

I'm staying on him, Ridge thought. *Anything you can do to keep the others from circling back and jumping on our tail would be appreciated. Tell Jaxi I like her flames.*

He's cackling inside too, Jaxi said.

The bronze flier dipped its left wing, then spiraled downward, more smoke flowing from its belly. Sardelle could not tell if it was a ploy, or if the craft had succumbed to the damage done.

I haven't let any new bullets get to him, Jaxi said, *but his flier was shot up already when we got here.*

The Cofah on its tail dipped after it, machine guns blazing. Ridge angled downward, choosing a course that would shave seconds off the descent and perhaps allow him to catch up.

Sardelle was tempted to reach out to the pilot, try to sense whether he was unconscious, conscious and calm, or awake and terrified, but the rest of the Cofah formation was doing as Ridge had predicted, trying to circle back and get behind his flier. Bullets streaked through the air. She did her best to create shields on either side of them. She didn't want to stop Ridge's ability to use the machine guns, nor did she want to cut them off from the wind, so she couldn't protect them as completely as she would have liked.

The bronze flier continued to fall, spiraling toward houses on the outskirts of the capital.

"Sleepy," Ridge said, his voice utterly calm even though they were arrowing toward the ground at top speed and had bullets coming in from all sides, "if you crash them into the buildings of the city, the ghosts of a hundred past kings will haunt you."

Sardelle didn't think he was talking to her, but wasn't sure if he was hoping to communicate with the pilot in the other flyer or muttering to himself. He fired several more rounds at the Cofah stalking his fellow Iskandian, his fellow Iskandian who was only seconds from crashing into shops lining a wide boulevard below. Sardelle kept shielding them from the fliers trying to get behind Ridge, but found their bullets rarely struck her barrier. Ridge did an uncanny job of avoiding them, even as he stayed on his target's tail, almost as if he had eyes in the back of his head and could track every other aircraft in the sky.

The Iskandian flier, smoke still streaming from its belly, pulled up at the last second, just avoiding smashing into the roof of a three-story building. It wobbled, its wings shuddering, and it clipped a flagpole before gaining altitude. The Cofah was following, but one of Ridge's bullets hit him square in the head. The pilot stiffened, then slumped to the side. Instead of pulling up and hanging with the Iskandian, the enemy flier plunged into the street between two buildings. The wings flew off, the fuselage caved in and skidded three blocks, and the wreck ended up coming to a halt in front of the steps of a barber shop. People out in the street had pressed their backs to the closest buildings, and were gaping at the crash and at the sky.

That was the last Sardelle saw, for Ridge was pulling up now, flying through smoke as they gained altitude.

"Sorry, sir," came a voice over the crystal. That definitely wasn't Therrik. "I've taken damage, didn't think I could make it to the harbor. Thanks for shooting that ugly feller, but I was hoping he would crash due to my craftiness, rather than your marksmanship." The firing of a machine gun punctuated the pilot's words. He had already turned his nose toward the oncoming fliers.

"If you need to get to the base, do it," Ridge said. "We'll take care of the rest of these."

"No, sir. I'm sticking with you. They've got rockets that—"

"I've seen them before. Stay on my six until you get a chance to shoot. I've got a secret weapon."

That's me, Jaxi preened.

It could be me.

All you've done so far is generate air. Watch this.

A second Cofah flier burst into flame. This time, the fire emerged from the cockpit, burning the occupant. Sardelle winced as the man's screams pierced her ears, even over the sounds of wind and machine gun fire. The Cofah flier dipped sharply, arrowing toward the city. The pilot struck a control on the dashboard before losing all conscious thought. A sleek black cylinder shot out. At first, it looked like it would target a building, but then it swooped upward, turning toward the Iskandian fliers.

Oops, Jaxi thought.

Yes, Sardelle recognized the rocket from their desperate flight from the volcano lab. *Try to incinerate the vial of dragon blood,* she told Jaxi. That had worked once before. The dragon blood itself was impervious to everything, or everything they had tried at least, but once the glass holding it was destroyed, it leaked all over the inside of the machine and could no longer power and guide the weapon.

These vials aren't made from glass anymore, Jaxi thought.

What? Sardelle tried to concentrate on the conversation, but the three fliers filling the sky in front of them made her want to grip Ridge's shoulders for support.

Shooting with every tilt of his wings, Ridge wove through the formation as if the fliers were cones on some obstacle course. Sardelle felt it suicidal, and she flailed mentally for a second, not sure where to apply her shields to protect them. To her surprise, the number of bullets streaking through the air lessened. The Cofah pilots didn't want to risk shooting each other, she realized.

That rocket is about to fly up your Iskandian butts, Jaxi said.

"I've got this one, Jaxi," Ridge yelled. "Handle that rocket that the newcomer just launched, will you?"

Newcomer? Sardelle was about to shore up their rear shield,

certain the rocket would smash into them, when Ridge turned sharply to the left, more sharply than she would have thought these fliers could manage. He seemed to defy all of the rules of physics, and Sardelle ducked low in her seat as the belly of a Cofah flier filled her vision. Its propeller buzzed right over her head, the sound like an angry hornet's nest stuffed in her ears, and she thought all of her hair might be shaved off by its blades. But then they were past the other flier and streaking toward the clouds.

An explosion came from behind them, the force battering at Sardelle's shield. Their flier rocked in the air despite her protection. She glanced back in time to see the Cofah craft burst into a million pieces.

Nice, Jaxi crooned in her mind. *He got the rocket to hit one of their fliers. That's almost as good as spontaneous combustion.*

Sardelle took a few shaky breaths, seeking some of the calmness that radiated from Ridge. He had flown in hundreds of battles like this, she reminded herself. Her only dogfight had been with two unmanned fliers. The fact that they were killing people this time was part of what had her trembling. She vowed to do better, not to dwell on the humanness of their opponents until after she and Ridge were safely on the ground.

She focused on one of the two remaining Cofah fliers, finding the two rockets nestled in launchers under the belly of the craft. The pilot was busy firing the machine guns and cursing—Sardelle allowed herself a brief moment of satisfaction to know that Ridge was flummoxing these people. Then she examined the firing mechanism of the weapons, trying to figure out what attached to what, so she could sabotage the insides. Too complicated. Instead, she heated the ends of the machine gun barrels, pouring controlled energy into them. The metal grew cherry hot. She nudged the ends together, so the bullets would no longer fly out. Lastly, she brought in a gust of cool air to chill the muzzles.

Sooner than she expected, the pilot tried to fire his guns. She worried that the bullets would simply shoot through her obstruction, that the metal would still be pliable, but a small explosion boomed. The pilot jerked back in his seat, startled. Sardelle didn't think it would ultimately do anything except deny him a couple of weapons, but the barrel of the guns had blown open and peeled back like flower petals. A piece got in the way of the propeller blade, causing it to jam and freeze up. The flier's momentum carried it a ways, but it soon tilted downward, falling toward the ground. Sardelle stared, unable to take her gaze from its plummet, newly aware of how fragile these craft were, of how little it took to knock them out of the sky.

"Jaxi?" Ridge called aloud after downing the sixth flier with the help of the other Iskandian pilot. "Sardelle? I'm out of targets to send that rocket into, unless I crash it into the city, which I don't want to do. Anything you can do?"

Sardelle had almost forgotten about the second rocket. Ridge had been avoiding it so deftly that it seemed he could do it forever, but with the dragon blood powering it, the weapon kept after them, its speed not flagging at all.

I'm having trouble destroying the vial this time, Jaxi admitted, presumably speaking to both of them.

Their flier twisted through the air like a corkscrew, Ridge doing his best to avoid the rocket. He tried to turn in time to shoot at it, but it was too fast.

The other Iskandian flier had left Ridge's tail and came in from the side. The pilot unloaded bullets at the rocket. Most missed the sleek, narrow cylinder, but one caught. Sardelle hoped that might be enough to destroy it, and indeed, it was knocked from its path for a second, but it righted itself and sped after Ridge's flier again.

They switched from glass to iron, Jaxi added. *Specially treated iron. It's resisting my attempts to incinerate it.*

Sardelle peered into the innards of the rocket, trying to make sense of the circuit board and wires inside. She sensed the encapsulated dragon blood riding in the center near the front and understood what Jaxi meant. Either a shaman had treated that metal, or the Cofah had found some old stash of ingots treated long ago, perhaps in creating armor to battle dragons and sorcerers. It resisted her attempts to melt it.

Let's destroy the rest of that board and those wires, Sardelle told Jaxi. *They're not armored the way the vial is.* Even if she wasn't an engineer and most of the new contraptions of this century confused her, she assumed that those parts somehow controlled the rocket.

I think your soul snozzle has something else in mind.

Sardelle had sunk low into her seat, losing awareness of their surroundings as she focused on the rocket, so when she sat taller and had a look ahead of them, her stomach nearly dropped to her boots. Black jagged rock filled her vision. She was barely aware of the castle to their left. They couldn't be more than two seconds from crashing.

Pull up, she thought—or maybe she screamed it.

At the last instant, Ridge did so. The bottom of their flier's tail scraped across a jagged boulder protruding above the others. An angry shudder rocked the craft, and Sardelle thought they were dead. Before she could tell if they would be able to rise up again and escape, an explosion ripped the air behind them. She barely had the presence of mind to shore up her shields and protect them from the shockwave.

Their flier soared away from the angry orange fireball churning the air. The rocks skimming past below disappeared, replaced by the gray waters of the harbor.

"Sorry," Ridge said. "It had to be close. As I found out last time, those rockets are not easily fooled."

"I understand," Sardelle rasped, her voice barely able to escape her tight throat.

"Nice flying, sir," came the other pilot's voice over the crystal. "Though that explosion got the guards in the castle towers all riled up."

"Yeah, I've heard they've had a bad week."

He sounded as casual as if they were all sitting at a bar and sharing drinks. He probably wasn't even sweating.

Sardelle mopped moisture from her own forehead as she slumped back in the seat.

At least you didn't throw up like Colonel Therrik did, Jaxi observed.

Once the flier had sailed to a safe height again—one where it was not in danger of hitting rocks, buildings, or crashing into the castle, Ridge twisted in his seat to grin back at her. He found her hand and clasped it—he didn't seem to notice that her knuckles were white from gripping the edge of her seat.

"Thanks for your help," he said. "Sleepy never would have made it if we had been any later."

"That's the other pilot?" she asked.

Ridge nodded. "Tiger Squadron. He's just a kid. I'm going to ask him about where the rest of his squadron is, but wanted to say thanks." He squeezed her hand again, then turned back to his controls.

He thanked me too. Jaxi sounded pleased. Or pleased with herself. Sometimes it was hard to tell the difference.

Jaxi sniffed haughtily in her mind.

"Sleepy," Ridge said over the crystal, "want to tell me what you're doing down here by yourself? Did—"

A wailing alarm emanated from the city below, drowning out his words. Sardelle had heard it before, the night the pirates had attacked.

They're a little late, Sardelle thought to Ridge.

He turned to look back at her, his usually warm and cheerful eyes grave. "No, they're not."

He tilted his chin toward the sea, past Sardelle's shoulder.

You don't want to look, Jaxi said.

She did, anyway. She looked... and stared.

About three miles out over the ocean, beneath grim gray clouds that promised more rain, a massive fortress floated in the air. It reminded her of the floating pirate city they had dealt with earlier that winter, but it appeared much more sophisticated, much more impenetrable. There weren't any balloons holding it up that one might target. Sardelle had no idea *what* was holding it up. Dragon blood had to be involved, but an energy source, no matter how powerful, could not defy gravity.

A pair of dirigibles floated on either side, the oblong balloons appearing small next to the walls and towers of the fortress. Even from here, Sardelle could tell that cannons, guns, and rocket launchers were mounted on those towers. An open area lay visible, too, almost like the courtyard in the castle, except one could have walked right off the fortress platform and fallen into the ocean. Or *flown* off, she realized, squinting at the dark smudges lined up in rows in that open area. Fliers. A lot of them. Fifty? One hundred?

Bleakly, she thought of the empty hangar she and Ridge had visited.

"Sleepy," Ridge said, "I hope you had a good breakfast, because it doesn't look like our work is done."

"Oh, sir." The other pilot had spoken with relative calm during their battle, but his voice had a choked, mournful quality to it now. "What can we do against all that?"

"Pray," Sardelle whispered.

Chapter 15

RIDGE DID THE AERIAL EQUIVALENT of pacing; he flew from one end of the harbor to the other, then back again, never letting the floating fortress out of his sight. He had expected it to mount an attack as soon as he had seen it, but three hours had passed since he had first noticed it out there. It hovered as easily as the airships, in a way that seemed to defy gravity. He could only assume some dragon-blood-powered thrusters lined the underside of the platform that the massive structure sat upon. A *lot* of dragon-blood-powered thrusters. He had hoped that his team had deprived the Cofah of their reserves, but they must have had many more vials squirreled away on different bases. And this monstrosity had to have been far along in the construction process when Ridge and his squadron had been on the continent.

"What are they waiting for?" He drummed his fingers on the metal first-aid kit strapped to the side of his seat.

He shouldn't be impatient. Their delay had allowed eight more fliers to join him in the air, patrolling the harbor, ready to face impossible odds when they had to. They were all Wolf Squadron, pilots who had received his telegraph message and risked punishment to come back and join him. It felt good to have Crash and Masser in the air behind him, but even if all of Wolf and Tiger Squadrons had returned, it wouldn't have been enough to equal the seventy-five fliers he had counted sitting on that launching pad. The city's big artillery weapons, mounted on towers at the north and south ends of the harbor, were pointing toward the fortress, but the Cofah seemed to know their range and hovered outside of it. Ridge didn't even know how effective the weapons would be against those walls. The fortress appeared to be made of metal. His mind boggled at the idea of keeping that much weight in the air.

I don't know, Sardelle projected into his mind, *but I'm going to have to use that tube soon if we stay up here.*

Probably better to do it before the next fight. Keeps things from happening unexpectedly when something alarms you.

Ridge did not have to look back to know Sardelle was raising her eyebrows.

Are you suggesting I might urinate on myself? she asked.

You wouldn't be the first passenger who's done that while flying into battle with me. In fact, I'm fairly certain Therrik did it while we were cruising through Crazy Canyon.

No, he just vomited. I cleaned the seat, remember?

Ah, too bad.

As long as we're sharing funny stories about people peeing on themselves, Jaxi spoke into Ridge's mind, both of their minds probably, *I noticed Sardelle left out a few details when sharing the events of our castle infiltration.*

I included all of the important *details,* Sardelle thought.

Ridge tapped the communication crystal. "Therrik, how's the flier round-up going?"

Several times, Ridge had thought about landing, so that he could expedite the orders he had given Therrik, but he worried that as soon as he left the sky, the fortress would attack. He also thought he might get punched if he presumed to order Therrik around without a few thousand feet of air between them.

"We've got four more in the hangar. The maintenance team is working its hardest to make them airworthy."

"Only four? Did you get the ones out of the flight museum?"

"Zirkander, I'm not sending people up in—"

"I'm not talking about pulling out the wrecks," Ridge snapped. "The Eagle-7s are perfectly serviceable. And I know we've got extra crystals stored in some vault somewhere. They came back with me from Galmok Mountain."

"Good, Zirkander. Talk about state secrets over an open radio that all of your pilots can listen in on."

"Just get the damned fliers into the hangar, Therrik." Ridge noticed he was gripping the flight stick hard enough to rip it off.

He forced his fingers to relax and took a deep breath. "Duck and Ahn ought to be there any minute." He almost forgot and said Apex would be there, too, but squashed that addition with a mix of frustration and sorrow. "If you can find any other pilots down there that you didn't send off on your idiotic witch-hunt, we'll want them in the air too."

A hand came to rest on his shoulder. Sardelle squeezed him through his jacket. She didn't presume to tell him to cool off—though it would have been prudent, since Therrik was the only one on the ground that he could deal with, and if he started ignoring Ridge, they would be in trouble. Also, any minute now, Therrik was going to realize that he still had orders saying he ran the flier battalion.

"Please," Ridge added, though forcing the word out nearly broke his jaw.

"Shit, Zirkander. Was that as hard for you as it sounded?"

"Just... get me more fliers. Please."

I wouldn't have guessed I could get you to be polite to him just by touching your shoulder, Sardelle thought.

You're serene; you make me want to be serene. Or at least less of an irritable jackass.

Nice to know I can have that effect. What I wanted to tell you is that the king made it to town.

Good.

He's in the tram now, heading up to the hangar with Tolemek, Cas, Duck, and Kaika. Jaxi says that Tolemek is carrying a huge bag—Duck is helping him with it.

Any chance it's full of weapons instead of dirty laundry? Ridge asked.

Perhaps a slight chance.

"Anyone know what they're waiting for?" came Captain Crash's voice over the crystal.

"I figured they saw the colonel blow up six of their fliers and wet themselves," Pimples said.

Ridge snorted. It felt good to have the men bantering around him again. Even if they were looking at suicidal odds, he had missed this.

"I had help," Ridge said.

"From your archaeologist?" Crash asked.

Several people snorted this time. Apparently, nobody believed that cover story anymore.

"Yup," Ridge said. "I wasn't sure if you all would be able to make it on time, what with being on vacation, touring the countryside."

Crash hesitated before answering. "I wouldn't have minded missing that tour."

His tone told Ridge he didn't want to discuss it further, at least not now, not with Sardelle right behind him. He wouldn't try to hide the truth from her, but he wouldn't want her to hear a first-hand accounting of her distant relatives being slain, either. Breyatah's Breath, he hoped the squadrons hadn't had much luck finding people.

Thank you. Sardelle squeezed his shoulder again.

"Zirkander?" Therrik asked. "You there?"

"No, I stepped out to lunch."

Someone giggled. Probably Pimples. The boy did *not* have a manly laugh.

"The king says to get your ass down here for a meeting."

"Everyone?" Ridge glanced at the fortress. Even if it hadn't moved closer yet, he hated to leave it.

"Just you," Therrik said.

"Am I in trouble?" Ridge tilted his wings to drop out of the formation and head downward.

"What kind of stupid question is that? You've been in trouble for the last month straight."

"Well, I suppose I was wondering about *new* trouble."

"There's no time to waste, Zirkander," a new voice said. The *king's* voice. "Get down here."

"Yes, Sire." Ridge had been descending, anyway, but now he wished he hadn't made it sound like he was dawdling. He also wished he knew how that conversation between Angulus and Kaika had gone. The king had been cordial enough toward Sardelle that afternoon—well, perhaps cordial wasn't exactly the word. Indifferent? Unfazed? Bland? How he felt now after learning about the queen... there had not been time to ask. He trusted that there wouldn't be an armed escort waiting to arrest Sardelle. Or himself. After all, he hadn't been back to the base since fleeing his cell.

Ridge ignored the thrusters when the flier reached the airstrip and simply landed with the wheels, his momentum carrying him to the hangar. He circled and parked outside, the nose toward the end of the runway again. He didn't want any delays if he needed to take off in a hurry.

Sardelle climbed to the ground before him and immediately jogged toward the hangar.

"I didn't know you'd missed the king that much," Ridge called after her.

I didn't use the tube.

Ah.

That armed escort would be in for a surprise if they tried to apprehend her, especially if someone tried to throw her over his shoulder.

With one more glance toward the sky to make sure that fortress wasn't coming yet, Ridge jogged into the hangar after her. The back doors had been rolled open in addition to the front, with cool wind gusting through. Several old fliers had been added to the empty floor, and a forklift was bringing in crates of parts. One of the decommissioned fliers had nearly naked women painted on the side.

"That must have come from someone's barnstorming show," Ridge muttered, then spotted Tolemek, Ahn, Duck, Therrik, and the king standing around a table. Therrik was glowering and glaring at Tolemek. Tolemek was ignoring him. He had a hand on a big, lumpy canvas bag lying on the table. It could have held a body. Ridge hoped it held weapons instead. Kaika sat against a wall behind the group, checking no less than six guns, two knives, and the detonation apparatuses on ten bombs. Several men in the deep blue uniforms of the castle guard stood by the door, rifles in hand. Either the king had stopped to pick up his usual contingent of bodyguards, or they had found him.

"Am I late for the meeting?" Ridge asked, walking as he talked, lest the king think he needed to give him another order.

"We don't know why they're waiting," Angulus said, "but I've radioed the other bases personally and ordered them to send the rest of our people back, as well as help from the other squadrons."

"Thank you, sir." Ridge did some calculations in his head. They might get help in as little as four hours. Would the flotilla out there wait that long?

"Deathmaker has brought something that may help," Angulus said.

Tolemek's eyebrows lifted at the use of his old moniker, but he did not correct the king. Ridge looked at Ahn, wondering if she was in a better state of mind than she had been a few hours earlier. Her bleak expression did not suggest that was the case. At least she had her Mark 500 rifle across her back instead of that sword.

"As per Zirkander's order," Tolemek murmured. Ridge didn't know if that was to give him credit for having the foresight to get him to work on weapons, or if he simply wanted to absolve himself of any disasters that might result when the army used them. "I've been studying the dragon blood since we first found some. As you know, it's proven an incredible energy source and also seems to allow orders to be stored in some kind of cellular memory, thus to direct an unmanned craft or—"

"We need the short version right now," Angulus said, his gaze flickering toward the sky beyond the open hangar doors.

Tolemek dug into the bag. He pulled out a few casings. "These are smoke grenades that also do some damage. Simple weapons. I know you already have the technology to create them, but I had extra ingredients. Here are a handful of knockout grenades. These items may be useful for the incursion."

As he rummaged more deeply in the bag, Ridge asked, "The incursion?" and looked around the table to see if everyone else already knew.

Only Therrik appeared as unenlightened as Ridge felt.

"Yes," Tolemek said, pulling out a ceramic spray bottle protected by a metal frame. "We'll need to get close to the dragon blood to destroy it."

Ridge stared at this decidedly unmilitary and un-dangerous-looking "weapon."

"I've been running tests, and I've managed to find something that kills even dragon blood. I embedded it in an acidic compound that can eat through glass or metal, using the assumption that they've got the blood in containers. If you encounter ceramic containers, you'll have to break them, then spray the blood. My peo—the Cofah don't have an equivalent to your power crystals, at least not the last I knew. Destroy the blood, and you should destroy their ability to launch fliers. That floating castle should fall out of the sky. You'll still have to deal with the dirigibles, but I trust you can handle that, Zirkander."

Therrik's nose wrinkled as he reached for the spray bottle. "That looks like something for cleaning the outhouse, not destroying an enemy stronghold."

Tolemek swatted his hand away and moved the bottle out of reach.

Therrik curled his lip and looked down at his hand, as if he couldn't believe Tolemek had presumed to do that.

"Unless you're going on the incursion team, then there's no need for you to touch that," Tolemek informed him.

Therrik curled his fingers into a fist and glanced at the king. Looking for permission to launch a punch? Angulus shook his head. Tolemek did not appear worried, perhaps because Ahn was standing at his side with her big gun. Or maybe he had already discussed this with the king and gotten approval. Angulus was wearing his hard-to-read face.

"Am I on the incursion team?" Ridge asked.

"We thought we'd let you *drive* the incursion team," Tolemek said.

Therrik smirked. Ridge resisted the urge to make a comment about being the flying rickshaw driver again, especially since the king was nodding. He and the others must have been planning this on the trip to town.

"The incursion team will infiltrate the fortress and destroy it from within," Angulus said. "Our pilots will take them there and pick them up."

"Pick them up? If the fortress falls out of the sky as soon as the dragon blood is destroyed..." Ridge grimaced, horror dawning over him as he stared at the spray bottle. "That's going to be a one-way trip for someone, isn't it?" Ridge glanced toward the big metal storage lockers in the back of the hangar. They had some prototype parachutes in there, but Tiger Squadron had lost a man during the trials the summer before. The things weren't reliable yet, and only a handful of pilots had even jumped with them.

"Not necessarily," Tolemek said. "I won't go so far as to say this is a slow-acting compound, but it *will* take time to eat through the container and break down the dragon blood."

"How much time?"

Tolemek spread one hand. "Impossible to say since I haven't seen the container, but maybe five minutes."

Ridge took a deep breath. Five minutes wouldn't be a lot of time to escape the bowels of that fortress, especially if Cofah were shooting at the team every step of the way, but maybe this wouldn't be a *guaranteed* death. He and his squadron could provide cover fire, help them get out.

"Who's on the team?" Ridge asked, glancing toward the lavatory in the back of the hangar. He hated the idea of volunteering Sardelle to go in somewhere, especially if *he* wasn't invited, but she was their greatest asset. And as dangerous as this sounded, it would be even more dangerous for the team if they didn't have her there.

Therrik lifted his chin and looked expectantly at the king.

Ridge's stomach sank. He didn't want to send Sardelle along if that loon was leading. Just because Therrik had let Ridge out of jail didn't mean Ridge had developed a fondness for his leadership style. Or any other style of his.

"Captain Kaika," Angulus said, "Tolemek, and Sardelle, if she'll go." He looked at Ridge.

"*What?*" Therrik demanded.

"Whether it makes sense or not—" Angulus paused to clench his jaw, "—you're in command of the flier battalion right now, Colonel Therrik. You'll stay here."

"But, Sire, you can't be serious about sending two witches along. They're not soldiers. They're not even Iskandian *subjects*."

"Zirkander," Angulus said, ignoring Therrik's meltdown, "you'll take Duck and Ahn to fly the team up and drop them off, using whatever camouflage you can to make sure they're not noticed."

Tolemek tapped one of his smoke grenades. "I can supply some of that camouflage for the pilots."

Ridge met his eyes, wondering why he had volunteered for this suicidal mission. Tolemek couldn't have read his mind, but when he looked away from Ridge, it was to look toward Ahn, and Ridge had his answer. Tolemek might not have risked his life to protect Iskandia, but he would do it to help ensure Ahn made it back from this battle.

Ridge hoped Ahn could appreciate that. Her face was a mask, but the haunted look in her eyes that he had seen earlier hadn't faded at all. He did not know if they'd had a chance to talk before leaving his mother's house, or even if Ahn had been in the right state of mind to listen to Tolemek, but he hoped sending her up in the air like this wasn't a mistake. He knew from past experience how reckless feelings of loss could make a person. Unfortunately, he had to order Ahn up there, no matter what her state of mind. They didn't have enough pilots to spare anybody.

"Every other flier we can muster will be in the air too," Angulus said, then grimaced as one of the old museum models wobbled through the back door on squeaking wheels. That one might need more attention from the maintenance team before it was ready. "Therrik, go clean out the barracks. Find enough pilots to get all of these old machines in the air. We need everything up there. The fliers will harry the Cofah, try to shoot any commanders that are visible, and do their best to keep that armada out over the sea and from coming in to bomb the city."

Ridge noticed Sardelle finally leaving the lavatory and walking toward them. She had been in there a while; he hoped there wasn't a problem. Especially since the king wanted her to go on a mission. Without him. He smiled at her as she approached, hoping his expression was not too bleak. He knew

Kaika could handle a lot of enemies, and Tolemek had his bag of torments, and Jaxi was Jaxi, but... he still wished he could go along. If Therrik wasn't such an unstable ass when the subject of magic came up, Ridge might have argued for him to go along and act as her bodyguard, but the man would probably kiss Ridge before considering Sardelle a human being. He was glowering at her now as she walked closer.

Sardelle wore a distracted look and didn't acknowledge Ridge's smile. She didn't seem to notice that the king, as well as the rest of the team, was staring in her direction, either. She looked toward the hangar door a few seconds before a corporal ran in.

"Sirs! My liege!" the man blurted, almost tripping over his own boots in his hurry to reach them. "Another Cofah dirigible showed up."

"What's one more dirigible matter?" Ridge asked, lifting a hand and inviting Sardelle to join them. She'd finally met his eyes, but hers were grave. Either something unpleasant had happened in that lavatory, or she already knew what the corporal was about to tell them.

"Yeah," Duck said, "the odds were already impossible." He flicked a dismissive finger toward Tolemek's spray bottle.

"It delivered someone," the corporal said. "I thought maybe it was their commander, and that's why they had been waiting."

"It was a sorceress," Sardelle said. "With a soulblade."

Ridge gaped at her. "Like you?"

If he had thought about it, he would have reasoned that other soulblades had survived, even if powerful sorcerers were rarities in this era, but since he had only seen Jaxi, he had started to think of her as a unique construction. He certainly thought of Sardelle as unique. They had encountered other magic users since he had met her, but she had usually called them shamans. He frowned, realizing he didn't quite know what the difference was. The shamans were from less sophisticated civilizations, was that it?

Yes and no, Sardelle spoke into his mind. *It refers to a master-apprentice tradition for teaching magic, with the education usually relayed in an oral manner. That does happen to be the style of teaching with most cultures in less developed civilizations. Sorcerer usually refers to someone who went to a formal school and studied history and other academic topics along with receiving a formal training in magic. The Cofah and Iskandians magic-users have primarily received that label.*

So, we're dealing with a Cofah sorceress.

Yes.

"Sardelle?" Tolemek frowned at her.

Ridge had more questions, but he held his mental tongue. People were probably wondering why she hadn't appeared to answer his last question.

"Like me," Sardelle said, "except... more powerful, I think."

Angulus sighed. "I didn't want to hear that."

"How can that be?" Tolemek pushed some of his ropes of hair away from his face. "We—the Cofah—had a period very much like the genocide in your time. There aren't trained sorcerers left."

Angulus winced at the word genocide.

"Sorcerers were hunted down and either chased out of the empire or destroyed by sheer numbers," Tolemek explained. "A few insiders helped with the betrayal, then were betrayed themselves. History says it wasn't a very happy time period."

"No, I imagine not," Sardelle murmured.

"So, where did they get this one?"

"There must have been some survivors over there, right?" Duck prodded Tolemek in the arm. "You're here."

"Only because nobody in my family ever showed off any of their odd talents. And I'm not anywhere near as powerful as Sardelle."

"Your sister might be," Sardelle said. "If she ever comes back, we can test her and find out. But... I'm not sure about this person. I won't be until I get closer. Which might not be healthy for me." Her lips flattened.

Maybe it was Ridge's imagination, but he thought he sensed fear, or at least hearty concern, from her. She must have faced Cofah sorcerers back in her day, but she wouldn't have been the only Iskandian sorceress then.

"Because she's more powerful than you?" Duck scratched his head. "How can you tell from so far away? How can you even tell there's a sorceress?"

"She has a powerful aura."

Therrik made a disgusted noise and stalked away from the table.

"This changes nothing," Angulus said. "We were in a desperate situation before, and we still are. We need to get this mission off the ground before the Cofah are ready to attack."

"Too late," Sardelle whispered, gazing out the hangar door.

* * *

Sardelle stood uselessly in the center of the hangar while pilots and crew members raced all about her. Well, not entirely uselessly since she was discussing their new enemy with Jaxi, but she worried someone else would think her in an unhelpful stupor.

I'm positive, Jaxi said. *She's not from this time any more than we are.*

You're judging this based on her clothing?

She's wearing ancient dragon-rider armor and a red cape. Who wears capes anymore?

Someone trying to scare us, perhaps? Sardelle suggested.

Can't you sense her power? I don't think her blood is as diluted as everyone else's we've seen in this century. And the soulblade... I can feel him from here.

Sardelle *could* sense the power, and it worried her. *Has it—he—spoken to you?*

Not yet. But they probably know we're here. Sardelle, that dragon stasis technology has existed for a long time, as evinced by our discovery of Phelistoth.

"Someone get some rope, so we can drop off and pick up our passengers," Ridge called across the busy hangar. "Tolemek, you better divvy up that explosive booty between all three fliers and all three people."

A throat cleared behind Sardelle. She turned and found

herself face-to-face with King Angulus.

"Sire," she said carefully, having no idea where she stood with him now that Kaika had shared the bad news. She hadn't had much of an idea where she stood with him *before* that, either.

"I think Zirkander forgot to ask you if you would be willing to go with the incursion team." Angulus tilted his head toward Tolemek and Kaika, who were sorting explosives on the table. "Or he assumed you would go for... reasons I'm not sure I understand, especially since the odds are not in our favor today."

"Well." Sardelle almost said *I love him* as her reason for going, but doubted the king would be impressed by that. He would probably think her some moon-eyed teenager willing to risk dying just for a boy. "He knows me," she said instead. "Before I came to be... here, I worked alongside our army—the Iskandian army—to keep the Cofah out of our country. Granted, I'm more of a healer than a combat sorceress, but I have a few tricks. And my sword has an incendiary streak."

Would it be inappropriate to demonstrate by lighting one of his buttons on fire?

Yes, it would.

I thought so, but the notion tickled me so that I had to make sure.

"A soulblade," the king said, looking down at her scabbard. Had he done some research? Did he know what that meant?

"Yes."

"It's sentient?"

"She is, yes. Jaxi."

"She."

Ridge ran past, carrying a bag of explosives, and Angulus stirred. Sardelle thought he would return to the table or perhaps let the bodyguards who had found him take him to the castle or some other compound from which to observe the battle. Instead, he met her eyes and offered her his hand.

"Ms. Terushan," he said gravely, "if you go up there with them and by some miracle of the seven gods find a way to keep the Cofah from leveling the city, you'll always have a place here in Pinoth. Down the hall from me in the castle if that's what it takes to keep people from bothering you." A tic in his cheek was the only indication that he might be thinking of the queen's death—and what she had been doing when she had been alive.

That sounds much nicer than Ridge's cabin, Jaxi said. *The castle even has that fancy indoor plumbing.*

Sardelle would gladly accept the king's protection, but she would prefer to stay with Ridge, wherever that might end up being.

Don't tell me you would miss the cat soaps.

Maybe we can get his mom to make some shaped like swords for you.

"Thank you, Sire," Sardelle said, realizing he was waiting for an answer. She accepted his handclasp. "I would certainly like to be able to live in the city without anyone trying to blow me up." She wondered if he had heard about the archives building.

Alarms continued to wail outside, and the earth shuddered slightly as an artillery gun fired from the nearby tower. Angulus nodded to her, released her hand, and turned toward the door. He paused to let Tolemek run past, a smaller but still bulging bag thrown over his shoulder. Kaika followed, carrying a bulging bag of her own. She could barely see over it. A big, double-barreled rifle hung across her back and four pistols were jammed into her belt.

"Did you pack enough explosives, Captain?" Angulus asked.

Kaika winked at him, then jerked her chin toward Tolemek's back. "Can't let *his* bag be bigger than mine, Sire."

"Good luck," he said softly as she continued past.

"Sardelle," Ridge called from his cockpit. "Are you ready?"

"Yes, coming."

Tolemek and Kaika were already climbing into the backs of Cas's and Duck's fliers. All of the pilots had boarded and were starting their propellers. In addition to those carrying the small incursion team, twelve craft were lined up, ready to harry the enemy. Sardelle hoped Tolemek's plan worked, because without it, all the brilliant flying in the world wasn't going to keep them alive against the force out there.

I'm more worried about the sorceress and her blade, Jaxi said as Sardelle pulled herself into the seat behind Ridge.

As usual, his flier was at the head of the formation. When she sat down, she had to share her foot space with a bag that had already been strapped in. More of Tolemek's explosives, she presumed. There was also a coil of rope tied to an eyelet. Her stomach fluttered as she anticipated carrying that bag and sliding down into the waiting arms of the enemy—and their sorceress.

She hasn't communicated with me yet, she responded to Jaxi. For which Sardelle was glad. She'd rarely had encouraging conversations when talking to enemy magic users. That first shaman she had met in this time period had offered to breed with her to make powerful babies. She still shuddered at the thought.

I'm guessing this woman won't make you that offer. After a second, Jaxi added, *She might make it to Ridge. To make powerful pilot babies.*

Thanks. That's exactly what I want to think about now.

Oblivious to her thoughts, Ridge turned around and thrust something toward her. His wooden dragon figurine.

"For luck?" His eyes crinkled behind his goggles.

She always felt silly doing so, but she rubbed the thing's head. He looked pleased as he returned it to his pocket and ordered Wolf Squadron to roll out. Apparently, even those pilots who came from other squadrons had been recruited into his. Even the one flying the craft with the nude women dancing on the hull. Nobody objected.

A pilot with dragon blood could be an impressive sight, Jaxi said. *Imagine if Ridge could fling fireballs while chasing down enemies. And just imagine the ability to sense enemies all around you.*

He seems to have a knack for that already.

Yes, but a flying sorceress would be amazing. Makes me think about how it must have been back in the dragon-rider days.

Figure out how to take human form, and you can marry one of Ridge's pilots and try to make that happen. I hear Pimples is available.

The moist, noisy snort Sardelle heard in her mind was impressively realistic for a sword.

Wind beat at Sardelle's cheeks as they rolled out of the hangar and picked up speed. Ridge pulled up on the flight stick, and the flier soared into the air, the sea breeze buffeting them. He compensated easily and streaked inland to gain altitude and wait for the rest of his team to join him before attacking.

The fortress had floated closer in the time they had been in the hangar. The dirigibles, three of them now, lurked farther back, but the Cofah fliers were taking off. Ten already buzzed through the air around the fortress. In addition to machine guns, each craft had two of those awful rockets mounted under the nose.

"Why didn't they fly themselves across the sea?" someone wondered over the communication crystal. "Why did they need a ride on that thing?"

"Maybe the flying fortress has lavatories inside," the one female pilot here besides Cas said, sounding wishful. Lieutenant Solk, that was her name.

"Actually," came Tolemek's voice, distant and barely audible as he leaned toward the crystal from the back seat, "my research has shown that the dragon blood, despite being so powerful, actually is burned as fuel when the Cofah use it in their rockets, unmanned fliers, and fliers. An infinitesimal amount goes a long way, yes, but they would have realized by now that a vial does eventually run out. It's probably more efficient for them to carry all of the aircraft that way than to have them fly across the ocean individually."

"Thank you for the science lesson, Tee," Ridge said. "Everyone ready to take it to them? Crash, you'll take point on the first run. I'll lead the incursion team plus Solk and Pimples, and we'll see if we can wreak some havoc on that fortress while finding a spot to drop off our passengers without anyone noticing. Anyone who can make smoke to cover their landing, do so. I'll try to find something to shoot that can blow up and make that smoke seem realistic."

A dozen yes-sirs came back to him over the crystal, and one of the fliers streaked into the lead, its nose pointed toward the fortress. As the others fell into a V-formation behind it, the guns boomed from the artillery towers below. The fortress must have flown into their range. Yes, a massive black shell arced across the sky and slammed into one of the front walls of the flying castle.

Sardelle expected it to do damage, but it simply bounced off.

Several of the pilots cursed.

"Is Cofah metal really hard, or is that... magicked?" another asked.

"Cut the chatter," Ridge said. "We're going in. Do as much damage as you can on this first run, before they have all their fliers in the sky. And don't get hit."

Someone snorted, but he got another round of yes-sirs.

The sorceress has reinforced the walls, Jaxi said. *That's probably why they were waiting for her to arrive.*

Are we going to be able to get to the platform and jump on? Sardelle imagined a big invisible bubble protecting the fortress, and the Iskandian fliers bouncing off as they tried to approach.

I don't sense anything like that. They wouldn't be able to fire through a barrier, if it were up, and it looks like they're planning to do that.

Yes, as if the fliers filling the sky like angry wasps driven from a nest weren't enough, giant rotating shell guns squatted on each of the fortress's towers. Even as Sardelle watched, the first one launched toward the north side of the city. Toward the castle?

She grimaced, picturing the damage that had already happened to the ancient structure. As the shell streaked toward its target, she located the gunpowder-like substance packed inside of it and lit a spark. The projectile exploded several hundred feet above the castle.

That might not have been the best idea, Jaxi said. *The sorceress is going to have an eye on us now, and we're trying to sneak in.*

If we felt her and knew where she was, I'm sure she already felt us. Sardelle bristled at the idea of letting the city take damage if she could stop it.

She might have been aware of us, but not worried about us. Now we'll represent a problem she has to deal with, and we're up here in this flimsy little flier at the moment.

Several arguments floated into her mind, but the fortress was firing more artillery weapons, and the Iskandian fliers had reached gun range of the Cofah fliers. Ridge was already swooping to stay out of the sights of the oncoming enemies. There were so many of them that Sardelle couldn't help but feel the inevitability of being struck. She and Jaxi could shield their flier, but what of the others in the group?

She forced herself to concentrate on what she *could* do and blew up another shell arcing toward the city. The sounds of firing guns and explosives filled her ears, drowning out the roar of the ocean. Just as she detonated a third shell, she felt a presence sweep over her.

Yup, she noticed us, Jaxi said. *And her sword too. Wreltad.*

Wreltad? You recognized it? Him?

No, he introduced himself.

That was polite.

He said he eagerly looked forward to engaging in battle with me and cleaving my blade from my hilt. Jaxi sounded like she was ready to cleave something of her own.

Perhaps not so polite, after all.

He also used the word forsooth. If I can't melt him down, I'm at least going to mock him.

Forsooth? Sardelle thought of Jaxi's argument that this sorceress and her sword had come from the past.

"Incursion team," Ridge said, "they're not patrolling the air beneath the fortress. We'll do a run under it, doing any damage we can to the bottom, then come up on the other side and drop off the team. Follow my lead. Crash, keep the rest of their fliers busy."

"Doing my best, sir." Crash already sounded tense.

I'm trying to burn bullets before they strike our people's fliers, Jaxi said, *but there are hundreds of them streaking through the sky. It feels like millions.*

I'm sure they appreciate your help. Though Sardelle did not want to abandon the city, she shifted her own focus to shielding Ridge and the others whenever she could. She left cutting down bullets to Jaxi, who had much faster reflexes. She also tried to ignite some of the vials of dragon blood powering the Cofah craft. As with the fliers they had encountered earlier in the day, the vials were metal and resistant to her attacks. Had the new sorceress been the one to imbue the containers with protective power? If so, she had been busy over there.

As Ridge weaved and dove on his way to his target, Sardelle focused on the engine of a craft following them. She poured heat into the workings, hoping to melt something important. To her surprise, at a certain temperature, the oil lubricating the pistons turned to vapor, and her heated air caused the vapor to explode.

That's delightful, Jaxi said as smoked poured out of the flier dogging them. It veered off Ridge's tail and headed for the fortress platform. An explosion came from within the engine, and the craft didn't make it. It spiraled downward, heading for the rocks of the harbor far below.

Look out! Jaxi barked at the same time as several other pilots cried the same warning over the crystal.

Ridge swerved so hard that Sardelle was thrown against the side of the flier. If not for her harness, she would have been thrown *out* of the flier.

A massive ball of crackling white energy streaked toward them from one of the towers. It filled the air with the intensity of the sun, scorching the air around it as it drew closer.

Aware of Jaxi throwing her power up in a shield in front of it, Sardelle struggled to regain her equilibrium and add her energy to the shield. Their combined forces only slowed down the ball, stealing some but not all of its power. Fortunately, Ridge had reacted quickly enough and steered them out of the energy ball's path. Even so, its heat seared their cheeks and crinkled the paint on the flier's wing as it soared past.

Seven gods, she's strong, Sardelle thought.

At least we know exactly where she is now, Jaxi responded.

That's a good thing?

Well, she's up on a tower instead of down on the platform that we want to land on.

I haven't checked closely, but she probably has legs.

"You all right, Colonel?" Cas asked. She and Duck were keeping their fliers close to Ridge's with the other two pilots he had selected flanking them.

"Yeah, just got some nose hairs singed." Ridge led the team under the platform. That had been his plan all along, but Sardelle sensed that he hoped the sorceress wouldn't be able to target him if she couldn't see him. She wouldn't count on that. "It's a little alarming when the *other* side has a sorceress," Ridge added.

His alarm didn't keep him from flying close to the banks of thrusters lining the bottom of the platform. All manner of pipes and conduits snaked around under there. He fired indiscriminately. Sardelle would have even less of a guess as to what might be critical to the operation of the massive craft.

A dozen Cofah fliers cruised under the platform in pursuit. They were a ways behind, so Sardelle let her senses stretch up through the layers of metal and machinery, trying to get a sense of what awaited them and also where the dragon blood was located. A large amount of it powered the flying fortress, so she found it quickly. The power it emitted sang to her, as it would to anyone sensitive enough to feel its energy. It sloshed in a hollow metal sphere that was about two-thirds of the way full. If Tolemek's hypothesis was correct, that the Cofah were burning the blood as fuel, perhaps that indicated that they had already spent a third of their reserve in flying across the ocean to reach Iskandia. That could mean that they would have to turn around and fly back once they used up another third. Even if Tolemek was only partially successful in destroying that sphere, it might be enough to halt the attack. But even if they could avoid the Cofah soldiers, getting to the sphere would be a challenge. She sensed the maze of metal and conduits, bulkheads and pipes, and had no idea how to reach the blood. Logic suggested there must be an access panel somewhere, but she would have to get closer to have a hope of finding it.

"Good shot, Ahn," Ridge said, at the same time as someone warned, "I hope you know what you're doing with that rocket, sir."

Sardelle brought her awareness back to the battle. They were snaking back and forth near the back edge of the Cofah platform, shooting at the squadron that had followed them. What had been a dozen Cofah fliers was down to eight. At the mention of a rocket, Sardelle twisted to look behind her. Her eyes grew wide as she took in the ominous black cylinder arrowing right for her.

Ridge dove down, as if to plunge thousands of feet into

the ocean. The rocket followed. Ridge's flier twisted in the air as he pulled up immediately, heading straight for one of those thrusters. By now, Sardelle had a notion of what he meant to do, but that didn't keep her from clinging to her seat with her heart hammering in her chest as they whipped about at breakneck speed. He held course for the thruster for so long that she started to believe he might actually plunge straight up into it. She almost said something into his mind, a warning that they couldn't reach the platform above that way, but she did not want to risk distracting him.

At the last second—and maybe a hair after it—he pulled the flier to the side. Afraid their momentum would carry them into the unyielding metal, Sardelle formed a cushion of air to deflect them. They came so close to the framework supporting the thrusters that she could have reached up and touched it—the heat from the combustion washed over them, baking them as would the most intense desert sun—but Ridge had calculated the turn correctly. They didn't touch anything. The rocket, however, flew up into the thruster. Unable to turn, it banged against the inner wall and bounced into the stream of heat.

The explosion that followed would have impressed Kaika. Orange flames burst out of the thruster housing like magma from a volcano. Sardelle had just enough time to shift her cushion of air to protect their flier from the shockwave that roiled out. Ridge would have missed most of it, anyway—he hadn't hesitated one iota after escaping the rocket—but she was pleased that no damage came to their craft. The thruster, however, after spitting that cloud of fire, fell cold and dark.

"Too bad there are two hundred more of them," Ridge muttered.

Sardelle was surprised nobody congratulated him on the fancy flying, but utter silence had fallen over the crystals. Only the whirring of the propellers and the bangs from machine guns continued, relentless in Sardelle's ears.

"The fireball—whatever the hells it was—got Masser," Crash announced.

Ridge slammed his fist against his control panel, fury blazing in his mind. But he quickly regained control, cordoning off his feelings to deal with later. All he said aloud was, "Keep doing what you're doing, Wolf Squadron. We're whittling them down. Ahn, Duck, we're going in for the drop off. Sardelle, Tolemek, Kaika, get those ropes ready. We're not going to be able to come to a full stop and let you off easy."

"Kaika says she'd be disappointed if it was easy," Duck said.

"Tolemek is ready," Cas said, her voice flat. Duck's was too. All of their humor had vanished at Crash's announcement.

Sardelle wished she could have done something to stop that loss, but she was barely aware of the other flier team. They had shifted from assaulting the fortress to diving in and out around the dirigibles, probably hoping the sorceress wouldn't risk flinging energy weapons toward the Cofah balloons.

"Sardelle?" Ridge twisted to look back at her.

She nodded firmly. *I'm ready.*

If you see that sorceress...

I'll try to deal with her. She had no idea how, but with this unknown sorceress up here, Sardelle was afraid Ridge's squadron wouldn't survive the wait while she and the others fought their way to the blood.

I was going to say run the other way, Ridge thought. He had turned around to pilot them out from under the platform, but she knew he wore a wry expression.

That won't save Iskandia.

Just take out that blood. Gravity will take care of the sorceress, along with everyone else on that platform.

Good point, Sardelle thought, pleased—and relieved—that there might be a way to avoid a confrontation she knew she could not win.

You make sure you get back to the pick-up point when you're done. I'm hoping Tolemek's spray takes a few minutes to eat through the metal, so there will be time for you to escape. Sardelle. He glanced back at her again. *You better come back to me.*

She leaned forward and gripped his shoulder. *You better be here when I come back.*

I'll be here, one way or another.

"Double-check your watches," Ridge said to everyone. "Unless I hear differently, we'll pick you up in twenty minutes."

"Yes, sir."

"Kaika has smoke grenades ready to throw," Duck announced.

"Good," Ridge said, his voice all business, though Sardelle knew his mind was as battered by fear and emotion as hers was. "We're pretending to aim for that tower," he said as he led the team along the back wall of the fortress. "Watch out for the gunner at the top."

"Yes, sir."

Sardelle glimpsed Tolemek as Cas flew close to Ridge's wing. He had something in his hand, as well, ready to throw. Nobody had given her instructions on how to use any of the grenades that had been stuffed into the bag at her feet, so she simply readied her mind to fan the smoke, to try to make the cloud bigger, so they could hide in it.

Better get your rope ready unless you're going to jump, Jaxi advised.

Sardelle tossed the end over the side as Ridge flew around the tower, then dipped toward its inner wall. Cofah soldiers with rifles raced out of a hangar-like building and ran toward them. She hadn't realized Ridge had anything other than his machine guns, but he must have pilfered from Tolemek's stash. He threw the first grenade. The soldiers halted when it clanged to the metal floor. One paused to shoot at Ridge, but the others scurried back. He ducked and tilted his wings, swooping around the tower again.

Wait until the next pass, Ridge thought.

Understood.

If you need me before the twenty minutes, or you need me at all, for anything, you know how to get in touch.

Sardelle blinked back tears, touched by his concern and afraid because of it too. *I do,* she thought, glad she did not have to use her voice, because she wouldn't have trusted it to work right. *Thank you.*

Tolemek and Kaika also threw grenades at the base of the tower. Ridge rose to the top, the nose of his flier peeking above the crenellations. He had come up behind the big artillery gun, and before the craft's momentum took him over the tower, he pounded rounds into the soldiers reloading the weapon. Neither had time to do more than scream as they were cut down. Even though it was all over in two seconds, those screams—and the horrified expressions on the men's faces—burned into Sardelle's mind. Another time, she would lament the ludicrousness of this everlasting war the Cofah forced on those it conquered— or tried again and again to conquer—but there was no time for contemplation now. Her hands shook as she gripped the rope, prepared to jump over the side.

Plumes of thick black smoke roiled from the base of the tower and also the top of it. Ridge swooped in, taking the place that Ahn's craft had just vacated. Sensing that Tolemek and Kaika already crouched at the base of the ruined tower, Sardelle wasted no time. She grabbed the bag of explosives and slung herself over the edge.

The rope burned her hands as she slid down it, but she had to hurry. Ridge's flier could not hover there, and its nose was already tilted upward, firing at the gunmen on the next tower over. Sardelle hit the ground hard and almost lost her footing. The awareness that she carried a bag of volatile—and combustible— weapons gave her the tenacity to keep from tumbling onto them.

Kaika gripped her arm and pointed. Between the booms of the fortress's artillery weapons and the constant bangs of the fliers' guns, Sardelle couldn't have heard her allies if they had been yelling in her ear. She couldn't see Tolemek but sensed him ahead of her, waving for them to follow. Even standing right next to Sardelle, Kaika was almost invisible in the dense smoke. Jaxi must be helping to thicken it, because it hung around them like a heavy fog, despite the constant blowing of the sea breeze.

You're welcome.

Sardelle raced after Kaika, who took the lead. Did Kaika have any idea where to go? She had to be even less familiar with the layout than Sardelle was. Once they reached a modicum of cover, Sardelle would use her senses to try to guide them to the blood without being seen.

Good luck. The sorceress knows where we are.

She's not coming, is she?

No, she seems to have the goal of burning every Iskandian flier out of the sky.

Sardelle clenched her teeth, wishing she dared fight her way to the sorceress and attack her. But Ridge was right. If they could pull this off, gravity might do what she could not achieve with magic alone.

She did just call an officer up to the top of her tower, Jaxi added. *She may be about to inform him of our presence.*

Wonderful.

Kaika found a low door leading into the space inside of the wall. She opened it and ducked inside, rifle leading. Before Sardelle could warn her that two soldiers were walking down the corridor inside, two shots fired. The men went down silently and swiftly, the bullets taking each of them in the heart. Sardelle hadn't realized Kaika was as deadly with firearms as she was with explosives, but couldn't be surprised. She just hoped it would be enough to keep their team alive.

Yup, Jaxi said. *She told the men about you. Expect a lot more company.*

As Sardelle ducked inside, she couldn't help but glance over her shoulder and through the smoke, hoping for a glimpse of Ridge, unable to shake the feeling that she might never see him again. But only enemy fliers filled the sky.

Chapter 16

Ridge fought back tears as he dove away from the tower. He wouldn't be able to wipe his eyes without removing his goggles, and that would take seconds when he dared not be inattentive up here. Sardelle would be fine. He had to believe that. He had to focus on staying alive, because if his mind wandered for even a second, he risked death, especially since attacking the tower had riled up the Cofah even further. So long as they hadn't seen the drop-off.

Ridge led Ahn, Duck, Solk, and Pimples back under the platform, staying close to it, weaving between the thrusters. It was the only place where the gunners in the fortress could not target them, nor did the dirigibles shoot at them. He wasn't sure yet whether the sorceress could curve her energy balls around the edge, but she hadn't yet. So far, they only had to deal with the other fliers down here, and those rockets. Evading those things was terrifying and exhilarating at the same time. Ridge shouldn't want more of them fired at him, but he couldn't help but imagine himself taking out some more of those thrusters. How many would it take before the massive fortress started to sag? The Cofah engineers would have built in redundancy, but still, there had to be a limit to how many thrusters they could afford to lose.

He leaned toward the communication crystal, "Report, Crash."

"We're harrying this here weather balloon, sir, pretending it's a mission-critical target. Mostly just trying to stay away from that she-witch. Even if you dodge those big lightning balls, they melt the fabric off your wings on their way by."

"I noticed. Good, yes. Stay away from her." Ridge had the sense that the fortress was moving, whereas before, it had been hanging stationary over the water. He glanced toward the ground and grimaced. Yes, it was definitely heading inland. To bomb the capital? Or worse?

"Figure I should invite you to do the same, sir," Crash said. "I'm sure the Cofah would miss these airships terribly if they fell out of the sky. This one here's about ready to drop. Come and work on the other two with us."

Ridge flew between two Cofah pilots trying to pin him against the bottom of the platform. One pulled out a sniper rifle. Ridge tilted his wings and banked, aiming his craft right at the cockpit. Even though he couldn't hear the man's curses, the alarmed—and furious—look on his face sufficed. Ridge would not have risked his own flier by crashing into another in midair, but the other pilot didn't seem to know that. He dropped his rifle, and grabbed his flight stick with flustered hands, shoving it down. Ridge skimmed over his head as the Cofah flier dipped, nearly giving the pilot a haircut. The maneuver did not do any damage to the man's craft, but Ridge had the satisfaction of seeing that rifle tumble over the side and plummet toward the ocean.

"Flying and shooting isn't easy." Ridge nodded in Ahn's direction.

"We've got more company coming, sir," Ahn said, pointing toward six more fliers cruising under the shadow of the platform. That made almost twenty soaring around down here, taking shots at Ridge's small team. The Cofah hadn't figured out that there were too many of them—they kept getting in each other's way. Ridge wouldn't complain. Since they were outnumbered and outgunned, greater experience was the only advantage he and his team had.

"Should we join the others, sir?" Duck asked. "Until it's time to do the pickup?"

Ridge hated the idea of leaving the platform in case Sardelle needed help. He also hated the idea of simply waiting and trying to avoid being hit. A man could die doing nothing useful at all. When Fate chose to sink his gravestone into the earth, he wanted it to be because he had been fighting to accomplish something. What *could* he accomplish here? Unfortunately, the fliers under the platform had stopped shooting rockets, at least at his team. Someone must have reported the thruster incident.

An appealing idea popped into his mind. It might not have been *sane*, but it was appealing.

"Anyone want to stay here with me and try to blow up the tower the sorceress is standing on?" Ridge asked.

A few heartbeats of silence answered him. Was he being too presumptuous? Maybe it was suicidal, but if they could take out the sorceress, it would demoralize the rest of the Cofah. She might even be the mission commander. Without her leadership, they might decide to retreat. At the least, it wouldn't be a bad idea to keep the sorceress distracted while Sardelle and the others sneaked around inside the fortress.

"I'll do it," Ahn said, her voice deadpan. Or maybe just dead. Ridge hadn't seen an iota of positive emotion from her since Apex's death. He hadn't seen much emotion of any kind at all, aside from dejection.

"Don't think that's a good idea, sir," Crash said. "You saw what she can do, and I'm figuring she's got more tricks in her magic bag."

"Aren't the walls reinforced?" Pimples asked, his voice squeaky as he dove to avoid three fliers gunning for him.

Ridge veered toward his pursuers, loosing bullets of his own. One of the pilots who was focused on chasing Pimples didn't see him swooping in like a hawk from above. Ridge shot him in the head. The other two scattered in a disorganized fashion. He didn't think the Cofah had thought of adding an equivalent of the communication crystals. One more tiny advantage.

"Thank you, sir," Pimples said.

"I've got a few of Tolemek's grenades," Ridge said, not willing to let his idea drop. "They might accomplish what the shells shot from thousands of feet below lacked the power to do. I'm not ordering anyone to go with me, just asking for volunteers. Anyone besides Ahn?"

Duck sighed. "I'm with you, sir. Like the tick that goes off the cliff with the lemming it's clinging to."

Ridge steered for the far corner of the platform, the one

with the sorceress's tower above it. "Thank you, Duck, but in the future, I'd appreciate analogies that turn me into something fiercer than a lemming."

"No problem with me being a tick?"

"I like my pilots to have more self-esteem than that, in general, but if that's your animal of choice, so be it." Ridge knew his humor sounded forced, and it was probably unwelcome right now, but he felt it important to make the others believe that he was confident, that nothing happening here was alarming him.

"A tick's an insect, sir," Duck said.

"Thanks for clearing that up. Pimples, Solk, I see you following. You coming to the tower?"

"Yes, sir," Solk said, her voice calmer than Pimple's had been. "Don't have any explosives, but planning to stay on your back and keep the others off it."

"Like a tick?" Ridge asked.

"Wouldn't mind being something fiercer, either, sir."

"Ticks *are* fierce," Duck said. "Got a powerful bite for something so little."

"I'm going up." Ridge angled out from under the platform, then tilted his nose straight up, hoping to surprise the sorceress and anyone else at the top of the tower.

Three variations of, "Got your back, sir," followed him. Ridge also heard a soft, "Good luck, sir," from Crash before he pulled his flier upside down and pounded bullets into the top of the wall and the top of the tower.

For a second, and from his upside down position, he had the satisfaction of seeing surprise on the sorceress's face, a bronze-skinned face with aristocratic features framed by flowing black hair. She wore golden armor that looked like it was made from dragon scales. That was all Ridge had time to see as he zipped past, firing. His bullets took out two startled soldiers on the wall, but, surprised or not, the sorceress had time to shield herself and the gunners atop the tower. His bullets burst into flame instead of striking their targets. He almost crashed into that invisible barrier himself, but tilted his wings at the last second and righted himself. A soft bump to the belly of his craft was all he felt. He had time to arm and toss one of the grenades before flying out of range.

"She blew that up before it struck," Duck said.

"I can't hit her or anyone around her," Ahn said, a tinge of frustration entering her voice.

"Now she's looking to mow you down like thistles in a field, sir," Duck said.

Ridge had expected as much. He plunged down the length of the tower and curved under the platform again.

He flinched when two Cofah fliers came into view, right at the edge of the platform. He almost crashed into them, but had the wherewithal to shoot at the same time as he drove hard to the right. Bullets slammed into the back of his craft, riddling the side before he veered out of the line of fire.

"Glad Sardelle isn't back there now," he whispered, twisting through the air in case the Cofah came around and tried to target him again.

But Ahn and Duck plowed through the Cofah fliers after him. With guns ablaze, they finished the job he had started. The pilots slumped in their seats, dead, and their craft spiraled toward the ocean, smoke streaming from their engines.

"Appreciate the help back there," Ridge said, coming around again. He wanted another try at the sorceress, but he didn't know how he might make his try effective.

He peered up at the thrusters near the edge of the platform, wishing he might direct a rocket into one right under the tower. Still, he doubted that would matter. He had flown up and down around the fortress enough times now that he knew that a layer of machinery or who knew what lay between the bottom of the platform and the top of it.

"Sir," Duck blurted. "Your tail!"

Ridge gaped over his shoulder. The tail of his flier had burst into flames. Those bullets couldn't have been responsible for that. With a sick feeling, he knew the sorceress had targeted him, the same way Sardelle had targeted those Cofah fliers earlier in the day.

"I'm going up there for one more try before I can't maneuver anymore." He couldn't bring himself to say before he *crashed*.

"Sir, wait," Ahn said. "I'll fly under you and match your speed. You can climb down into my back seat."

"Then who takes Tolemek home?" Ridge already had no idea who would take *Sardelle* home. He had promised he would be there for her, damn it.

"Don't get suicidal on us, sir," Duck said. "It's a good idea. We'll figure out the rest later."

"Yeah," Pimples added. "We're supposed to be the ticks, not you."

"That didn't make sense, Pimples," Ahn said. "Colonel?"

"I agree. It didn't make sense." With his nose full of the stench of his own smoke, Ridge headed for the edge of the platform again. Already, his craft wobbled, the control affected.

"I meant you should jump down, sir," Ahn blurted. "I'm right behind you. I can get under you."

"Let's get under this sorceress. Or on top of her."

Ridge climbed as tremors wracked his craft. As much as he appreciated Ahn's offer, he didn't want to sit in someone's back seat like an invalid. If he was going to crash anyway, maybe he could crash in a way that would make a difference, like by taking out a tower with a sorceress on it. If he matched his direction with that of the fortress and cut down on the relative speed between them, maybe he could survive by jumping out before the flier crashed.

"Wishful thinking, soldier," he mumbled.

But it was all he could think to try. Ridge climbed above the height of the fortress wall, slouching as low in his cockpit as he could. His smoking tail would not keep the riflemen from targeting him. He could just see above the rim of the cockpit, and he spotted the sorceress looking up at him, a sword in her hand. It shimmered blue, ripples of energy coursing along the blade. Even before she pointed it in his direction, he suspected he would be the target. He turned, choosing what was destined to be his crash route carefully. And he hoped that sword wasn't about to utterly incinerate him.

Ahn rose above the level of the tower, firing at the sorceress from scant feet away. Without bothering to look worried, the woman waved her hand. Ridge did not see the invisible power that crashed into Ahn's flier, but it hit her like a tidal wave. Her craft flew backward, tumbling nose over tail.

Ridge wished he could do something, but his rudder and tail had burned entirely off. He had no directional control. The course he had set would be his final one.

Though Ahn hadn't damaged the sorceress, she *had* distracted the woman. By the time she turned her attention back toward Ridge, his flaming flier was almost upon her. He had already unbuckled his harness; he grabbed both sides of the cockpit, pulling his feet onto the seat. The sorceress lifted a hand, but fear—or at least mild concern—widened her eyes for the first time. She turned and jumped from the top of the tower. The gunners had already flown.

Ridge licked his lips—his timing would have to be precise. If he jumped too soon, he would miss any chance of landing on the fortress. If he was too late, the crash would kill him. A quick glance showed him that Cas wasn't anywhere nearby where she might fly under and catch him, not after she had been hurled across the sky like a bug. Ridge hoped Sardelle never had to face this woman.

"Now," he whispered to himself and jumped.

He sprang as far as he could, trying to land on the walkway along the wall. But he hadn't calculated the lightness of the flier well. Even with its rapid downward momentum, the seat—his springboard—gave slightly as he jumped. He stretched his arms toward the wall, terror leaping into his throat when he realized he wouldn't reach his target.

Ridge slammed into the metal barricade so hard, he almost blacked out. Pain struck him like a boulder to the chest, and his ribcage bent with the impact, bone crunching. Some primitive instinct kicked in, overriding the pain, and his fingers caught and curled around the top of the wall.

Shock clutched his torso, and he couldn't breathe—or think. He was scarcely aware of his flier crashing into the tower—it was probably the only thing that kept ten soldiers from running over to shoot him. He couldn't have done anything to stop them. He could barely fight back the intense waves of pain to keep holding on. When he could finally suck in a breath, that only made the pain worse. Unwelcome tears blurred his vision, and he lost sight of the smoke billowing from the top of the tower. He hoped he had taken out the gun, and that the gun had fallen over the edge and onto the sorceress. He wanted his last action in life to count, since he couldn't imagine how he was going to pull himself up with however many broken ribs he had just given himself. Even uninjured, it would have been a struggle. The smooth metal wall didn't offer so much as a deep scratch that he could wedge his boot into.

"Someone's hanging on over there," came a shout from the side.

Not good. Ridge's fingers were already quivering. He had his pistol and a knife belted at his waist, but neither would do him any good if someone leaned over and pointed a rifle in his face.

The buzz of propellers increased in volume behind him. Ridge risked more pain to glance over his shoulder. A Wolf Squadron flier barreled straight toward him. *Almost* straight toward him. Right away, he realized what the pilot had in mind. He was going to fly under Ridge, giving him a chance to drop down into that empty rear seat.

Not *he*, Ridge corrected, recognizing the slight form in the cockpit even before she turned, lifting her Mark 500 to fire twice behind her. It was Ahn. Coming in fast. Two Cofah fliers were on her tail, firing indiscriminately. Ridge winced as bullets bounced off the wall a few feet below him.

A soldier leaned out above him, staring down, his expression somewhere between surprise and delight. Ridge still hung from his fingers, helpless to do anything as his forearms quivered from the strain.

Ridge glanced down again. Ahn was almost there, and her aim was precise. She would fly right under him. But the drop would be more than twenty feet, even if she skimmed under the platform as close to it as she could. And the speed—who in all the hells could time that fall and not miss the flier?

Above him, the grinning soldier raised his rifle. Ridge wished he could pull himself up with some great feat of strength and punch that grin right off his face. But he was as good as dead if he stayed here. He might as well try the jump.

Another soldier leaned into view. Four seconds and he could drop. But it didn't look like they would give him that long.

"Wait," the second soldier said, pushing the rifle aside. "That's Colonel Zirkander."

As the man added, "If we can capture him..." Ridge glanced down, almost letting go. He met Ahn's eyes through their goggles as she flew under him. But his mind did an instant calculation, tracking the angle and the altitude of the Cofah craft right behind her. He wouldn't be a useless invalid in the back seat if he could take over *that* flier.

"Too dangerous," the first soldier said, swinging his rifle back toward Ridge's face.

He barely noticed. He was counting in his head. Two... one... now.

Ridge heard the bang of the rifle as he fell, but it fired into the space he *had* occupied. He was falling, the wind whipping his scarf, terror clutching his heart. His fear almost immobilized him, but he forced himself to yank out his knife as he dropped, to ignore the stabs of pain from his chest.

He slammed onto the body of the flier right *behind* the pilot. The entire craft shuddered under his weight, the give softening his landing somewhat, but he still came hard down. Pain erupted in his leg when one knee twisted the wrong way. He couldn't bite back a scream as his boot almost slid off the fuselage. Only his one-handed grip on the rim of the cockpit kept him from tumbling to his death.

The pilot jerked around as much as his harness would allow, surprised but already reaching for his pistol. Ridge turned his scream of agony into a battle roar and jabbed the man in the side of the neck with his dagger. Knowing he couldn't win a confrontation from his precarious perch, he stabbed the Cofah again and again, feeling more like a dying animal than an officer. Pain made his attacks clumsy, and had the man not been strapped in and unable to fight properly, Ridge never would have won. But from behind the cockpit, he overcame the pilot quickly. There was no time for relief. The flier was out of control and heading for a bank of thrusters.

With shaking hands, Ridge hacked at the dead pilot's shoulder harnesses. He nearly tumbled into the cockpit as he attempted to cut away the waist strap. Trying not to feel like a depraved maniac, Ridge pushed the pilot over the side. Without watching him fall, Ridge lunged into the vacated spot. For the first time, he was pleased that the Cofah had stolen the basic flier technology from his people, because the control panel was familiar to him. He wrenched the flight stick to the side, narrowly avoiding those thrusters.

Ahead of him, Ahn had twisted in her seat and was staring back at him. She shouted something that he couldn't hear over the sound of the propellers, but he was fairly certain it was, "You're a lunatic!" He doubted she added the sir at the end.

Ridge couldn't say she was wrong. His move had left him injured and flying an enemy craft, one his squadron would try to shoot down on sight, and without a crystal, he had no way to talk to any of them. The rockets in his new aircraft had been fired, but the machine guns still had half of their ammunition. It would be enough. He could keep attacking, keep helping his people.

He forced a smile and gave Ahn a cheerful wave, then pointed for her to pay attention to the enemies ahead of her. Little had changed, and they weren't done with this battle yet. No, one thing had changed, as he soon saw when he flew up to check. The sorceress had not returned to her post on the tower. He grimaced, afraid that meant she had gone to deal with Sardelle and the others.

* * *

Sardelle followed Kaika, keeping her senses stretched out, so she could warn the others when soldiers were heading their way. Tolemek trailed after her, a pistol in one hand, a knockout grenade in the other, and his special spray bottle clasped to a loop on his belt. He hadn't had an opportunity to knock anyone out yet. Kaika was too deadly, shooting any soldier that dared run toward them through the corridor. Right now, it was hard to think of her as the amiable lady who offered raunchy sex advice to anyone who would listen. She was a walking deliverer of death, and Sardelle could only be glad she was on their side.

I've found an access panel in the floor, Jaxi said. *But it's not anywhere near that tunnel in the wall you're walking through. You'll have to leave at the door ahead, sneak across the back of the flight deck, and enter double doors that lead into a big maintenance shop.*

Sneak across the back of the flight deck? How were they going to do that? With the fliers all in the air, that would be open ground.

Sneaking is optional, but you need to cross that space. There's only one entrance to the shop.

What about behind it? Can we blow our way in? Between us, we're carrying enough explosives to take out half of the Cofah continent.

We can try that, but it's not abutting this outer wall. You'll have to— More people coming. Six this time.

I sense them. Sardelle tapped Kaika on the shoulder and held up her hand. Their group paused between two of the oil lamps that lined the windowless interior and guttered with the vibrations of the fortress. Not sure her hand gesture would be seen, she whispered, "Six coming. I think they know to expect us."

Kaika nodded grimly, but Tolemek brushed past both of them before she could continue ahead.

"Let me." He held up one of his knockout grenades as he went by and gave Kaika a dark look. "No need to kill *everyone* here."

Kaika shrugged and let him go ahead, but whispered, "He knows that if we achieve our goal, this whole place is plummeting into the ocean, right? And that nobody's going to survive that?"

With the soldiers just around the corner, Sardelle held a finger to her lips as her answer. Besides, she didn't want to dwell too deeply on the mass killing they were attempting to perpetrate. It was war, and they were defending their homeland, but that did not make it easy to digest. She understood why this bothered Tolemek. These were his people, and he had once been a soldier in this very army.

Ahead, Tolemek knelt and rolled his grenade around the corner.

"There," one of the soldiers yelled. The man couldn't have been more than five feet from the corner.

Shots rang out, but Tolemek was already backing away. "Hold your breath," he warned as he pushed Sardelle and Kaika behind him.

The sorceress and her forsoothing sword are coming, Jaxi warned.

Two soldiers leaped around the corner, their rifles leading. Sardelle hurled a wall of air at them as Kaika's firearm rang out. The men didn't get their shots off, not with Kaika's deadly aim. They crumpled to the ground.

Kaika charged forward, ignoring Tolemek's sigh. She dropped to one knee at the corner and leaned around it just enough to target down the corridor. But she did not fire. Sardelle checked the soldiers with her senses. The other four were unconscious.

Lots more coming, Jaxi said. *If you don't want to fight that woman, you better go quickly. There's a door around the corner. Take that one, and I'll guide you to the maintenance shop.*

"Sorceress coming," Sardelle told the others. "This way."

"I heard," Kaika said, an incredulous expression on her face. Even as she ran to lead the way, she asked, "Was that you talking to me?"

"Jaxi, actually." Sardelle hadn't realized that Jaxi had spoken to everyone, but she had done that before in emergencies, whether everyone was used to the idea of telepathy or not.

They can get used to it. Hurry. I don't want to try and keep you alive against Wreltad.

Sardelle sensed more men on the other side of the door and whispered, "Wait," before Kaika pushed it open. "Four of them. They're walking past, not coming in, I think. Give them a minute." She scanned the area further and found the backside of the cavernous maintenance building a few meters from the door. It was large enough for several of those fliers to be worked on inside, and... She grimaced. No less than ten people were in there. "We're going to need more knockout grenades. Or an attack or something that draws them outside."

She almost reached out to Ridge, but she could sense him under the platform, dealing with countless enemies. No, she would not ask him for help. She dared not even contact him, lest she distract him.

The sorceress entered the corridor inside the wall. She's heading toward you.

The four men Sardelle had been tracking had gone around the corner of the maintenance shop. She waved for Kaika to open the door. She could have done it herself, but the grim determination on Kaika's face—and the blood that wasn't hers spattered on the sleeve of her uniform—said she intended to lead the way, to protect them so they could do their job.

Kaika peered out, checked in both directions, then strode out with her big rifle at the ready. Sardelle went straight to the back wall of the shop, though she glanced up and to the sides. There weren't any soldiers on the wall directly above where they had come out, but a tower loomed not that far away. If the men manning the gun on the top looked back into the compound instead of out at the fliers, they would easily spot Sardelle and the others. She closed her eyes for a second, focused on the insides of that big shell gun, then melted what appeared to be the firing mechanism. That ought to keep them busy for a minute.

She's halfway down the corridor. She's going to know you came out that door and right where you are.

If you're worried about Wreltad, how about you help with this wall?

Tolemek had applied some of his corrosive goo, and it was already steaming, but the concoction would take time to eat through the metal. A thunderous crack came from underneath the tower. Sardelle stared in confusion. Her small sabotage of the gun shouldn't have done that.

No, that was me. I found a water line and broke it, then tore up some of the wall. A nice spray is assaulting the sorceress as we speak.

Should I be worried that you're fighting that hard to ensure that person doesn't reach us?

You should be worried about what will happen if she does, yes.

Tolemek had donned gloves, and he pulled out the ragged, newly formed door that he had made in the wall. Before he set it down, he juggled it on his knee with one hand, so he could throw two more knockout grenades into the shop. Sardelle did not know how effective they would be in such a large space where the high ceiling would provide plenty of room for the gas to disperse. She tinkered with the airflow, trying to push the fumes toward the people on the ground.

Kaika lifted her leg and climbed through the hole before asking if it was safe. Smoke still wafted from the edges. Gunfire rang out, and Sardelle winced. If the sorceress knew their location, perhaps it didn't matter if they made noise, but she could easily envision the Cofah figuring out what they were up to and bringing a whole army down to block the way to the sphere of blood.

They don't need to bring an army, Jaxi thought grimly. *They're sending the sorceress.*

"Which way?" Kaika asked as soon as Sardelle joined her inside.

Tolemek did not bother trying to put the cut-out back in the hole when he stepped through after Sardelle.

"There's a trapdoor in the corner there that leads under the platform." As Sardelle was pointing, her chest tightened, harsh pain forming behind her sternum. She stumbled after the others, avoiding the unconscious men on the floor, but fear filled her mind. She could feel the other sorceress's power, the invisible fingers wrapping around her heart. Sardelle struggled to push back that power, to build a shield around herself—especially her heart.

I'm trying to distract her, Jaxi said, irritation and desperation mingling in her tone, *but you better put some more distance between you and her. She'll only be more powerful up close.*

"Sardelle?" Tolemek knelt beside an open trapdoor. Kaika had already disappeared into the dark space below.

Sardelle staggered toward him, her hand clutched to her chest, most of her focus on fighting off the attack. "Got anything in your bag to thwart a magical assault?" She tried to smile, but it was hard to manage when she felt like she was having a heart attack.

"Explosives?"

"She'd just make a shield." Sardelle pointed down. "We have to hurry. Jaxi is trying to delay her."

Tolemek offered her a hand to lower her down, but she waved him away, not out of pride, but because she had finally managed to erect a shield around herself. The pain in her chest had lessened, but she still felt the sorceress's power and had the sense she was poised to spring another trap.

Sardelle climbed down a metal ladder secured to the wall and into a space thirty degrees warmer than what they had left behind. Heat radiated from the clanking machinery she sensed in the darkness. The space was not lit, but she sensed a cavernous area that extended from one side of the platform to the other, supported only by sturdy posts. Boilers, engines, and other mechanical equipment she couldn't identify filled the space, with tangles of wires, tubes, and ductwork dangling everywhere.

Tolemek landed beside her with a curse as he banged his knee. He had shut the trapdoor, and not a hint of light seeped through from above. Usually, conjuring a sphere of illumination would be easy, but Sardelle was afraid to shift her energy from shielding herself to doing anything else. She could feel the sorceress coming closer, following them with the inevitability of a hound on a trail.

Kaika had not waited at the bottom of the stairs. She had disappeared into the maze of clanking machinery. If she had lit a lantern, Sardelle could not see its influence anywhere. She looked down, startled by intense heat resting against her thigh.

That wasn't all from the temperature of the room. Jaxi's pommel glowed like the embers in a stove.

Are you all right? Sardelle asked. *What are they doing now? Are they hurting you?*

Jaxi did not answer. Her silence alarmed Sardelle even more than a cry of pain would have.

After another curse, Tolemek managed to strike a match and light a lantern. "Want me to lead? I can feel where the blood is. Not sure how to get to it." He curled a lip at the wall of boilers and pipes that surrounded them.

"Go ahead," Sardelle said, distracted by Jaxi's heat. "I'll help if I can."

She thought about trying to put together an attack of her own to slow down the other woman, but if she was as powerful as Jaxi believed, she would easily bat away anything Sardelle threw at her. She ducked and followed Tolemek into the dark, hot maze. As they weaved through the chaotic rows of machines, Sardelle reached out to the other sorceress for the first time, trying to contact her. She doubted anything would come of talking to a Cofah, but maybe she could distract her with words if not power, slow her down slightly.

Where are you from? Why are you working with the Cofah?

She felt stupid asking the second question, because she anticipated the obvious answer, that the sorceress *was* Cofah. She only hoped to get the woman talking. If she was focused on talking, she wouldn't be hurting Jaxi.

When she didn't get an answer immediately, she doubted she would. Soft clangs echoed down from above. At first, she believed they were gunshots, but she realized they were boots—soldiers running across the floor of the machine shop. Sardelle reached up and melted the locking mechanism on the trapdoor. Her team might have to cut its way out later, but she doubted that would be the case. The sorceress could easily incinerate that entire door if she wished.

I am *Cofah*, a proud voice spoke into Sardelle's mind. *I am Tarshalyn Eversong. My family has always served the emperor. You are weak. I cannot believe someone gave you a soulblade.*

Which emperor? Sardelle ignored the insult. If this sorceress came from the distant past, from an ancestor closely descended from a dragon union, she *would* see Sardelle as weak. She would be right.

Magaroshi Toathor the Third.

Even as a student of history, Sardelle had to think for a long minute to place that ruler. Oh, she knew right away that he had died centuries ago, but how *many* centuries? More than ten, she was fairly certain. Fifteen? She believed he had ruled during the Tan'shan Dynasty. Sardelle hadn't seen the woman's armor and clothing yet, but from what Jaxi had described, fifteen hundred years might fit. *You lived during the time when dragons still flew the skies?*

I am descended directly from a silver named Jasholomodrin, the sorceress said, that pride coming through with her voice again. *My great-grandfather. He lives still. Or he did.* For the first time, Eversong's certainty—her arrogance—faltered.

I came from the past too. Sardelle was probably being delusional, but she couldn't help but think that she might form a rapport with the other woman, at least make Eversong hesitate to kill her. *Only three hundred years ago, though. The dragons were long gone by the time I was born.*

That is why you are so weak, your blood so diluted.

I can't claim any great-grand-dragons, no.

You aren't as puny as most of the magic users I've seen since waking up.

Such a compliment.

"Almost there," Tolemek whispered, squeezing between two long cylindrical boilers, the walls and rivets hot to the touch.

Sardelle stayed with him and kept herself from thinking of their plan, of what they meant to do down here. Even though she was guarding her thoughts as assiduously as she was guarding her body with a shield, she worried that Eversong would guess their intent.

Jaxi, is she still following us? When Sardelle checked the trapdoor, she found it was still sealed.

A soft moan whispered in her mind.

Jaxi, is there anything I can do to help? Sardelle worried Jaxi's nemesis, the other soulblade, had found a way to attack her, that they were engaged in some mental battle in a way she could not see or understand. Jaxi's hilt blazed with heat.

The world has changed a great deal, Sardelle told Eversong. She sensed the sorceress had entered the machine shop. She would find the trapdoor soon.

Some things never change. Eversong sounded amused as she sent a picture of the battle outside that still raged. *Our people are destined to war through all eternity it seems.*

Pointless. Sardelle banged her knee on a flywheel protruding from some machine. Tolemek glanced back, but she waved for him to continue, to hurry.

Eversong chuckled. *It is pointless for your people to continue to fight. A place awaits you in the empire, if only you succumb.*

That happened in the past. It didn't go well for Iskandia. Sardelle realized Eversong wouldn't know that history, unless she had been in this era long enough to study events of the last millennium.

It will be better this time, when I rule.

Sardelle almost tripped. *What?*

The new emperor has promised me Iskandoth for my assistance here. Eversong almost purred the words into Sardelle's mind. *With so few left in the world with any power, ruling will be a simple matter.*

So much for building a rapport with the woman. Sardelle couldn't even feign to share this interest with her. *You'll find that much has changed, that people fear magic, and will risk everything to get rid of it.* Sardelle thought of the queen and her organization and of those soldiers who had destroyed the Referatu three centuries ago.

Eversong sneered. *Their fear means nothing, except that they will be easy to cow, easy to lead. In time, they will accept me as their ruler. And their only choice.*

"I think I see it," Tolemek whispered. He pointed into the gloom ahead.

At least Sardelle had succeeded in distracting the sorceress. Nobody had opened the trapdoor yet. They ought to have time to—

A great screech ripped through the air, and light poured down from above. Sardelle staggered back, imagining some explosive had been launched. Her heel caught on a bolt sticking up out of the floor, and she barely managed to keep from falling. She gaped up a ten-foot-wide hole in the ceiling, at the gleaming golden armor of the woman standing on the rim of it. Eversong smirked down at Sardelle, even as she held her soulblade aloft, the weapon shimmering blue in the air.

Do it now, Tolemek, Sardelle cried into his mind, even as she stepped forward and reached for Jaxi's hilt.

She worried she would burn her hand on the pommel, but the leather wrapping the hilt wasn't so hot that she could not draw her blade. A good thing, because Eversong only held her smirk for a couple of seconds. Then she leaped down, landing lightly on her feet. In that move, she displayed an agility that Sardelle could only dream of unless Jaxi was helping her.

No, she was trained as a warrior at the same time as she learned magic. Jaxi sounded so weary that Sardelle feared her blade might go limp in her hand.

No, but he drained me. I'll do my best to help, but—

Eversong did not give them time to finish the conversation. She lunged forward, her blade leaving a blue streak in the sky as it swung toward Sardelle's head.

With Jaxi's help, Sardelle made the block in time, but the sheer power that rocketed up her arm made every joint from her knuckles to her shoulder hurt. More than a woman's usual strength lay behind those blows.

Sardelle ducked the second strike. Eversong's blade swept over her head and struck a machine so hard, it lodged into the metal. Steam spat out, startling the woman.

Sardelle tried to take advantage, leaping in and slashing toward Eversong's exposed side. Jaxi ought to be able to bite through that armor.

Before they could find out, Eversong lifted her free hand. Raw power hurled Sardelle ten feet, her boots torn from the ground. She slammed into the side of some machine, the blow knocking all the air from her lungs.

"Need thirty seconds," came a quick whisper from behind her. She had been flung in Tolemek's direction.

Only the knowledge that he was back there with a mission to accomplish gave Sardelle the strength to climb to her feet. She charged at Eversong. It might be suicidal, but she had to be the distraction. She was the only one who could keep Eversong from seeing what Tolemek was doing—and stopping him.

A firearm rang out as Sardelle swung. She half expected a bullet to slam into her back, but nothing hurt her except the power of Eversong's block.

That's Kaika. She's shooting the soldiers who have crept to the rim of the hole and are thinking of shooting you. Also, I can cut through that armor, but it won't be easy. Jaxi frowned. *Those are dragon scales that were molded with pure magic. I hate to say it, but this is the battle where Kasandral would have been more useful.*

There's no way he could be more useful than you. Sardelle hoped the encouragement would help. She kept raining blows at Eversong, but the woman blocked them easily. Only once did Sardelle manage to feint, then slip through her defenses. Jaxi left a knick in the fancy golden armor, but that was it.

Sorry.

Not your fault.

Eversong grew bored of defending and took back the offensive, her sword slicing through the air with the speed of bullets. Her soulblade's blue glow and Jaxi's red were a blur of color that mingled before Sardelle's eyes. A few times, Eversong hit the machinery again, and every time something clunked loudly or steam burst out, it seemed to surprise her. She would be even less familiar with modern technology than Sardelle had been when she had awakened. Sardelle wished she could think of a way to take advantage of that.

Eversong thrust her free hand toward Sardelle, fingers splayed. Sensing the wave of energy before it was released, Sardelle poured all of her energy into creating a shield, both to protect herself and also to protect Tolemek who was somewhere behind her. She felt Jaxi adding power to the shield an instant before the crackling blast of electricity flew from Eversong's fingers. It was identical to the energy ball she had hurled at the fliers. When it slammed into Sardelle's barrier, she deflected the burst, but the power staggered her, knocking her to her knees. The deflected electricity arced all over the room, throwing light and shadows and starting fires. The scent of charred wiring stung the air.

We can't block many like that, Jaxi said. *You should probably keep her from doing that.*

No kidding.

After flinging the energy ball, Eversong had advanced several steps. She must have sensed that Tolemek was back there doing something to the dragon blood. Though Sardelle wanted nothing more than to get out of the way, to accept that she was overmatched and would likely get herself killed, she gritted her teeth and pushed herself to her feet. She advanced to block the woman.

"Sardelle," came a warning from behind her. Tolemek.

Since Eversong had pushed her back, Sardelle was no longer under the hole in the ceiling. They had drawn close to where he was working on the dragon blood. Too close. Even though the battle was keeping Sardelle busy, and sweat streamed down her face, she could feel the power of that blood behind her. She tried to plant her feet, to defend without giving ground. If they failed here... they would fail everywhere. The capital would fall. Iskandia would follow.

"Duck," Tolemek yelled.

Even though she feared she would be cleaved in half when she did so, Sardelle obeyed. At Jaxi's behest, she also threw herself backward, rolling away from Eversong. The other soulblade came down like an axe, biting into the metal floor where Sardelle had been standing.

Thanks, Sardelle thought.

As she jumped to her feet, something flew over her head. A grenade?

Sardelle scrambled back even farther and would have kept going except that she smacked into Tolemek. He was rolling a second grenade across the floor, this one angled toward a big machine beside Eversong. As soon as Tolemek released his weapon, he grabbed her around the waist and hefted her from her feet. Sardelle tried to protest—his grenades wouldn't do anything to stop the sorceress; she would simply deflect or destroy them—but he was leaping over a snarl of pipes and dragging her away from the light of the hole.

"Tolemek, we—"

The first explosion went off, the roar of the boom echoing throughout the cavernous engine room. Sardelle glimpsed Eversong standing in the midst of the flames, an invisible shield shimmering around her, a bored expression on her face. Then Tolemek was hauling Sardelle down an aisle, and she lost sight of the sorceress. Between the fight and his manhandling, she had lost her sense of direction too. Was he running for the trapdoor? If so, they would climb out only to be surrounded by soldiers.

A second explosion rang out, this one ten times more powerful than the first. The floor shuddered, and machinery toppled as Tolemek ran. Bangs sounded all around them, almost like rifle shots, but she realized machinery was toppling over, and pieces of the ceiling were tumbling down. Tolemek almost smacked into a beam as it crashed to the floor in front of them. He backed up, coughing and wiping his eyes. Sardelle took the moment to squirm from his shoulder. Tiny particles of debris clouded the air. Shards of metal flew everywhere. Another boom came from behind them, an entire chain of booms. Something heavy crashed through the ceiling from back in the direction of the hole.

"This way," Tolemek rasped. He crawled his way over the beam.

Whatever was going on back there, the sorceress was not communicating to Sardelle anymore, nor did she feel that presence wrapping around her, threatening to smash her heart. She risked using her power to create a light in front of them. Tolemek picked up his speed, though when another explosion happened, this time to their side, he was pitched into a tangle of wires. Jaxi blazed, incinerating them.

Feeling better now that your twin isn't bothering you? Sardelle helped Tolemek to his feet. He grimaced, having twisted an ankle, but he led the way again.

No, and get moving. That acid of his is eating through the container quickly.

That was the idea. Sardelle leaped over another downed beam. *If they have time to find the problem and fix it...* She cut off the thought, worried the sorceress might be monitoring their conversation somehow.

Yes, but if you're still on this flying contraption when it falls out of the sky, that's going to be a problem.

I see your point. Sardelle ducked a tangle of wires and spotted the ladder leading to the trapdoor up ahead. Someone already stood beside it. Kaika, her face covered with soot again. *Can you tell Ridge we're ready for our pickup?* She wasn't sure if he would be close enough for her to contact.

I already told him.

And?

He's having some troubles and isn't in his original flier anymore, the flier with the back seat.

Erg?

He can't get in touch with the rest of his people, either.

How are we going to get out of here, Jaxi?

Working on it, but Mr. Forsooth is still harassing me from under his pile of machinery. He—

Jaxi?

"Hope you all liked my explosions," Kaika said as they approached. "And hope the witch didn't."

"Up." Tolemek leaped for the rungs. "We have seconds, not minutes."

Kaika cursed and followed him up.

Tolemek hefted the door, but only a few inches. He tossed a knockout grenade through before climbing out.

"Don't we need to wait?" Sardelle imagined running through the gas and dropping to the floor, unconscious. They could fall to their deaths without ever waking up.

One more boom echoed, this time from the floor above instead of the machine room below.

"Never mind," Sardelle said, realizing that had not been a knockout grenade.

Tolemek had already climbed out, with Kaika on his heels. Sardelle scampered up the ladder, but couldn't help but reach into the chaos behind them—bombs were *still* going off—to check on the sorceress. Eversong was alive, but under a pile of rubble. Even her shields hadn't been able to keep her from being buried. Kaika had been placing her bombs as a distraction, or perhaps to do damage to key machinery, but Tolemek must have thrown his very specifically, to drop the ceiling and a few tons of machinery on the woman. That first one had only been a distraction.

"Sardelle," Tolemek barked down. "We need your help."

"Coming." Hoping Eversong would still be pinned when the fortress fell from the air, Sardelle pulled herself out of the hole to join the others. They had to figure out how to get off this flying monstrosity before it was too late.

CHAPTER 17

IF RIDGE'S CHEST HADN'T HURT so much, he would have been grinning, huge battle notwithstanding. Given the overall situation, he shouldn't have been pleased, especially since he hadn't yet figured out how he was going to pick up Sardelle, but the mischief he was able to wreak from within the Cofah flier tickled him. Oh, the maneuverability of the craft left much to be desired, but he kept finding it possible to sneak up on the enemy formations. Though he wore a different uniform, he slouched in the cockpit, and his cap and goggles and scarf did not appear any different from what the other side used. After sailing along with the Cofah squadrons, he lit into them, tearing holes into their engines and pounding the backs of their cockpits. When the pilots looked behind to see who was firing on them, he looked behind *him*, as if craning his neck to spot some vile Iskandian. Then he ran off to torment other fliers before they figured out what was happening. It felt like cheating, but this was an attack on his homeland, and he would use any advantage he could find to get rid of these invaders. He took down eight aircraft with his new trick before Jaxi's voice sounded in his mind.

We need that pickup, or your favorite sword is going to drown.

Kasandral is here?

I'd melt your balls off for that, but I'm too tired. Jaxi did sound tired. Ridge hadn't heard that before, and his gut furled into a tense worried knot. Sardelle must have tangled with the sorceress.

Is she all right, Jaxi?

She will be if you get us off this smoking pile of dung in the next thirty seconds.

Thirty seconds? Ridge glanced at the spot on the control panel where there should have been a chronometer, but the Cofah had left out that feature. Cursing, he fumbled in his pocket for his watch, the slight touch to his chest causing a fresh blast of pain. They had four minutes until the scheduled pickup.

Tolemek's concoction is eating up the dragon blood right now, and Kaika set off a few million bombs too. We don't have *four minutes.*

Understood. I'll get the others. Get up on top of one of the back towers so we can see you.

How Ridge would "get the others" without being shot himself remained to be seen. Thus far, he had been avoiding the Iskandian fliers, so they wouldn't target him by accident. Now, he flew toward the other side of the platform, where Ahn, Pimples, Duck, and Solk had just swept back into view. With the sorceress gone, they had been flying up and shooting the soldiers atop the walls, then ducking back under the platform, so they could come up on the other side. Solk had another two-person flier, so if Ridge could figure out how to tell her to go to the pickup spot, they could successfully get their people out. Unfortunately, Solk and Duck were too distracted to look in his direction.

Wait, Jaxi? he thought as he veered in their direction to help. *Can you tell Cas to come get you? I'm not able to communicate with the others, right now.*

Jaxi did not respond. Ridge feared he had waited too long to remember that she had spoken with some of the others before and presumably could again. She was probably too busy fighting to monitor him constantly.

"Damn," he whispered, both because he had missed an opportunity and because his people were in trouble.

Eight of the Iskandian fliers were hanging with Ahn, Pimples, Duck, and Solk, shooting indiscriminately. Countless bullets riddled the side of Duck's craft, and Solk looked to be struggling with her steering. Ridge hoped the enemy squadron would run out of ammo. He also hoped that Ahn had told the others to watch out for a friendly Cofah flier, since he still had no way to communicate with the rest of his squadron.

Ridge would have preferred to go straight in and join his

squadron, but that would put him into the line of fire from the fliers chasing them. Instead, he angled in from ahead and to the side of them. Ignoring the pain it stirred, he stood slightly in his cockpit—something nobody else would do, because nobody else should have harnesses that had been cut away. He waved, his fingers curled into the Iskandian pilots' all right/ready gesture.

Ahn spotted him. She raised a hand toward him, and he pointed upward several times, making his gestures dramatic so she couldn't miss them. Two of the fliers on their tails had just fired rockets. For the last few minutes, Ridge hadn't had to worry about those, since they seemed to have a built-in command not to lock onto their own fliers. Solk and Duck didn't have that luxury.

Ahn and Pimples dove down, probably intending to loop and come up behind their pursuers. Ridge rose up to skim along near the thrusters, hoping the Cofah would pass him without a second glance, but he was already turning to follow those rockets. Solk and Duck were both good, but he wasn't sure they were good enough—or maybe the term was reckless enough—to perform the moves he had been doing to wreck the rockets. They zigzagged all over the sky to elude them, but he knew from experience that those blood-powered weapons would simply alter course and continue after their targets.

The sleek rockets were faster than fliers, so Ridge struggled to get behind them and put them in the sights of his guns without placing his own people there, as well. One zoomed so close to Solk that Ridge feared for her life. Some instinct warned her to duck in the cockpit and dive down as the rocket skimmed past, nearly knocking her cap from her head.

As it banked to come back toward her, Ridge saw his chance to catch up with it. Wishing for Ahn's deadly accuracy, he sprayed rounds at it. The slender, fast-moving cylinder did not offer a large target, but at least two of his bullets smacked off it; he was certain of it. The rocket wobbled briefly, then continued on its inexorable path, picking up speed as it chased Solk.

"Up," Ridge yelled, and pointed at the thrusters, though it was probably futile. She wouldn't hear him over all of the noise.

He pushed his flier, trying to gain ground again. For an instant, he was behind the rocket and Solk's flier was not square in front of him. He took a second to aim carefully and shot it in the back. Four directional flaps controlled its path, and he had the satisfaction of knocking one off. He would have preferred if the entire rocket blew up spectacularly, but the damage was enough. With its ability to steer compromised, the rocket sailed off uselessly into the distance.

Ridge searched around for Duck. He glimpsed him flying downward with smoke wafting from his engine. Ridge cursed, both because he didn't know if that damage was something that Duck would be able to land with and because that stole one more of his people who was supposed to be available for the pickup.

Before he could chase after Duck and check more closely on him, the snarling face of a Cofah pilot bore toward him from the right. Someone had figured out he wasn't on their side.

Ridge flew up, knowing the pilot wouldn't be able to correct his path quickly enough to follow. Bullets raked through the air under his flier's belly. Somehow, he misjudged the air around him, and he almost smacked into a roaring thruster. Confused, he jerked his craft to the side and toward a lower elevation as heat washed over him.

Once again, he did not compensate fully and get himself far enough away from the thrusters. Usually, his spatial orientation was as good as a bird's, so his first thought was to blame the craft. Then, with the abruptness of a cannon firing, he realized what was happening. The platform was sinking. In seconds, it might be dropping a lot faster.

All thought of helping other pilots and fighting the Cofah fled from his mind. He arrowed straight for the back side of the platform. He had to get Sardelle. He *did* look around as he flew, searching for the others. He needed their help to get his team. They needed to pick up three people, and he didn't have a rope or another seat.

Ridge did not see anybody except Ahn. He cursed. He glanced toward the dirigibles—only one remained in the sky, thanks to Crash's team's work, but if Iskandian fliers were still over there, he couldn't see them. He certainly couldn't communicate with them.

As he soared out from underneath the platform, all he could do was hope that Ahn had called for someone else to come over. At least the Cofah fliers were not chasing them anymore. Those pilots also must have realized the platform was sinking and that they had more problems than enemy bullets now.

Ridge spotted Sardelle, Kaika, and Tolemek standing atop a tower and waving. Relief and worry mixed in his throat, making a tight ball he couldn't swallow around. Having no idea what he intended to do, he soared toward them. Ahn was ahead of him, her rope dangling down from her back seat. At least *one* person would get the ride off that he expected. Could her flier possibly carry the weight of three people instead of two? Ahn was the lightest pilot in the squadron, but neither Kaika nor Tolemek was exactly small.

Ridge? Sardelle asked into his head.

Changed rides. Long story.

How do we...

My lap, he thought. *Can Jaxi help you jump?*

Uhm. Sardelle glanced over the side at the ocean far, far below.

Something huge inside the fortress snapped, the noise echoing for miles around. The platform lurched downward to a thirty-degree slope. Kaika caught Sardelle and threw her weight back, and Ridge's heart nearly flew out through his throat. He couldn't hover in this cursed bucket, so all he could do was fly around in circles, trying to figure out how he was going to pick up Sardelle.

Since the two-man Iskandian fliers had thrusters, Ahn was able to activate them and drop low enough for the rope to dangle down to the tower. She shouted for Tolemek to get on.

Tolemek waved, but pushed Kaika toward the rope. Kaika hesitated, glancing at Sardelle.

"Hurry," Ridge yelled, knowing it was useless, but if that fortress tilted further sideways, or simply fell out of the air, he would lose all three of them. And that could *not* happen.

An idea popped into his mind as Kaika leaped and caught

Ahn's rope. Ridge thrust his knee against the stick for a second, yanked out his knife, and cut off a length of what remained of the shoulder harness. He jammed the blade back in its sheath and rushed to tie the strip to the ends of the lap harness he had cut the pilot out of earlier. He tied it so tightly that he would risk stopping the circulation to his legs, but he could worry about that later.

When he finished, he swooped back toward the tower, irritated with how far the craft had flown while he had been cutting and tying. All around him, smoke rose and structures burned. Ahead of him, Sardelle and Tolemek were still on the tower, gripping the crenelated edge to keep from sliding off. Ahn was waving down to Tolemek, urging him to come up, even as Kaika climbed into the back seat.

Tolemek shook his head, pointed, and yelled something. With his fancy scientist mind, he had probably more accurately performed the calculation that Ridge had been worrying over earlier. With him *and* Kaika in the back, that craft would be too heavy to fly. An anguished expression contorted Ahn's face, but she must have seen Ridge turning to come in, for she maneuvered away from the tower top.

Ridge empathized and approved of Tolemek's selfless choice, but he could only pick up one of them, and there was no way it wasn't going to be Sardelle. As he swooped down toward the tower, he flipped over, flying upside down toward her.

Stick your arm up, and get ready, he thought, praying she was listening and praying that his battered body would hold together so he could do this.

Sardelle's eyes widened, but she did as he ordered, standing as straight as she could on the tilted tower and stretching her arm upward. Hanging upside down, he headed in, lowering his own hand. His brain hurt at the thought of how precise he had to be with his flying to grab her. The harness cut into his lap, and he was all too aware of how little kept him from tumbling out of the craft.

He lined it up for the final approach and reached for her hand. Another tremendous snap sounded from within the fortress.

Ridge lunged, afraid the platform would fall lower and that she would drop out of his range, that he would lose her.

The tower *did* tilt farther downward, but Sardelle jumped and clasped his arm as his fingers wrapped around her wrist. The extra weight suddenly hanging from his body sent such intense pain through Ridge that he almost lost her.

He gritted his teeth, black dots darting through his vision, as the flier engine groaned, and he lost altitude. Fortunately, he was already past the tower, and there was nothing but five thousand feet of air between him and the sea. As slowly as he could, he rotated the craft back to upright. As he did, he pulled Sardelle into the cockpit with him, panting to try and control the pain. As a fresh torment, her sword scabbard jammed against his crotch—Jaxi perhaps making up for not being able to melt his balls earlier. But he had Sardelle. That was all that mattered. He pulled her close with one arm and guided the flier away from the fortress with the other. Sardelle gripped his shoulders so tightly, they would probably fall off when he landed, along with his legs and his ribs, but he wouldn't have it any other way.

Ridge was half-tempted to ask her if she could heal him while they were in such awkward positions, but he had left Tolemek up there, so he couldn't relax yet. He searched the sky, still hoping one of the other fliers in the squadron would realize someone needed help and sail over. Ridge's own craft was sinking slightly, and he knew he had to go straight down and land before his engine overheated. This flier was not designed to carry two any more than Ahn's could carry three.

"Look," Sardelle said, gazing behind Ridge's head.

He craned his neck and spotted two things: Crash's two-man flier had come out from behind the dirigible and was arrowing toward the platform, and something else much larger than his craft was also arrowing toward the platform.

"Uhhh," was all Ridge could manage, not sure whether the great silver dragon soaring through the air was *their* dragon, the one they had released from the pyramid, or if the Cofah had found another one buried in a stasis chamber along with their sorceress. Even if it was the dragon they had saved, that didn't mean the creature was working for their side now.

"It's Phelistoth," Sardelle said as Ridge spotted someone riding atop the dragon's neck, unfazed by the wings flapping behind her. Tolemek's sister.

That made Ridge feel better. Even if Tylie was Cofah, she wouldn't do anything to harm Tolemek. Indeed, as the dragon swept toward the tilted tower—toward the entire tilted platform—he realized what she intended to do. Phelistoth spread his wings, coasting down and landing, the great claws wrapping around those low wall of the tower top. Tolemek appeared small next to the massive creature, but he did not hesitate in approaching. Phelistoth crouched low and Tolemek scrambled up his side to join his sister on the dragon's neck.

Sardelle leaned away from Ridge's chest, frowning down at him. *You're injured.* She lowered one of her hands from his shoulder to his ribs, her touch so light that he barely felt it.

Yeah, my chest challenged a wall to a duel. The wall won.

A warm sensation radiated from Sardelle's fingers, like some balm sinking through his skin and soothing his battered nerves. *I don't think I can heal you until we're on the ground, but I'll try to lessen the pain.*

Thank you. Ridge glanced over his shoulder, wondering how much longer that fortress could float up there. His flier had already descended a thousand feet, but that did not keep him from spotting movement on a tower at the far side of the platform. A Cofah flier swept down in a maneuver that wasn't quite as fancy as Ridge's had been and picked someone up. Sardelle groaned. Sunlight glinted off armor, and Ridge had a good idea as to who had been rescued.

As Phelistoth leaped away from the tower, Tolemek's added weight doing nothing to bother him, the final snap came from within the fortress. One second, Ridge was flying along beside and below it, contemplating his route to the hangar. In the next second, the final thrusters gave out, and the entire structure plummeted. The draft it created was enough to rock his flier as it passed, but then it was gone, sinking into the ocean far below, no longer a threat to Iskandia.

The lone dirigible left in the air limped out to sea. The remaining Cofah fliers—Ridge was proud of his people when he saw how few remained—also headed for home. If Ridge had been able to communicate with his squadron, he might have ordered a pursuit, to take down the Cofah before they could return home and report, but he couldn't continue to fly with Sardelle in his lap and his engine groaning pitifully. He doubted many of his people's craft were in any better shape. He hoped they hadn't lost anyone else.

No, Sardelle murmured into his mind as she stroked his chest lightly. *Going after them would be a bad idea. Despite our best effort to bury her, they still have their sorceress.*

You buried enough. Ridge would savor the memory of the giant fortress sinking into the blue ocean for a long time. *Shall we go home, my lady?*

Please. I know Jaxi is squishing something that I want to see working later tonight.

I assure you that with your healing skills and the proper motivation, everything will be working. He had better not promise too much since he did not know how much being healed would take out of him. He also couldn't feel his legs at the moment.

I'll think of some good motivation. Kaika has been offering tips.

Ridge snorted, but admitted to a sense of intrigue, as well. *Then I shall look forward to being motivated.*

Good. She kissed him on the neck and laid her head on his shoulder.

Ridge tilted them toward the airbase far below, more ready than ever to go home.

Epilogue

Sardelle clasped her hands in her lap so she would not fidget. In her past, three hundred years in her past, she wouldn't have been nervous about being invited to a dinner gathering with the king at Harborgard Castle. Oh, she might have felt out of place, but mage advisers had often been brought in to political meetings, and she had gone along on a few. That had been before she had played a role in killing the king's wife and demolishing a section of his castle.

"I think he's decided not to throw you into the harbor," Ridge whispered, leaning close enough to brush her shoulder with his.

He didn't look nervous. His eyes gleamed with good humor, and he was as handsome as ever, with his hair freshly cut and his face shaven. His dress uniform, the breast of the jacket full of medals, added to his dashing air. Alas, he did not smell like lavender today, having moved back on base and returned to using military-issue bathing products. Fortunately, he also did not smell like pine trees or cockpits, or any of the other things he had thought would make a pleasing scented soap for men.

"Are you sure?" Sardelle murmured back. "He's hard to read. Half the time, when he's joking, I'm not sure if he's joking."

"I think if he's joking at all, then it's a good sign. I've heard from General Ort that Angulus can have quite the temper when riled."

King Angulus had not yet joined them at the gathering, so Sardelle did not know if he would be joking tonight or not. She and Ridge sat along one side of a long wrought-iron table, sharing it with their comrades from the last few weeks and enjoying the fragrant air in the solarium. The glass-lined and plant-filled room had been far enough away from Kaika's bombs that it did not appear to have suffered damage, and through luck or fortune, none of the flying fortress's artillery weapons had slammed into the castle during the battle. Other parts of the city had not been so fortunate, and nobody would soon forget that attack.

"Is General Ort back on duty?" Sardelle asked. She knew Ridge had been eager to return all of the bigger problems to his C.O.'s lap, so he could go back to being a simple squadron leader.

"Yes. He refused to take any time off, even though *his* lighthouse prison was apparently less opulent than the king's. He and the other officers that the queen ordered rounded up lost a lot of weight while they were crammed into a dank, windowless room for weeks, and that was on top of having received injuries during the initial kidnapping. But I think it was not being able to keep his boots polished and his uniform ironed that really riled Ort up. When we broke down the door, he came out swinging and looked ready to chew bullets. I'm just glad Angulus knew where they were, so we could collect them easily enough." Ridge swirled the beer in his mug and smiled. "I didn't mind being the one leading that rescue. A few of the generals stuck with Ort aren't my biggest cheerleaders. Maybe they'll feel more kindly toward me now."

"You don't think that would be more likely to happen if you stopped strolling irreverently into their offices and throwing your boots up on their desks?" Sardelle asked.

He snorted. "Who's been telling you that I do such things?"

Sardelle sipped from her glass and smiled innocently over at him.

"He would have liked this," Duck mumbled from the other side of Ridge, a beer stein cupped in his hands.

"The beer or the castle?" Ridge asked.

"The castle. The history. Apex would have had stories."

"Yes." Ridge patted Duck on the shoulder, then lifted his mug. He looked around the table, meeting the eyes of his comrades.

All of the Wolf Squadron men and women who had fought had been invited to the gathering, along with Tolemek, Sardelle, and Kaika. Some sat around the table with them and others stood in twos and threes, talking quietly while they waited for the king. Only Cas was missing, a fact that had left Tolemek brooding and silent tonight. Even the return of his sister did not seem to have brightened his mood for long. Tylie was staying at Ridge's mother's house tonight, washing up after her travels and playing with the cats. Sardelle had no idea where the dragon had gone off to.

Better you not know, Jaxi said. *When last he flew into my range, he was munching on a sheep.*

A wild sheep or a shepherd's sheep?

I didn't ask.

"To Apex," Ridge said when everyone was looking. "And to Masser, as well. Fallen comrades taken from us too soon."

The others raised their mugs and thumped their fists on the tables three times as they drank. Sardelle did not feel like one of Ridge's pilots, even after all they had been through, but she replicated the gesture quietly and sipped a dry white wine from her glass. Tolemek only stared into his mug, the beverage barely touched. Like her, he would probably never feel entirely comfortable here, a white wolf amid all the grays. Still, none of the pilots were making superstitious hex signs at either of them. It was an improvement, the first of many, she dared let herself believe.

The somber moment was replaced by laughter as Pimples tried to convince Duck to take him to visit some noble ladies they had been discussing off and on tonight, vintners who lived in the countryside. Sardelle assumed they were the same women Duck and Tolemek had helped kidnap the night of the castle infiltration, but she could not imagine how Duck had turned them into friends. He must have been charming, to keep those women from holding a grudge.

Jaxi snorted. *He convinced the ladies that he had rescued them from an evil sorceress who had stolen their carriage.*

He rescued them, eh?

Nobly and bravely, yes.

Was Tolemek noble and brave too? In the chaos of the following day, Sardelle never had gotten a chance to ask what had happened with those women.

He played the role of Duck's loyal henchman.

No wonder he's been in a dour mood.

I think that has more to do with the fact that he helped kill hundreds of his people. Either that, or he's upset over Cas.

Some of both, perhaps. Sardelle had started thinking of Tolemek as a dependable ally and sometimes forgot he had grown up in Cofahre and fought in their army for years before becoming a pirate.

More laughter broke out as the squadron made bets and speculated on Pimples's likelihood of "making it to the end of the runway" with a noblewoman.

Sardelle squeezed Ridge's arm, then left her seat to sit in the empty one next to Tolemek.

"Are you going to be all right?" she asked softly.

"There's nothing wrong with me," Tolemek said.

"Which is why you're scowling into your mug so fiercely that you're making the foam wither."

Tolemek did not smile at her attempt at humor.

More soberly, Sardelle said, "I hope the king has already said as much, but please know how much Ridge and I appreciate your help with destroying the fortress. I'm sure all of the pilots do here, and in time, I hope everyone in the city will learn how instrumental you were in protecting them."

"I don't care if anyone knows. I don't want a prize."

Sardelle groped for something else to say, but she did not have any words that would take the blood from his hands. Maybe he wanted nothing more than to be left alone.

"I chose to study the field I did," Tolemek said. "I don't need sympathy—I don't *deserve* it. You pick a path where you don't know what lies at the end, then that's your fault for not checking a map. I'm just... in an uncomfortable position now. Your king wants more weapons, more defenses, and I know exactly who they'll be used on."

Sardelle turned her palm upward and spread her fingers. "So what if you pick a new path?"

Tolemek frowned at her. "What do you mean?"

"Not every scientist makes weapons. There are other ways

to be useful, perhaps ways that would help humankind. *All* of humankind, not just Iskandians."

Tolemek grunted noncommittally, but the faintest hint of speculation entered his eyes.

She would not press him. She wasn't even sure if she should, since she did not know what deal he had made with the king for his lab.

"Have you been able to talk with Cas at all?" Sardelle hadn't seen much of her since the air battle. She knew Cas wasn't staying on base, though, and she knew Ridge was worried about her. Everyone in her squadron was, especially since the true story hadn't come out, so they didn't understand her absence.

"Some, but she's mostly avoiding me. I don't know why. It's not as if *I* would judge her." Tolemek took a deep swallow from his mug.

"I'm afraid it's about her judging herself." Sardelle had thought about seeking her out a couple of times, but suspected she was one of the last people that Cas wanted to see right now. "She probably needs some time, so the edge dulls somewhat."

"I know. I'm not pushing her to talk. But I wish she would let me—" Tolemek glanced around, then lowered his voice. "I wish she would let me take care of her. And that she would stop trying to resign."

"Ridge is doing his best to thwart that." Sardelle smiled faintly. "Apparently, she's left three resignation letters on General Ort's desk this week, which have all accidentally flown out the window, become illegible due to ink spills, or burst into flames. I suspect Jaxi of colluding with him to make these accidents happen."

I know nothing of these letters of which you speak.

You're a worse liar than I am, Jaxi.

That can't be possible.

"I heard she saved Zirkander's ass up there." Tolemek looked pleased, either at the idea of Ridge needing his lower cheeks saved or out of pride that Cas had performed well. Maybe both.

"There's a reason he doesn't want her to resign."

More servants were coming in with drinks, and a set of six guards filed into the sunroom. Assuming Angulus would join them soon, Sardelle left Tolemek to his drink and returned to Ridge's side.

"Any news about Ahn?" Ridge asked as she sat down.

"How do you know that was the subject of our conversation?"

"For a second there, Tolemek looked wistful instead of brooding."

"No news."

"Ah. Too bad," Ridge said. "I'd thought she might come out of hiding for this. If only to ask about that sword and make sure it had been stuck somewhere safe."

"Has it?" Sardelle had seen evidence of construction crews when they had entered the castle, but she did not know if the sword had been uncovered yet.

Oh, yes. He throbbed and glowed so fiercely that the construction workers nearly wet themselves. Such an uncouth monster.

I'm trying to refrain from mentioning that you caused something similar to happen.

Yes, but I did it cunningly, not uncouthly, Jaxi assured her.

Odd, that's not how I remember it.

No? Perhaps you were hit in the head by rubble during that explosion. As for where he's located now, the king ordered Kasandral locked back in his box and returned to Therrik's family crypt.

Sardelle grimaced. *So, Therrik can get at the sword any time he likes?*

No, the king had a lock installed, and he has the key.

I'm surprised he didn't have the sword destroyed.

Are you? I don't think kings are in the habit of destroying powerful weapons. I'm sure he got the full report on that other sorceress and knows Kasandral might be the best bet for killing her if she shows up again.

Sardelle supposed that made sense—it wasn't as if she and Jaxi had been able to hurt the Cofah sorceress—but Sardelle shuddered at the idea of the hateful blade being wielded anywhere near her again.

Better that than being killed by Eversong, Jaxi said. *Given how few people were found during that witch-hunt, I doubt there are a lot of undiscovered powerful sorceresses in Iskandia who could stand against her. We may be it.*

Even if Sardelle longed to have colleagues again, she was glad the witch-hunt hadn't turned up many people, since that would have resulted in those people being killed. Unfortunately, that did not mean that nobody had died. Ridge had reported the truth to her as soon as he had learned it. His pilots hadn't fired any guns, but they *had* flown the infantry soldiers around who had done so. They had also helped with the "testing." She had yet to see this device that could supposedly detect the presence of dragon blood and couldn't guess if it was accurate or who had designed it. Though she wanted to know more about it—or perhaps arrange for it to fall off a cliff—she hadn't been able to bring herself to ask any of the pilots who had gone along for details. It was bad enough that they avoided her eyes whenever she crossed their paths.

Kaika strolled over, a frothy mug of beer in hand, and Sardelle tried to put the grim thoughts out of her mind, at least for tonight. Tonight, she would celebrate being alive and having Ridge alive at her side. He hadn't shared the details of the air battle with her, but she had healed those ribs, and she had also heard enough from Duck to know Ridge had nearly gotten himself killed multiple times. Even if she had assured his mother that she did not object to Ridge's career, she could understand why it might have driven other women away.

Kaika plopped into the empty chair next to Sardelle. Like Ridge and the other officers, she wore her dress uniform, wool slacks, a button-down shirt with a collar, and a fitted jacket full of medals, pins, and ribbons. With her height, she would be stunning in a dress, but Sardelle wasn't sure she could imagine Kaika in one.

"Didn't get to say it," Kaika said, "but I appreciate you keeping that witch busy while I planted explosives."

"I didn't do much." Sardelle certainly hadn't wounded Eversong in any way. The only victory she could claim had been leaving a dent in that armor, and Jaxi had done that.

Yes, I did. It was all I could manage. I couldn't convince her to pee on herself.

Sardelle had been sipping from her glass and snorted,

inhaling a few drops of wine. How ladylike. She made a note to avoid drinking anything when the king was around.

Wise. He might not be impressed by involuntary nostril spasms.

Kaika lifted her eyebrows and glanced at the glass.

"Jaxi agrees that I didn't do much," Sardelle said.

"Hm, well, you were making a nice target and keeping her busy. That let me skulk around in the shadows and set my explosives. I took out eight of the engines in there. I figure the fortress would have gone down even if the blood hadn't been destroyed. But I'm glad that happened too." She waved across the table toward Tolemek. "That witch woman felt me, too, I'm sure of it. I got this real creepy sense of her noticing me and checking me out, like ants were crawling all over my skin."

"We're lucky she didn't read your intentions in your mind then," Sardelle said. "Some sorceresses are telepaths."

"That *is* creepy. Yup, good thing you were keeping her busy then."

"It's possible she didn't realize what the ramifications were of the bombs you were setting. I exchanged a few words with her and believe she's from fifteen hundred years in the past. I don't think we even had fireworks yet back then. She seemed confused by the machinery down there." Sardelle still wished she had found a way to use that to her advantage. While Iskandia may have won the day, she regretted that Eversong had survived and that she would likely return.

Her and her snooty sword.

You found him snooty? He didn't speak to me. He actually sounded kind of noble from the way you described him, eagerly looking forward to engaging in battle with you.

Please, he wanted to forsooth me out of existence. That's not noble. Can you imagine a world without me?

Forsooth, I cannot.

Don't start.

"Did you say fifteen hundred *years*?" Kaika asked. "How is that possible?"

"I was busy dodging her attacks and didn't get all of the details, but the dragons had stasis technology millennia ago. I don't know why she would have been put to sleep in the prime of her life, but I will definitely see if I can find a historical record of her."

"Stasis, what?" Kaika frowned over at Ridge, who had turned to listen to the conversation. "Sir, did you know your woman talks about confusing and unsettling things that don't make sense?"

The corners of Ridge's eyes crinkled. "I know my world has become much more interesting since she came into it."

Thank you for that heartfelt defense, Sardelle thought into his mind.

His eye crinkles deepened.

"So long as she isn't doing that creepy telepathing stuff."

Sardelle blushed and glanced at Ridge.

He slid his arm around her back. *You can be creepy with me anytime.*

"Mind reading." Kaika shuddered. "That is *not* something I want my enemies to be able to do. Although..." She ticked a fingernail against the side of her mug. "I can see where it could have some interesting bedroom applications."

Sardelle blushed harder, sank back into her seat, and avoided Ridge's eyes. They had explored a few interesting methods of motivation the night after the battle, and the memory could have made her blush even without Kaika's comment.

"If you had power like that, you could tell exactly what your partner enjoyed," Kaika went on. "Groaning is all right as a guide, but this would be even better. Of course, then you'd have to listen to all the dirty sick thoughts men usually have romping around in their heads during sex. Some of them let those thoughts out, and it's bad enough having to hear that. The idiots ought to just be happy enough that you're with them and keep their lurid fantasies to themselves."

"Really," came a dry voice from the head of the table.

Sardelle had been too busy feeling mortified to notice the king's entrance. Pimples, Solk, and the pilots on the other side of the table from Kaika all snickered.

"Evening, Sire," Kaika said, as if she had been discussing

nothing more contentious than the weather.

Sardelle almost snorted her wine again when Kaika gave Angulus a wink and a look that bordered on brazen. Since she tended to look at *any* man she found attractive like that, she probably wasn't truly thinking of wooing the recently widowed king. Though Angulus *did* look quite handsome tonight, especially in comparison to the rumpled, unshaven man that Ridge had first brought to the house. His clothing was simple, trousers and a velvet tunic, but there was also a fur-trimmed cloak held back from his shoulders with a golden chain and clasp that looked like it might be part of some official royal attire. The garb fit him well.

He did not return Kaika's wink as he slid into the chair at the head of the table, but he did offer a cordial nod to the men and women seated around him.

Ridge still had his arm around Sardelle's waist, and he squeezed her. *You don't find my fantasies lurid, right?*

It depends. The ones about me, or the ones where you're thinking of your flier and slaying enemies?

A faintly concerned crease furrowed his brow. *Uhm, the ones about you.*

Then not at all. They've been quite flattering. Sardelle dropped her hand and threaded her fingers through his, letting him know she was teasing about the rest. He *did* think about flying a lot, but she knew it was the chance to pit himself against another man in battle that appealed to him, not the killing itself.

His concerned expression shifted to a roguish smile, and he shared a lurid thought, one of making an excuse to leave the table and take her off behind some of the potted trees for a tryst.

I'm not sure you should be dreaming of any naughty actions in the solarium, especially not ones that could endanger the foliage, Sardelle told him. *I understand you already destroyed one of the king's vining plants.*

I—what?

Jaxi finally shared the story.

I don't know if it's fair that you brought an omniscient sword into our relationship. Unless she's going to share the embarrassing things that you do with me.

A tickled cackle emanated inside Sardelle's head.

Didn't we discuss how alarming it is when you cackle like that, Jaxi? Sardelle must have made an odd face, because Ridge asked, "What?"

"I think you just opened yourself up to receiving *frequent* updates from Jaxi."

"Oh." He scratched his jaw, probably not certain if he had won a victory there or not.

"Thank you all for joining me tonight," Angulus said as a server walked around, refilling wine glasses and replacing empty beer mugs with new ones.

Sardelle shifted her attention toward him, though she kept her fingers twined with Ridge's and listened for any thoughts he wanted to share. Knowing him, he would add some irreverent mental commentary.

"I want to thank you for keeping the Cofah out of our city," Angulus said. "You'll all receive awards."

"My first award?" Pimples blurted, then clasped a hand over his mouth. The pilots on either side of him elbowed him in the ribs.

Sardelle marveled that Cas was the youngest of the pilots. Surely, Pimples and Duck both acted younger. Once again, she wished Cas had come tonight, that she had allowed herself to be acknowledged for risking her life.

"Everyone will receive one," Angulus said, "even Zirkander, despite the fact that he lost his perfectly good Iskandian flier and came back with a feeble Cofah imitation, one that doesn't even include a crystal."

"Ah." Ridge usually would have waved away any criticism—or found an equally critical retort for it—but he didn't look like he was quite sure where he stood with the king. Unlike with most of the senior officers in his life, he *did* care what the king thought. "Did I mention that Sardelle may be able to make crystals, Sire?"

Sure, deflect his attention toward me. Sardelle looked down at the table, aware that she had *everybody's* attention now.

You're much more attractive than I and worthy of his attention.

I think I prefer your lurid thoughts to your flattery.
I'll keep that in mind for later.

"Oh?" Angulus asked. "Then I hope she will indeed stay in the city and work with us. My offer of a room at the castle is still open. I've already seen to it that Deathmaker has his lab back, with a lock on it that only he will have the key to."

"Mrs. Zirkander will be relieved to have the spiders and snakes moved out of her house," Tolemek said.

You're getting a room at the castle? Ridge asked. *Am I invited? I've never done lurid things in a castle before.*

We'll see.

"I've talked with General Ort," Angulus said. "I asked him if there was any way his star pilot would accept a promotion, since he's received enough awards in his career that he's probably started stuffing them into a box in the attic."

Ridge's eyebrows rose and that concerned look returned to his face, almost a panicked how-do-I-escape-this-horrible-fate look.

"Your methodology is somewhat questionable at times, Zirkander—" Angulus's eyes narrowed as he pinned Ridge with a stare, "—but there's no doubting your loyalty to Iskandia and your officers. I understand you've turned down a few offers of promotions in the past."

"Yes, Sire," Ridge said firmly, hope entering his eyes that he might be able to turn down this one too.

"Ort said that we'd have to give you command of the flier battalion, along with the training program to make sure we get more quality recruits in the air. And that I would have to promise that you would still fly, and that we would find you an extremely capable assistant who would handle all of the paperwork that crossed your desk."

Sardelle thought these suggestions sounded quite reasonable—who else would receive such a hand-tailored promotion?—but Ridge still appeared faintly panicked.

"Desk, Sire?"

"Yes," Angulus said dryly. "It's like a cockpit, but without wings."

"Do it, sir," Duck whispered. "You'd be a great general. Much more fun than General Ort."

Sardelle was not sure generals were supposed to be *fun*, but she kept her mouth shut.

"I—what about General Ort, Sire? You're basically describing his job."

"I thought I would recommend his promotion to brigade commander. You would still report to him, and he could still come with you on any trips to the castle, so someone is there to kick you under the table and remind you of proper protocol." Angulus's eyelids drooped even lower.

"Er."

Snickers came from the opposite side of the table.

Kaika nudged Sardelle. "Remind him that he would outrank Therrik. That ought to seal the wax on the scroll."

Ridge snorted, though his eyes *did* grow speculative.

"Colonel Therrik shouldn't cross your path for a while," Angulus said. "Even though I understand that he did not lift his own hand to betray me, his silence was unacceptable. He'll be contemplating his mistakes from his new command station, the Magroth Crystal Mines."

Ridge grinned, far more excited by this pronouncement than he had been at the promise—or threat—of a promotion. "I'm sure he'll enjoy his time there *immensely*, Sire."

"I have no doubt."

You better send him a gift, Sardelle commented. *Since he did let you out of jail.*

The only gift a man in those mines can use is a crate of alcohol. Or a mysterious sorceress.

"I'll see to it that your new orders are on your desk in the morning, Zirkander," Angulus said.

"Uh." Ridge hadn't said yes, but it was probably too late now. One didn't truly have the option to refuse orders from one's king. "Yes, Sire."

The rest of the pilots clapped. Ridge looked like he was still worried about getting a desk. Sardelle patted his hand reassuringly.

"The last thing I would like to discuss before dinner is brought out is this dragon." Angulus looked at Sardelle, as if she were a dragon expert.

"I understand it has Cofah leanings," Angulus said, "and that Tolemek's sixteen-year-old sister is the only reason it's here in a non-predatory capacity."

Non-predatory? Jaxi snorted. *Phelistoth is hunting sheep in the mountains right now. It takes a lot to feed a dragon.*

So long as he's not eating people.

Since the king was still looking at her, Sardelle supposed she was the one who had to come up with an answer. "I haven't spoken with Phelistoth since we left Owanu Owanus," she said slowly, "but he did seem to have Cofah origins. And Tylie does, too, of course." She nodded down at Tolemek.

"There's nothing left for us there," Tolemek said. "Our family... Tylie could never go back and study magic. Father wouldn't allow that. She'll stay wherever there's a teacher willing to train her." He nodded back at Sardelle.

Sardelle thought of Eversong and was glad the woman had never crossed paths with Tylie. Tylie didn't need to know that there was a powerful Cofah sorceress she might turn to. Besides, Eversong might not consider teaching even if she knew of a potential student. Sardelle hadn't sensed a nurturing quality in her; that was a certainty.

You would definitely be a better teacher, Jaxi said. *Those overpowered sorcerers of the past had no sense of subtlety. Such as how to give people rashes.*

"Considering that the Cofah seem to have achieved our level of technology, we have no advantage left over them anymore," Angulus said, "no sure way to defend ourselves. I'd like that dragon on our side."

He was still looking at Sardelle. Did he think *she* could make that happen?

"If you want to teach Tylie or anyone else who wants to come to the capital to learn from you, I will make sure you have that opportunity." His eyes and voice hardened when he added, "And woe to he—or she—who tries to stop you."

"I... thank you, Sire," Sardelle said, not sure she could say anything else. She wanted to teach and to seek out others with dragon blood, but his implication that he expected her to get the dragon on their side... That made her nervous about the deal.

It's like a desk, Ridge thought.

What?

You get a dragon you don't want. I get a desk I don't want. Rewards from the king come with stipulations. It's the perk of working for royalty.

Sardelle leaned back against him, feeling dazed. Ridge chuckled and kissed the side of her head. At least she had been offered protection, sanctuary even. Even if she felt daunted about the future, it was a far more promising future than she'd had a few weeks ago.

THE END

The Blade's Memory

Bonus Extras

Interview with Jaxi

I asked on Facebook if anyone would be interested in an interview with one of the characters from the series, and Jaxi nudged out Tolemek. Actually, she may have poked him in the backside to make sure she was the most prominent choice.

Here are answers to the questions readers asked:

Kantami asks: Have you ever been tempted to annoy your companions by beaming images into their minds when they are being intimate?

I see this is an interview about the important things in the world. Tempted, perhaps. But there are lines one does not cross. Not many of them, mind you, but I try to give my handler her privacy when she's being intimate. Otherwise, I get locked in the closet. Besides, you can more easily mock a person later if they're not on guard against your comments during the moment...

Meera asks: How would you feel about getting romantic with a dragon?

I don't know. Is the dragon going to shape shift into a sword? I'm not sure we would be compatible. And dragons are such tedious know-it-alls. I've only met one, mind you, but I've read plenty of books. I'm practically an expert. Those people who had liaisons with dragons back in the day probably had stars in their eyes. Or horny itches in their pants. Dragons are pretty, and I've heard they shape shift into fine-looking humans.

Averill asks: Are you lonely? Or content with your choice?

Now? Or in the past? The three hundred years I spent entombed in rock with nobody to talk to was slightly lonely.

I'm glad to have Sardelle back, and it's even better now that I can share my whimsical but insightful thoughts with Ridge too.

I do miss all the other sorcerers and soulblades I used to speak with all the time back before our home was destroyed and everyone... went away. It was difficult to be lonely then. Sometimes, there was so much chatter going on that you wished for the opportunity to be lonely.

Now, I'm hoping Sardelle and I can find some new people with talent and with whom I can converse. I'm sure there must be young would-be sorcerers out there who are in need of my wisdom.

Bekki asks: Is it possible for you to have romantic feelings for someone?

I don't know. Send me a handsome young man prepared to polish my blade and worship me appropriately, and we'll see.

Heidi asks: If you could regain a body and live as a person, would you choose something else? Like a cat or a dragon?

A cat?? Who would come back as a cat? With nothing to do but lie around and lick your nether regions and rub fur on people's trousers?

I suppose a dragon would be all right, but they're tediously arrogant. I wouldn't want to be like that.

Excuse me. I see Sardelle smirking about something. I'll be right back.

Mirian asks: Does it ever get old? Being cognizant forever?

Not really. I take naps if I need to. Three-hundred-year ones, sometimes.

All right, honestly, it's tough because the world changes so much and so fast, especially now, and you can get tired trying to adapt to everything. Magic seems less and less important, and I wonder if there will be a time when I'm buried in some tomb like Kasandral, and I'll continue going on but no longer have anyone to talk to. Even a sword could go mad like that, surely?

It's even tougher getting attached to people and having them die. I've had nine handlers now. My memory is better than it was when I was flesh and blood, but the details still grow fuzzy over time. I hate the idea of forgetting anyone who was so close to me for so long.

Sarah asks: What magical skill do you wish you had but you don't? What do you miss about having a body? What don't you miss?

I have every magical skill that I could possibly need. I'm a powerful sorceress, you know. I've mastered all that's important.

But maybe sometimes, it would be handy to have a knack for healing. There have been times when Sardelle or my previous handlers were injured and unconscious, and I couldn't do much more than float some bandages over to wrap around them. And I wasn't even that good at that. Did you know you can cut off a person's circulation if you tie a bandage too tight? And that circulation is apparently important? I'm fair at cauterizing wounds, at least...

As to what I miss, it's been so long since I had a body that I don't remember much about it. Swords do not have female concerns, so that's a perk. We can't have children. Also a perk. I suppose I miss eating quite a bit. We had this dessert called almond honey cakes. Do they still have those? Fabulous. And maybe I lament that I didn't get to do more with the ah, moist achy bits, as Sardelle calls them. But mostly I miss the almond honey cakes.

Lindsay answers questions about the books

Over the last few months, I've received a few questions multiple times via email. I thought I would answer them here in case you're interested, as well.

How many books will there be in the Dragon Blood series?

It depends. Oh, did you want a better answer than that? Hm, let's see...

When I wrote *Balanced on the Blade's Edge*, I squeezed it in between other projects and didn't have any plans to turn it into a series. But by the time I finished, I realized I wanted to spend more time in that world. I had never written about pilots and air battles before, so it was a fun change, and we got to see so little of Iskandia in that first novel, I was curious to explore it further. When the sales and reviews of the first book were promising, that cemented it.

Looking back, I'm surprised I didn't continue Ridge and Sardelle's story, but at the time, I thought it would be interesting to do all of these adventures (and romances) that centered around the pilots in the flier squadron. I came up with the idea for *Deathmaker* when one of my beta readers said something to effect of, "What if that Lieutenant Ahn, the one who inadvertently caused all of the Book 1 adventures for Ridge, turned out to not be dead?"

I had fun writing that book, but by the end, I realized I was more interested in writing more about Ridge and Sardelle again rather than introducing a third couple or continuing with the idea of Wolf Squadron Romances. The world had expanded, too, and we had this war going on in the background. I figured I should focus more on that and liked the idea of using the aggression between Cofahre and Iskandia as a backdrop to make the story bigger.

When I started Book 3, *Blood Charged*, I knew that story would span two or three novels. I wrapped up a lot of the threads that I had introduced in that one here in Book 5, but clearly left myself some options for going forward with a few more stories. At the least, I would feel bad leaving Cas where she is now without some resolution.

So, while I haven't committed to anything yet, I'm open to doing more if there's an interest!

Who are your favorite characters? Have any of them surprised you?

I have a lot of fun writing Ridge and Sardelle (and Jaxi... making this my first threesome, I guess!). They come the easiest for me, probably because I share a lot of Ridge's humor. (I shouldn't confess to sharing Jaxi's sense of humor, since she's had an inordinate number of pee lines lately.) I would have loved to be that irreverent when I was in the army. The things you thought but could never say...

Tolemek is too broody to be a favorite for me, but he's certainly got the most interesting background to work with. I want to explore more of Cas's background, too, if I keep going with the series, put her face-to-face with Dad again.

Captain Kaika has been my surprise character in that she and Nowon were both supposed to die in Book 3. I had designed them to be red shirts from the beginning and even asked the readers on Facebook to throw out names for them (and Therrik), because I wasn't invested in them. When Kaika and Nowon went off to the volcano laboratory, neither was supposed to come out again. You can imagine my surprise when Cofah started showing up dead, and Kaika walked out of the shadows at the end. I had to go back and rewrite the scene where the team found the bodies hanging on the doors and make sure it was impossible to be sure Kaika was one of them.

Will there be more about the dragon?

As you could probably guess from the epilogue, I would like

to do more with the dragon and Tylie. I've even been kicking around the idea of having our guys find some more dragons, but we shall see. The sheep population of Iskandia might be in danger if that happened.

Will you go back into the past and do any stories about Jaxi or Sardelle before their world collapsed?

I've thought about doing a Jaxi story, perhaps the one about how she ends up in a sword, but that would be a sad tale to write. Also, it's tough going back in time and writing things that happened in the past, because you have to worry about contradicting the facts that have been presented in the existing timeline. There's also less suspense, because the reader already knows what happens to the hero. You're not too worried that someone might die when he or she has already shown up in the future!

I never say never, but right now, I doubt I'll jump back in time.

Will we see any more soulblades? There must still be some buried in the rocks under that mountain, right?

Well, we got an introduction to a new one at the end of this story, but in general, they're sturdier than humans, so there should definitely be some left in the world. Maybe Tylie will have to go on a quest to find one as part of her training. I may have to bring Ridge's dad back to Iskandia to help with some archaeological digs.

~

Printed in Great Britain
by Amazon